my LiTTLE
PONY
Friendship
is Magic

SEASON 10

VOLUME
3

Facebook: **facebook.com/idwpublishing**
Twitter: **@idwpublishing**
YouTube: **youtube.com/idwpublishing**
Instagram: **@idwpublishing**

Cover Artist
JustaSuta

Series Editor
Megan Brown

Group Editor
Bobby Curnow

Collection Editors
Alonzo Simon
& Zac Boone

Collection Designer
Jessica Gonzalez

Licensed By:

ISBN: 978-1-68405-876-1   25 24 23 22   1 2 3 4

Originally published as MY LITTLE PONY: FRIENDSHIP IS MAGIC issues #98–102.

Special thanks to Ed Lane, Beth Artale, and Michael Kelly.

Nachie Marsham, Publisher
Blake Kobashigawa, VP of Sales
Tara McCrillis, VP Publishing Operations
John Barber, Editor-in-Chief
Mark Doyle, Editorial Director, Originals
Erika Turner, Executive Editor
Scott Dunbier, Director, Special Projects
Joe Hughes, Director, Talent Relations
Anna Morrow, Sr. Marketing Director
Alexandra Hargett, Book & Mass Market Sales Director
Keith Davidsen, Senior Manager, PR
Topher Alford, Sr. Digital Marketing Manager
Shauna Monteforte, Sr. Director of Manufacturing Operations
Jamie Miller, Sr. Operations Manager
Nathan Widick, Sr. Art Director, Head of Design
Neil Uyetake, Sr. Art Director Design & Production
Shawn Lee, Art Director Design & Production
Jack Rivera, Art Director, Marketing

Ted Adams and Robbie Robbins, IDW Founders

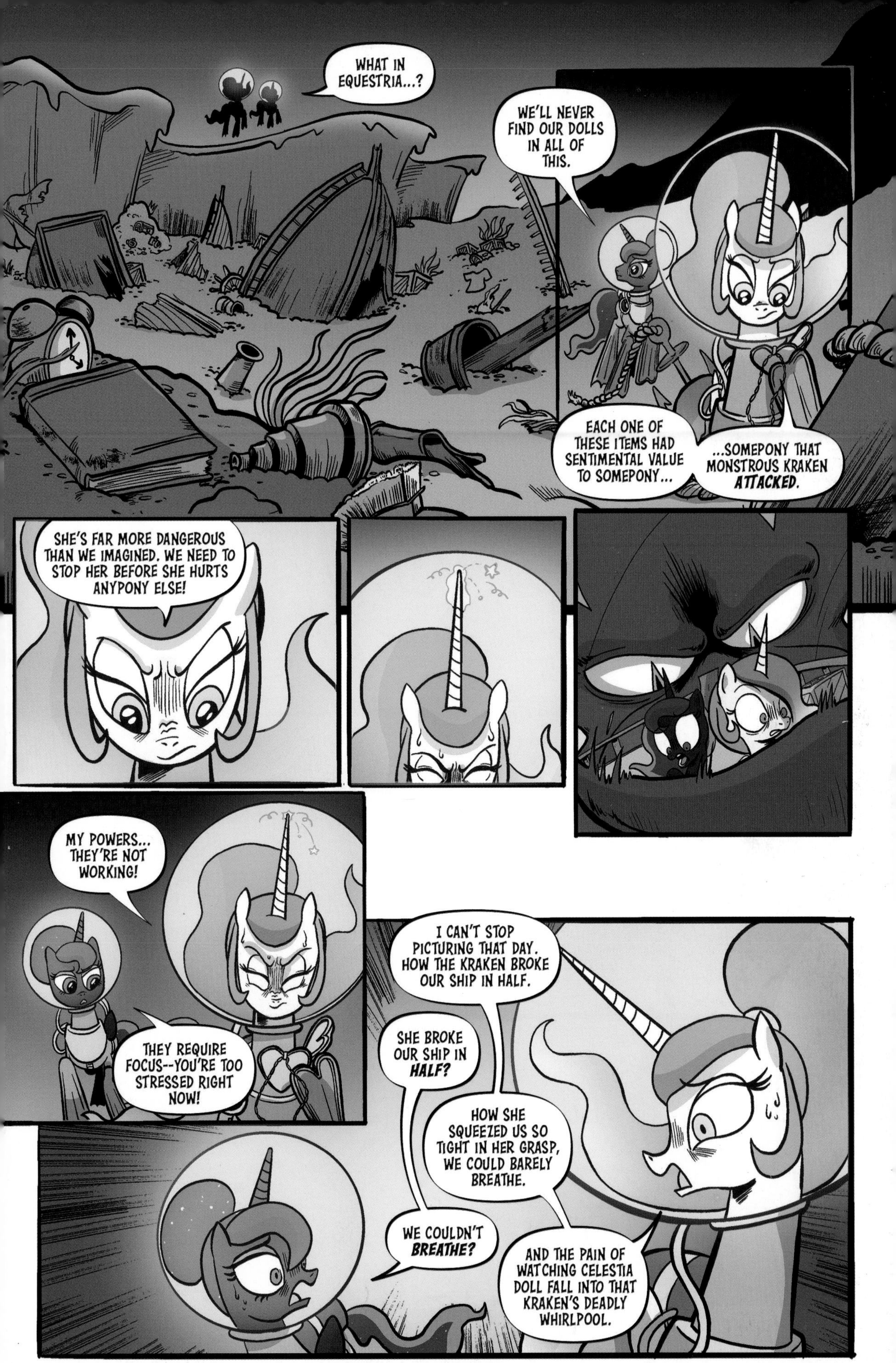
WHAT IN EQUESTRIA...?
WE'LL NEVER FIND OUR DOLLS IN ALL OF THIS.
EACH ONE OF THESE ITEMS HAD SENTIMENTAL VALUE TO SOMEPONY...
...SOMEPONY THAT MONSTROUS KRAKEN ATTACKED.
SHE'S FAR MORE DANGEROUS THAN WE IMAGINED. WE NEED TO STOP HER BEFORE SHE HURTS ANYPONY ELSE!
MY POWERS... THEY'RE NOT WORKING!
THEY REQUIRE FOCUS--YOU'RE TOO STRESSED RIGHT NOW!
I CAN'T STOP PICTURING THAT DAY. HOW THE KRAKEN BROKE OUR SHIP IN HALF.
SHE BROKE OUR SHIP IN HALF?
HOW SHE SQUEEZED US SO TIGHT IN HER GRASP, WE COULD BARELY BREATHE.
WE COULDN'T BREATHE?
AND THE PAIN OF WATCHING CELESTIA DOLL FALL INTO THAT KRAKEN'S DEADLY WHIRLPOOL.

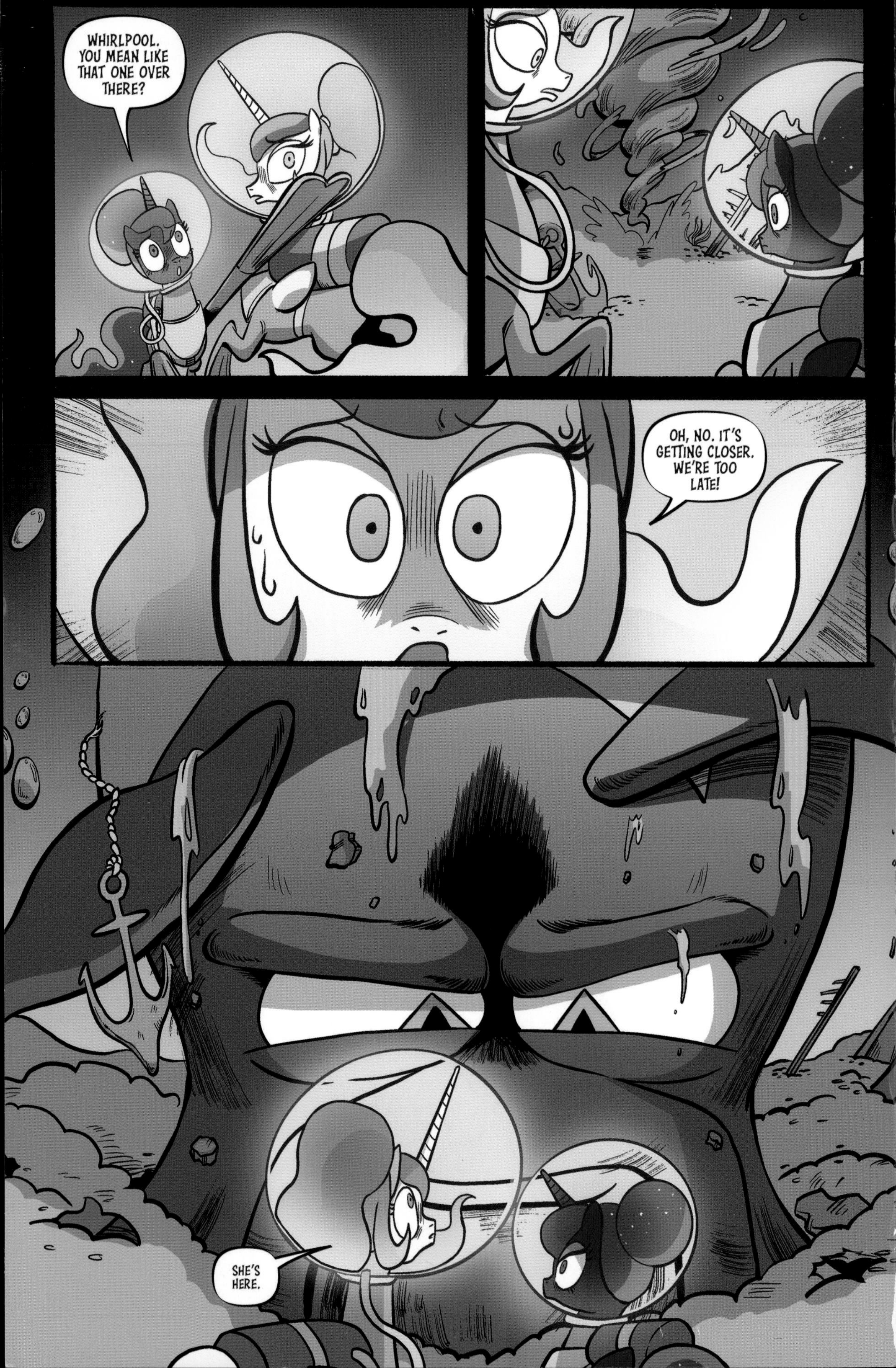
WHIRLPOOL. YOU MEAN LIKE THAT ONE OVER THERE?
OH, NO. IT'S GETTING CLOSER. WE'RE TOO LATE!
SHE'S HERE.

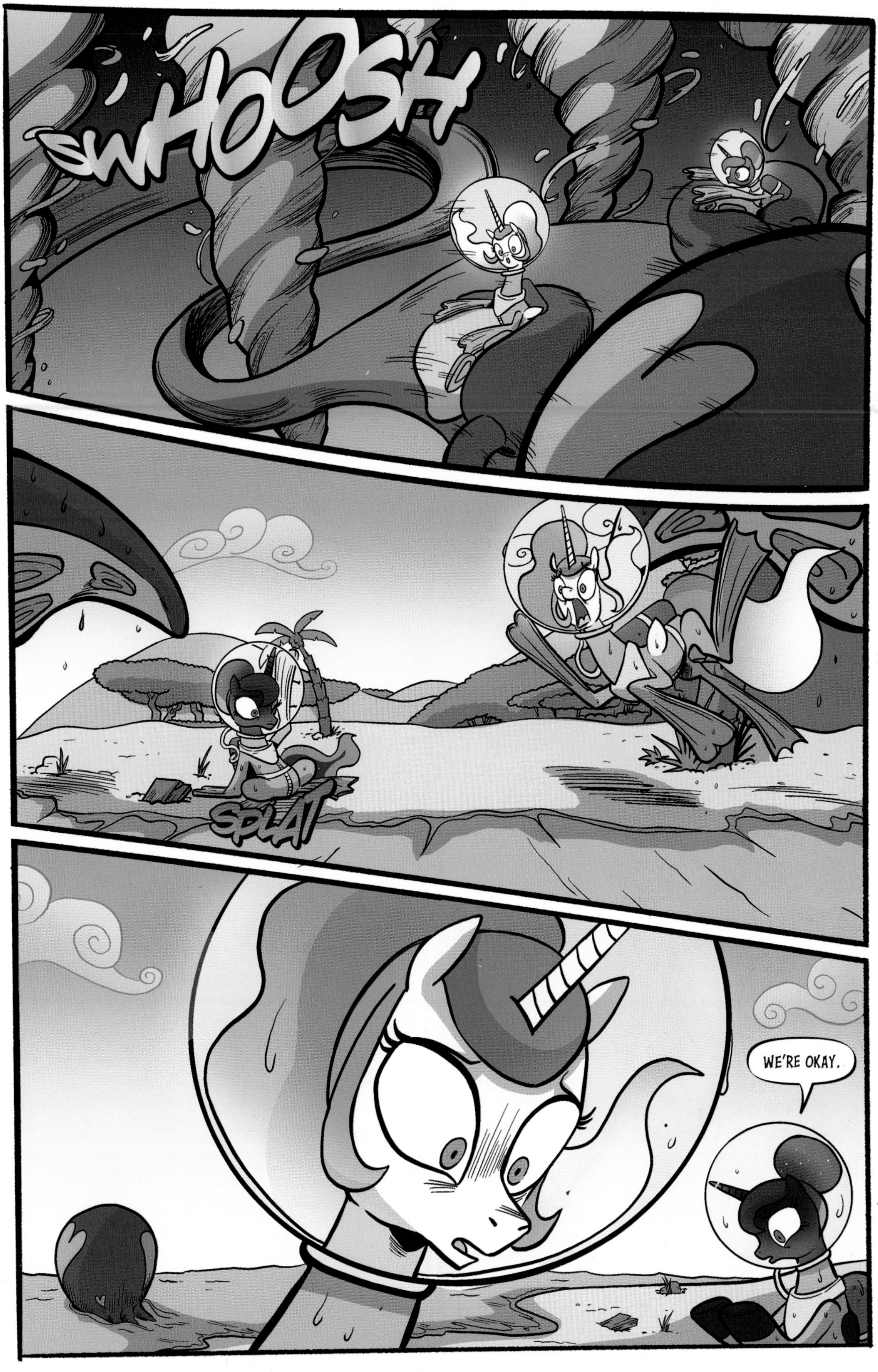
SWHOOSH
SPLAT
WE'RE OKAY.

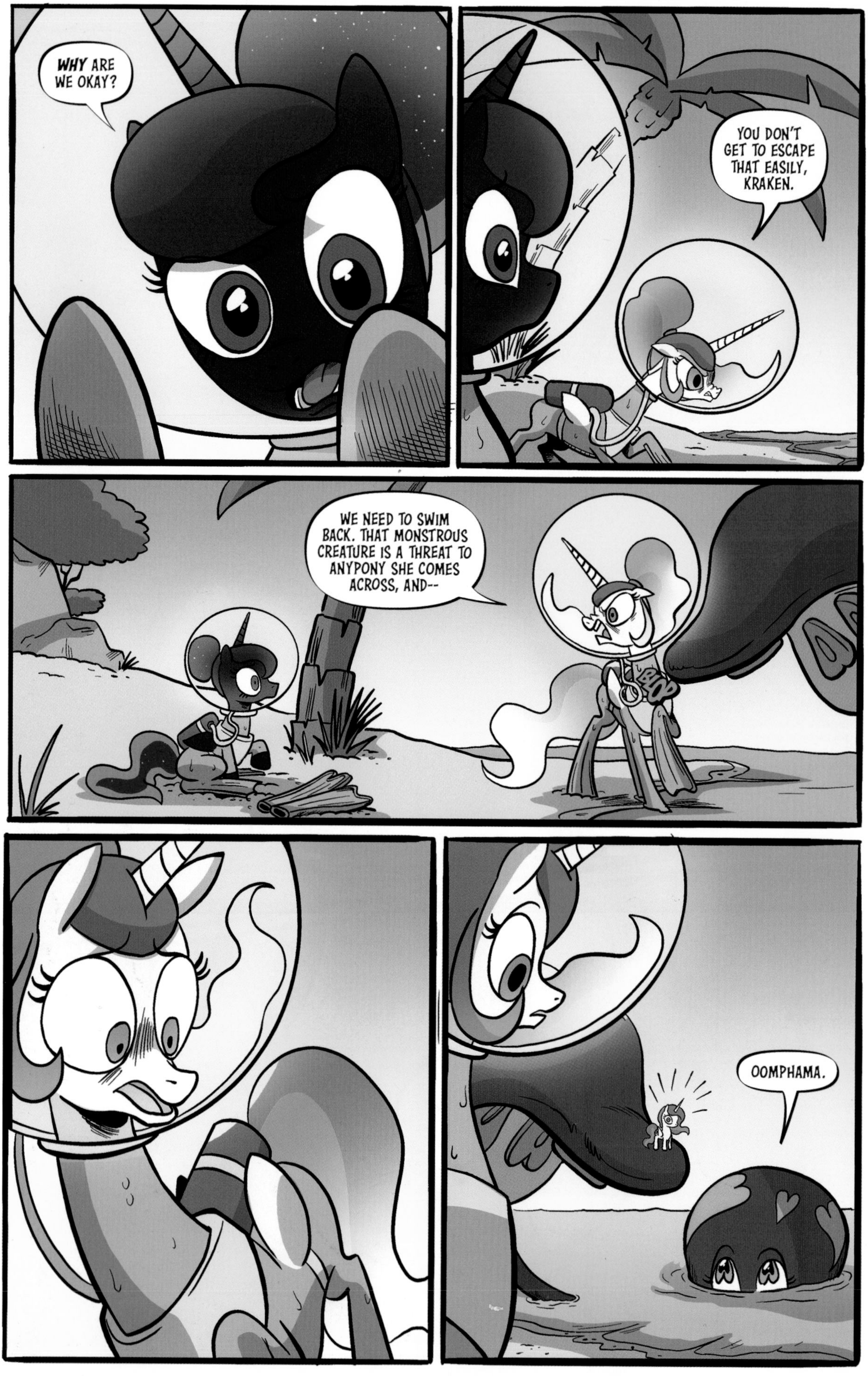
WHY ARE WE OKAY?
YOU DON'T GET TO ESCAPE THAT EASILY, KRAKEN.
WE NEED TO SWIM BACK. THAT MONSTROUS CREATURE IS A THREAT TO ANYPONY SHE COMES ACROSS, AND--
OOMPHAMA.

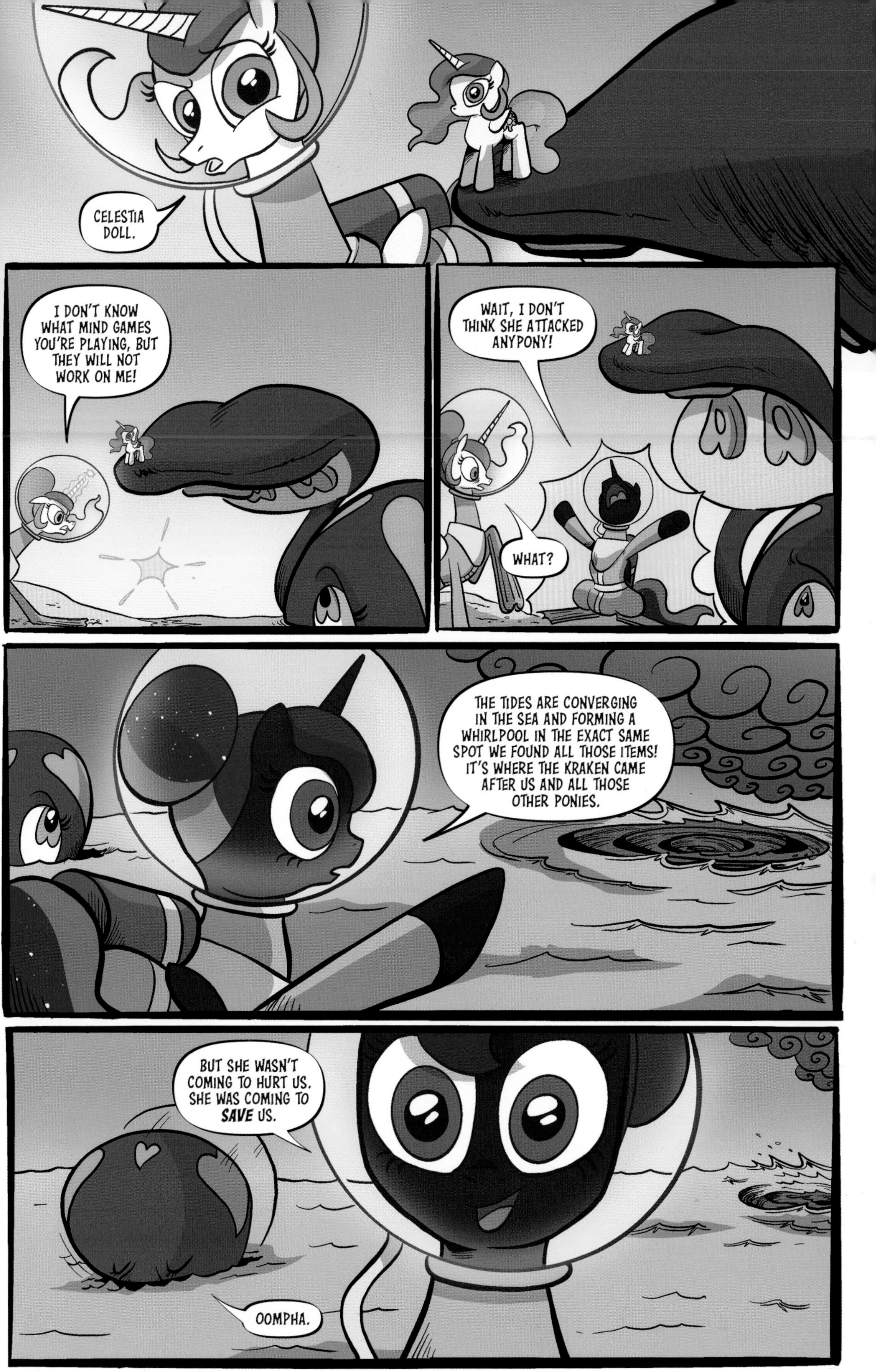
CELESTIA DOLL.
I DON'T KNOW WHAT MIND GAMES YOU'RE PLAYING, BUT THEY WILL NOT WORK ON ME!
WAIT, I DON'T THINK SHE ATTACKED ANYPONY!
WHAT?
THE TIDES ARE CONVERGING IN THE SEA AND FORMING A WHIRLPOOL IN THE EXACT SAME SPOT WE FOUND ALL THOSE ITEMS! IT'S WHERE THE KRAKEN CAME AFTER US AND ALL THOSE OTHER PONIES.
BUT SHE WASN'T COMING TO HURT US. SHE WAS COMING TO **SAVE** US.
OOMPHA.

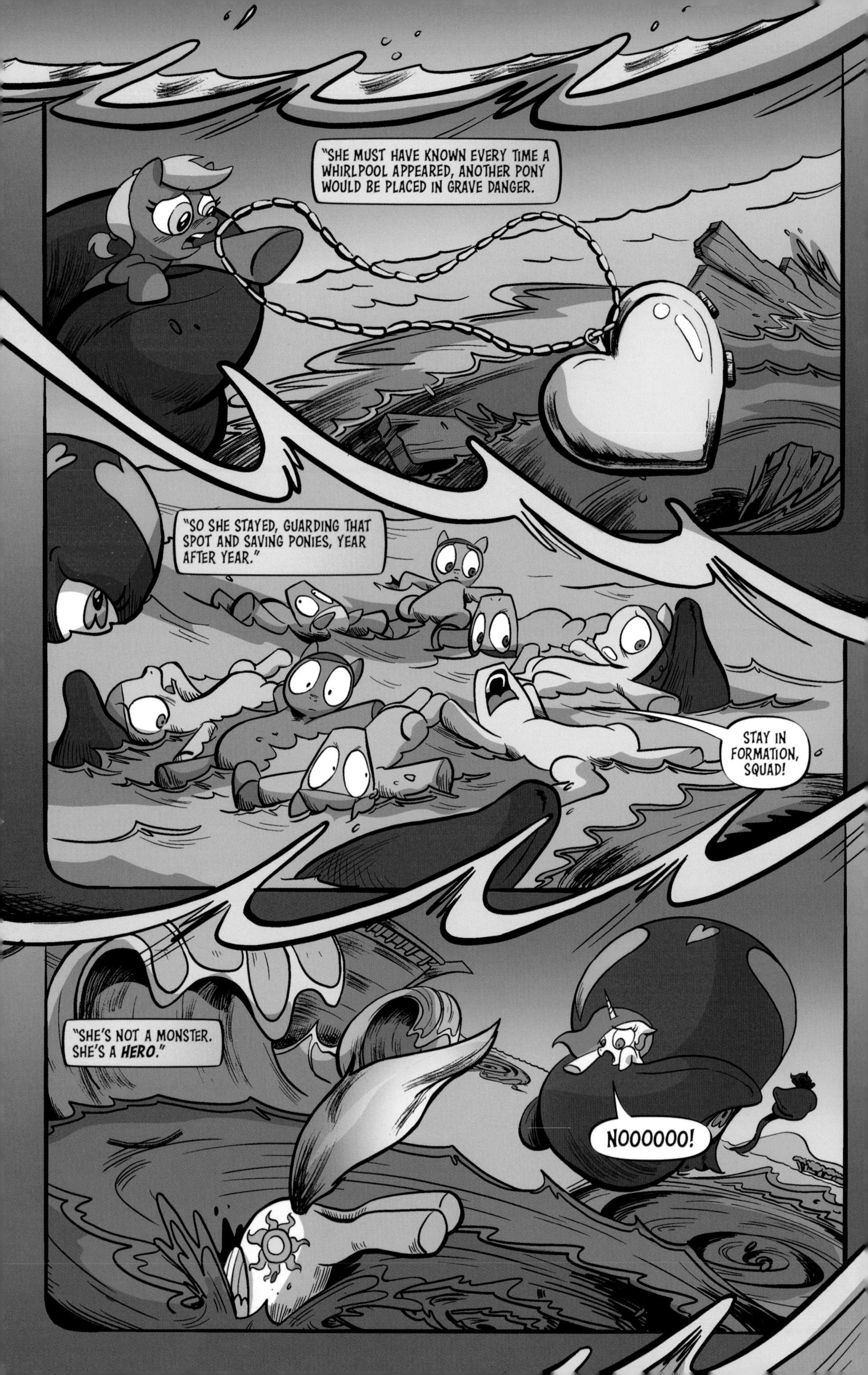
"SHE MUST HAVE KNOWN EVERY TIME A WHIRLPOOL APPEARED, ANOTHER PONY WOULD BE PLACED IN GRAVE DANGER.
"SO SHE STAYED, GUARDING THAT SPOT AND SAVING PONIES, YEAR AFTER YEAR."
STAY IN FORMATION, SQUAD!
"SHE'S NOT A MONSTER. SHE'S A *HERO*."
NOOOOOO!

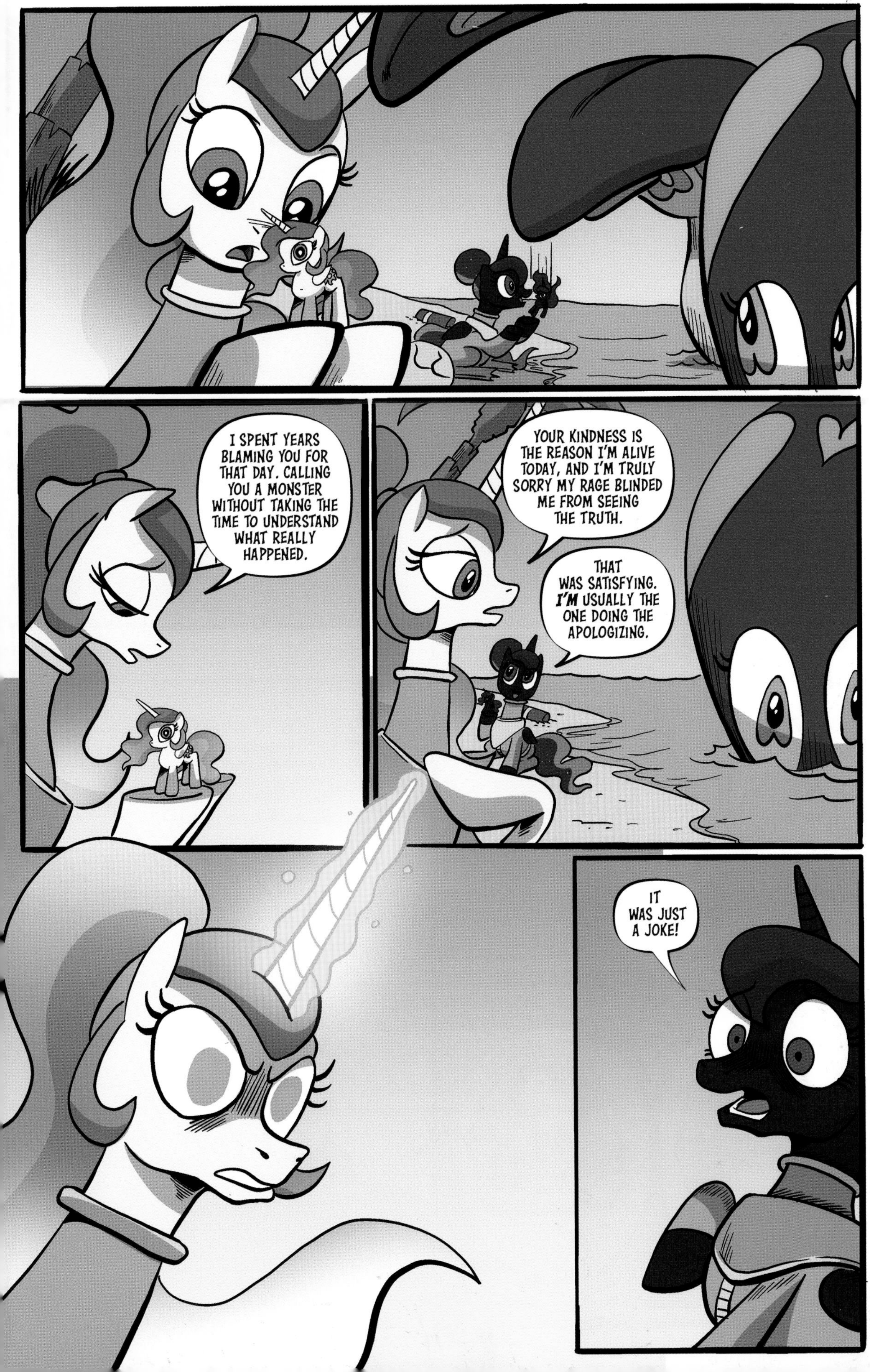
I SPENT YEARS BLAMING YOU FOR THAT DAY. CALLING YOU A MONSTER WITHOUT TAKING THE TIME TO UNDERSTAND WHAT REALLY HAPPENED.
YOUR KINDNESS IS THE REASON I'M ALIVE TODAY, AND I'M TRULY SORRY MY RAGE BLINDED ME FROM SEEING THE TRUTH.
THAT WAS SATISFYING. *I'M* USUALLY THE ONE DOING THE APOLOGIZING.
IT WAS JUST A JOKE!

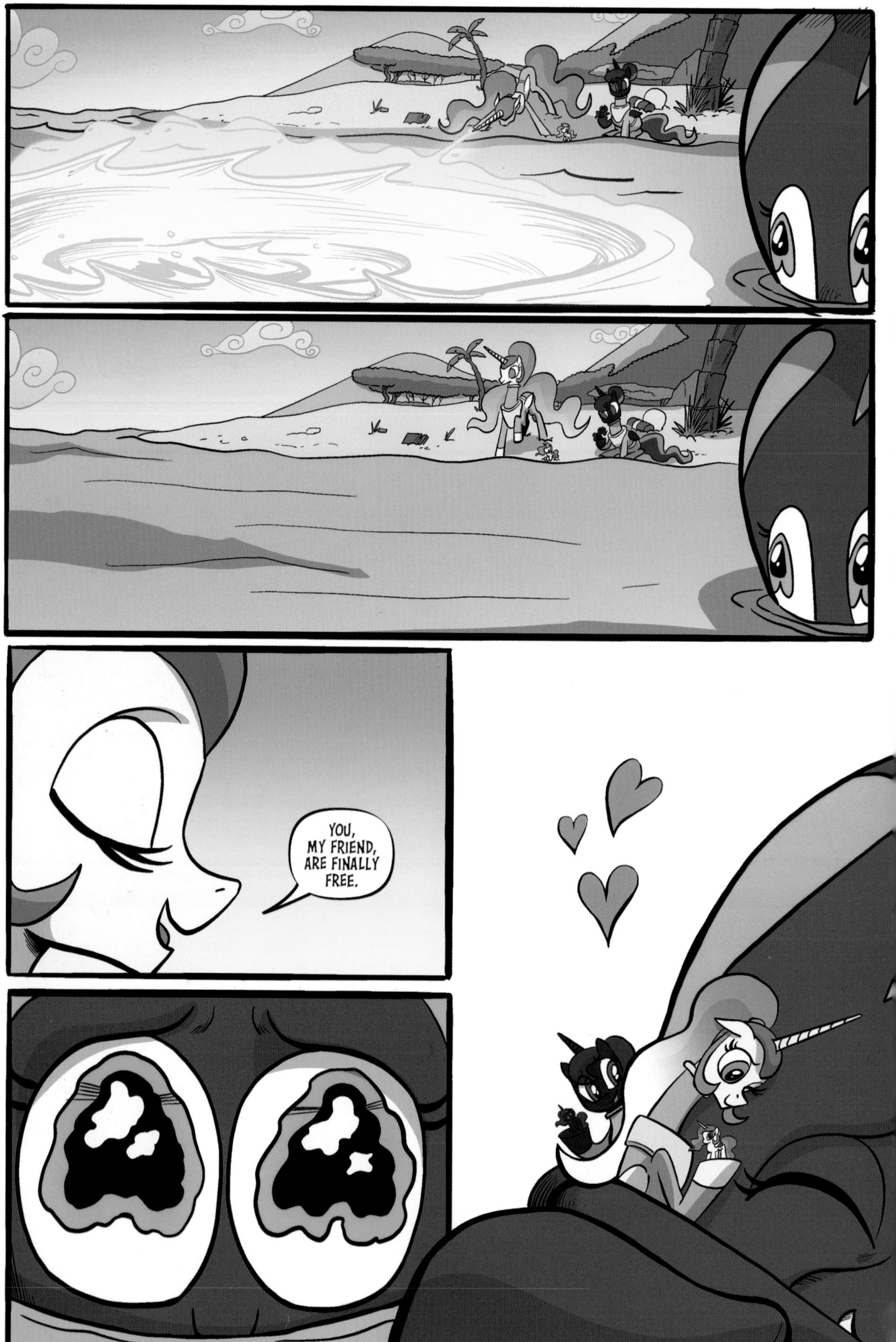
YOU, MY FRIEND, ARE FINALLY FREE.

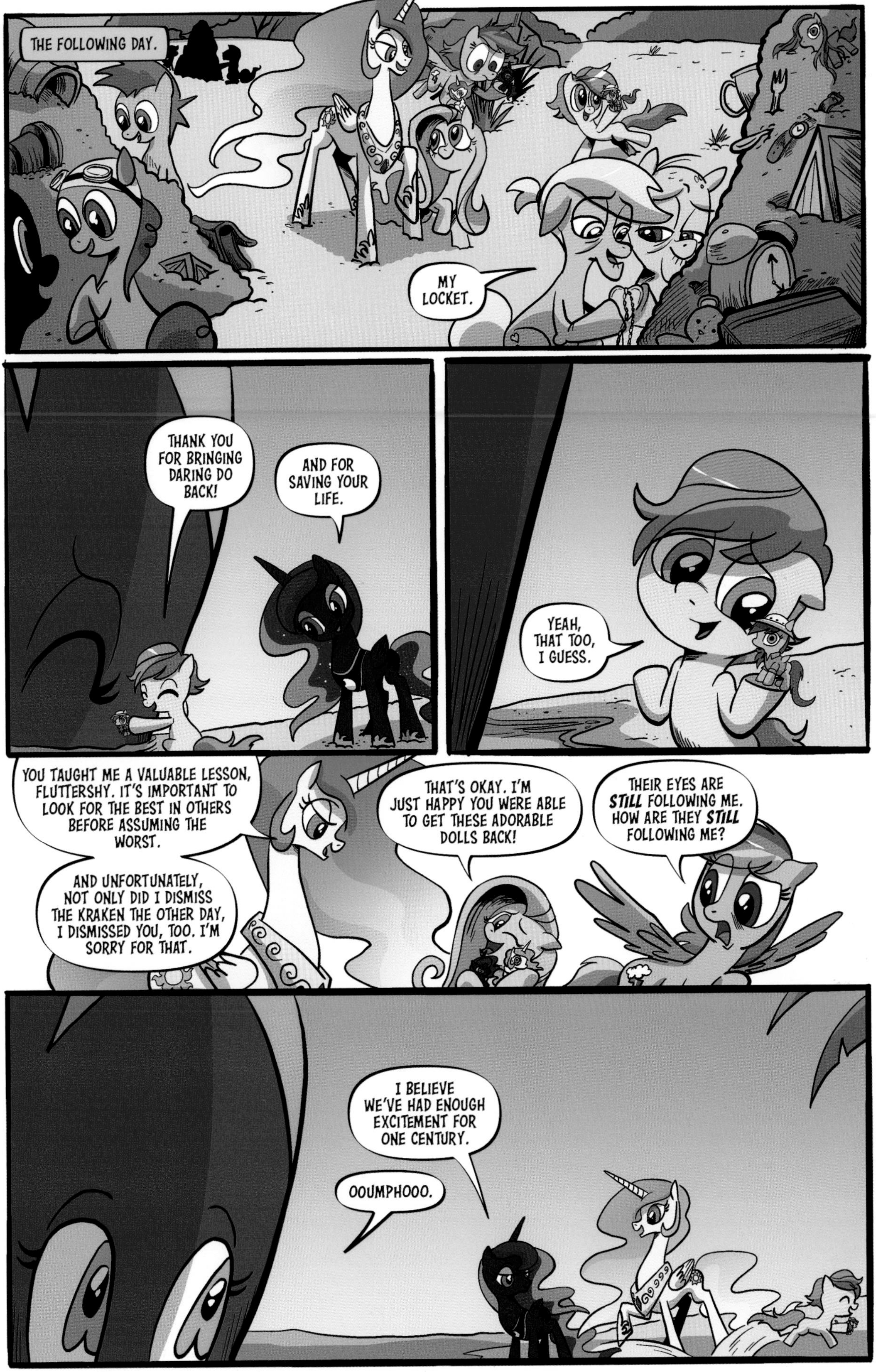
THE FOLLOWING DAY.
MY LOCKET.
THANK YOU FOR BRINGING DARING DO BACK!
AND FOR SAVING YOUR LIFE.
YEAH, THAT TOO, I GUESS.
YOU TAUGHT ME A VALUABLE LESSON, FLUTTERSHY. IT'S IMPORTANT TO LOOK FOR THE BEST IN OTHERS BEFORE ASSUMING THE WORST.
AND UNFORTUNATELY, NOT ONLY DID I DISMISS THE KRAKEN THE OTHER DAY, I DISMISSED YOU, TOO. I'M SORRY FOR THAT.
THAT'S OKAY. I'M JUST HAPPY YOU WERE ABLE TO GET THESE ADORABLE DOLLS BACK!
THEIR EYES ARE STILL FOLLOWING ME. HOW ARE THEY STILL FOLLOWING ME?
I BELIEVE WE'VE HAD ENOUGH EXCITEMENT FOR ONE CENTURY.
OOUMPHOOO.

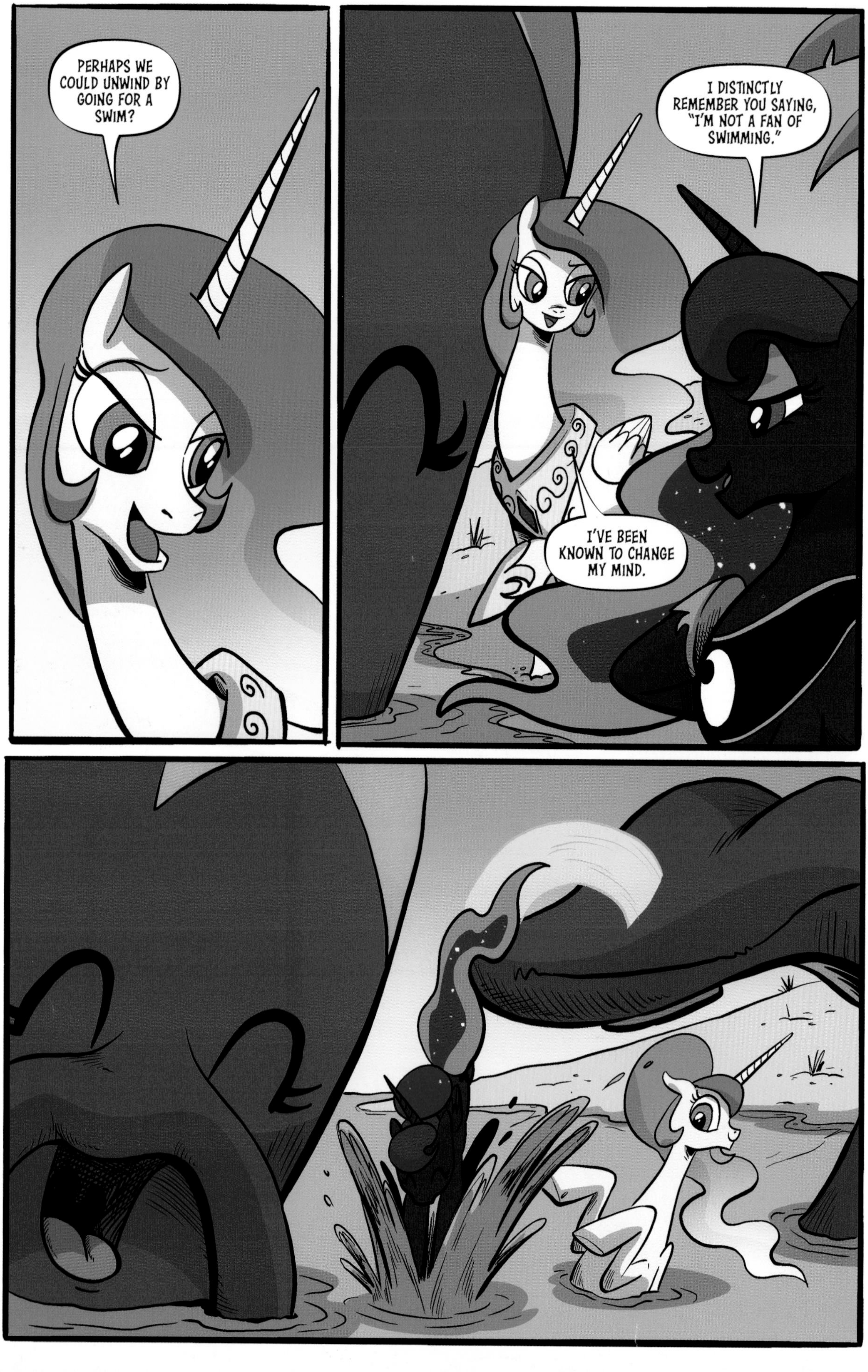
PERHAPS WE COULD UNWIND BY GOING FOR A SWIM?
I DISTINCTLY REMEMBER YOU SAYING, "I'M NOT A FAN OF SWIMMING."
I'VE BEEN KNOWN TO CHANGE MY MIND.

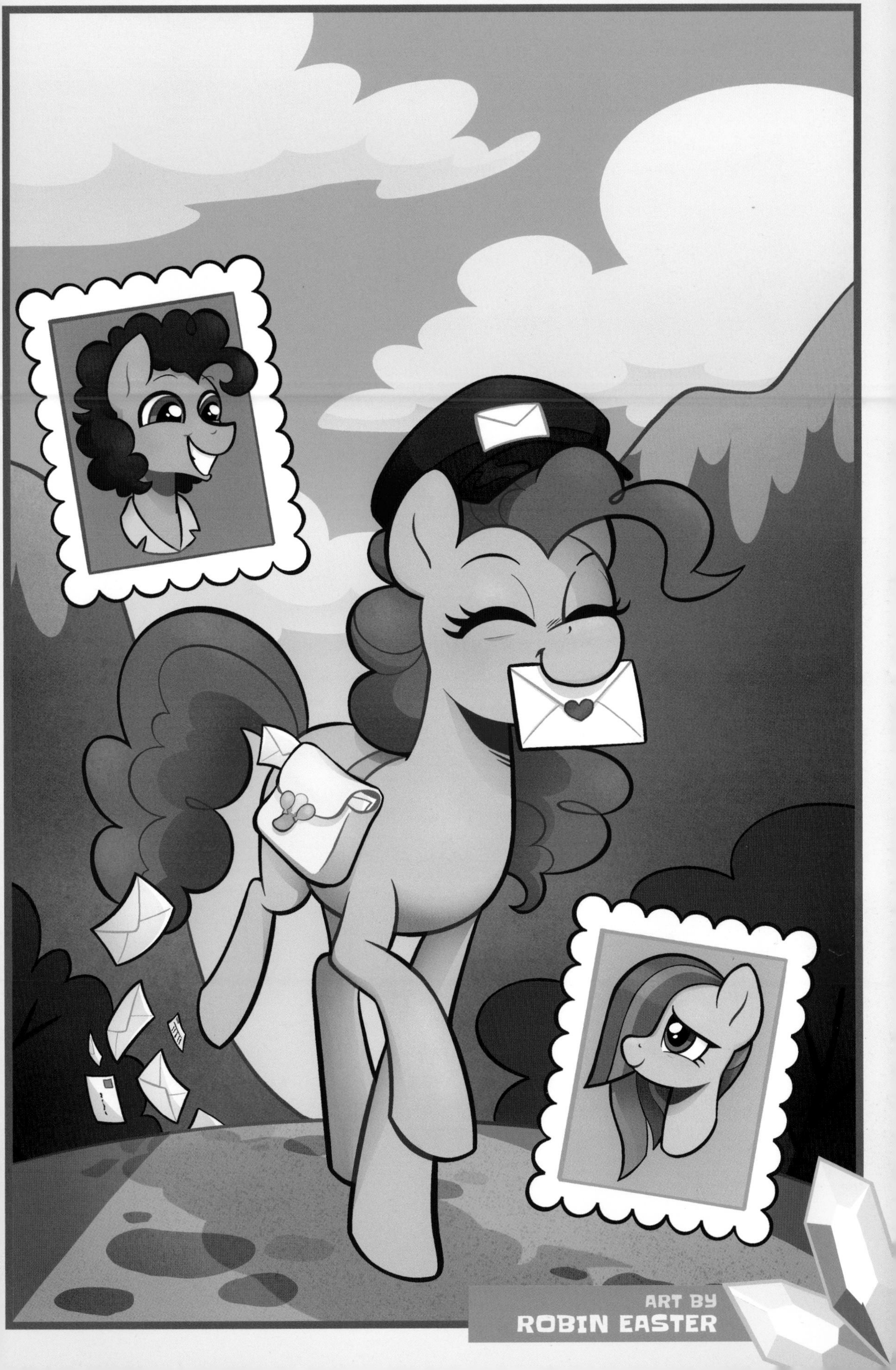
ART BY
ROBIN EASTER

See You Later

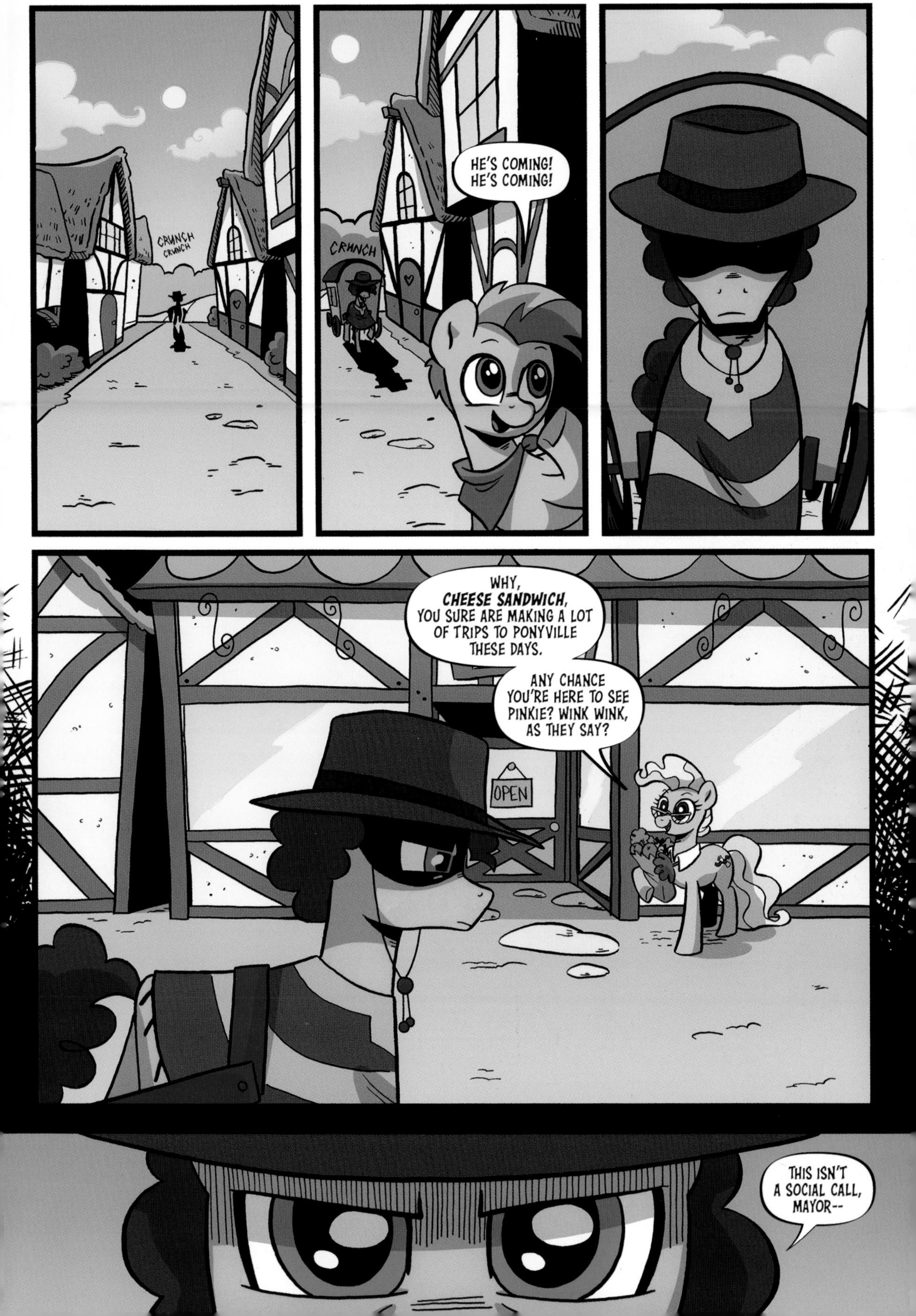
CRUNCH
CRUNCH
CRUNCH
HE'S COMING! HE'S COMING!
WHY, ***CHEESE SANDWICH***, YOU SURE ARE MAKING A LOT OF TRIPS TO PONYVILLE THESE DAYS.
ANY CHANCE YOU'RE HERE TO SEE PINKIE? WINK WINK, AS THEY SAY?
OPEN
THIS ISN'T A SOCIAL CALL, MAYOR--

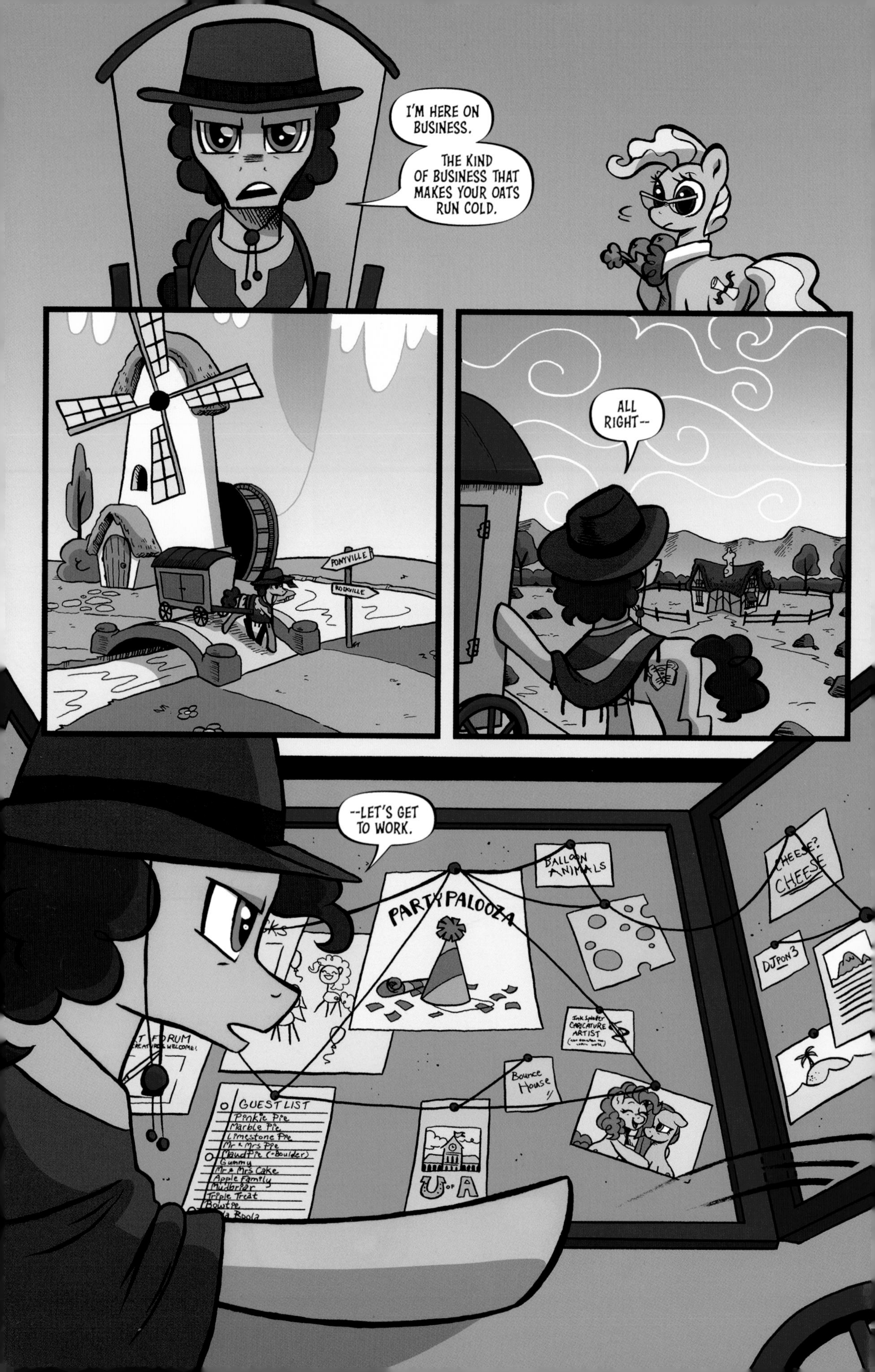

I'M HERE ON BUSINESS.
THE KIND OF BUSINESS THAT MAKES YOUR OATS RUN COLD.
PONYVILLE
ROCKVILLE
ALL RIGHT--
--LET'S GET TO WORK.
BALLOON ANIMALS
CHEESE? CHEESE
PARTYPALOOZA
DJPON3
Ink Splatter CARICATURE ARTIST
Bounce House
GUEST LIST
Pinkie Pie
Marble Pie
Limestone Pie
Mr & Mrs Pie
Maud Pie (+Boulder)
Gummy
Mr & Mrs Cake
Apple Family
Mudbriar
Triple Treat
Bowtie
U of A

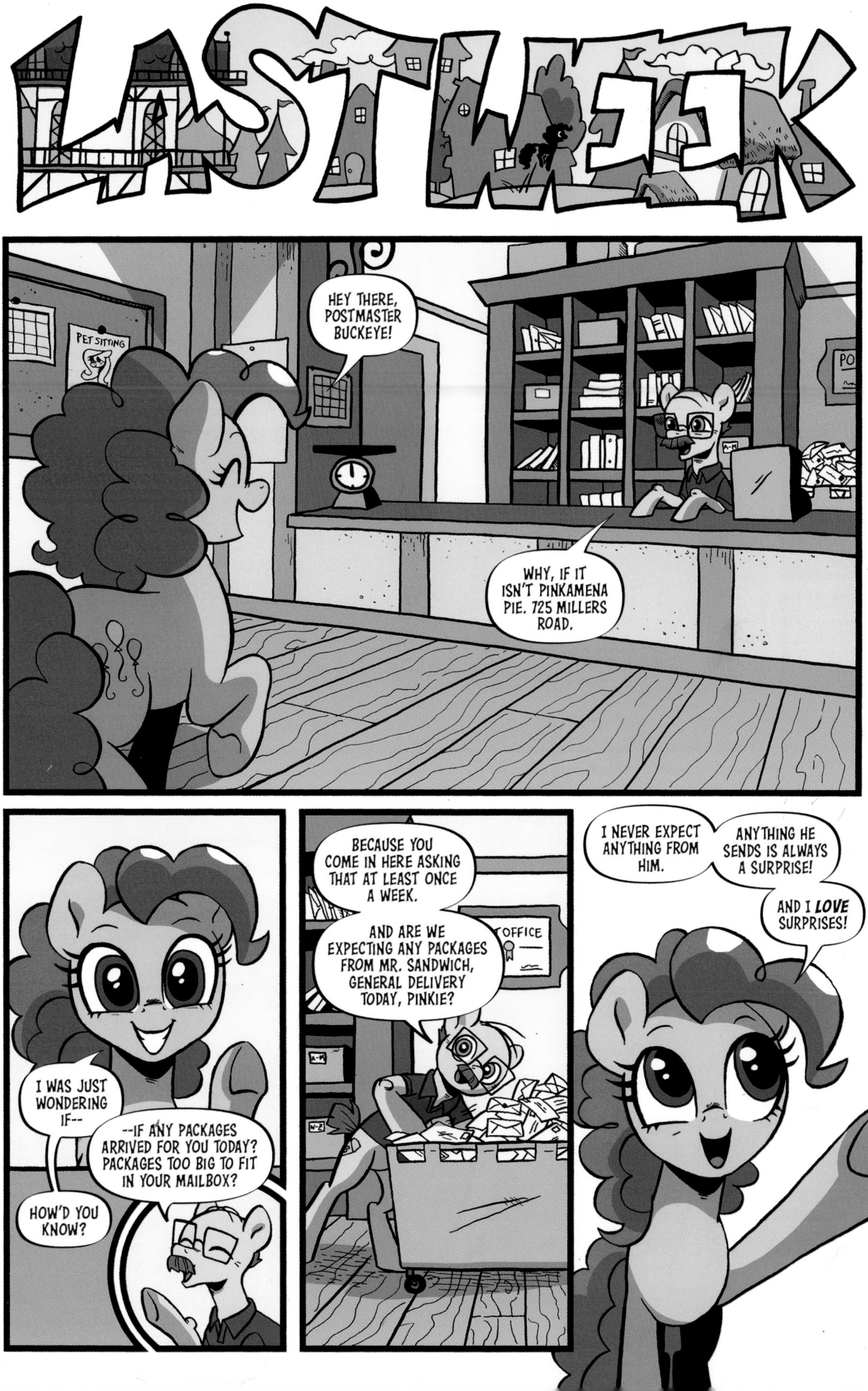
LAST WEEK
PET SITTING
HEY THERE, POSTMASTER BUCKEYE!
WHY, IF IT ISN'T PINKAMENA PIE. 725 MILLERS ROAD.
I WAS JUST WONDERING IF--
--IF ANY PACKAGES ARRIVED FOR YOU TODAY? PACKAGES TOO BIG TO FIT IN YOUR MAILBOX?
HOW'D YOU KNOW?
BECAUSE YOU COME IN HERE ASKING THAT AT LEAST ONCE A WEEK.
AND ARE WE EXPECTING ANY PACKAGES FROM MR. SANDWICH, GENERAL DELIVERY TODAY, PINKIE?
OFFICE
I NEVER EXPECT ANYTHING FROM HIM.
ANYTHING HE SENDS IS ALWAYS A SURPRISE!
AND I *LOVE* SURPRISES!

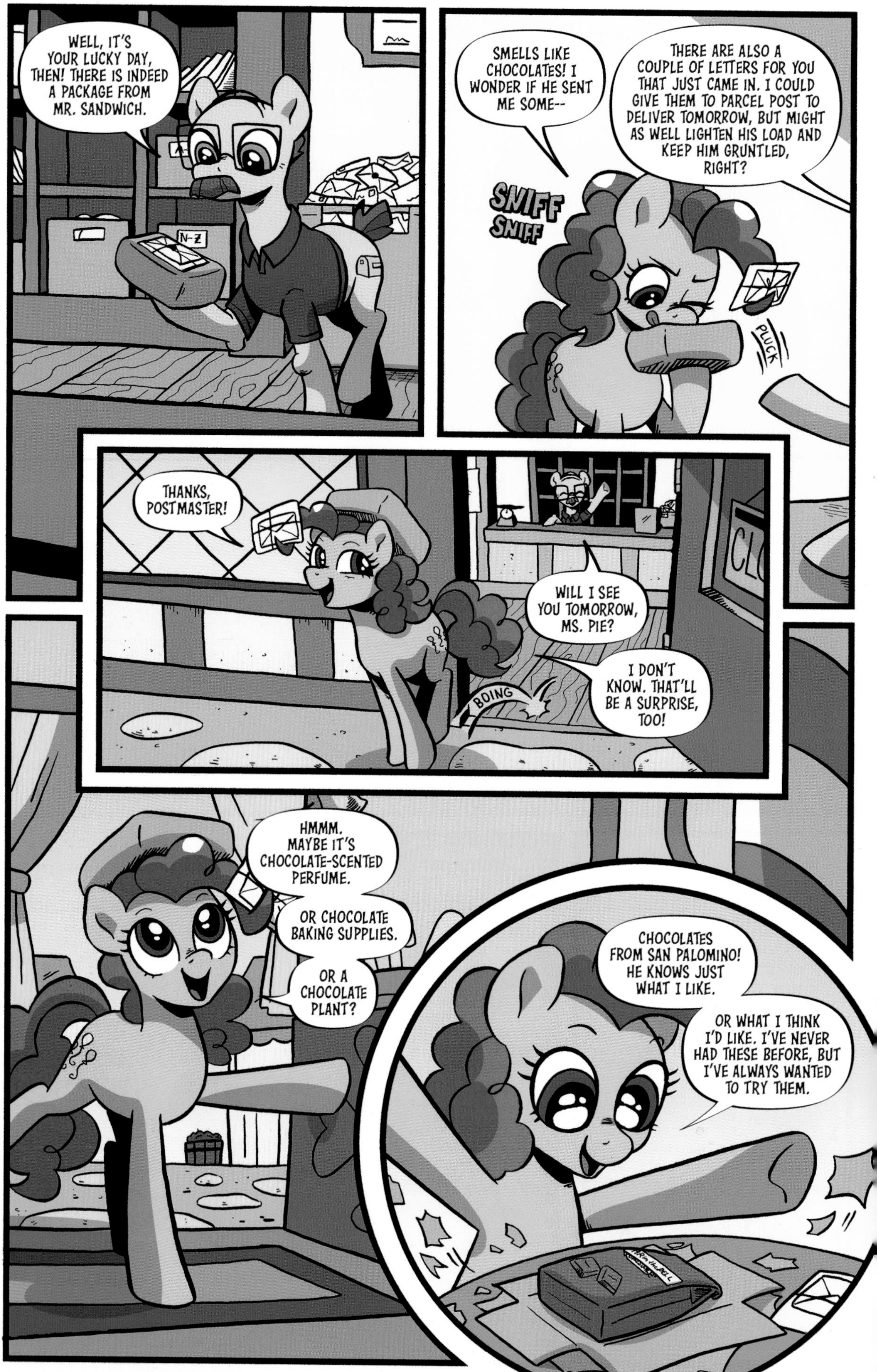
WELL, IT'S YOUR LUCKY DAY, THEN! THERE IS INDEED A PACKAGE FROM MR. SANDWICH.
N-Z
SMELLS LIKE CHOCOLATES! I WONDER IF HE SENT ME SOME--
SNIFF SNIFF
THERE ARE ALSO A COUPLE OF LETTERS FOR YOU THAT JUST CAME IN. I COULD GIVE THEM TO PARCEL POST TO DELIVER TOMORROW, BUT MIGHT AS WELL LIGHTEN HIS LOAD AND KEEP HIM GRUNTLED, RIGHT?
PLUCK
THANKS, POSTMASTER!
WILL I SEE YOU TOMORROW, MS. PIE?
I DON'T KNOW. THAT'LL BE A SURPRISE, TOO!
BOING
HMMM. MAYBE IT'S CHOCOLATE-SCENTED PERFUME.
OR CHOCOLATE BAKING SUPPLIES.
OR A CHOCOLATE PLANT?
CHOCOLATES FROM SAN PALOMINO! HE KNOWS JUST WHAT I LIKE.
OR WHAT I THINK I'D LIKE. I'VE NEVER HAD THESE BEFORE, BUT I'VE ALWAYS WANTED TO TRY THEM.

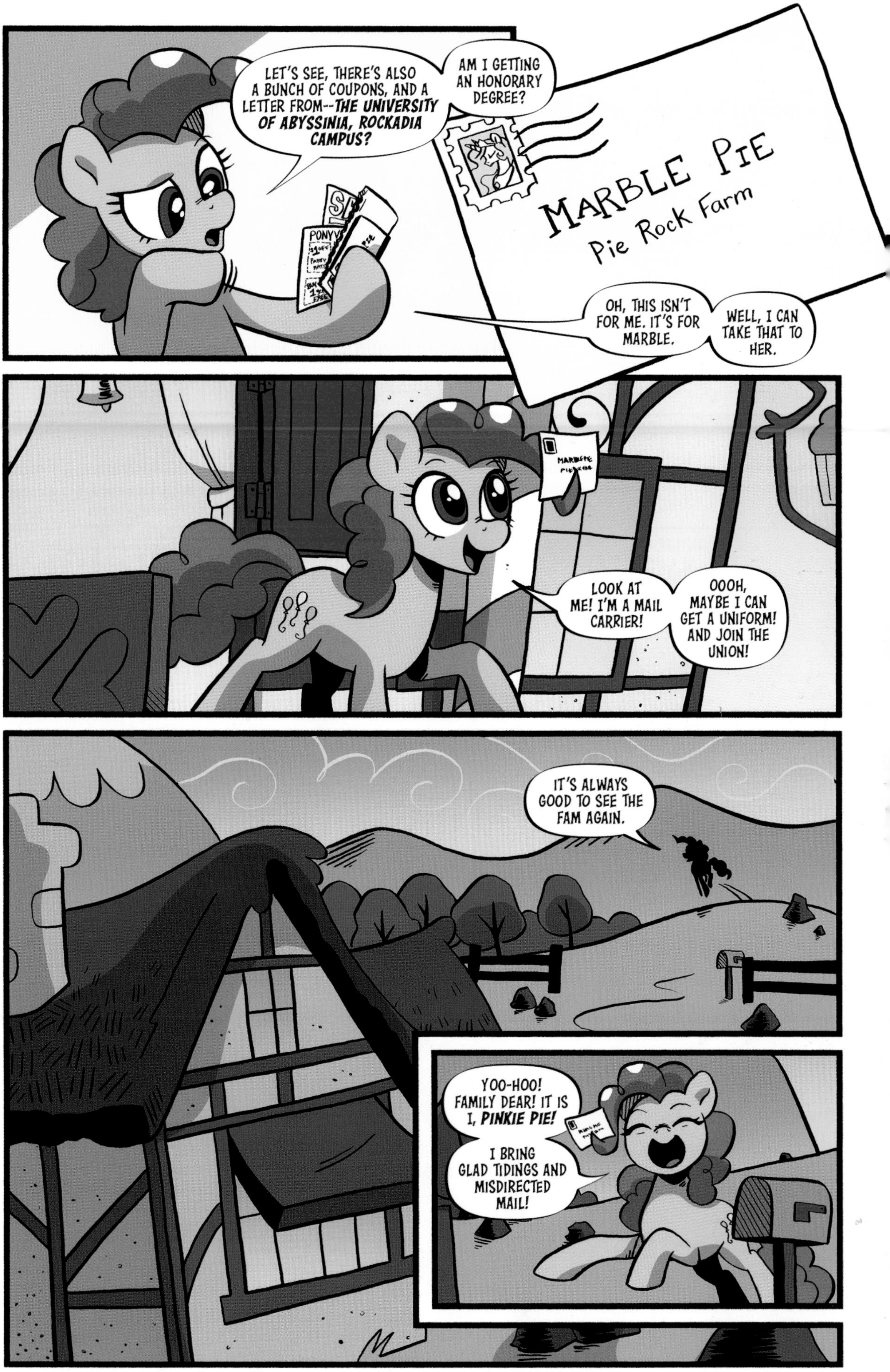
LET'S SEE, THERE'S ALSO A BUNCH OF COUPONS, AND A LETTER FROM--THE UNIVERSITY OF ABYSSINIA, ROCKADIA CAMPUS?
AM I GETTING AN HONORARY DEGREE?
MARBLE PIE
Pie Rock Farm
OH, THIS ISN'T FOR ME. IT'S FOR MARBLE.
WELL, I CAN TAKE THAT TO HER.
LOOK AT ME! I'M A MAIL CARRIER!
OOOH, MAYBE I CAN GET A UNIFORM! AND JOIN THE UNION!
IT'S ALWAYS GOOD TO SEE THE FAM AGAIN.
YOO-HOO! FAMILY DEAR! IT IS I, PINKIE PIE!
I BRING GLAD TIDINGS AND MISDIRECTED MAIL!

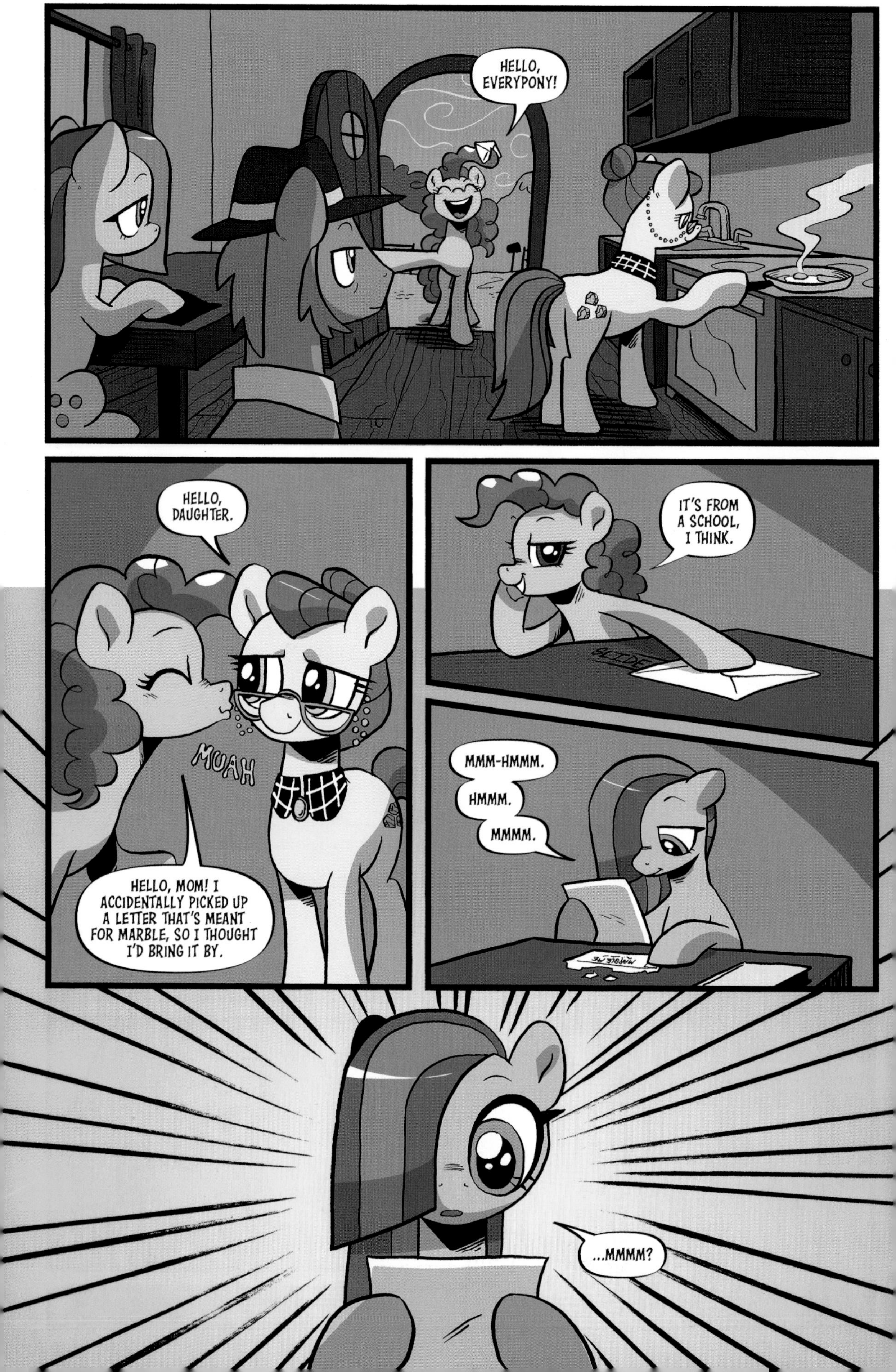
HELLO, EVERYPONY!
HELLO, DAUGHTER.
HELLO, MOM! I ACCIDENTALLY PICKED UP A LETTER THAT'S MEANT FOR MARBLE, SO I THOUGHT I'D BRING IT BY.
MUAH
IT'S FROM A SCHOOL, I THINK.
SLIDE
MMM-HMMM.
HMMM.
MMMM.
...MMMM?

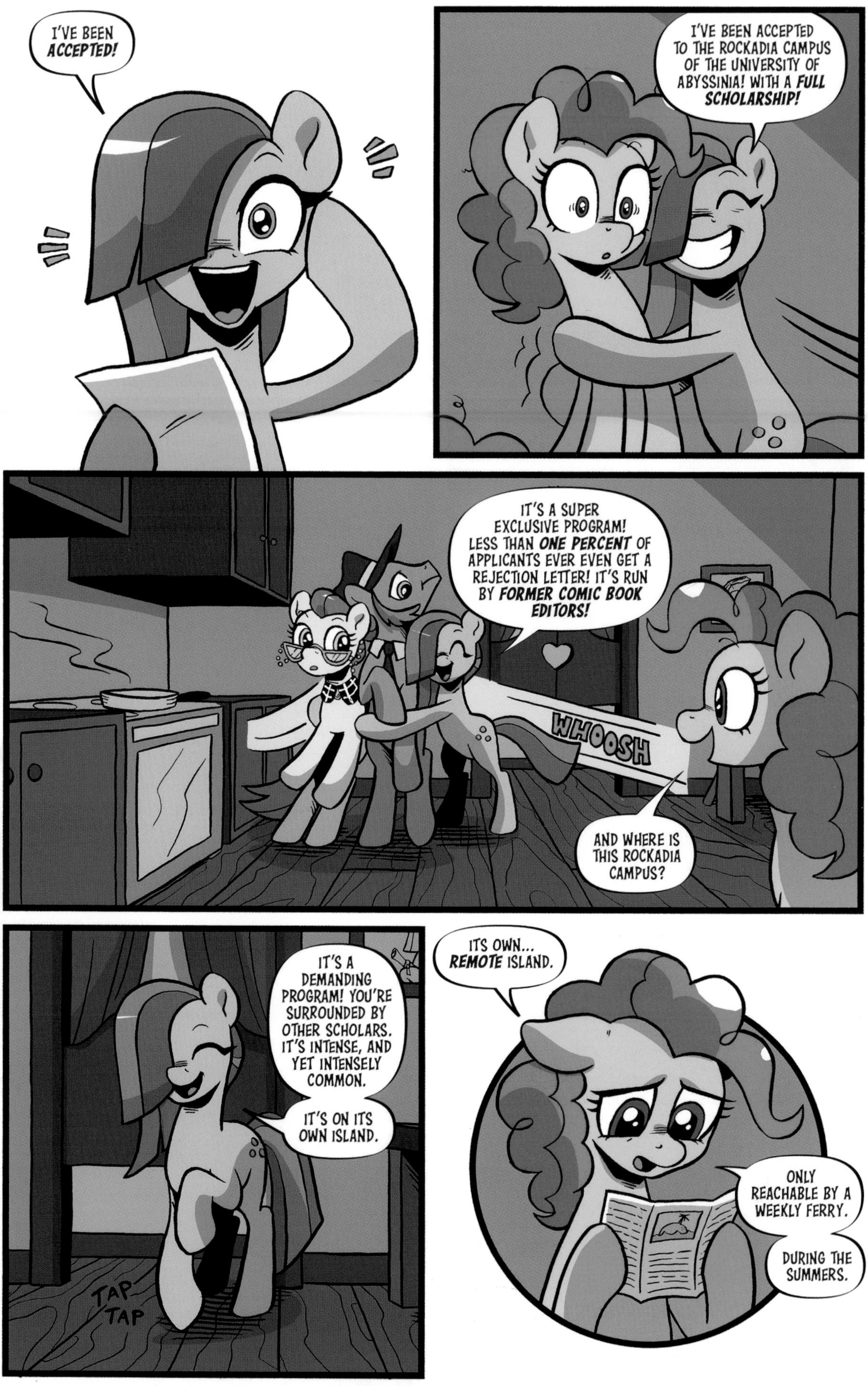
I'VE BEEN ACCEPTED!
I'VE BEEN ACCEPTED TO THE ROCKADIA CAMPUS OF THE UNIVERSITY OF ABYSSINIA! WITH A FULL SCHOLARSHIP!
IT'S A SUPER EXCLUSIVE PROGRAM! LESS THAN ONE PERCENT OF APPLICANTS EVER EVEN GET A REJECTION LETTER! IT'S RUN BY FORMER COMIC BOOK EDITORS!
WHOOSH
AND WHERE IS THIS ROCKADIA CAMPUS?
IT'S A DEMANDING PROGRAM! YOU'RE SURROUNDED BY OTHER SCHOLARS. IT'S INTENSE, AND YET INTENSELY COMMON.
IT'S ON ITS OWN ISLAND.
TAP TAP
ITS OWN... REMOTE ISLAND.
ONLY REACHABLE BY A WEEKLY FERRY.
DURING THE SUMMERS.

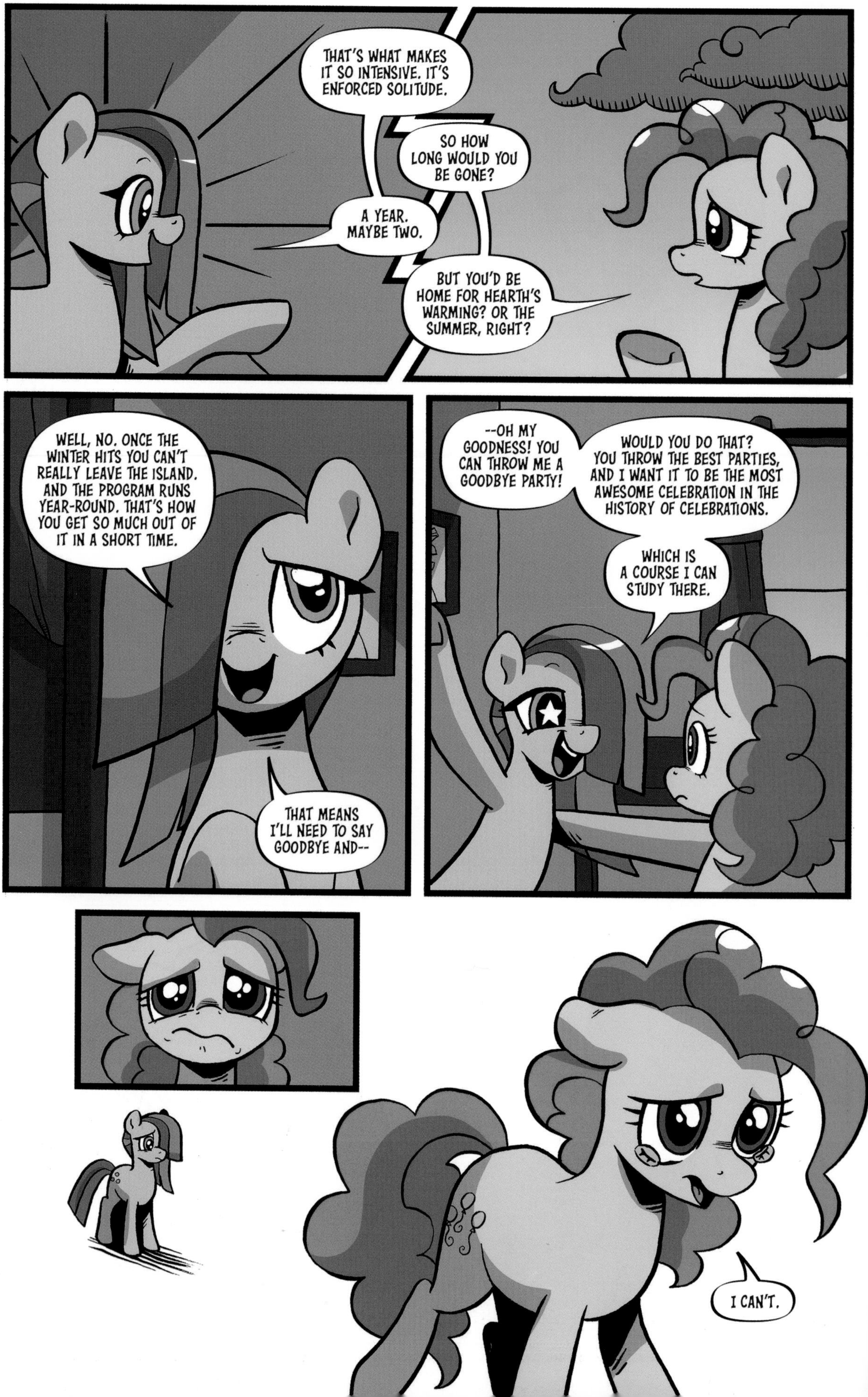
THAT'S WHAT MAKES IT SO INTENSIVE. IT'S ENFORCED SOLITUDE.
SO HOW LONG WOULD YOU BE GONE?
A YEAR. MAYBE TWO.
BUT YOU'D BE HOME FOR HEARTH'S WARMING? OR THE SUMMER, RIGHT?
WELL, NO. ONCE THE WINTER HITS YOU CAN'T REALLY LEAVE THE ISLAND. AND THE PROGRAM RUNS YEAR-ROUND. THAT'S HOW YOU GET SO MUCH OUT OF IT IN A SHORT TIME.
THAT MEANS I'LL NEED TO SAY GOODBYE AND--
--OH MY GOODNESS! YOU CAN THROW ME A GOODBYE PARTY!
WOULD YOU DO THAT? YOU THROW THE BEST PARTIES, AND I WANT IT TO BE THE MOST AWESOME CELEBRATION IN THE HISTORY OF CELEBRATIONS.
WHICH IS A COURSE I CAN STUDY THERE.
I CAN'T.

DID PINKIE JUST TURN DOWN THE CHANCE TO PLAN A PARTY?

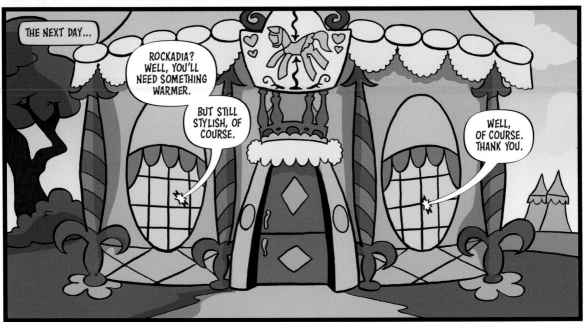

THE NEXT DAY...

ROCKADIA? WELL, YOU'LL NEED SOMETHING WARMER.

BUT STILL STYLISH, OF COURSE.

WELL, OF COURSE. THANK YOU.

IS YOUR SISTER PLANNING A GIANT GOODBYE PARTY FOR YOU?

NO. SHE'S NOT.

IN FACT, SHE'S BARELY SPOKEN TO ME SINCE I GOT THE ACCEPTANCE.

PINKIE? SILENT? THAT'S UNUSUAL.

I THINK THIS BEARS SOME INVESTIGATION.

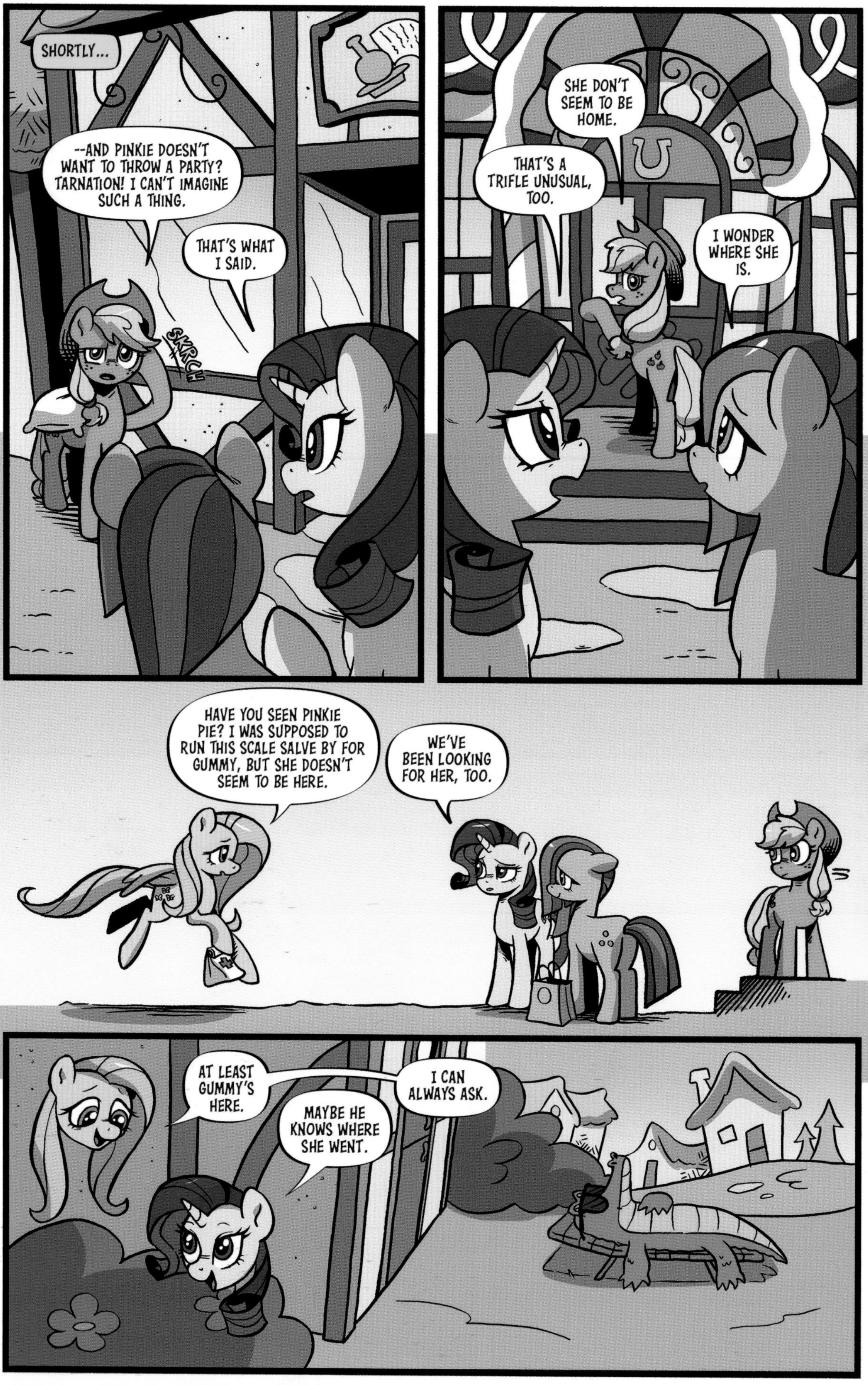
SHORTLY...
--AND PINKIE DOESN'T WANT TO THROW A PARTY? TARNATION! I CAN'T IMAGINE SUCH A THING.
THAT'S WHAT I SAID.
SKRCH
SHE DON'T SEEM TO BE HOME.
THAT'S A TRIFLE UNUSUAL, TOO.
I WONDER WHERE SHE IS.
HAVE YOU SEEN PINKIE PIE? I WAS SUPPOSED TO RUN THIS SCALE SALVE BY FOR GUMMY, BUT SHE DOESN'T SEEM TO BE HERE.
WE'VE BEEN LOOKING FOR HER, TOO.
AT LEAST GUMMY'S HERE.
I CAN ALWAYS ASK.
MAYBE HE KNOWS WHERE SHE WENT.

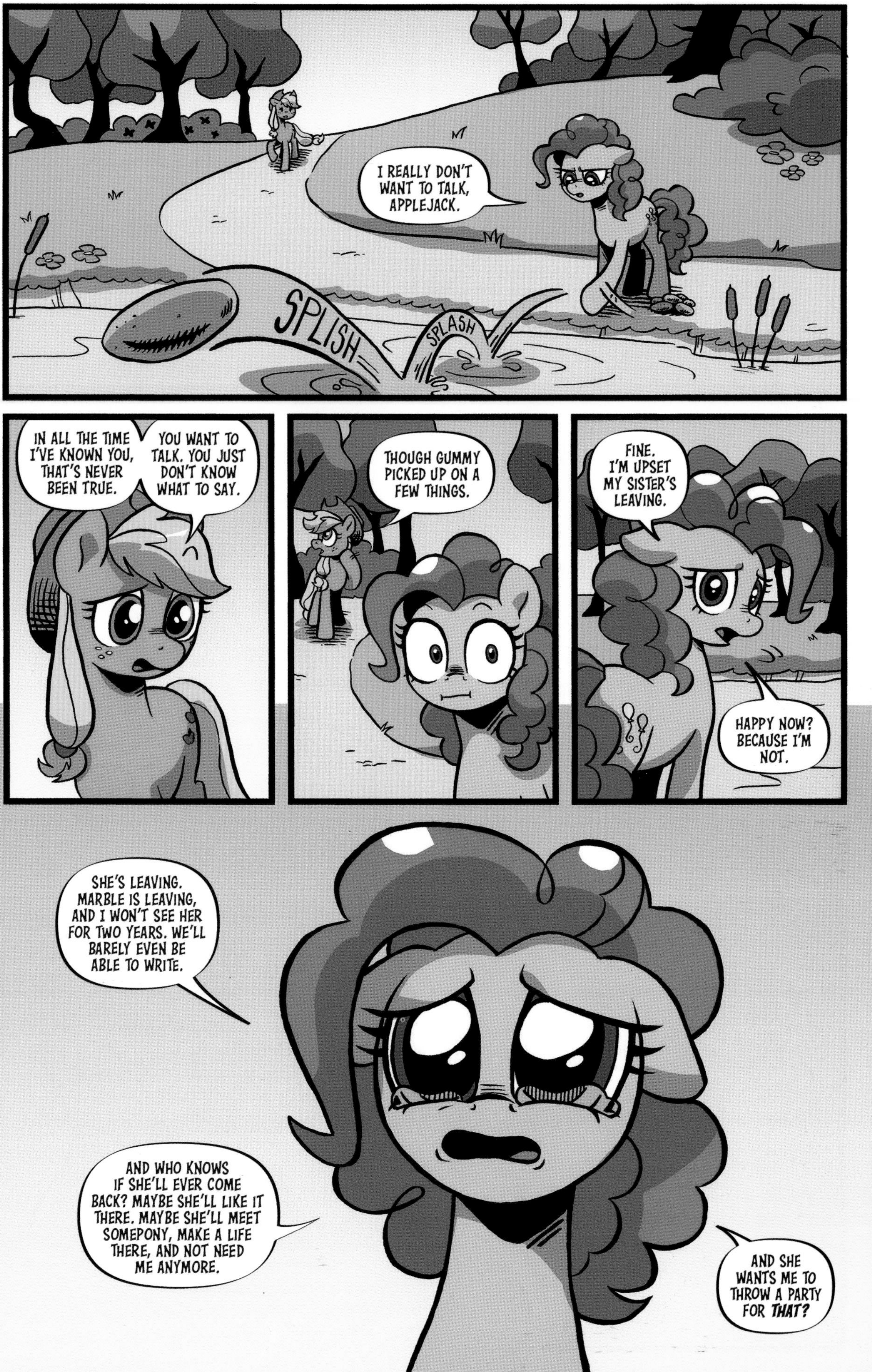
I REALLY DON'T WANT TO TALK, APPLEJACK.
SPLISH
SPLASH
IN ALL THE TIME I'VE KNOWN YOU, THAT'S NEVER BEEN TRUE.
YOU WANT TO TALK. YOU JUST DON'T KNOW WHAT TO SAY.
THOUGH GUMMY PICKED UP ON A FEW THINGS.
FINE. I'M UPSET MY SISTER'S LEAVING.
HAPPY NOW? BECAUSE I'M NOT.
SHE'S LEAVING. MARBLE IS LEAVING, AND I WON'T SEE HER FOR TWO YEARS. WE'LL BARELY EVEN BE ABLE TO WRITE.
AND WHO KNOWS IF SHE'LL EVER COME BACK? MAYBE SHE'LL LIKE IT THERE. MAYBE SHE'LL MEET SOMEPONY, MAKE A LIFE THERE, AND NOT NEED ME ANYMORE.
AND SHE WANTS ME TO THROW A PARTY FOR ***THAT?***

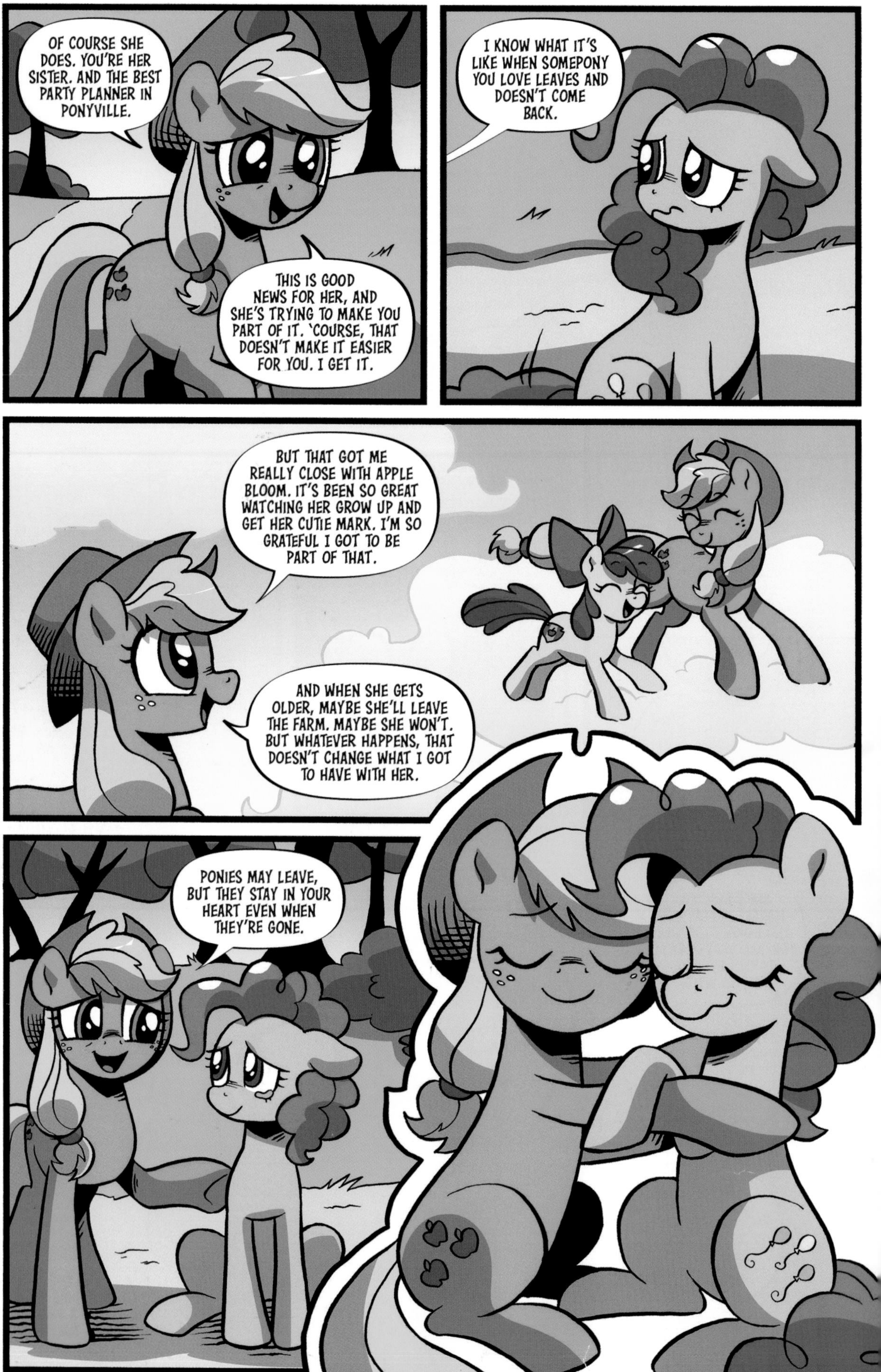
OF COURSE SHE DOES. YOU'RE HER SISTER. AND THE BEST PARTY PLANNER IN PONYVILLE.
THIS IS GOOD NEWS FOR HER, AND SHE'S TRYING TO MAKE YOU PART OF IT. 'COURSE, THAT DOESN'T MAKE IT EASIER FOR YOU. I GET IT.
I KNOW WHAT IT'S LIKE WHEN SOMEPONY YOU LOVE LEAVES AND DOESN'T COME BACK.
BUT THAT GOT ME REALLY CLOSE WITH APPLE BLOOM. IT'S BEEN SO GREAT WATCHING HER GROW UP AND GET HER CUTIE MARK. I'M SO GRATEFUL I GOT TO BE PART OF THAT.
AND WHEN SHE GETS OLDER, MAYBE SHE'LL LEAVE THE FARM. MAYBE SHE WON'T. BUT WHATEVER HAPPENS, THAT DOESN'T CHANGE WHAT I GOT TO HAVE WITH HER.
PONIES MAY LEAVE, BUT THEY STAY IN YOUR HEART EVEN WHEN THEY'RE GONE.

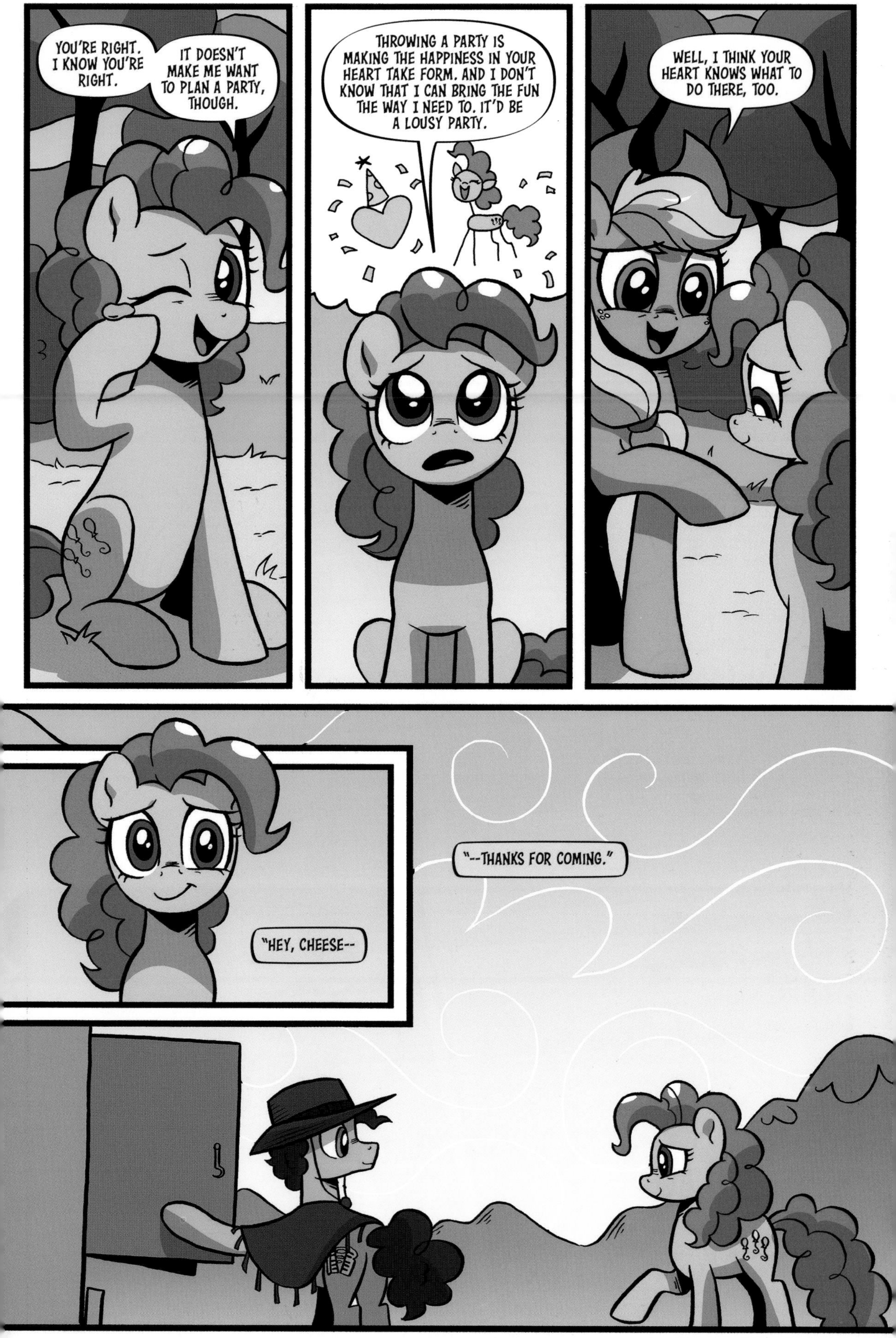

YOU'RE RIGHT. I KNOW YOU'RE RIGHT.
IT DOESN'T MAKE ME WANT TO PLAN A PARTY, THOUGH.
THROWING A PARTY IS MAKING THE HAPPINESS IN YOUR HEART TAKE FORM. AND I DON'T KNOW THAT I CAN BRING THE FUN THE WAY I NEED TO. IT'D BE A LOUSY PARTY.
WELL, I THINK YOUR HEART KNOWS WHAT TO DO THERE, TOO.
"HEY, CHEESE--
"--THANKS FOR COMING."

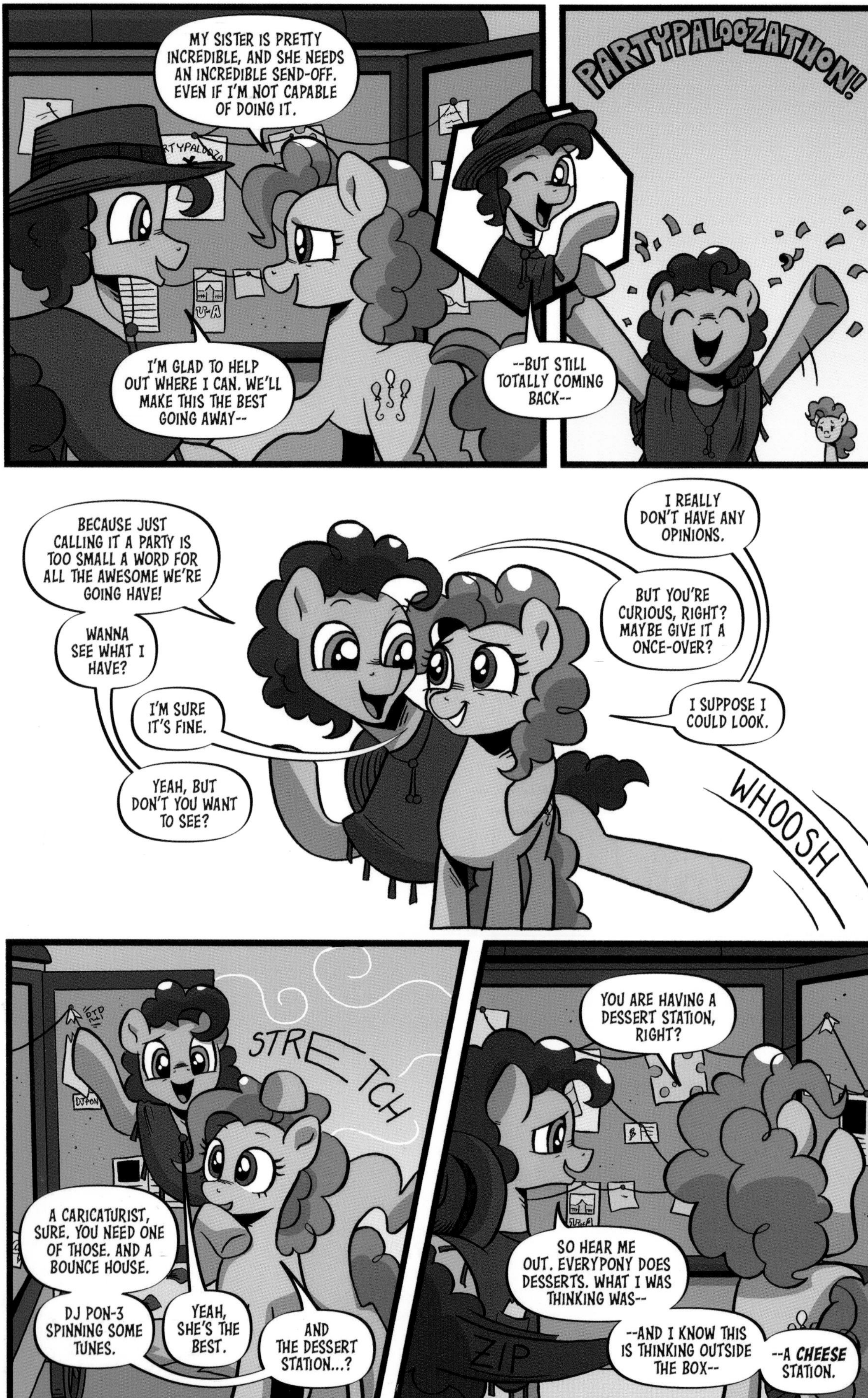
MY SISTER IS PRETTY INCREDIBLE, AND SHE NEEDS AN INCREDIBLE SEND-OFF. EVEN IF I'M NOT CAPABLE OF DOING IT.
I'M GLAD TO HELP OUT WHERE I CAN. WE'LL MAKE THIS THE BEST GOING AWAY--
--BUT STILL TOTALLY COMING BACK--
PARTYPALOOZATHON!
BECAUSE JUST CALLING IT A PARTY IS TOO SMALL A WORD FOR ALL THE AWESOME WE'RE GOING HAVE!
WANNA SEE WHAT I HAVE?
I'M SURE IT'S FINE.
YEAH, BUT DON'T YOU WANT TO SEE?
I REALLY DON'T HAVE ANY OPINIONS.
BUT YOU'RE CURIOUS, RIGHT? MAYBE GIVE IT A ONCE-OVER?
I SUPPOSE I COULD LOOK.
WHOOSH
STRETCH
A CARICATURIST, SURE. YOU NEED ONE OF THOSE. AND A BOUNCE HOUSE.
DJ PON-3 SPINNING SOME TUNES.
YEAH, SHE'S THE BEST.
AND THE DESSERT STATION...?
YOU ARE HAVING A DESSERT STATION, RIGHT?
SO HEAR ME OUT. EVERYPONY DOES DESSERTS. WHAT I WAS THINKING WAS--
ZIP
--AND I KNOW THIS IS THINKING OUTSIDE THE BOX--
--A *CHEESE* STATION.

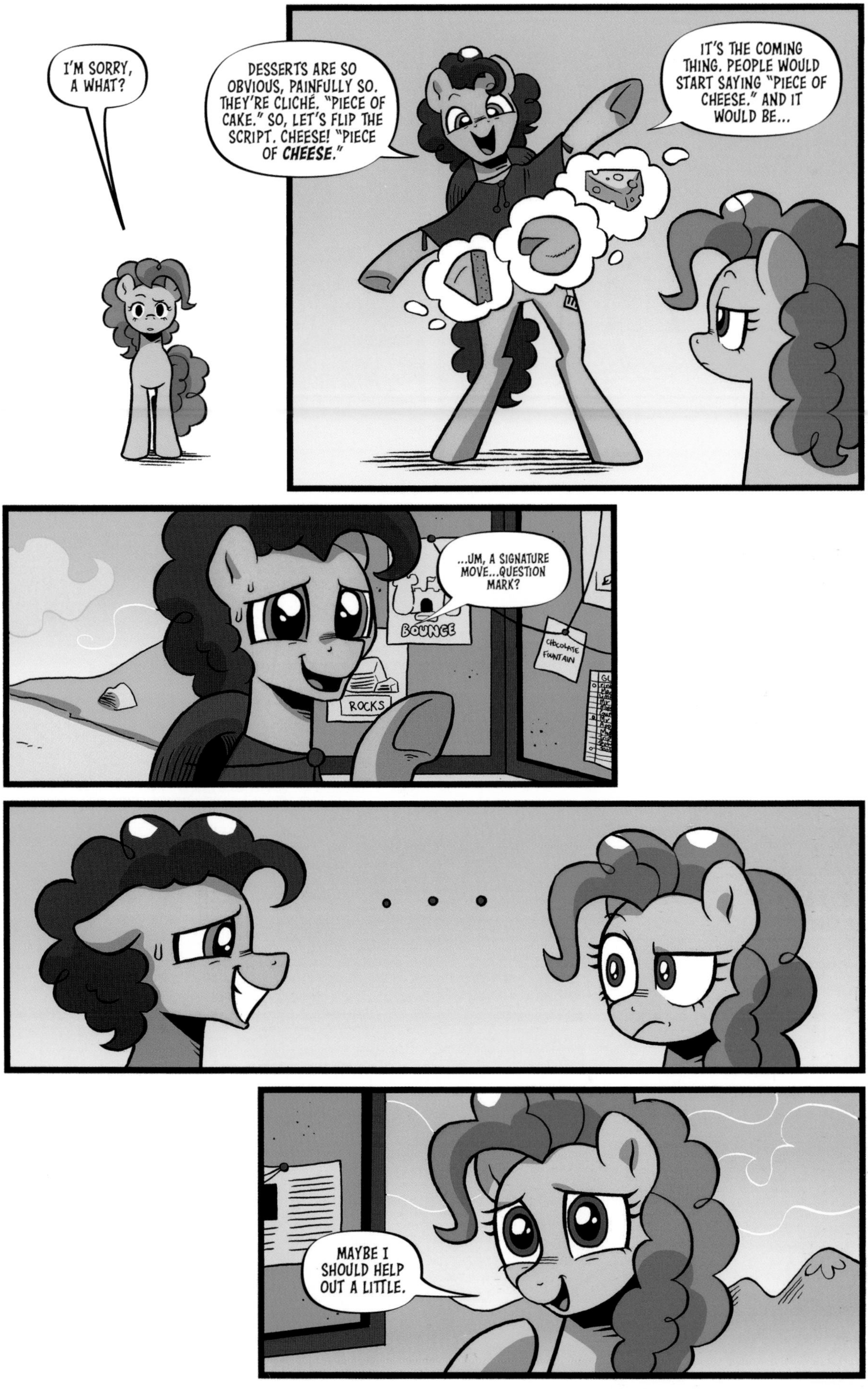
I'M SORRY, A WHAT?
DESSERTS ARE SO OBVIOUS, PAINFULLY SO. THEY'RE CLICHÉ. "PIECE OF CAKE." SO, LET'S FLIP THE SCRIPT. CHEESE! "PIECE OF CHEESE."
IT'S THE COMING THING. PEOPLE WOULD START SAYING "PIECE OF CHEESE." AND IT WOULD BE...
BOUNCE
ROCKS
CHOCOLATE FOUNTAIN
...UM, A SIGNATURE MOVE...QUESTION MARK?
. . .
MAYBE I SHOULD HELP OUT A LITTLE.

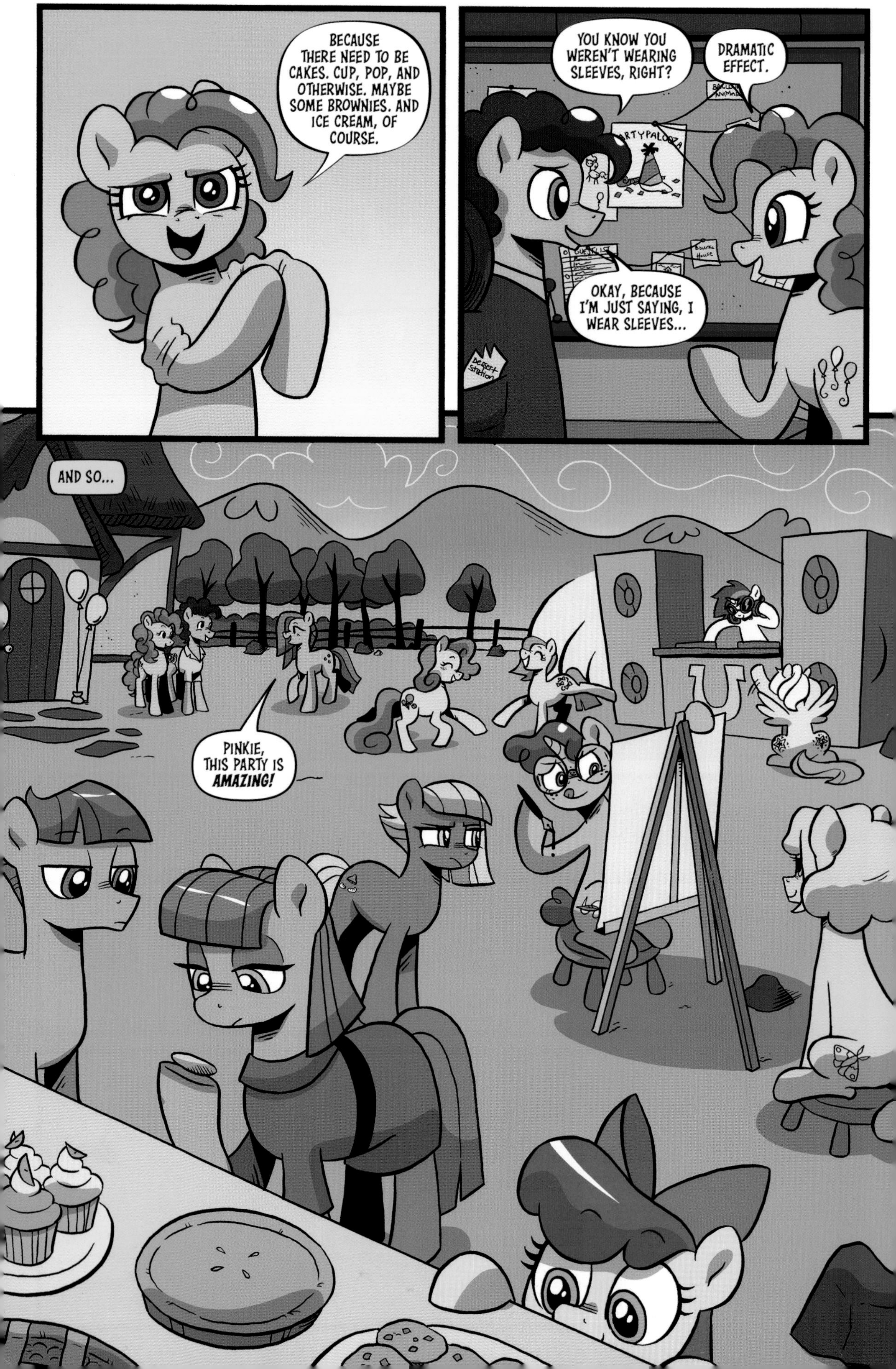

BECAUSE THERE NEED TO BE CAKES. CUP, POP, AND OTHERWISE. MAYBE SOME BROWNIES. AND ICE CREAM, OF COURSE.
YOU KNOW YOU WEREN'T WEARING SLEEVES, RIGHT?
DRAMATIC EFFECT.
OKAY, BECAUSE I'M JUST SAYING, I WEAR SLEEVES...
AND SO...
PINKIE, THIS PARTY IS AMAZING!

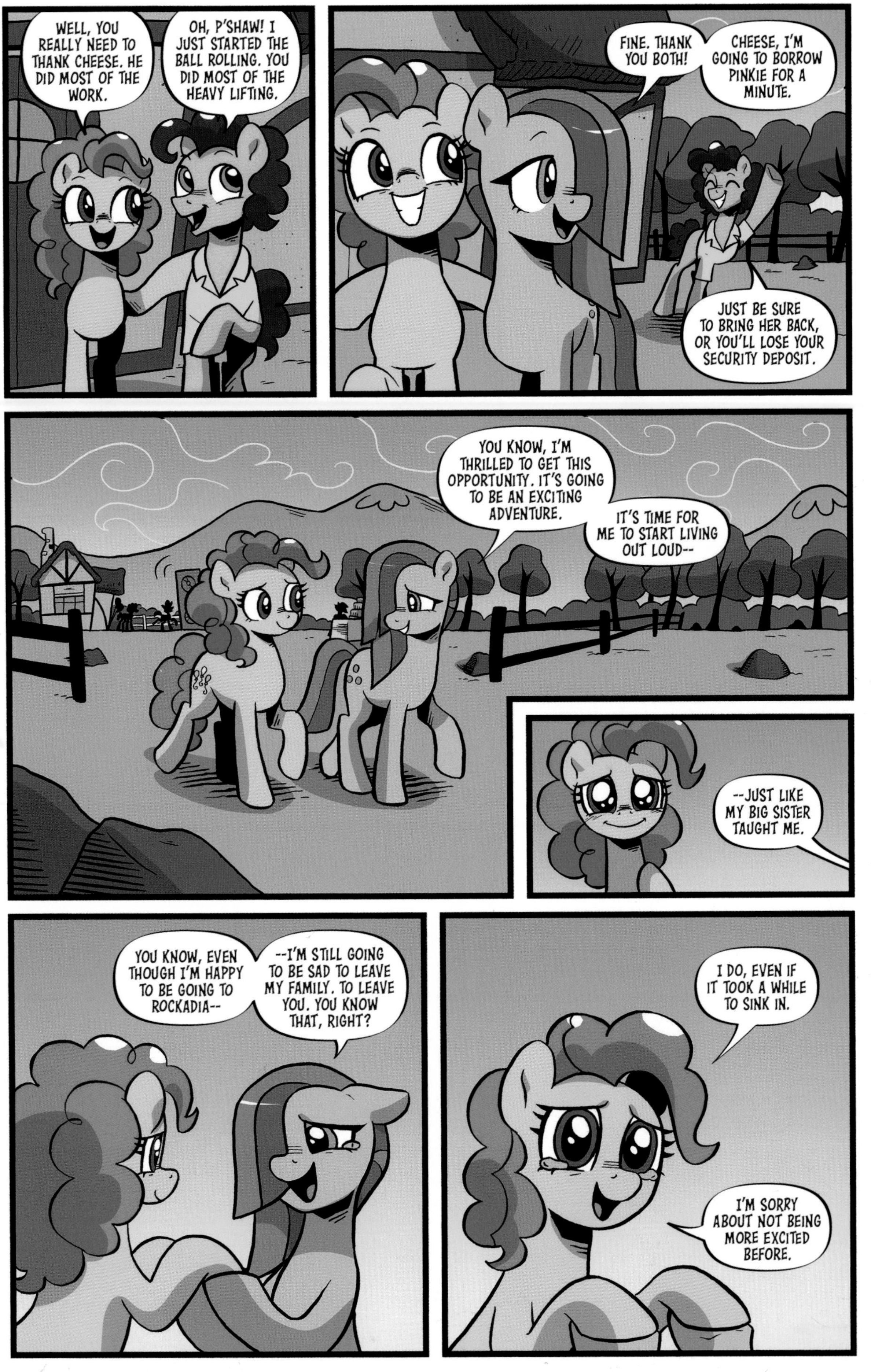
WELL, YOU REALLY NEED TO THANK CHEESE. HE DID MOST OF THE WORK.
OH, P'SHAW! I JUST STARTED THE BALL ROLLING. YOU DID MOST OF THE HEAVY LIFTING.
FINE. THANK YOU BOTH!
CHEESE, I'M GOING TO BORROW PINKIE FOR A MINUTE.
JUST BE SURE TO BRING HER BACK, OR YOU'LL LOSE YOUR SECURITY DEPOSIT.
YOU KNOW, I'M THRILLED TO GET THIS OPPORTUNITY. IT'S GOING TO BE AN EXCITING ADVENTURE.
IT'S TIME FOR ME TO START LIVING OUT LOUD--
--JUST LIKE MY BIG SISTER TAUGHT ME.
YOU KNOW, EVEN THOUGH I'M HAPPY TO BE GOING TO ROCKADIA--
--I'M STILL GOING TO BE SAD TO LEAVE MY FAMILY. TO LEAVE YOU. YOU KNOW THAT, RIGHT?
I DO, EVEN IF IT TOOK A WHILE TO SINK IN.
I'M SORRY ABOUT NOT BEING MORE EXCITED BEFORE.

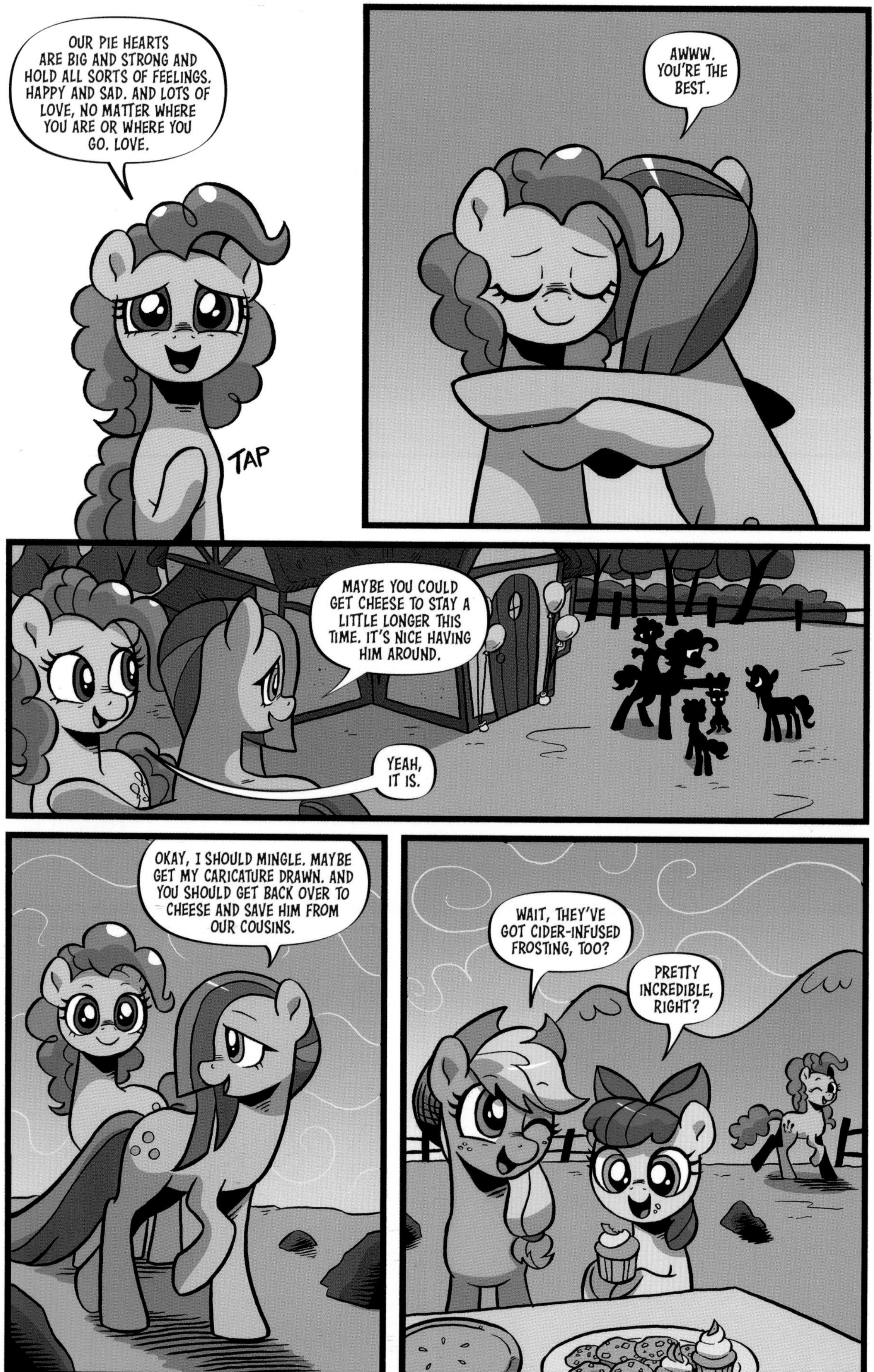
OUR PIE HEARTS ARE BIG AND STRONG AND HOLD ALL SORTS OF FEELINGS. HAPPY AND SAD. AND LOTS OF LOVE, NO MATTER WHERE YOU ARE OR WHERE YOU GO. LOVE.
TAP
AWWW. YOU'RE THE BEST.
MAYBE YOU COULD GET CHEESE TO STAY A LITTLE LONGER THIS TIME. IT'S NICE HAVING HIM AROUND.
YEAH, IT IS.
OKAY, I SHOULD MINGLE. MAYBE GET MY CARICATURE DRAWN. AND YOU SHOULD GET BACK OVER TO CHEESE AND SAVE HIM FROM OUR COUSINS.
WAIT, THEY'VE GOT CIDER-INFUSED FROSTING, TOO?
PRETTY INCREDIBLE, RIGHT?

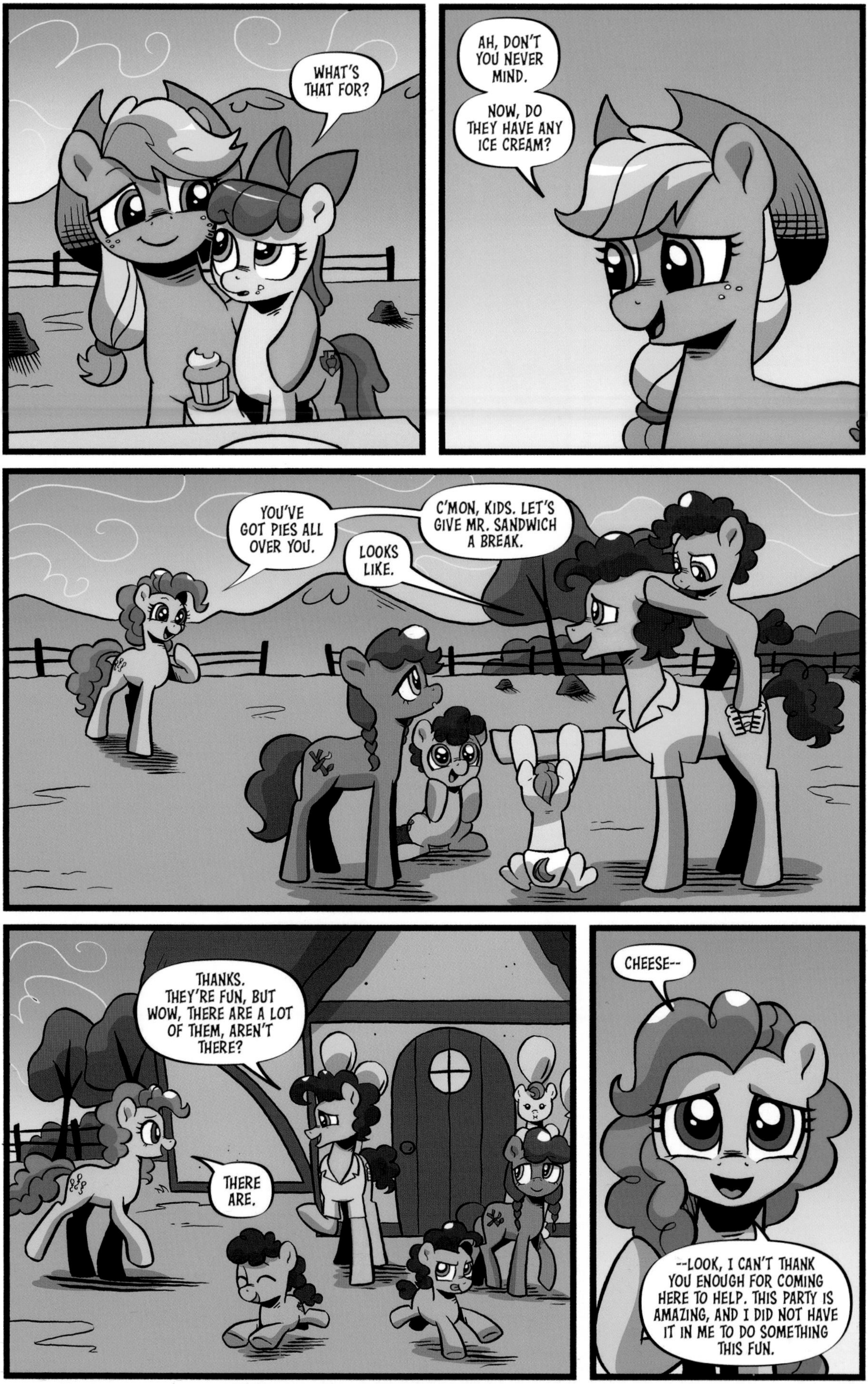
WHAT'S THAT FOR?
AH, DON'T YOU NEVER MIND.
NOW, DO THEY HAVE ANY ICE CREAM?
YOU'VE GOT PIES ALL OVER YOU.
C'MON, KIDS. LET'S GIVE MR. SANDWICH A BREAK.
LOOKS LIKE.
THANKS. THEY'RE FUN, BUT WOW, THERE ARE A LOT OF THEM, AREN'T THERE?
THERE ARE.
CHEESE--
--LOOK, I CAN'T THANK YOU ENOUGH FOR COMING HERE TO HELP. THIS PARTY IS AMAZING, AND I DID NOT HAVE IT IN ME TO DO SOMETHING THIS FUN.

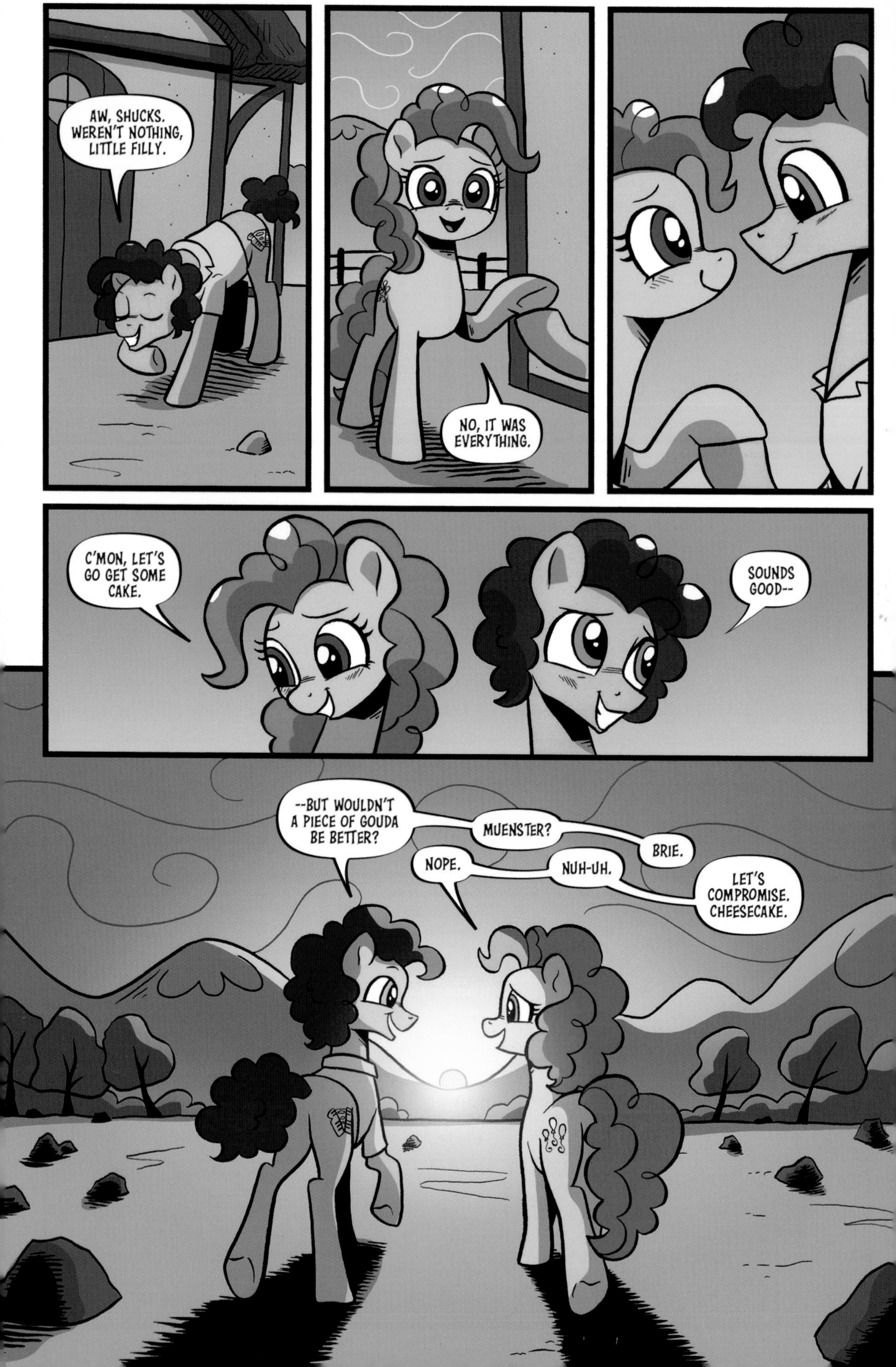
AW, SHUCKS. WEREN'T NOTHING, LITTLE FILLY.
NO, IT WAS EVERYTHING.
C'MON, LET'S GO GET SOME CAKE.
SOUNDS GOOD--
--BUT WOULDN'T A PIECE OF GOUDA BE BETTER?
NOPE.
MUENSTER?
NUH-UH.
BRIE.
LET'S COMPROMISE. CHEESECAKE.

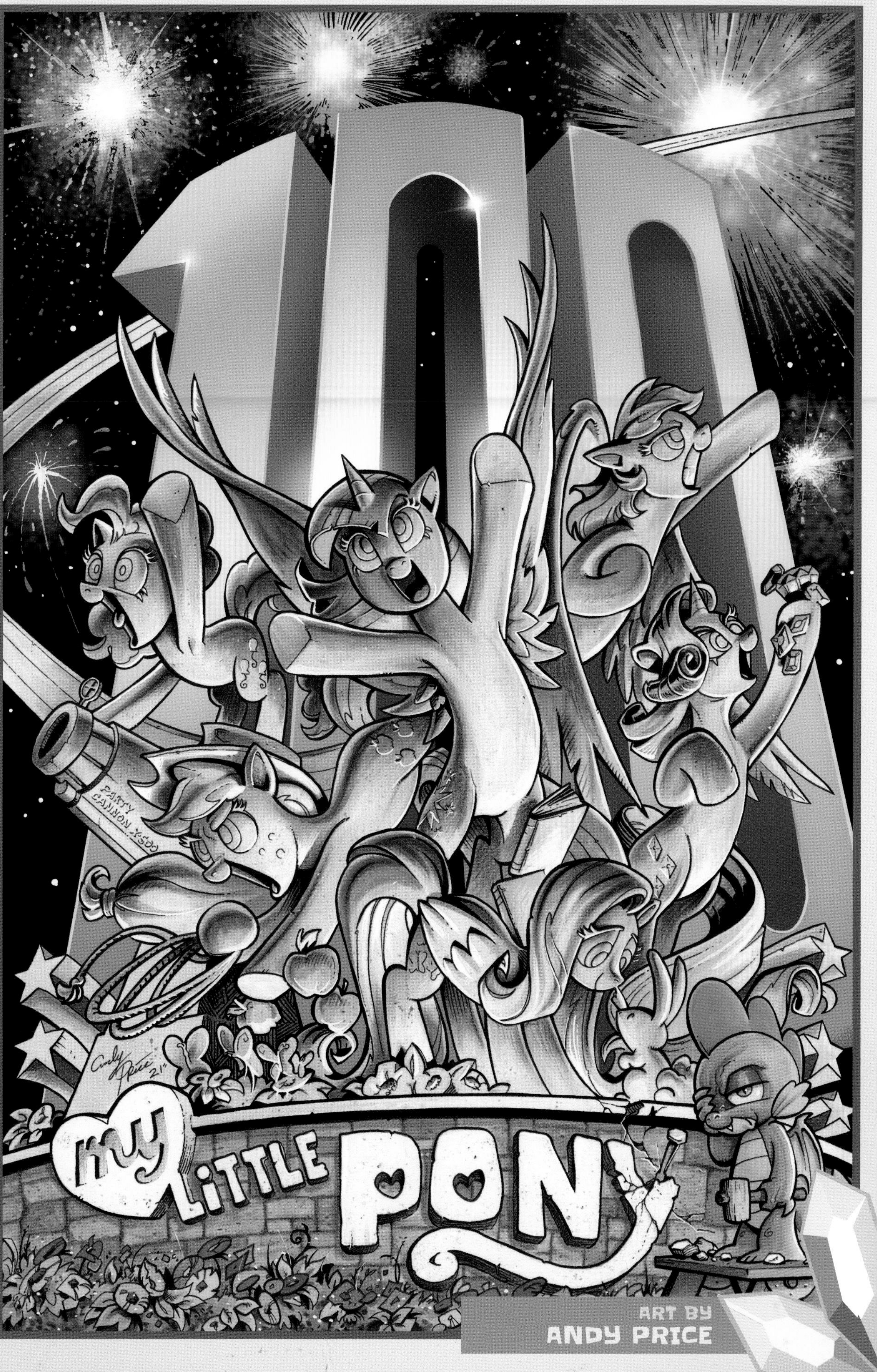
100
PARTY CANNON X-500
My Little Pony
ART BY
ANDY PRICE

The Finale

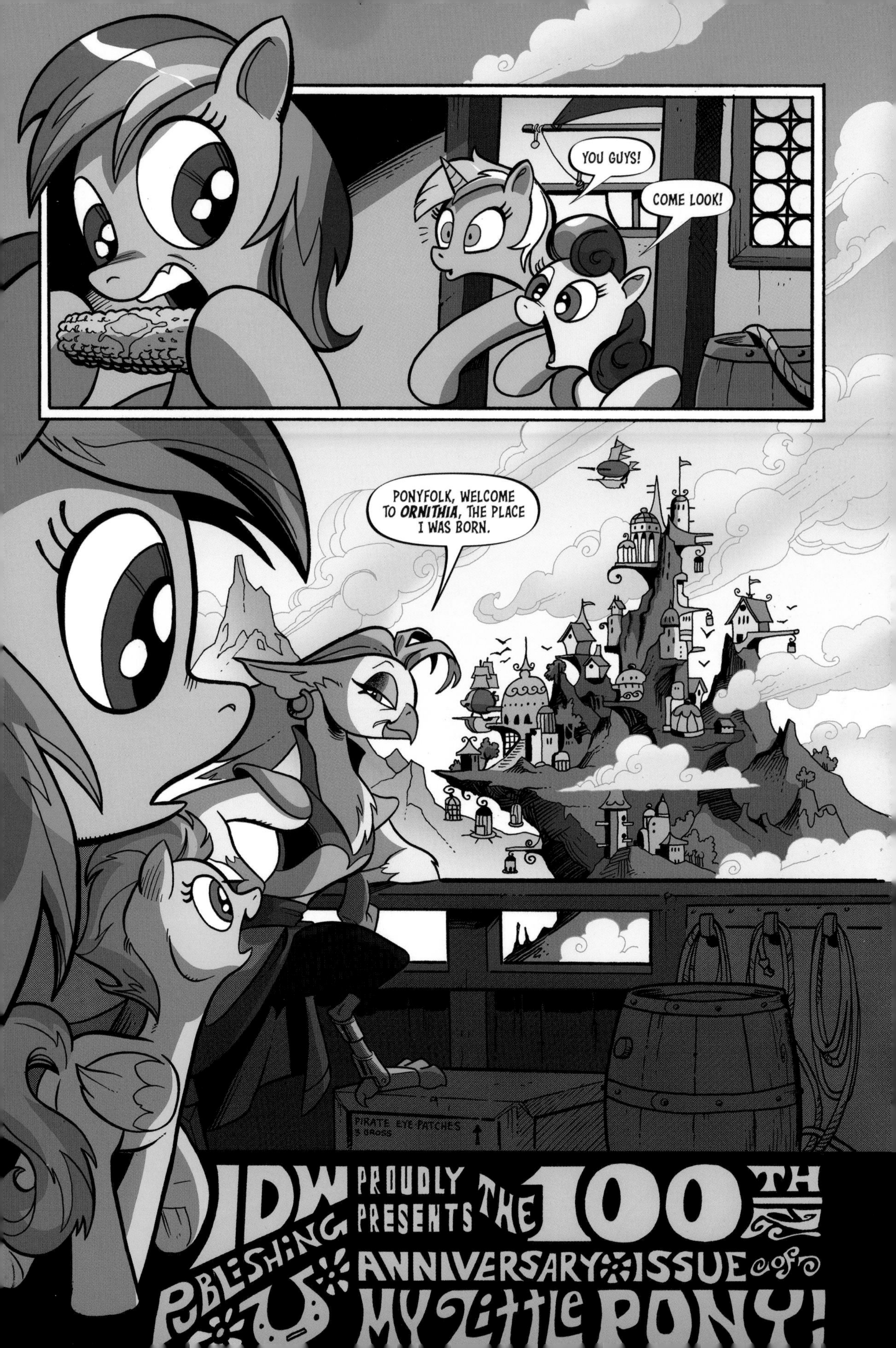
YOU GUYS!
COME LOOK!
PONYFOLK, WELCOME TO *ORNITHIA*, THE PLACE I WAS BORN.
PIRATE EYE PATCHES
3 GROSS
IDW PUBLISHING PROUDLY PRESENTS THE 100TH ANNIVERSARY ISSUE of MY Little PONY!

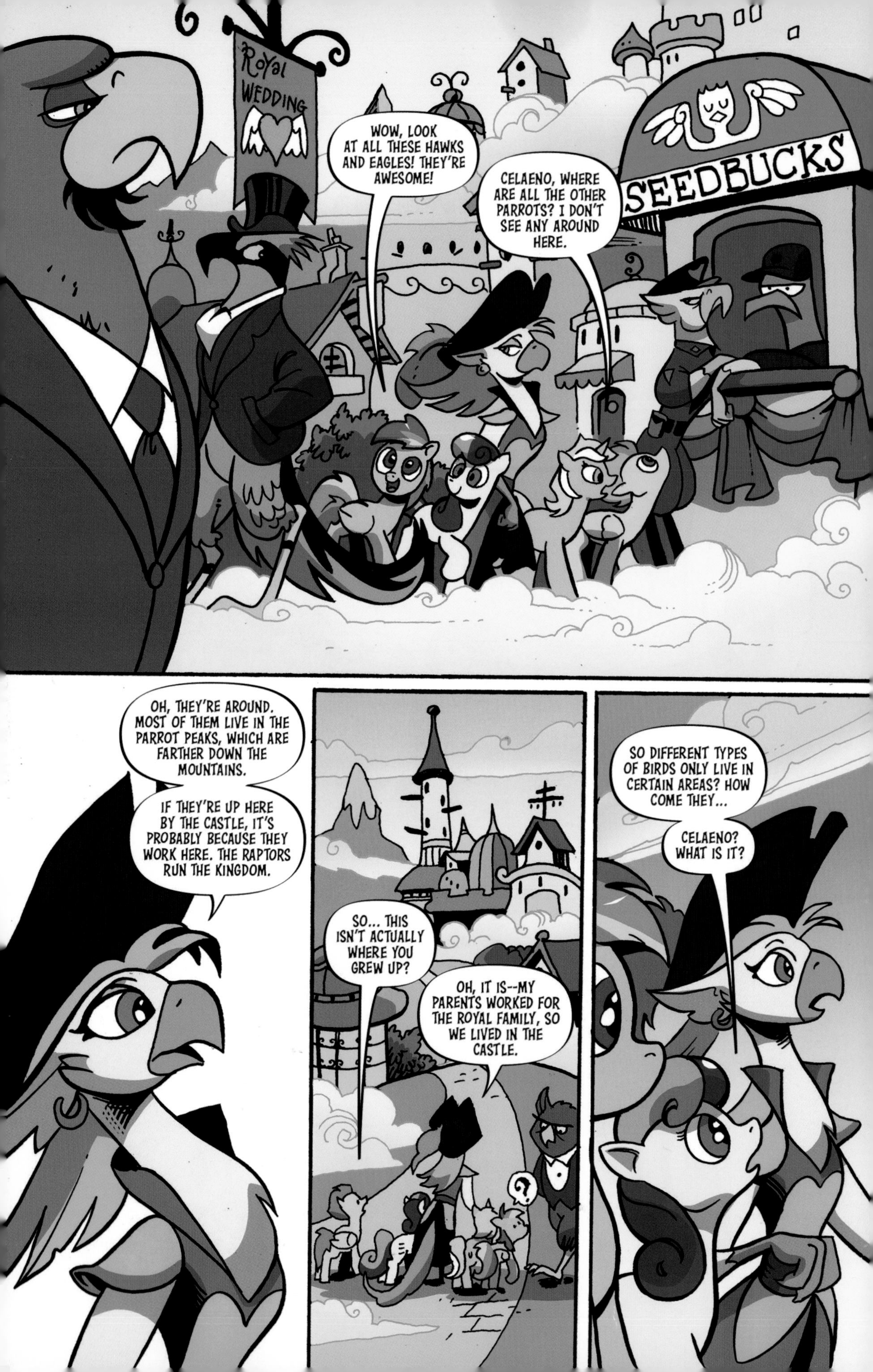
Royal WEDDING
SEEDBUCKS
WOW, LOOK AT ALL THESE HAWKS AND EAGLES! THEY'RE AWESOME!
CELAENO, WHERE ARE ALL THE OTHER PARROTS? I DON'T SEE ANY AROUND HERE.
OH, THEY'RE AROUND. MOST OF THEM LIVE IN THE PARROT PEAKS, WHICH ARE FARTHER DOWN THE MOUNTAINS.
IF THEY'RE UP HERE BY THE CASTLE, IT'S PROBABLY BECAUSE THEY WORK HERE. THE RAPTORS RUN THE KINGDOM.
SO... THIS ISN'T ACTUALLY WHERE YOU GREW UP?
OH, IT IS--MY PARENTS WORKED FOR THE ROYAL FAMILY, SO WE LIVED IN THE CASTLE.
?
SO DIFFERENT TYPES OF BIRDS ONLY LIVE IN CERTAIN AREAS? HOW COME THEY...
CELAENO? WHAT IS IT?

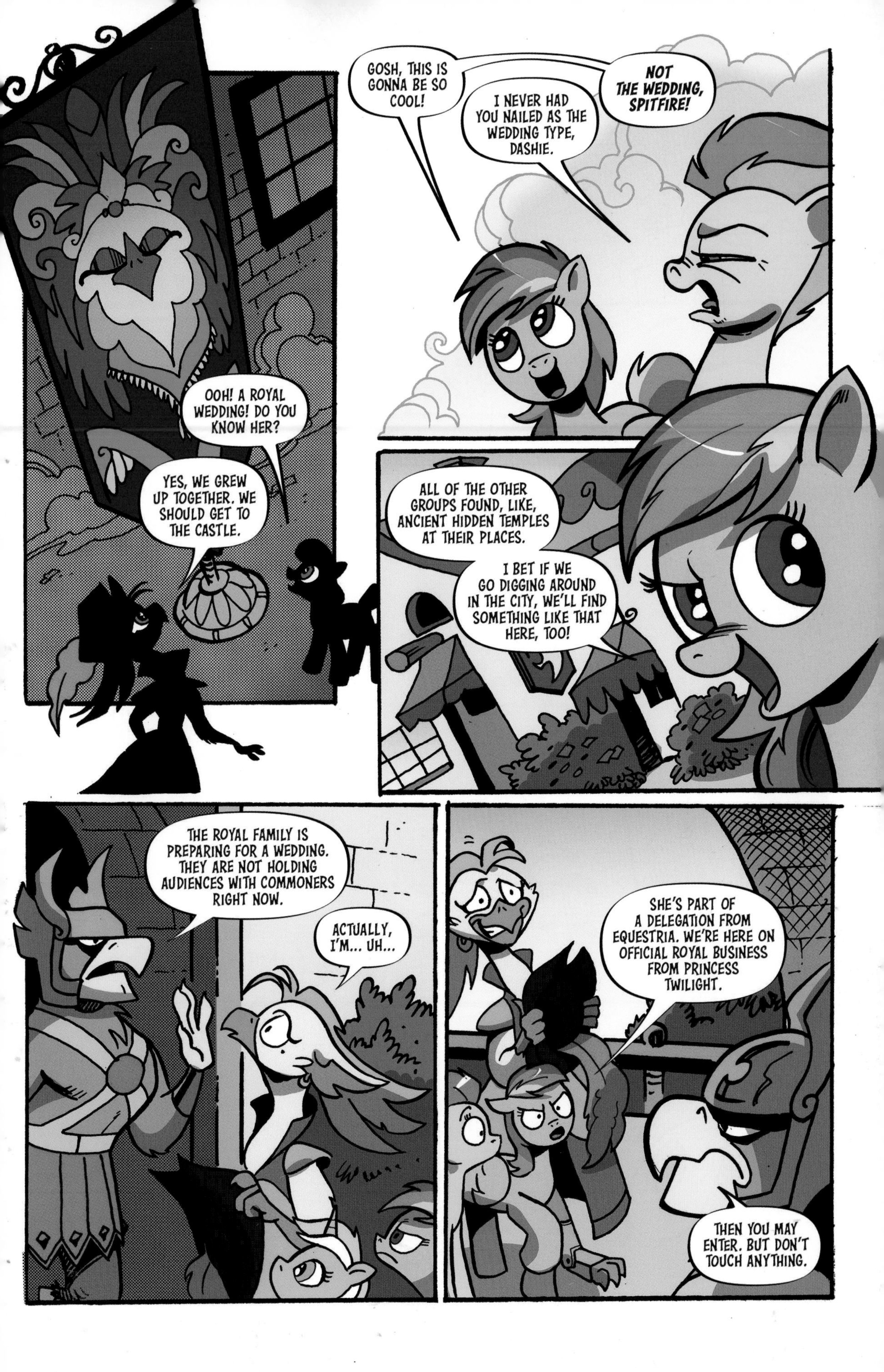
OOH! A ROYAL WEDDING! DO YOU KNOW HER?
YES, WE GREW UP TOGETHER. WE SHOULD GET TO THE CASTLE.
GOSH, THIS IS GONNA BE SO COOL!
I NEVER HAD YOU NAILED AS THE WEDDING TYPE, DASHIE.
NOT THE WEDDING, SPITFIRE!
ALL OF THE OTHER GROUPS FOUND, LIKE, ANCIENT HIDDEN TEMPLES AT THEIR PLACES.
I BET IF WE GO DIGGING AROUND IN THE CITY, WE'LL FIND SOMETHING LIKE THAT HERE, TOO!
THE ROYAL FAMILY IS PREPARING FOR A WEDDING. THEY ARE NOT HOLDING AUDIENCES WITH COMMONERS RIGHT NOW.
ACTUALLY, I'M... UH...
SHE'S PART OF A DELEGATION FROM EQUESTRIA. WE'RE HERE ON OFFICIAL ROYAL BUSINESS FROM PRINCESS TWILIGHT.
THEN YOU MAY ENTER. BUT DON'T TOUCH ANYTHING.

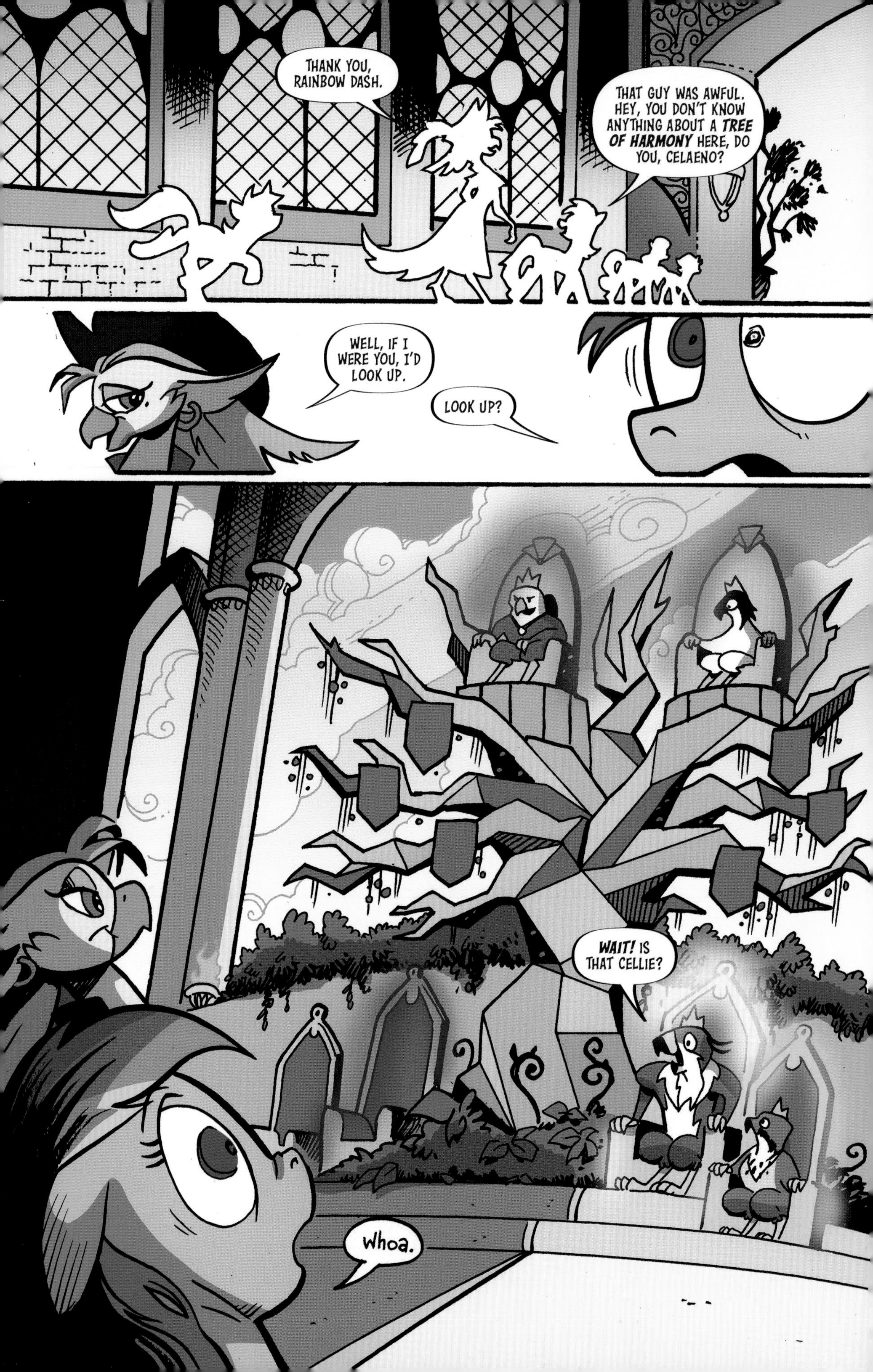
THANK YOU, RAINBOW DASH.
THAT GUY WAS AWFUL. HEY, YOU DON'T KNOW ANYTHING ABOUT A *TREE OF HARMONY* HERE, DO YOU, CELAENO?
WELL, IF I WERE YOU, I'D LOOK UP.
LOOK UP?
WAIT! IS THAT CELLIE?
Whoa.

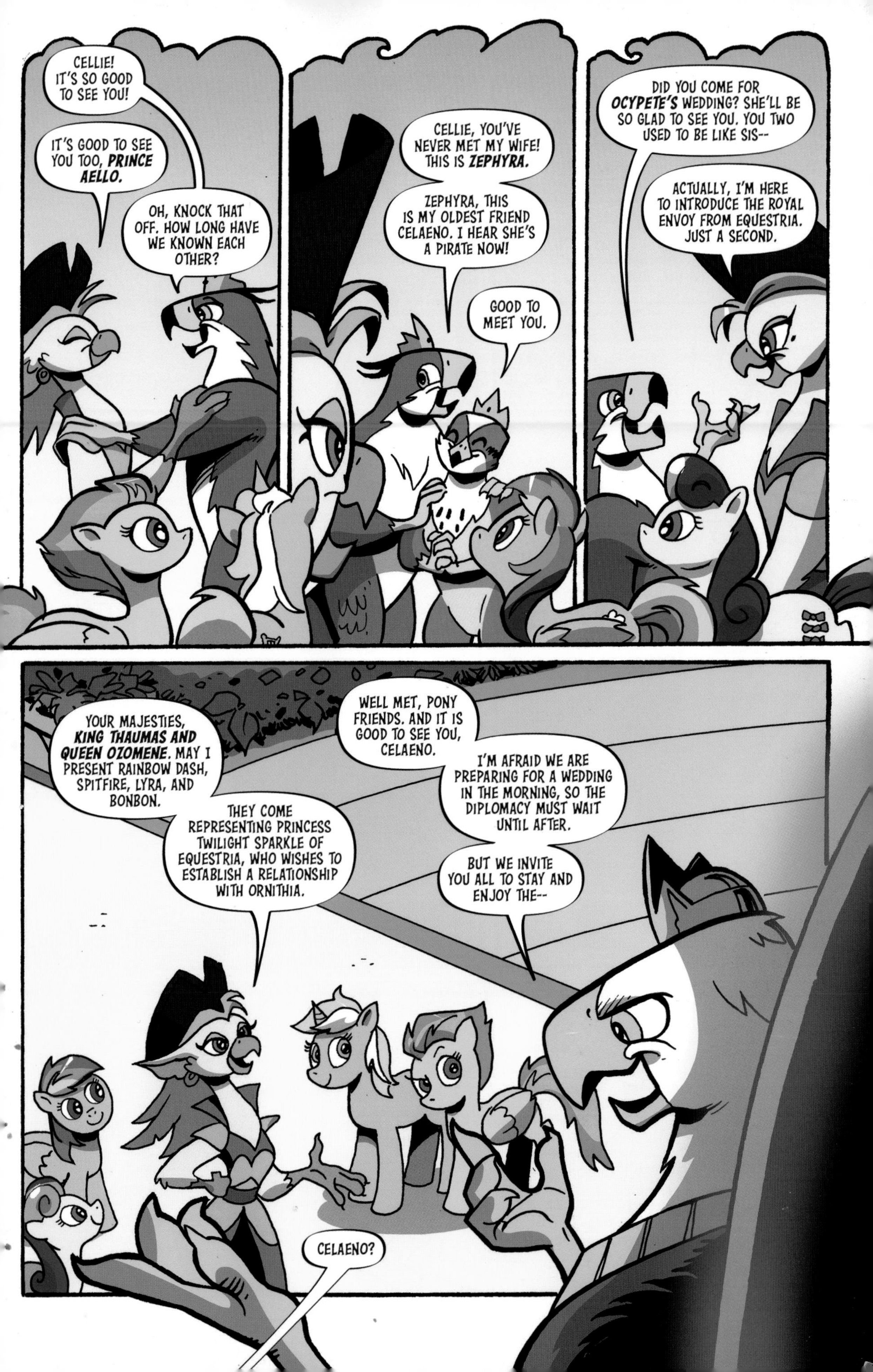
CELLIE! IT'S SO GOOD TO SEE YOU!
IT'S GOOD TO SEE YOU TOO, **PRINCE AELLO.**
OH, KNOCK THAT OFF. HOW LONG HAVE WE KNOWN EACH OTHER?
CELLIE, YOU'VE NEVER MET MY WIFE! THIS IS **ZEPHYRA.**
ZEPHYRA, THIS IS MY OLDEST FRIEND CELAENO. I HEAR SHE'S A PIRATE NOW!
GOOD TO MEET YOU.
DID YOU COME FOR **OCYPETE'S** WEDDING? SHE'LL BE SO GLAD TO SEE YOU. YOU TWO USED TO BE LIKE SIS--
ACTUALLY, I'M HERE TO INTRODUCE THE ROYAL ENVOY FROM EQUESTRIA. JUST A SECOND.
YOUR MAJESTIES, **KING THAUMAS AND QUEEN OZOMENE.** MAY I PRESENT RAINBOW DASH, SPITFIRE, LYRA, AND BONBON.
THEY COME REPRESENTING PRINCESS TWILIGHT SPARKLE OF EQUESTRIA, WHO WISHES TO ESTABLISH A RELATIONSHIP WITH ORNITHIA.
WELL MET, PONY FRIENDS. AND IT IS GOOD TO SEE YOU, CELAENO.
I'M AFRAID WE ARE PREPARING FOR A WEDDING IN THE MORNING, SO THE DIPLOMACY MUST WAIT UNTIL AFTER.
BUT WE INVITE YOU ALL TO STAY AND ENJOY THE--
CELAENO?

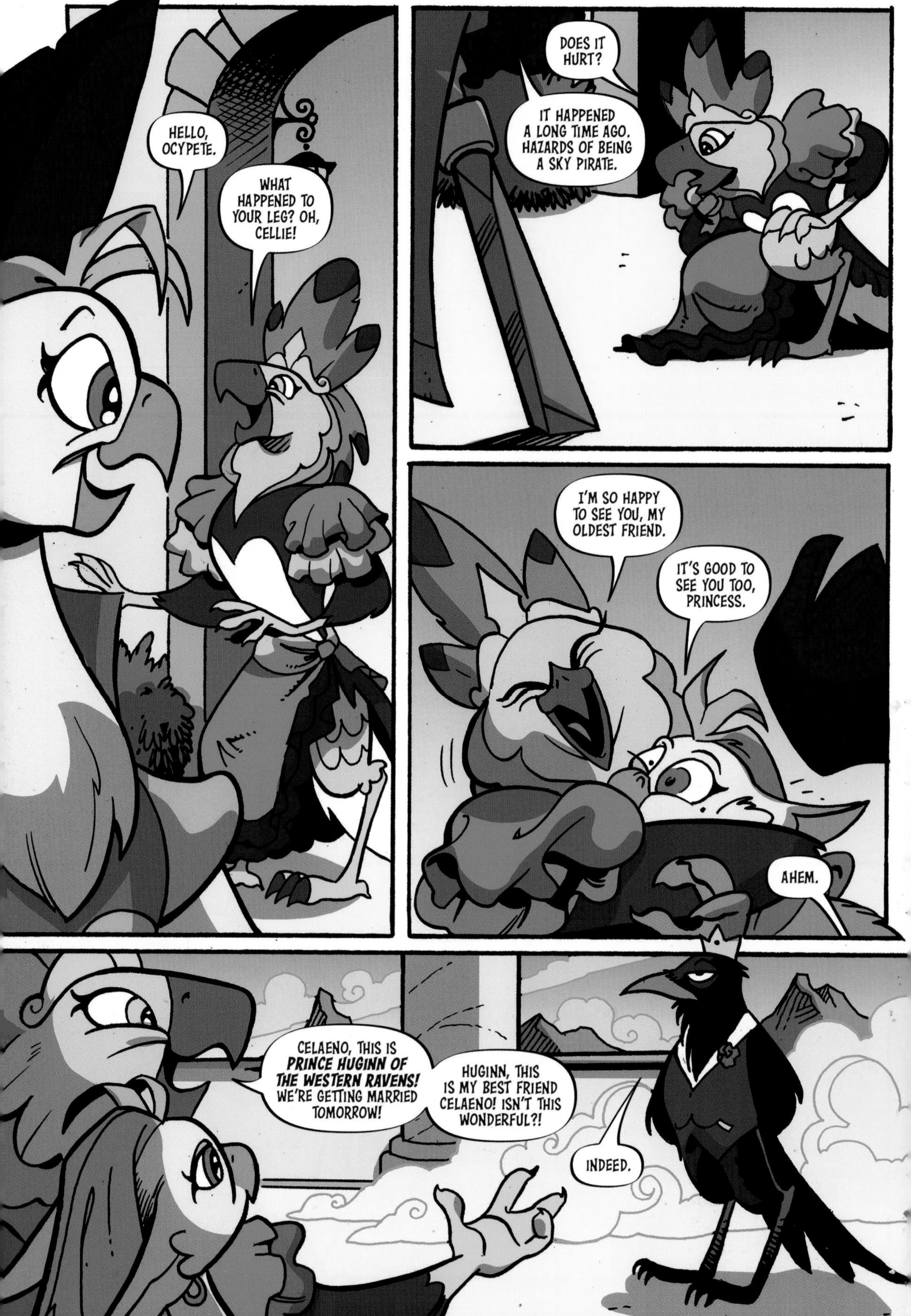
HELLO, OCYPETE.
WHAT HAPPENED TO YOUR LEG? OH, CELLIE!
DOES IT HURT?
IT HAPPENED A LONG TIME AGO. HAZARDS OF BEING A SKY PIRATE.
I'M SO HAPPY TO SEE YOU, MY OLDEST FRIEND.
IT'S GOOD TO SEE YOU TOO, PRINCESS.
AHEM.
CELAENO, THIS IS ***PRINCE HUGINN OF THE WESTERN RAVENS!*** WE'RE GETTING MARRIED TOMORROW!
HUGINN, THIS IS MY BEST FRIEND CELAENO! ISN'T THIS WONDERFUL?!
INDEED.

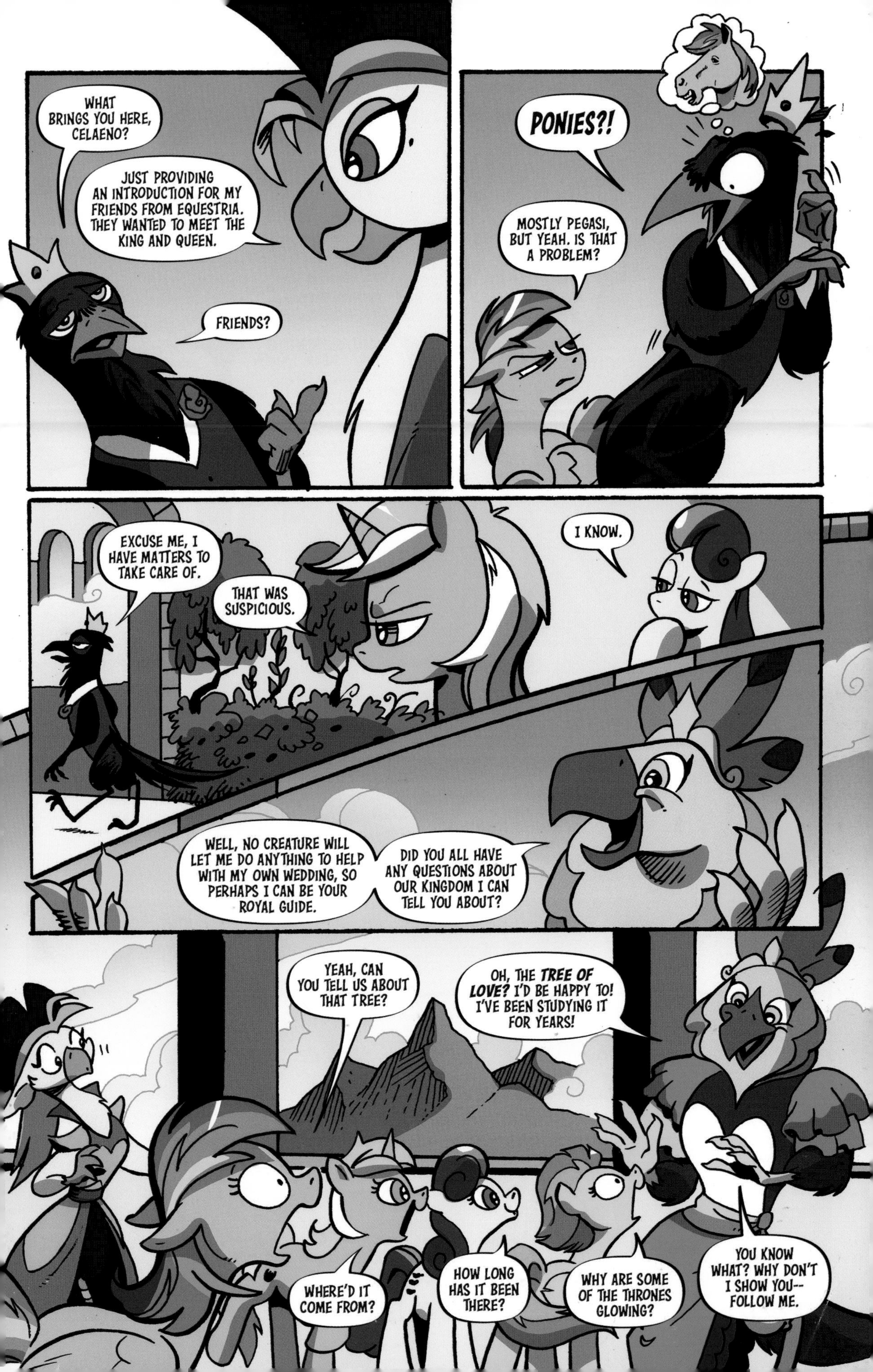
WHAT BRINGS YOU HERE, CELAENO?
JUST PROVIDING AN INTRODUCTION FOR MY FRIENDS FROM EQUESTRIA. THEY WANTED TO MEET THE KING AND QUEEN.
FRIENDS?
PONIES?!
MOSTLY PEGASI, BUT YEAH. IS THAT A PROBLEM?
EXCUSE ME, I HAVE MATTERS TO TAKE CARE OF.
THAT WAS SUSPICIOUS.
I KNOW.
WELL, NO CREATURE WILL LET ME DO ANYTHING TO HELP WITH MY OWN WEDDING, SO PERHAPS I CAN BE YOUR ROYAL GUIDE.
DID YOU ALL HAVE ANY QUESTIONS ABOUT OUR KINGDOM I CAN TELL YOU ABOUT?
YEAH, CAN YOU TELL US ABOUT THAT TREE?
OH, THE TREE OF LOVE? I'D BE HAPPY TO! I'VE BEEN STUDYING IT FOR YEARS!
WHERE'D IT COME FROM?
HOW LONG HAS IT BEEN THERE?
WHY ARE SOME OF THE THRONES GLOWING?
YOU KNOW WHAT? WHY DON'T I SHOW YOU-- FOLLOW ME.

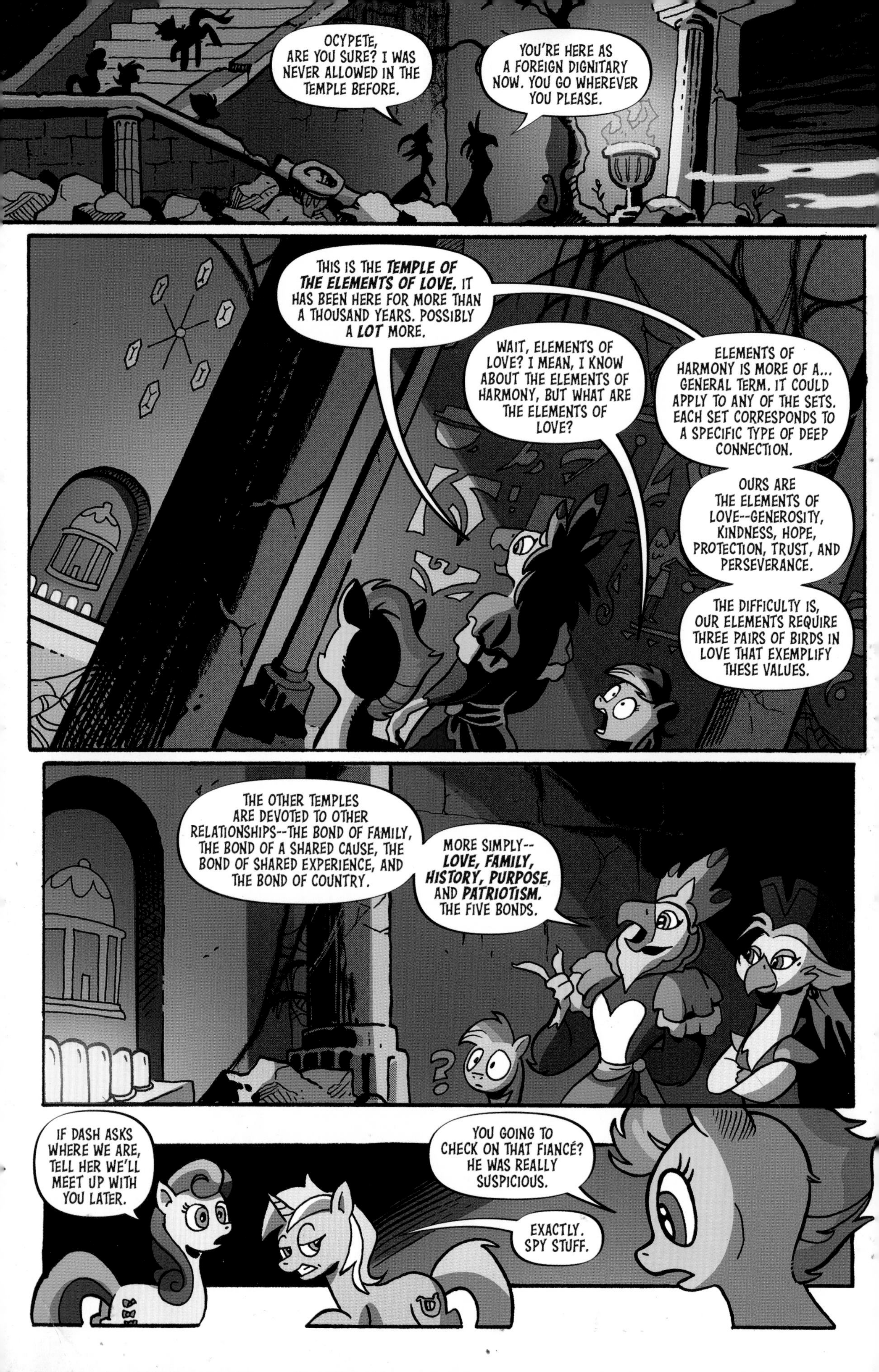
OCYPETE, ARE YOU SURE? I WAS NEVER ALLOWED IN THE TEMPLE BEFORE.
YOU'RE HERE AS A FOREIGN DIGNITARY NOW. YOU GO WHEREVER YOU PLEASE.
THIS IS THE ***TEMPLE OF THE ELEMENTS OF LOVE.*** IT HAS BEEN HERE FOR MORE THAN A THOUSAND YEARS. POSSIBLY A ***LOT*** MORE.
WAIT, ELEMENTS OF LOVE? I MEAN, I KNOW ABOUT THE ELEMENTS OF HARMONY, BUT WHAT ARE THE ELEMENTS OF LOVE?
ELEMENTS OF HARMONY IS MORE OF A... GENERAL TERM. IT COULD APPLY TO ANY OF THE SETS. EACH SET CORRESPONDS TO A SPECIFIC TYPE OF DEEP CONNECTION.
OURS ARE THE ELEMENTS OF LOVE--GENEROSITY, KINDNESS, HOPE, PROTECTION, TRUST, AND PERSEVERANCE.
THE DIFFICULTY IS, OUR ELEMENTS REQUIRE THREE PAIRS OF BIRDS IN LOVE THAT EXEMPLIFY THESE VALUES.
THE OTHER TEMPLES ARE DEVOTED TO OTHER RELATIONSHIPS--THE BOND OF FAMILY, THE BOND OF A SHARED CAUSE, THE BOND OF SHARED EXPERIENCE, AND THE BOND OF COUNTRY.
MORE SIMPLY-- ***LOVE, FAMILY, HISTORY, PURPOSE,*** AND ***PATRIOTISM.*** THE FIVE BONDS.
?
IF DASH ASKS WHERE WE ARE, TELL HER WE'LL MEET UP WITH YOU LATER.
YOU GOING TO CHECK ON THAT FIANCÉ? HE WAS REALLY SUSPICIOUS.
EXACTLY. SPY STUFF.

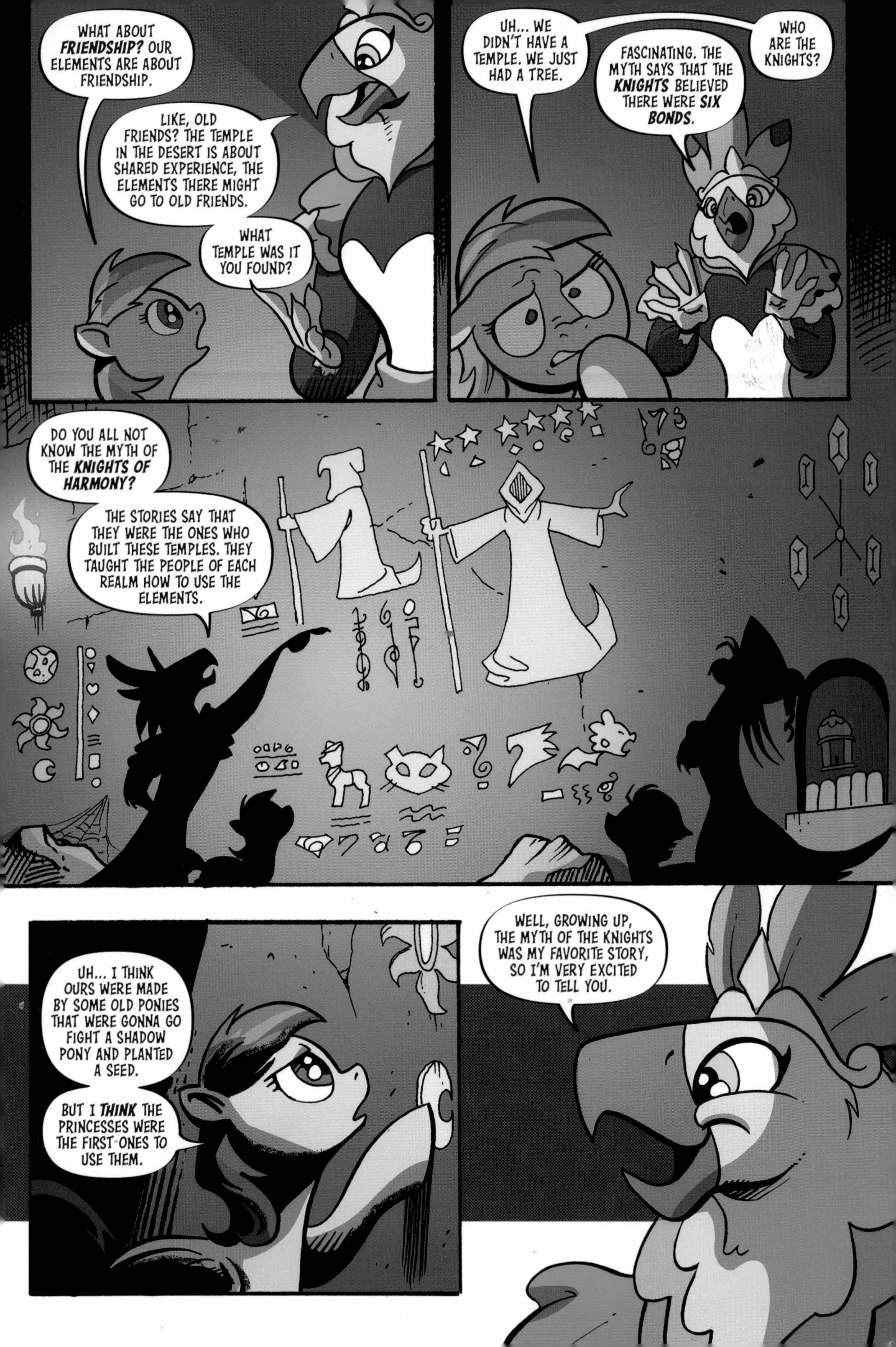
WHAT ABOUT FRIENDSHIP? OUR ELEMENTS ARE ABOUT FRIENDSHIP.
LIKE, OLD FRIENDS? THE TEMPLE IN THE DESERT IS ABOUT SHARED EXPERIENCE, THE ELEMENTS THERE MIGHT GO TO OLD FRIENDS.
WHAT TEMPLE WAS IT YOU FOUND?
UH... WE DIDN'T HAVE A TEMPLE. WE JUST HAD A TREE.
WHO ARE THE KNIGHTS?
FASCINATING. THE MYTH SAYS THAT THE KNIGHTS BELIEVED THERE WERE SIX BONDS.
DO YOU ALL NOT KNOW THE MYTH OF THE KNIGHTS OF HARMONY?
THE STORIES SAY THAT THEY WERE THE ONES WHO BUILT THESE TEMPLES. THEY TAUGHT THE PEOPLE OF EACH REALM HOW TO USE THE ELEMENTS.
WELL, GROWING UP, THE MYTH OF THE KNIGHTS WAS MY FAVORITE STORY, SO I'M VERY EXCITED TO TELL YOU.
UH... I THINK OURS WERE MADE BY SOME OLD PONIES THAT WERE GONNA GO FIGHT A SHADOW PONY AND PLANTED A SEED.
BUT I THINK THE PRINCESSES WERE THE FIRST ONES TO USE THEM.

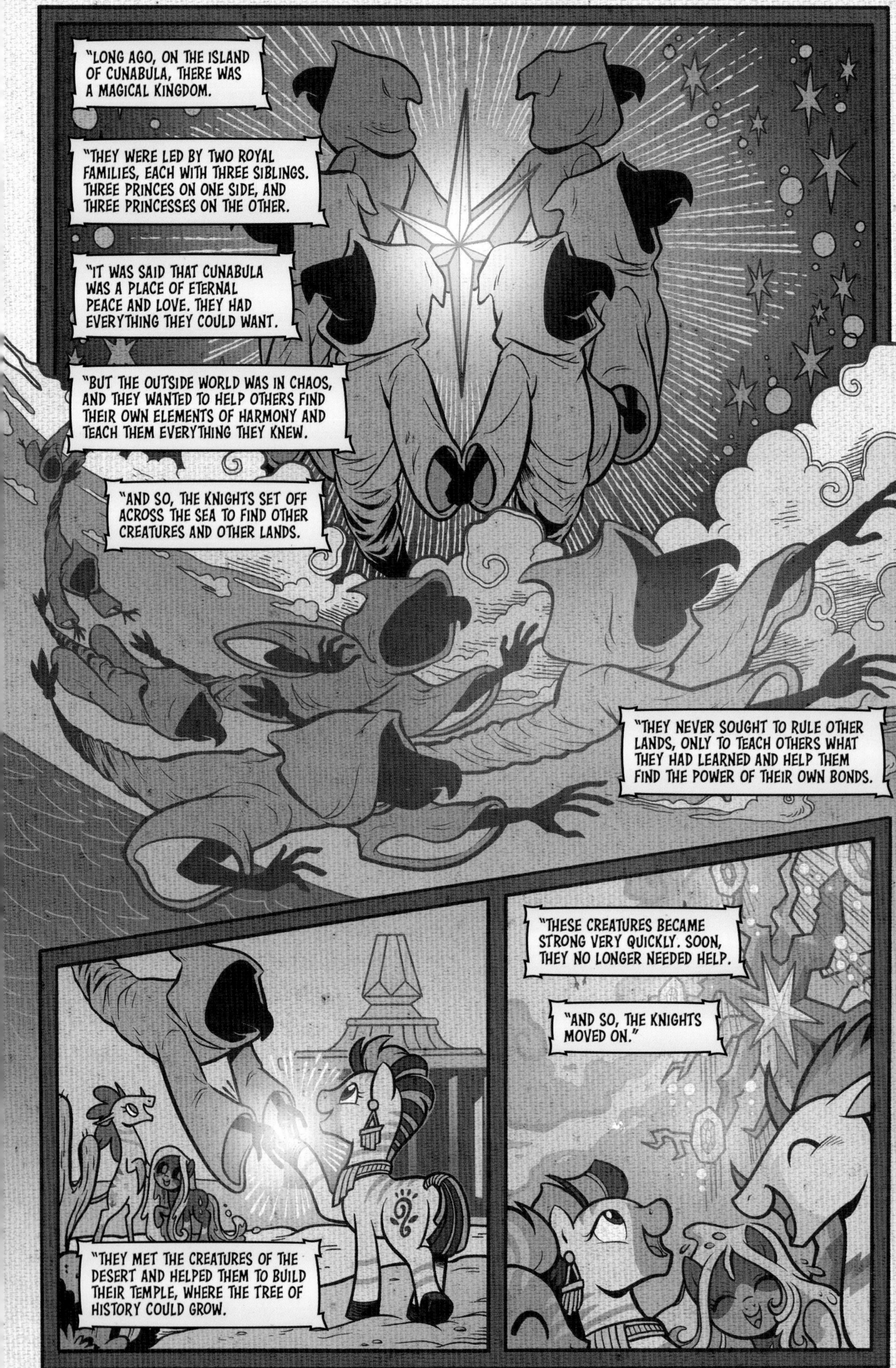
"LONG AGO, ON THE ISLAND OF CUNABULA, THERE WAS A MAGICAL KINGDOM.
"THEY WERE LED BY TWO ROYAL FAMILIES, EACH WITH THREE SIBLINGS. THREE PRINCES ON ONE SIDE, AND THREE PRINCESSES ON THE OTHER.
"IT WAS SAID THAT CUNABULA WAS A PLACE OF ETERNAL PEACE AND LOVE. THEY HAD EVERYTHING THEY COULD WANT.
"BUT THE OUTSIDE WORLD WAS IN CHAOS, AND THEY WANTED TO HELP OTHERS FIND THEIR OWN ELEMENTS OF HARMONY AND TEACH THEM EVERYTHING THEY KNEW.
"AND SO, THE KNIGHTS SET OFF ACROSS THE SEA TO FIND OTHER CREATURES AND OTHER LANDS.
"THEY NEVER SOUGHT TO RULE OTHER LANDS, ONLY TO TEACH OTHERS WHAT THEY HAD LEARNED AND HELP THEM FIND THE POWER OF THEIR OWN BONDS.
"THEY MET THE CREATURES OF THE DESERT AND HELPED THEM TO BUILD THEIR TEMPLE, WHERE THE TREE OF HISTORY COULD GROW.
"THESE CREATURES BECAME STRONG VERY QUICKLY. SOON, THEY NO LONGER NEEDED HELP.
"AND SO, THE KNIGHTS MOVED ON."

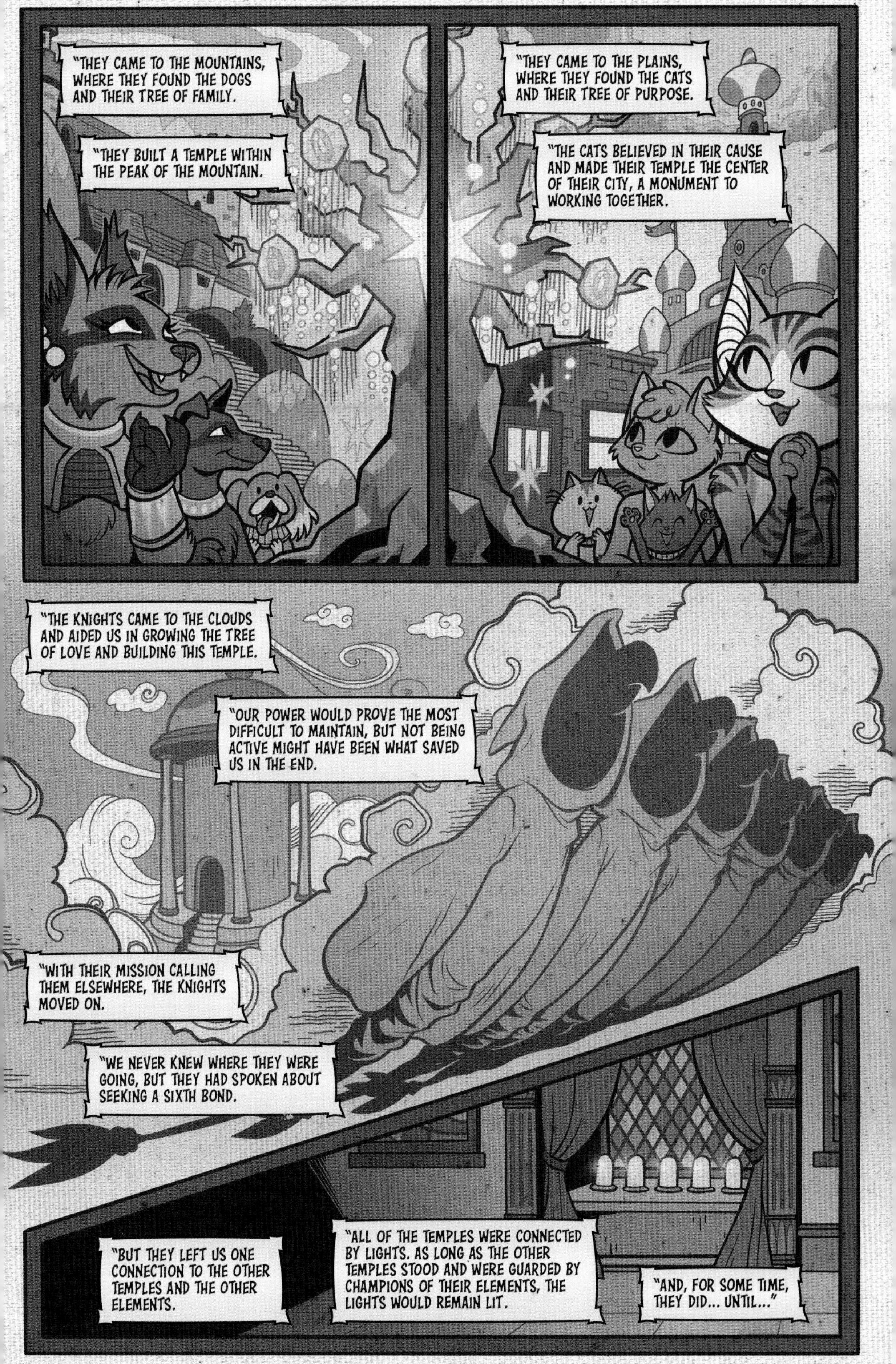
"THEY CAME TO THE MOUNTAINS, WHERE THEY FOUND THE DOGS AND THEIR TREE OF FAMILY.
"THEY BUILT A TEMPLE WITHIN THE PEAK OF THE MOUNTAIN.
"THEY CAME TO THE PLAINS, WHERE THEY FOUND THE CATS AND THEIR TREE OF PURPOSE.
"THE CATS BELIEVED IN THEIR CAUSE AND MADE THEIR TEMPLE THE CENTER OF THEIR CITY, A MONUMENT TO WORKING TOGETHER.
"THE KNIGHTS CAME TO THE CLOUDS AND AIDED US IN GROWING THE TREE OF LOVE AND BUILDING THIS TEMPLE.
"OUR POWER WOULD PROVE THE MOST DIFFICULT TO MAINTAIN, BUT NOT BEING ACTIVE MIGHT HAVE BEEN WHAT SAVED US IN THE END.
"WITH THEIR MISSION CALLING THEM ELSEWHERE, THE KNIGHTS MOVED ON.
"WE NEVER KNEW WHERE THEY WERE GOING, BUT THEY HAD SPOKEN ABOUT SEEKING A SIXTH BOND.
"BUT THEY LEFT US ONE CONNECTION TO THE OTHER TEMPLES AND THE OTHER ELEMENTS.
"ALL OF THE TEMPLES WERE CONNECTED BY LIGHTS. AS LONG AS THE OTHER TEMPLES STOOD AND WERE GUARDED BY CHAMPIONS OF THEIR ELEMENTS, THE LIGHTS WOULD REMAIN LIT.
"AND, FOR SOME TIME, THEY DID... UNTIL..."

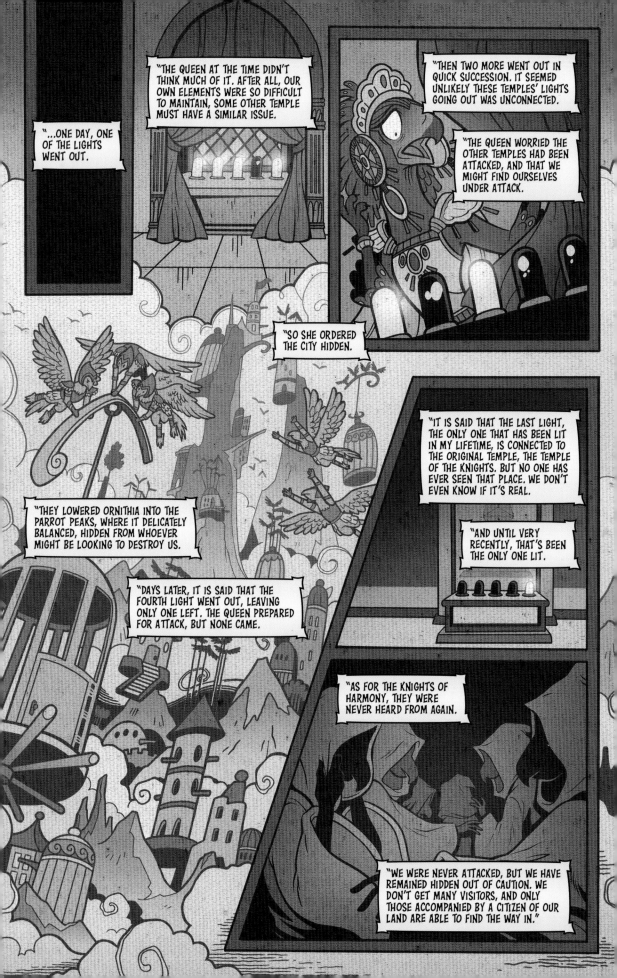

"...ONE DAY, ONE OF THE LIGHTS WENT OUT.

"THE QUEEN AT THE TIME DIDN'T THINK MUCH OF IT. AFTER ALL, OUR OWN ELEMENTS WERE SO DIFFICULT TO MAINTAIN, SOME OTHER TEMPLE MUST HAVE A SIMILAR ISSUE.

"THEN TWO MORE WENT OUT IN QUICK SUCCESSION. IT SEEMED UNLIKELY THESE TEMPLES' LIGHTS GOING OUT WAS UNCONNECTED.

"THE QUEEN WORRIED THE OTHER TEMPLES HAD BEEN ATTACKED, AND THAT WE MIGHT FIND OURSELVES UNDER ATTACK.

"SO SHE ORDERED THE CITY HIDDEN.

"IT IS SAID THAT THE LAST LIGHT, THE ONLY ONE THAT HAS BEEN LIT IN MY LIFETIME, IS CONNECTED TO THE ORIGINAL TEMPLE, THE TEMPLE OF THE KNIGHTS. BUT NO ONE HAS EVER SEEN THAT PLACE. WE DON'T EVEN KNOW IF IT'S REAL.

"THEY LOWERED ORNITHIA INTO THE PARROT PEAKS, WHERE IT DELICATELY BALANCED, HIDDEN FROM WHOEVER MIGHT BE LOOKING TO DESTROY US.

"AND UNTIL VERY RECENTLY, THAT'S BEEN THE ONLY ONE LIT.

"DAYS LATER, IT IS SAID THAT THE FOURTH LIGHT WENT OUT, LEAVING ONLY ONE LEFT. THE QUEEN PREPARED FOR ATTACK, BUT NONE CAME.

"AS FOR THE KNIGHTS OF HARMONY, THEY WERE NEVER HEARD FROM AGAIN.

"WE WERE NEVER ATTACKED, BUT WE HAVE REMAINED HIDDEN OUT OF CAUTION. WE DON'T GET MANY VISITORS, AND ONLY THOSE ACCOMPANIED BY A CITIZEN OF OUR LAND ARE ABLE TO FIND THE WAY IN."

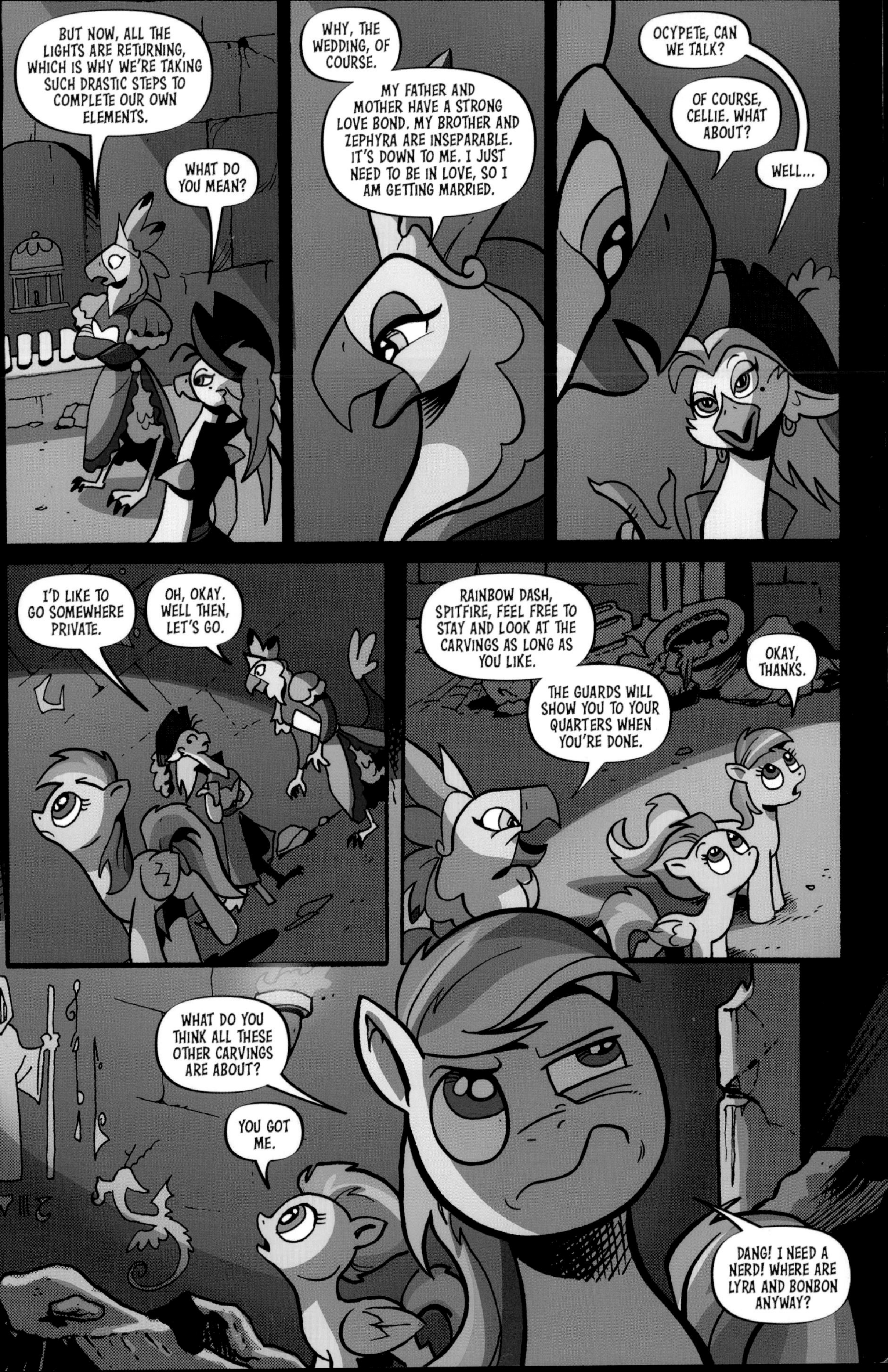

BUT NOW, ALL THE LIGHTS ARE RETURNING, WHICH IS WHY WE'RE TAKING SUCH DRASTIC STEPS TO COMPLETE OUR OWN ELEMENTS.
WHAT DO YOU MEAN?
WHY, THE WEDDING, OF COURSE.
MY FATHER AND MOTHER HAVE A STRONG LOVE BOND. MY BROTHER AND ZEPHYRA ARE INSEPARABLE. IT'S DOWN TO ME. I JUST NEED TO BE IN LOVE, SO I AM GETTING MARRIED.
OCYPETE, CAN WE TALK?
OF COURSE, CELLIE. WHAT ABOUT?
WELL...
I'D LIKE TO GO SOMEWHERE PRIVATE.
OH, OKAY. WELL THEN, LET'S GO.
RAINBOW DASH, SPITFIRE, FEEL FREE TO STAY AND LOOK AT THE CARVINGS AS LONG AS YOU LIKE.
THE GUARDS WILL SHOW YOU TO YOUR QUARTERS WHEN YOU'RE DONE.
OKAY, THANKS.
WHAT DO YOU THINK ALL THESE OTHER CARVINGS ARE ABOUT?
YOU GOT ME.
DANG! I NEED A NERD! WHERE ARE LYRA AND BONBON ANYWAY?

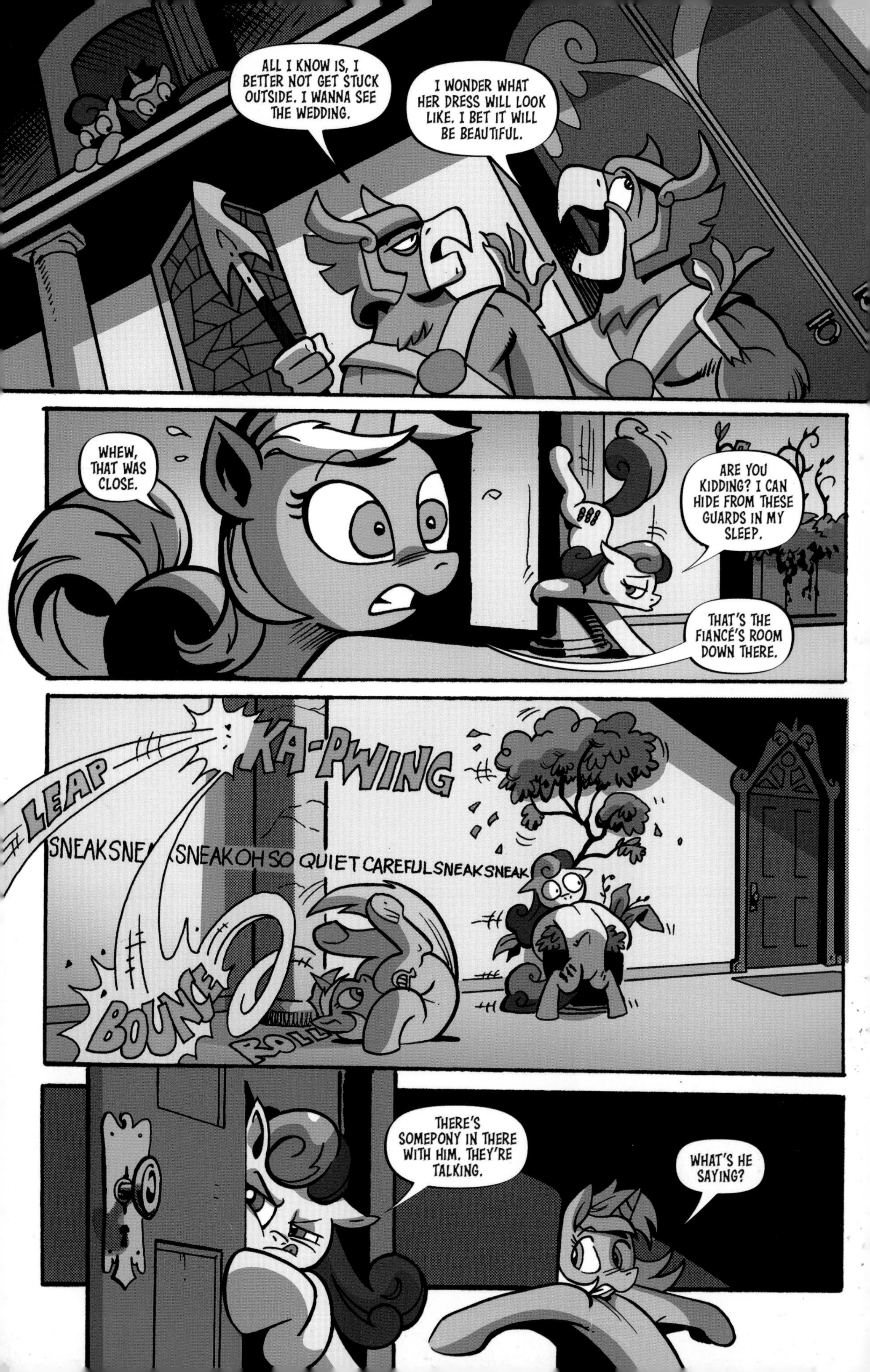
ALL I KNOW IS, I BETTER NOT GET STUCK OUTSIDE. I WANNA SEE THE WEDDING.
I WONDER WHAT HER DRESS WILL LOOK LIKE. I BET IT WILL BE BEAUTIFUL.
WHEW, THAT WAS CLOSE.
ARE YOU KIDDING? I CAN HIDE FROM THESE GUARDS IN MY SLEEP.
THAT'S THE FIANCÉ'S ROOM DOWN THERE.
LEAP
KA-PWING
SNEAKSNEAKSNEAKOHSO QUIET CAREFULSNEAKSNEAK
BOUNCE
THERE'S SOMEPONY IN THERE WITH HIM. THEY'RE TALKING.
WHAT'S HE SAYING?

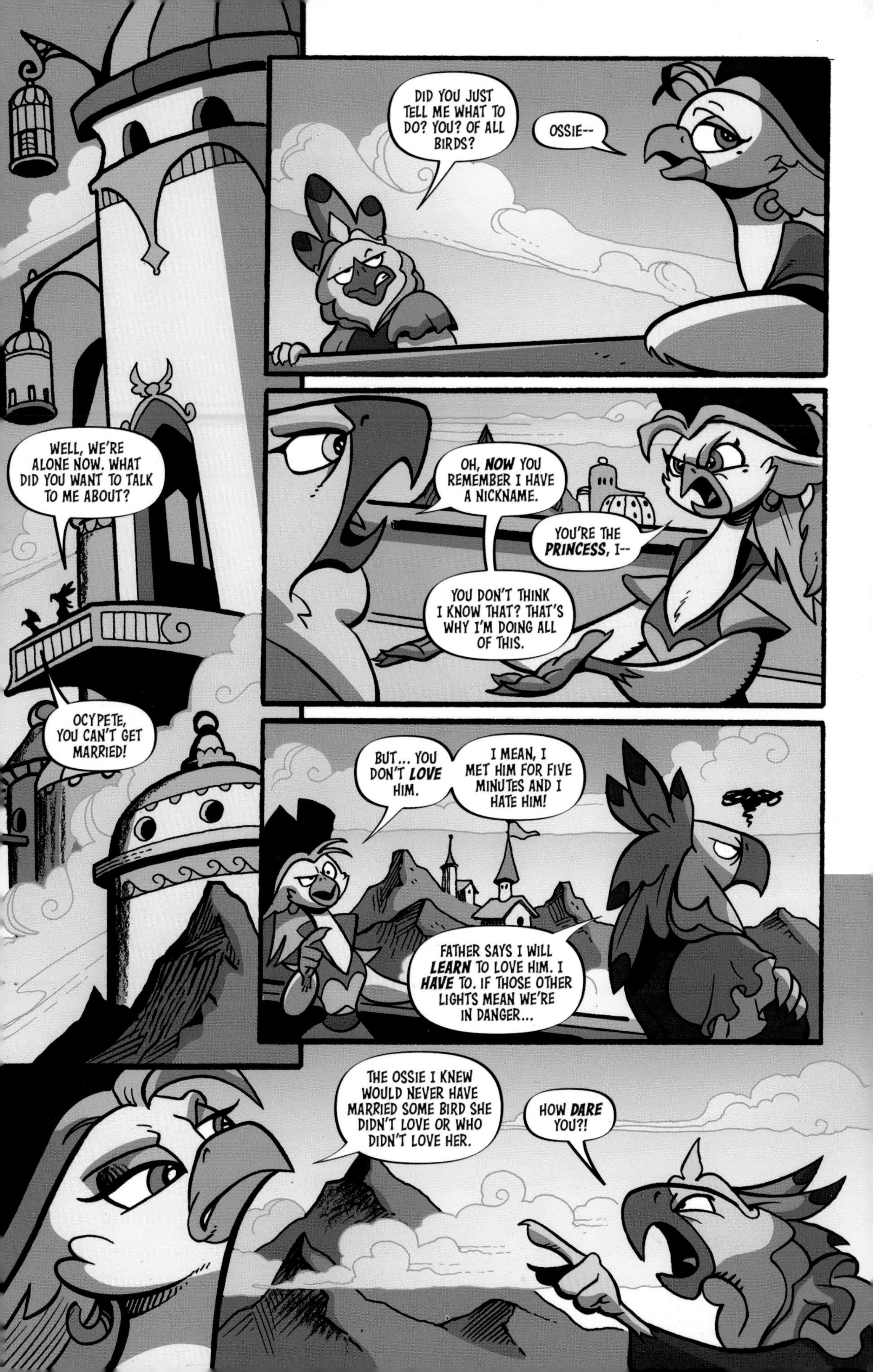
WELL, WE'RE ALONE NOW. WHAT DID YOU WANT TO TALK TO ME ABOUT?
OCYPETE, YOU CAN'T GET MARRIED!
DID YOU JUST TELL ME WHAT TO DO? YOU? OF ALL BIRDS?
OSSIE--
OH, NOW YOU REMEMBER I HAVE A NICKNAME.
YOU'RE THE PRINCESS, I--
YOU DON'T THINK I KNOW THAT? THAT'S WHY I'M DOING ALL OF THIS.
BUT... YOU DON'T LOVE HIM.
I MEAN, I MET HIM FOR FIVE MINUTES AND I HATE HIM!
FATHER SAYS I WILL LEARN TO LOVE HIM. I HAVE TO. IF THOSE OTHER LIGHTS MEAN WE'RE IN DANGER...
THE OSSIE I KNEW WOULD NEVER HAVE MARRIED SOME BIRD SHE DIDN'T LOVE OR WHO DIDN'T LOVE HER.
HOW DARE YOU?!

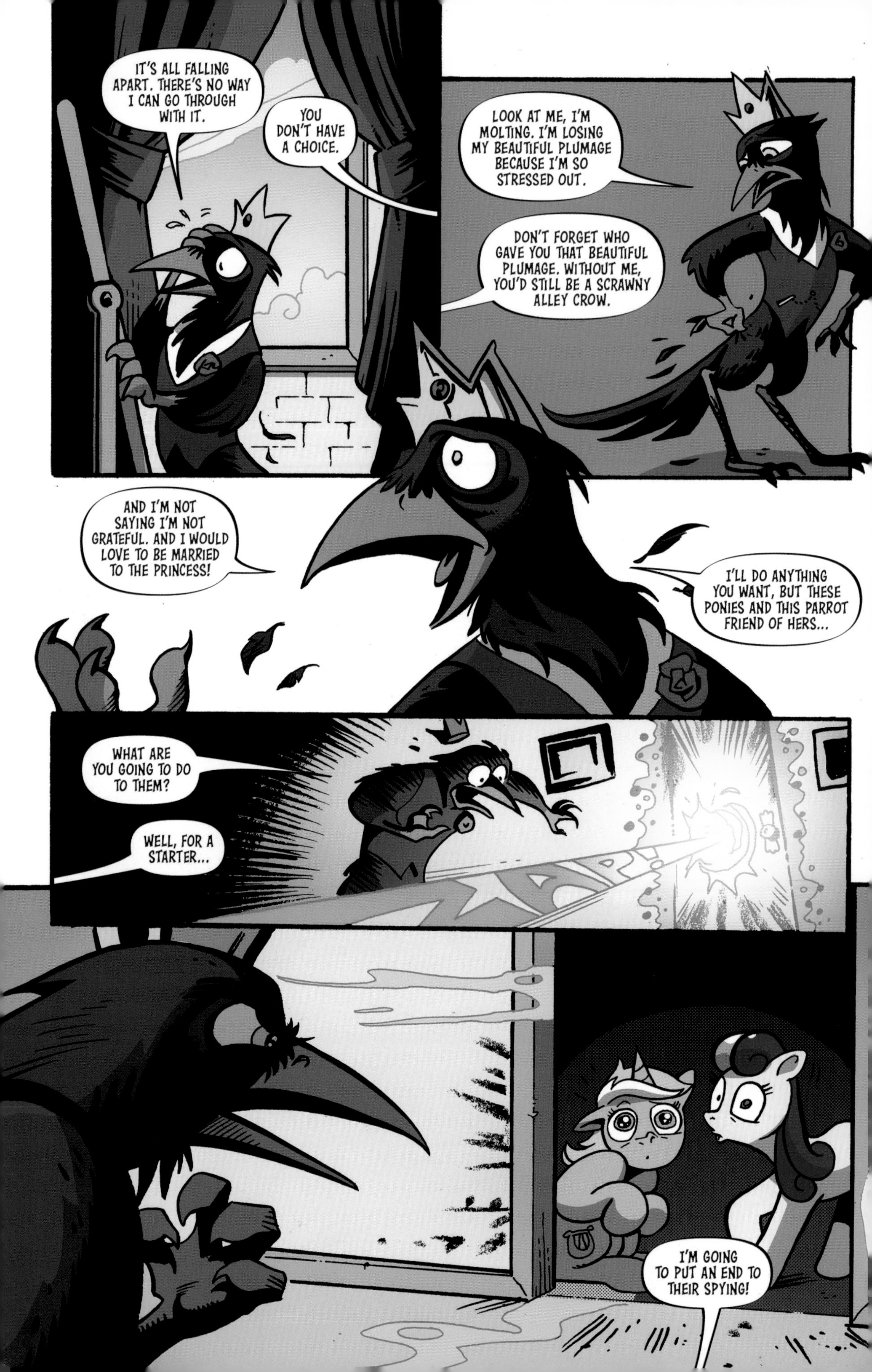
IT'S ALL FALLING APART. THERE'S NO WAY I CAN GO THROUGH WITH IT.
YOU DON'T HAVE A CHOICE.
LOOK AT ME, I'M MOLTING. I'M LOSING MY BEAUTIFUL PLUMAGE BECAUSE I'M SO STRESSED OUT.
DON'T FORGET WHO GAVE YOU THAT BEAUTIFUL PLUMAGE. WITHOUT ME, YOU'D STILL BE A SCRAWNY ALLEY CROW.
AND I'M NOT SAYING I'M NOT GRATEFUL. AND I WOULD LOVE TO BE MARRIED TO THE PRINCESS!
I'LL DO ANYTHING YOU WANT, BUT THESE PONIES AND THIS PARROT FRIEND OF HERS...
WHAT ARE YOU GOING TO DO TO THEM?
WELL, FOR A STARTER...
I'M GOING TO PUT AN END TO THEIR SPYING!

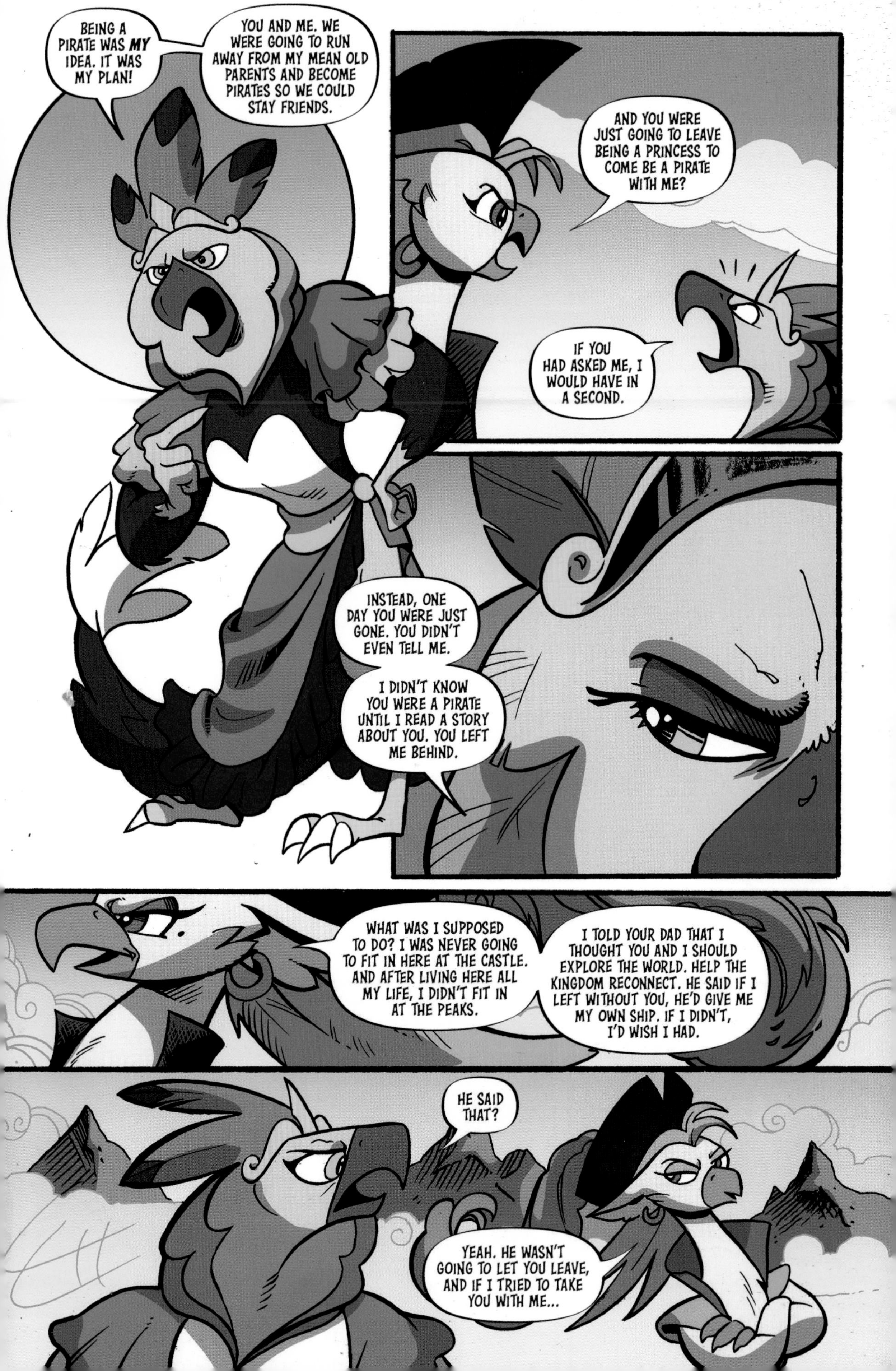
BEING A PIRATE WAS *MY* IDEA. IT WAS MY PLAN!
YOU AND ME. WE WERE GOING TO RUN AWAY FROM MY MEAN OLD PARENTS AND BECOME PIRATES SO WE COULD STAY FRIENDS.
AND YOU WERE JUST GOING TO LEAVE BEING A PRINCESS TO COME BE A PIRATE WITH ME?
IF YOU HAD ASKED ME, I WOULD HAVE IN A SECOND.
INSTEAD, ONE DAY YOU WERE JUST GONE. YOU DIDN'T EVEN TELL ME.
I DIDN'T KNOW YOU WERE A PIRATE UNTIL I READ A STORY ABOUT YOU. YOU LEFT ME BEHIND.
WHAT WAS I SUPPOSED TO DO? I WAS NEVER GOING TO FIT IN HERE AT THE CASTLE. AND AFTER LIVING HERE ALL MY LIFE, I DIDN'T FIT IN AT THE PEAKS.
I TOLD YOUR DAD THAT I THOUGHT YOU AND I SHOULD EXPLORE THE WORLD. HELP THE KINGDOM RECONNECT. HE SAID IF I LEFT WITHOUT YOU, HE'D GIVE ME MY OWN SHIP. IF I DIDN'T, I'D WISH I HAD.
HE SAID THAT?
YEAH. HE WASN'T GOING TO LET YOU LEAVE, AND IF I TRIED TO TAKE YOU WITH ME...

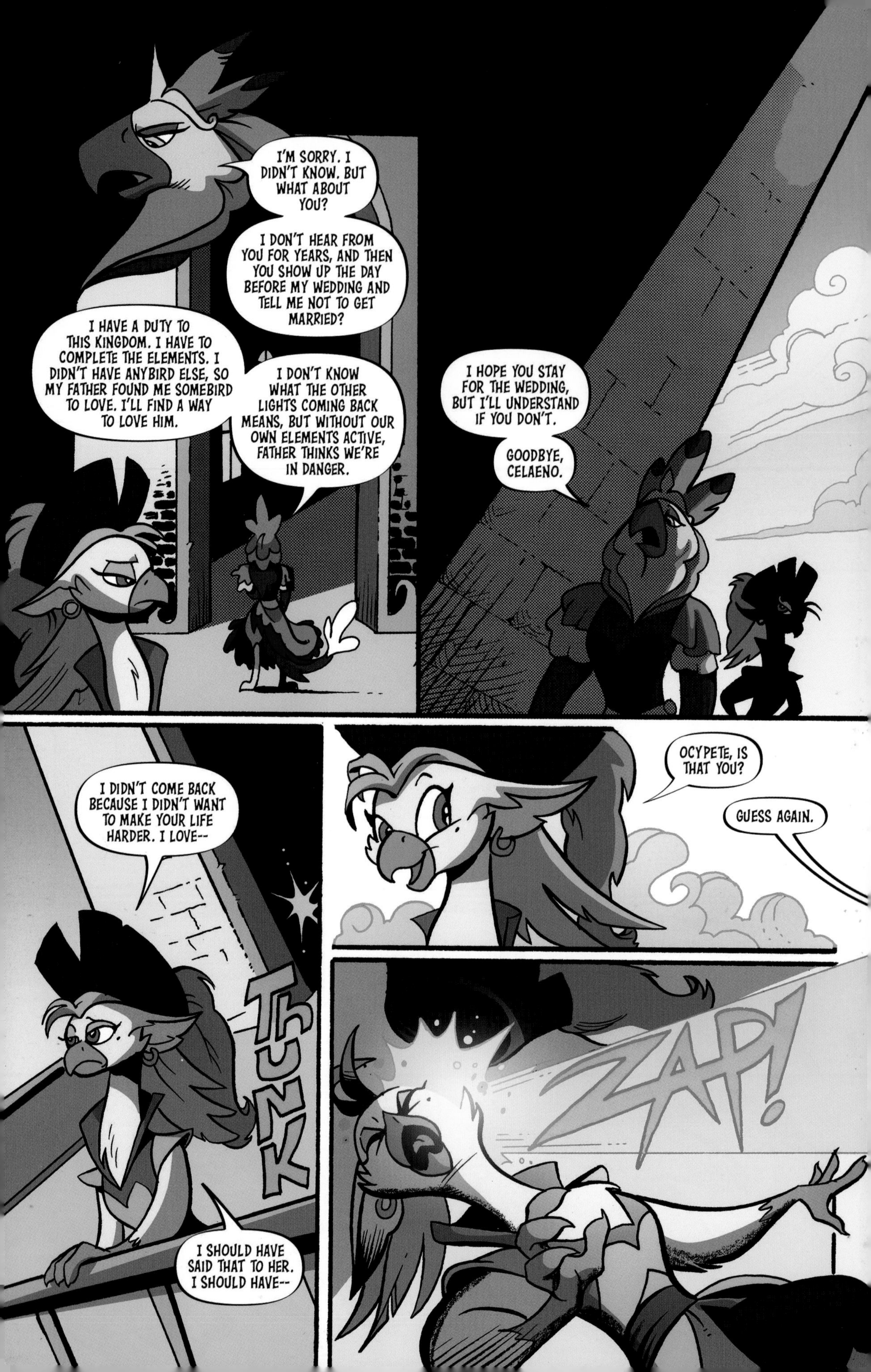
I'M SORRY. I DIDN'T KNOW. BUT WHAT ABOUT YOU?
I DON'T HEAR FROM YOU FOR YEARS, AND THEN YOU SHOW UP THE DAY BEFORE MY WEDDING AND TELL ME NOT TO GET MARRIED?
I HAVE A DUTY TO THIS KINGDOM. I HAVE TO COMPLETE THE ELEMENTS. I DIDN'T HAVE ANYBIRD ELSE, SO MY FATHER FOUND ME SOMEBIRD TO LOVE. I'LL FIND A WAY TO LOVE HIM.
I DON'T KNOW WHAT THE OTHER LIGHTS COMING BACK MEANS, BUT WITHOUT OUR OWN ELEMENTS ACTIVE, FATHER THINKS WE'RE IN DANGER.
I HOPE YOU STAY FOR THE WEDDING, BUT I'LL UNDERSTAND IF YOU DON'T.
GOODBYE, CELAENO.
I DIDN'T COME BACK BECAUSE I DIDN'T WANT TO MAKE YOUR LIFE HARDER. I LOVE--
THUNK
I SHOULD HAVE SAID THAT TO HER. I SHOULD HAVE--
OCYPETE, IS THAT YOU?
GUESS AGAIN.
ZAP!

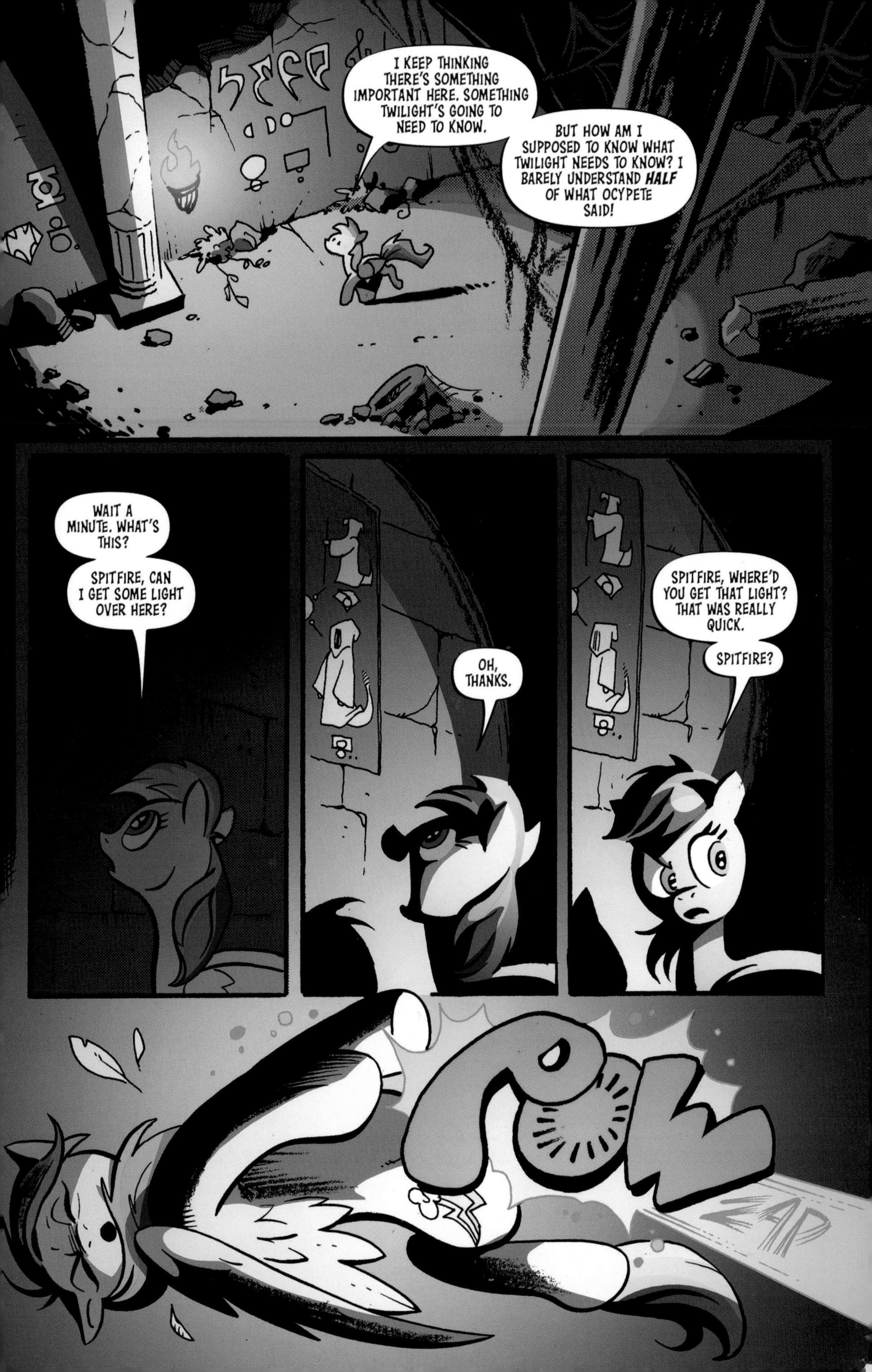
I KEEP THINKING THERE'S SOMETHING IMPORTANT HERE. SOMETHING TWILIGHT'S GOING TO NEED TO KNOW.
BUT HOW AM I SUPPOSED TO KNOW WHAT TWILIGHT NEEDS TO KNOW? I BARELY UNDERSTAND **HALF** OF WHAT OCYPETE SAID!
WAIT A MINUTE. WHAT'S THIS?
SPITFIRE, CAN I GET SOME LIGHT OVER HERE?
OH, THANKS.
SPITFIRE, WHERE'D YOU GET THAT LIGHT? THAT WAS REALLY QUICK.
SPITFIRE?
POW
ZAP

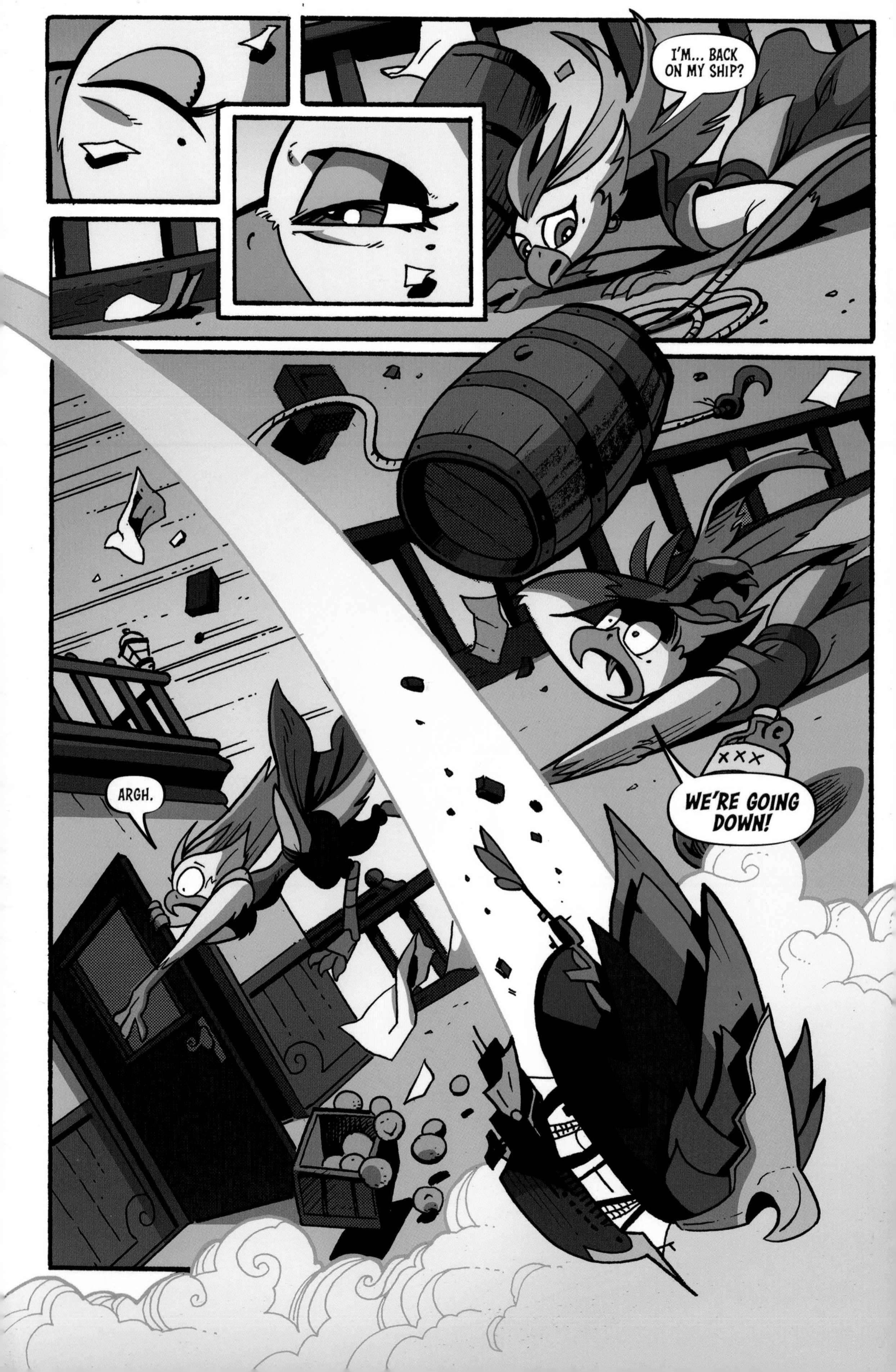
I'M... BACK ON MY SHIP?
ARGH.
WE'RE GOING DOWN!
XXX

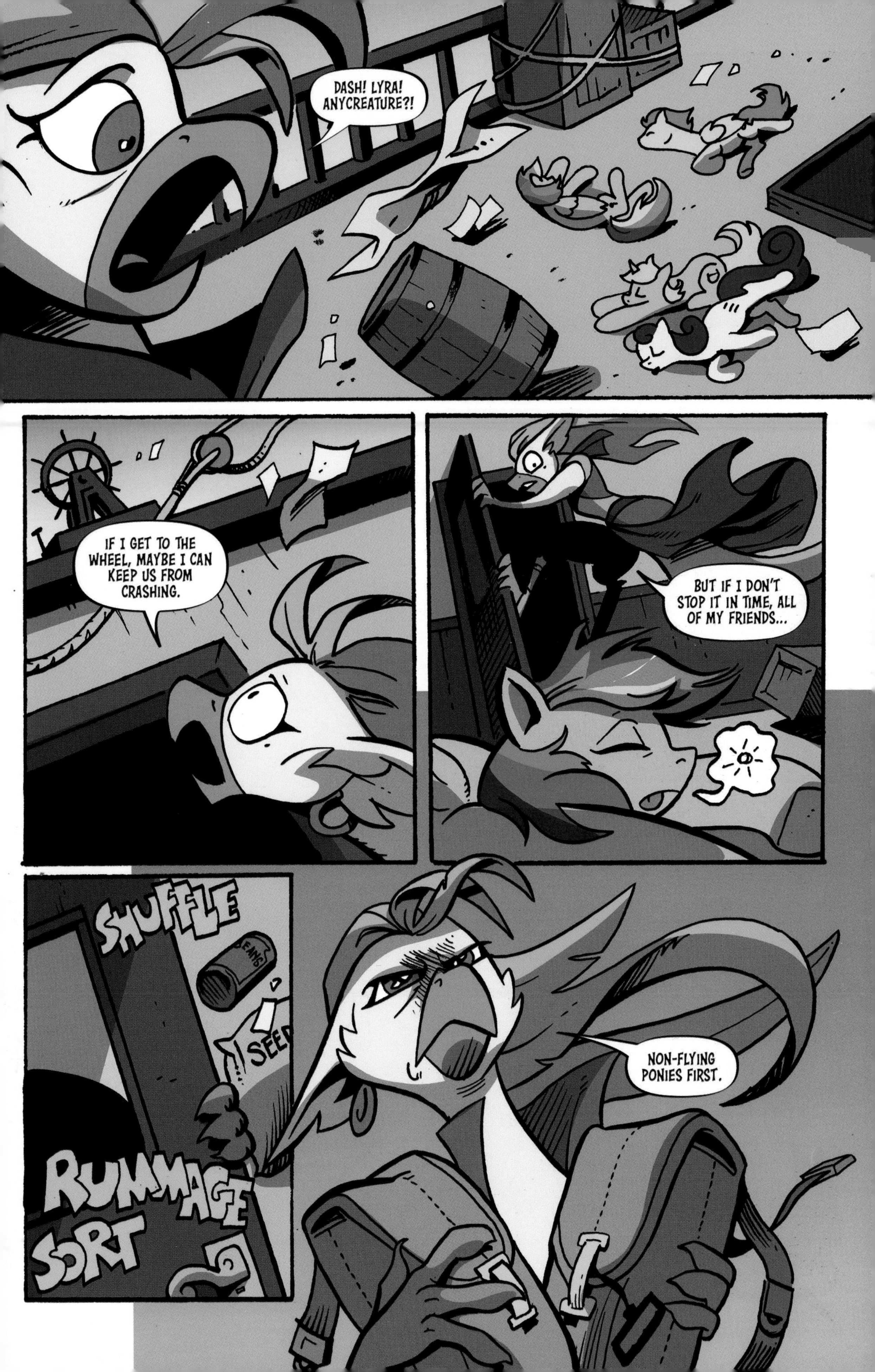
DASH! LYRA! ANYCREATURE?!
IF I GET TO THE WHEEL, MAYBE I CAN KEEP US FROM CRASHING.
BUT IF I DON'T STOP IT IN TIME, ALL OF MY FRIENDS...
SHUFFLE
BEANS
SEED
RUMMAGE
SORT
NON-FLYING PONIES FIRST.

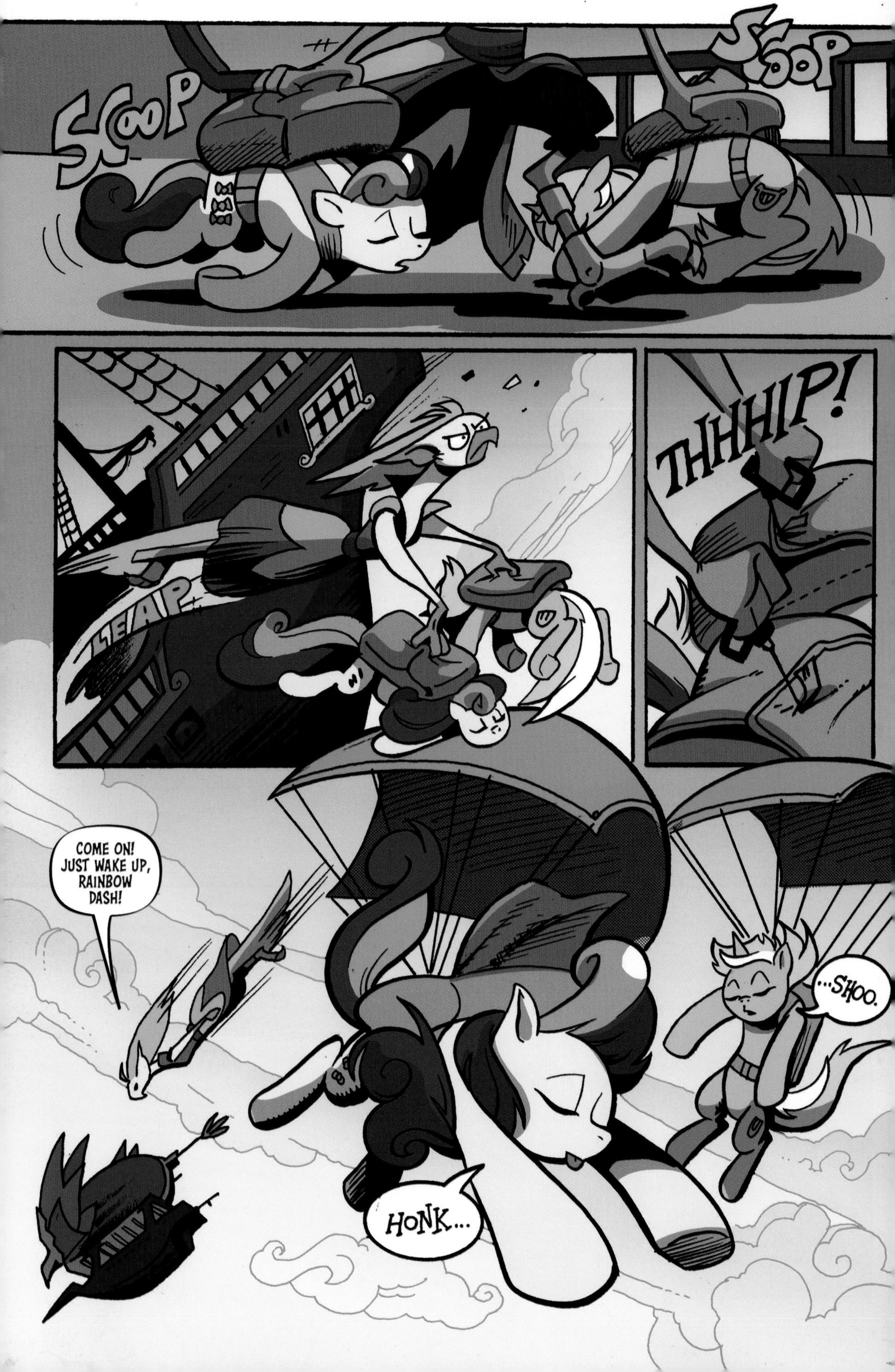
SCOOP
SCOOP
LEAP
THHHIP!
COME ON! JUST WAKE UP, RAINBOW DASH!
...SHOO.
HONK...

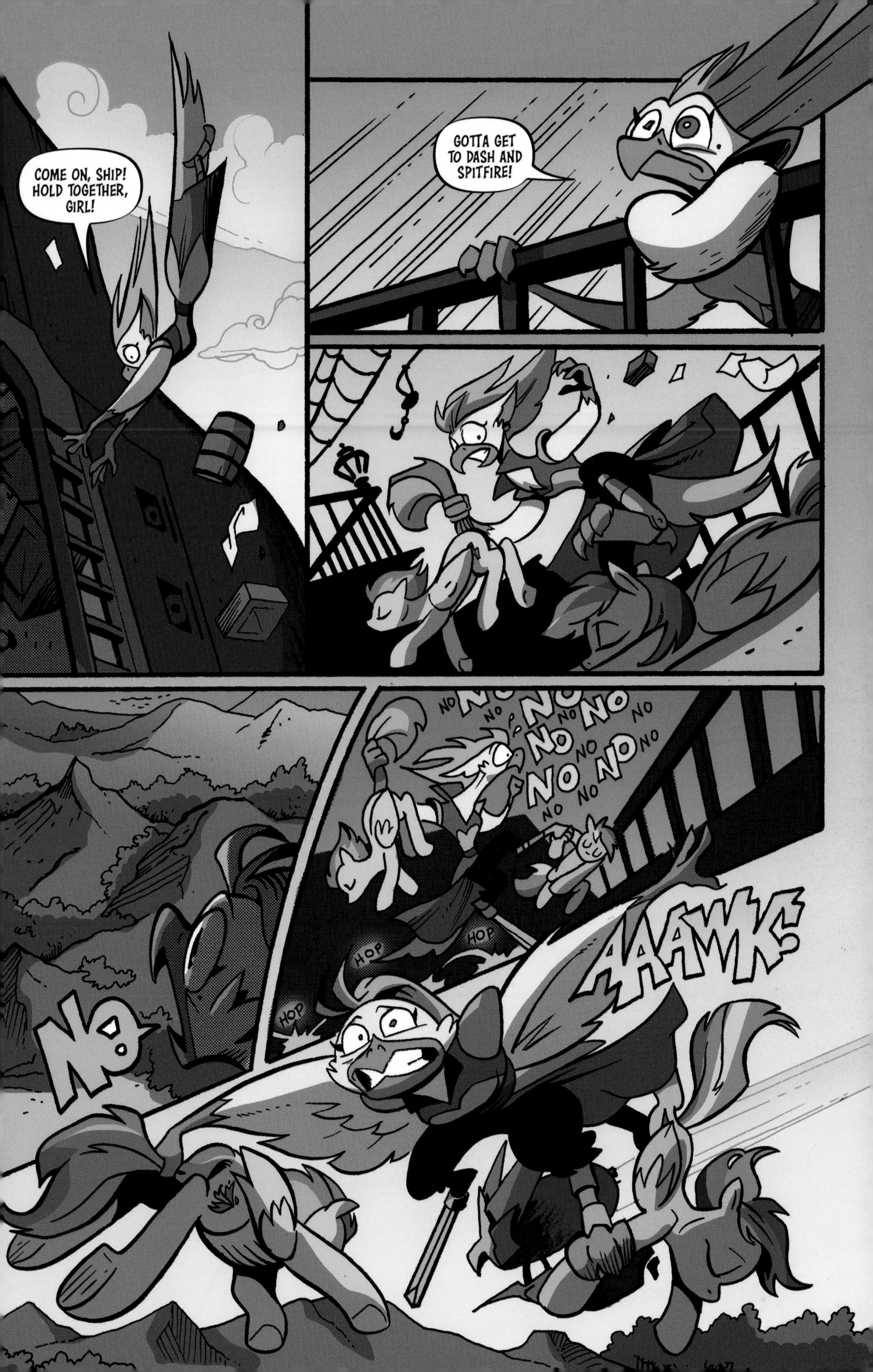
COME ON, SHIP! HOLD TOGETHER, GIRL!
GOTTA GET TO DASH AND SPITFIRE!
NO NO NO NO NO NO NO NO NO NO NO NO NO NO NO NO NO NO
HOP HOP HOP HOP
AAAWK!
NO!

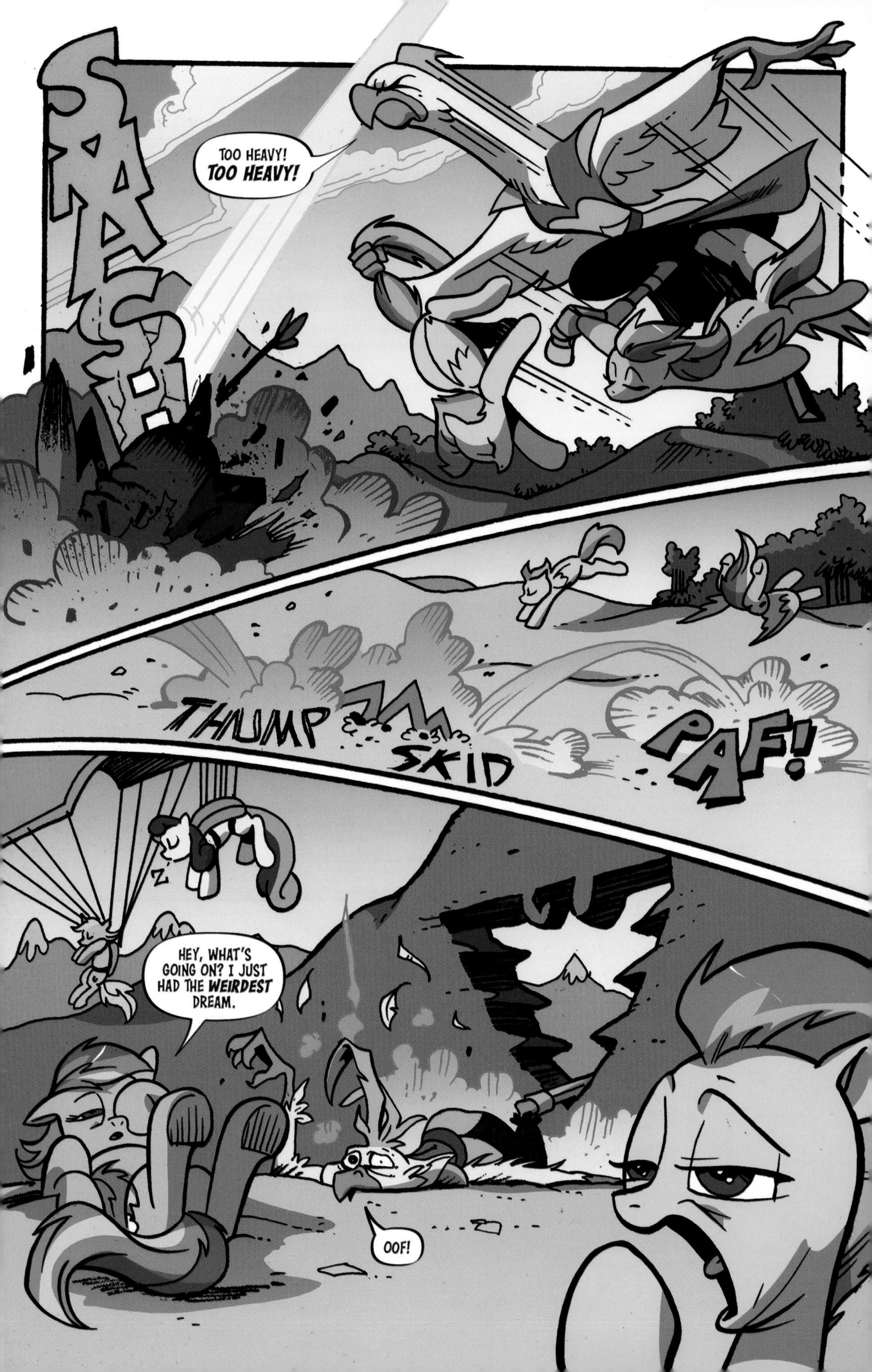
SPAASH!
TOO HEAVY! TOO HEAVY!
THUMP
SKID
PAF!
Z
HEY, WHAT'S GOING ON? I JUST HAD THE WEIRDEST DREAM.
OOF!

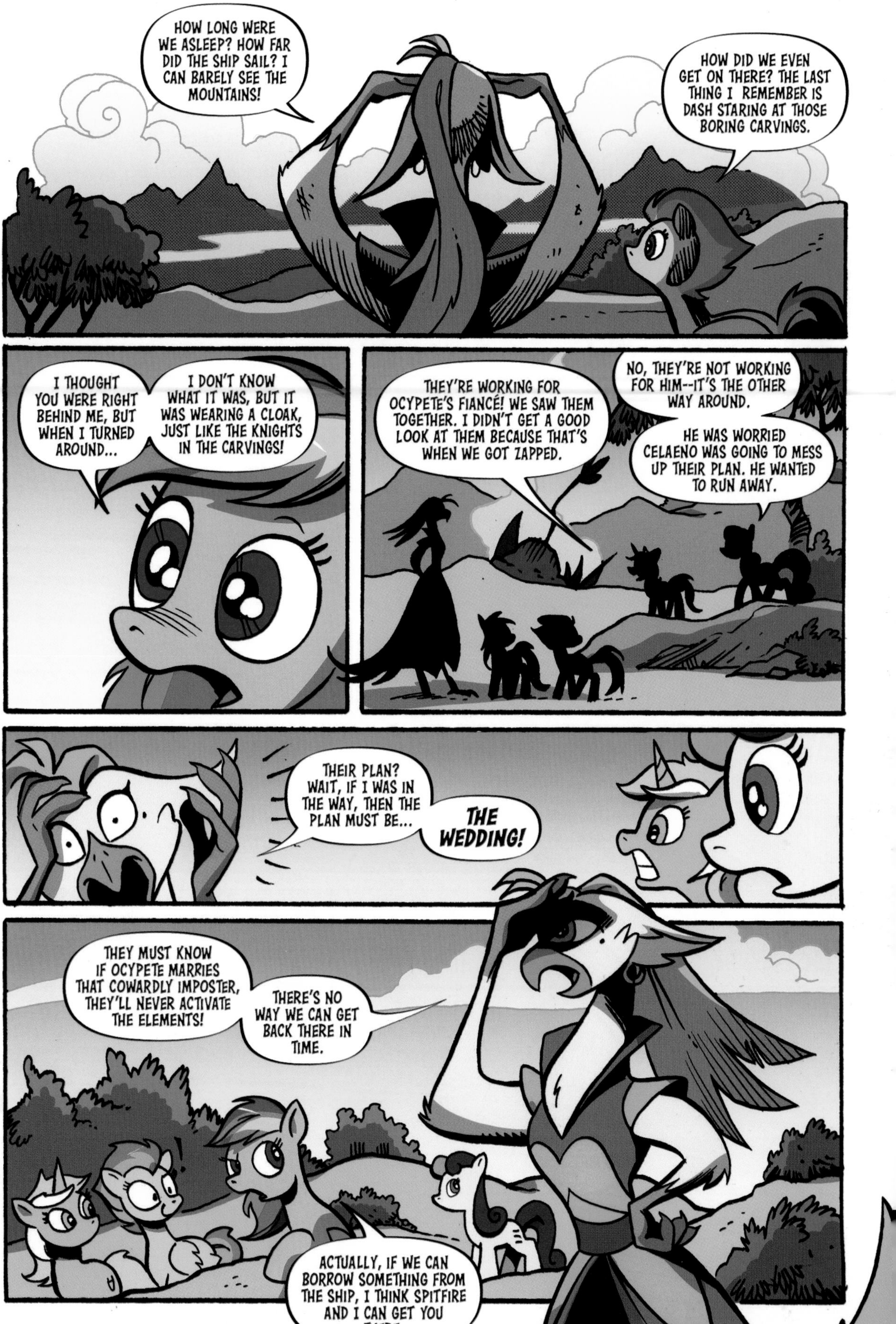
HOW LONG WERE WE ASLEEP? HOW FAR DID THE SHIP SAIL? I CAN BARELY SEE THE MOUNTAINS!
HOW DID WE EVEN GET ON THERE? THE LAST THING I REMEMBER IS DASH STARING AT THOSE BORING CARVINGS.
I THOUGHT YOU WERE RIGHT BEHIND ME, BUT WHEN I TURNED AROUND...
I DON'T KNOW WHAT IT WAS, BUT IT WAS WEARING A CLOAK, JUST LIKE THE KNIGHTS IN THE CARVINGS!
THEY'RE WORKING FOR OCYPETE'S FIANCÉ! WE SAW THEM TOGETHER. I DIDN'T GET A GOOD LOOK AT THEM BECAUSE THAT'S WHEN WE GOT ZAPPED.
NO, THEY'RE NOT WORKING FOR HIM--IT'S THE OTHER WAY AROUND.
HE WAS WORRIED CELAENO WAS GOING TO MESS UP THEIR PLAN. HE WANTED TO RUN AWAY.
THEIR PLAN? WAIT, IF I WAS IN THE WAY, THEN THE PLAN MUST BE...
THE WEDDING!
THEY MUST KNOW IF OCYPETE MARRIES THAT COWARDLY IMPOSTER, THEY'LL NEVER ACTIVATE THE ELEMENTS!
THERE'S NO WAY WE CAN GET BACK THERE IN TIME.
ACTUALLY, IF WE CAN BORROW SOMETHING FROM THE SHIP, I THINK SPITFIRE AND I CAN GET YOU THERE.

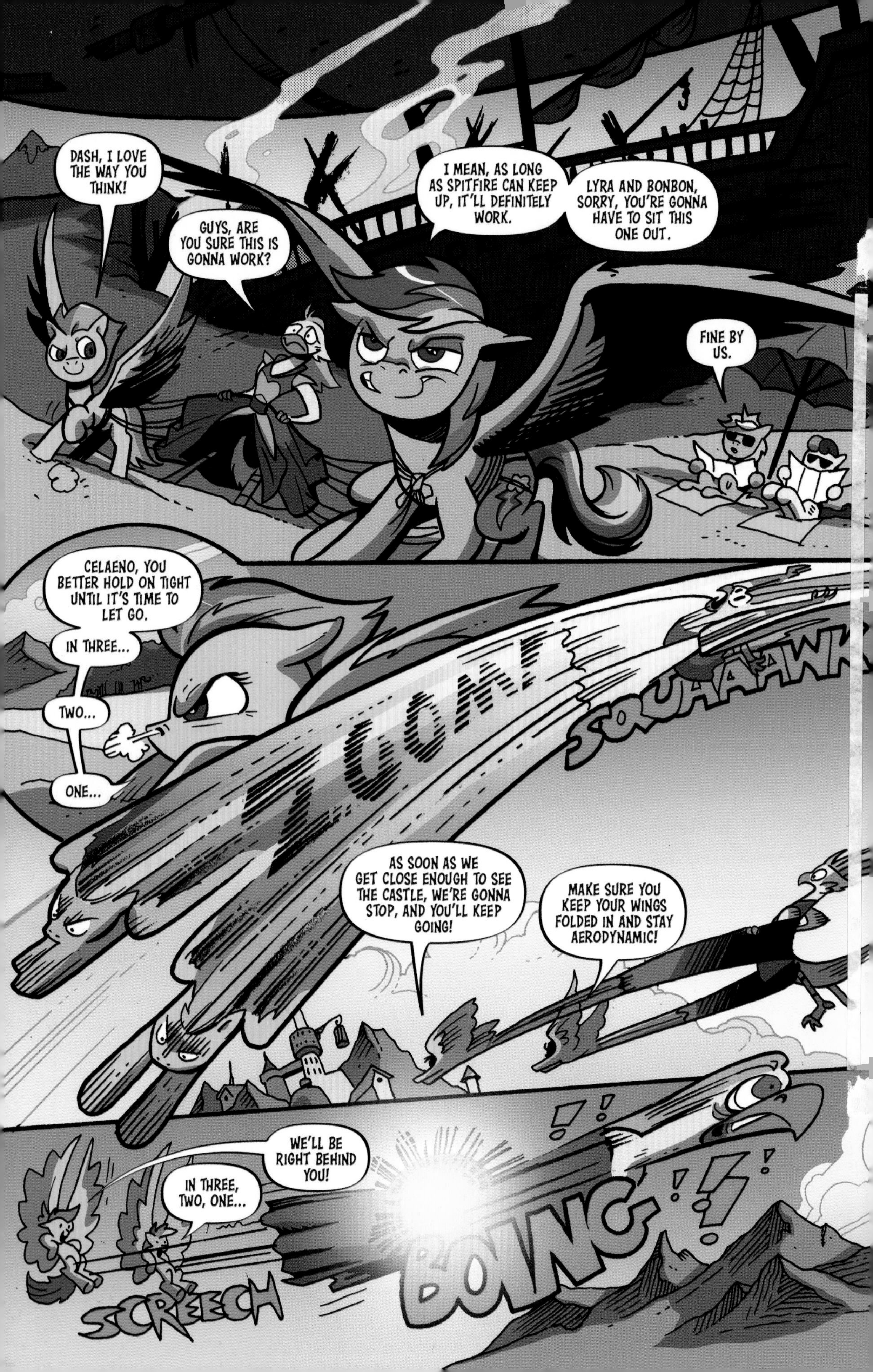
DASH, I LOVE THE WAY YOU THINK!
GUYS, ARE YOU SURE THIS IS GONNA WORK?
I MEAN, AS LONG AS SPITFIRE CAN KEEP UP, IT'LL DEFINITELY WORK.
LYRA AND BONBON, SORRY, YOU'RE GONNA HAVE TO SIT THIS ONE OUT.
FINE BY US.
CELAENO, YOU BETTER HOLD ON TIGHT UNTIL IT'S TIME TO LET GO.
IN THREE...
TWO...
ONE...
ZOOM!
SQUAAAWK
AS SOON AS WE GET CLOSE ENOUGH TO SEE THE CASTLE, WE'RE GONNA STOP, AND YOU'LL KEEP GOING!
MAKE SURE YOU KEEP YOUR WINGS FOLDED IN AND STAY AERODYNAMIC!
WE'LL BE RIGHT BEHIND YOU!
IN THREE, TWO, ONE...
BOING!?!
SCREECH

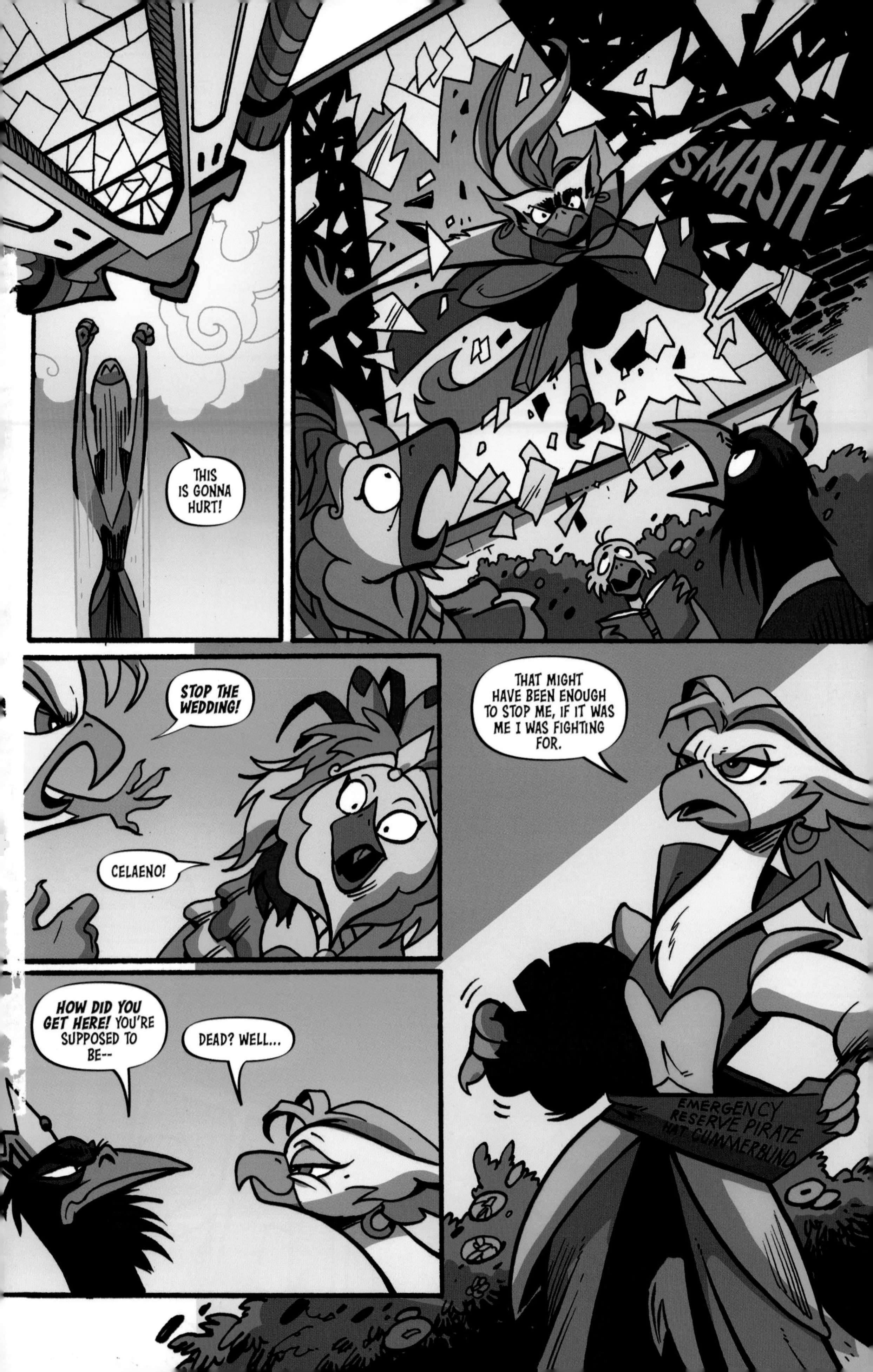
THIS IS GONNA HURT!
SMASH
STOP THE WEDDING!
CELAENO!
HOW DID YOU GET HERE! YOU'RE SUPPOSED TO BE--
DEAD? WELL...
THAT MIGHT HAVE BEEN ENOUGH TO STOP ME, IF IT WAS ME I WAS FIGHTING FOR.
EMERGENCY RESERVE PIRATE HAT CUMMERBUND

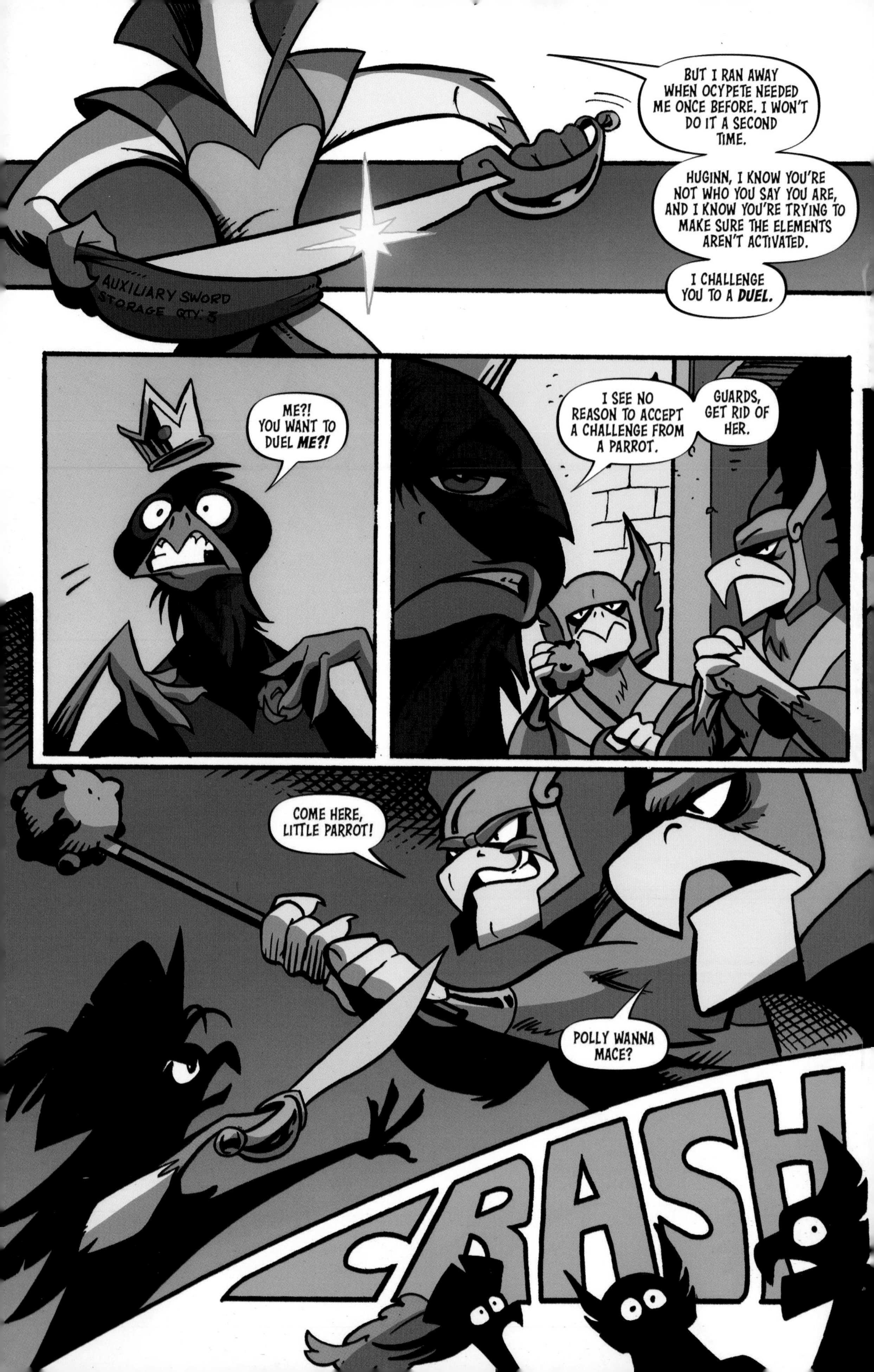
BUT I RAN AWAY WHEN OCYPETE NEEDED ME ONCE BEFORE. I WON'T DO IT A SECOND TIME.
HUGINN, I KNOW YOU'RE NOT WHO YOU SAY YOU ARE, AND I KNOW YOU'RE TRYING TO MAKE SURE THE ELEMENTS AREN'T ACTIVATED.
I CHALLENGE YOU TO A **DUEL.**
AUXILIARY SWORD STORAGE QTY: 3
ME?! YOU WANT TO DUEL **ME?!**
I SEE NO REASON TO ACCEPT A CHALLENGE FROM A PARROT.
GUARDS, GET RID OF HER.
COME HERE, LITTLE PARROT!
POLLY WANNA MACE?
CRASH

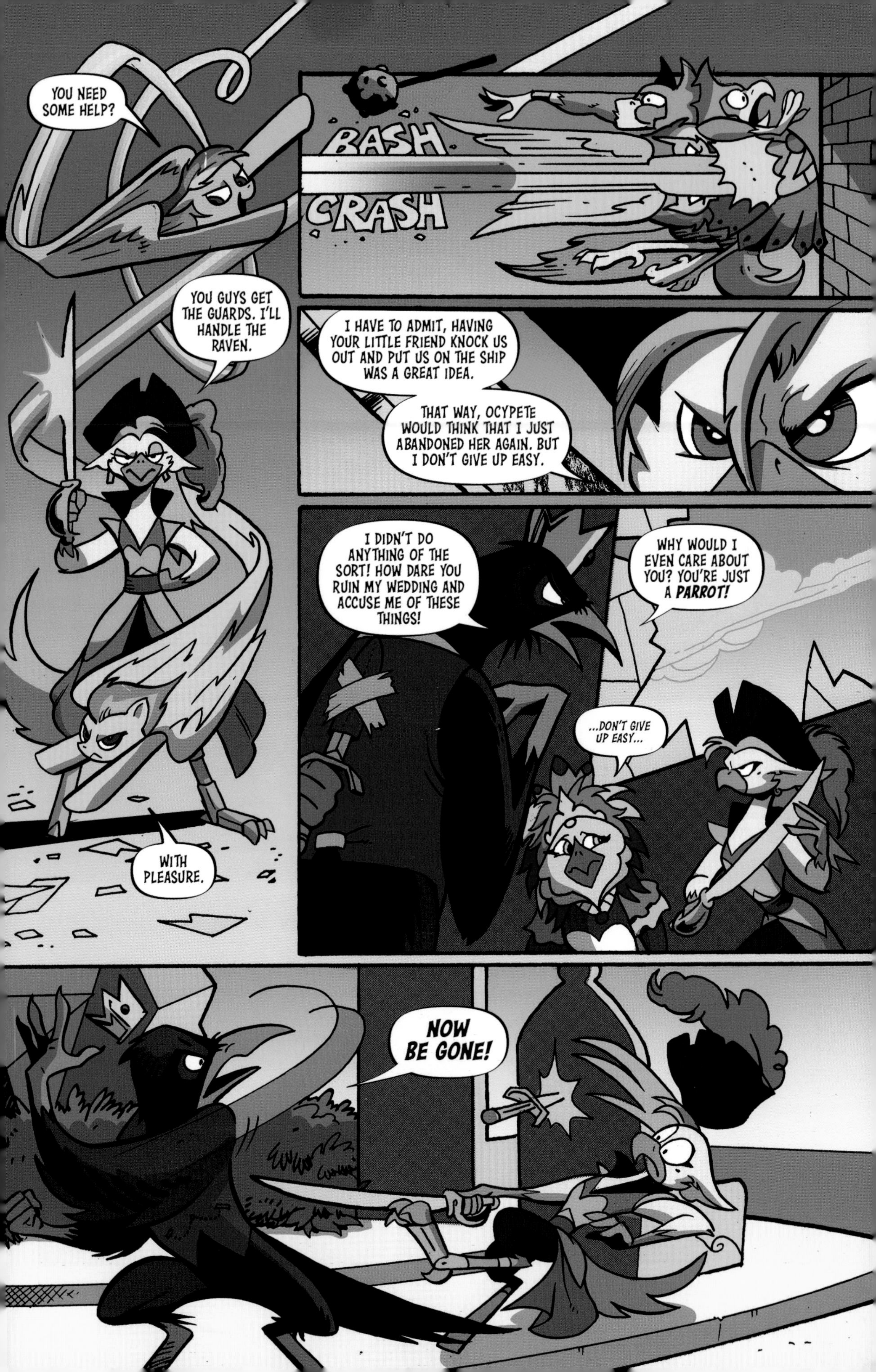
YOU NEED SOME HELP?
BASH
CRASH
YOU GUYS GET THE GUARDS. I'LL HANDLE THE RAVEN.
WITH PLEASURE.
I HAVE TO ADMIT, HAVING YOUR LITTLE FRIEND KNOCK US OUT AND PUT US ON THE SHIP WAS A GREAT IDEA.
THAT WAY, OCYPETE WOULD THINK THAT I JUST ABANDONED HER AGAIN. BUT I DON'T GIVE UP EASY.
I DIDN'T DO ANYTHING OF THE SORT! HOW DARE YOU RUIN MY WEDDING AND ACCUSE ME OF THESE THINGS!
WHY WOULD I EVEN CARE ABOUT YOU? YOU'RE JUST A PARROT!
...DON'T GIVE UP EASY...
NOW BE GONE!

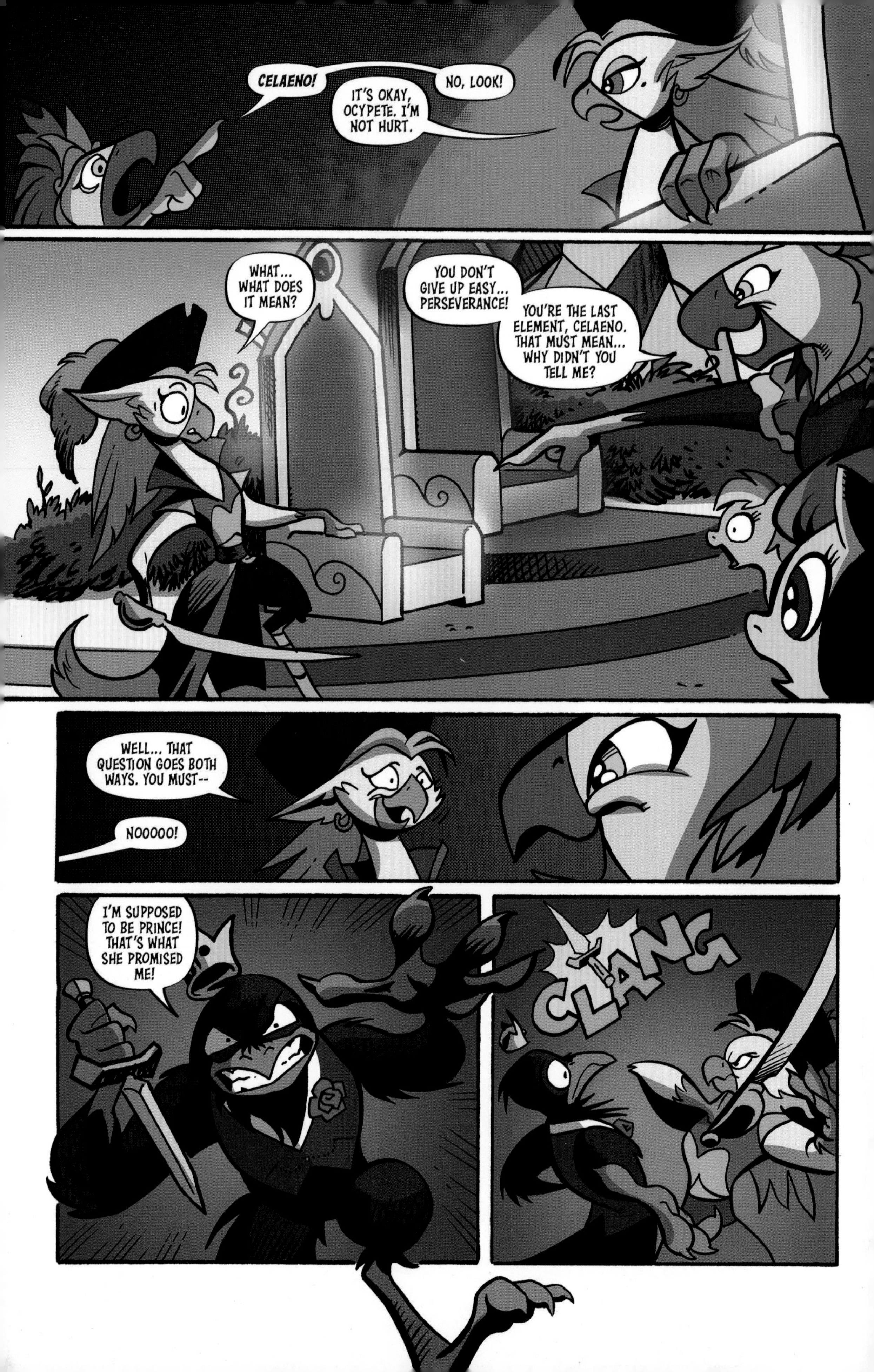

CELAENO!
NO, LOOK!
IT'S OKAY, OCYPETE. I'M NOT HURT.
WHAT... WHAT DOES IT MEAN?
YOU DON'T GIVE UP EASY... PERSEVERANCE!
YOU'RE THE LAST ELEMENT, CELAENO. THAT MUST MEAN... WHY DIDN'T YOU TELL ME?
WELL... THAT QUESTION GOES BOTH WAYS. YOU MUST--
NOOOOO!
I'M SUPPOSED TO BE PRINCE! THAT'S WHAT SHE PROMISED ME!
CLANG

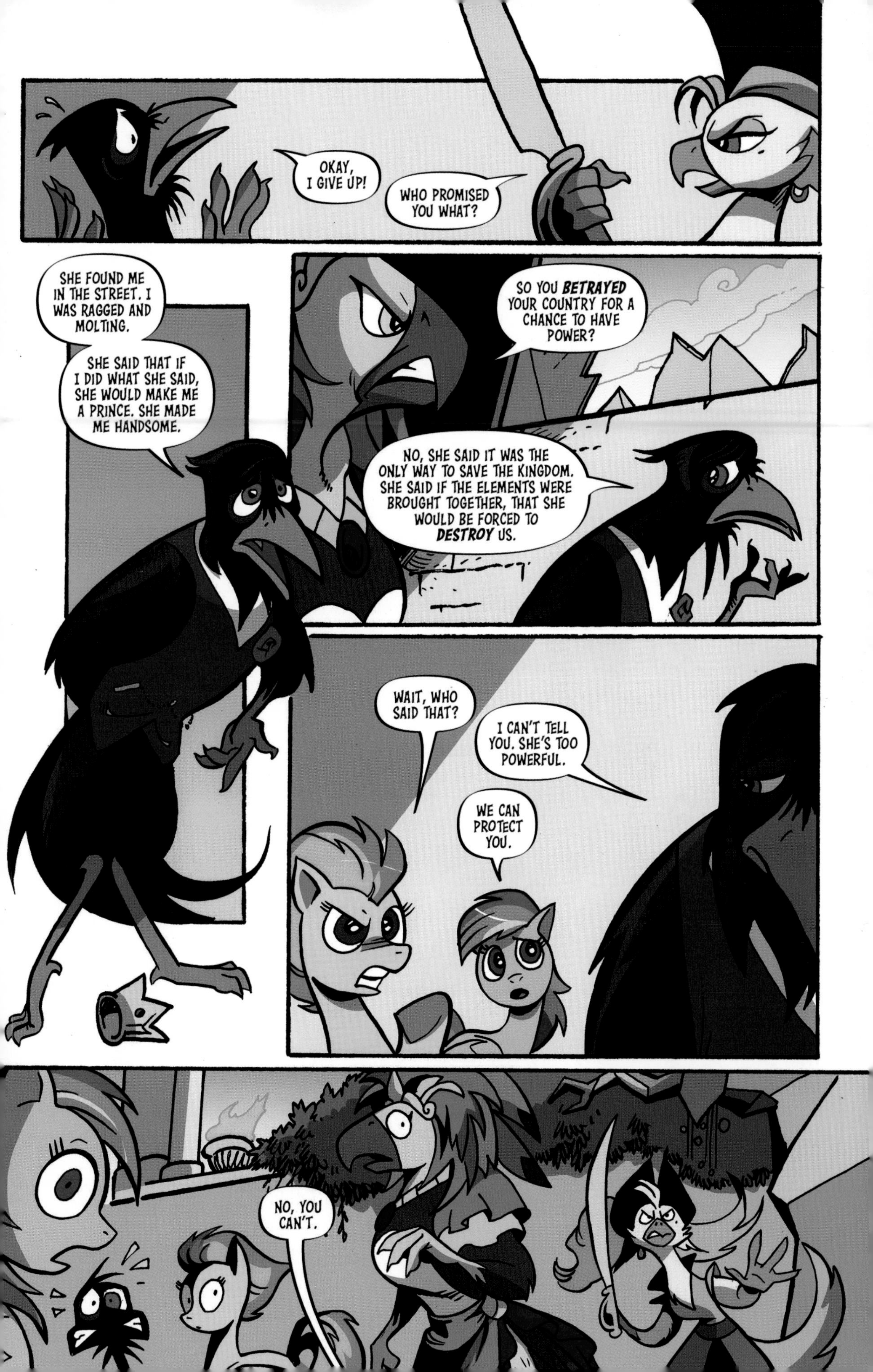
OKAY, I GIVE UP!
WHO PROMISED YOU WHAT?
SHE FOUND ME IN THE STREET. I WAS RAGGED AND MOLTING.
SHE SAID THAT IF I DID WHAT SHE SAID, SHE WOULD MAKE ME A PRINCE. SHE MADE ME HANDSOME.
SO YOU BETRAYED YOUR COUNTRY FOR A CHANCE TO HAVE POWER?
NO, SHE SAID IT WAS THE ONLY WAY TO SAVE THE KINGDOM. SHE SAID IF THE ELEMENTS WERE BROUGHT TOGETHER, THAT SHE WOULD BE FORCED TO DESTROY US.
WAIT, WHO SAID THAT?
I CAN'T TELL YOU. SHE'S TOO POWERFUL.
WE CAN PROTECT YOU.
NO, YOU CAN'T.

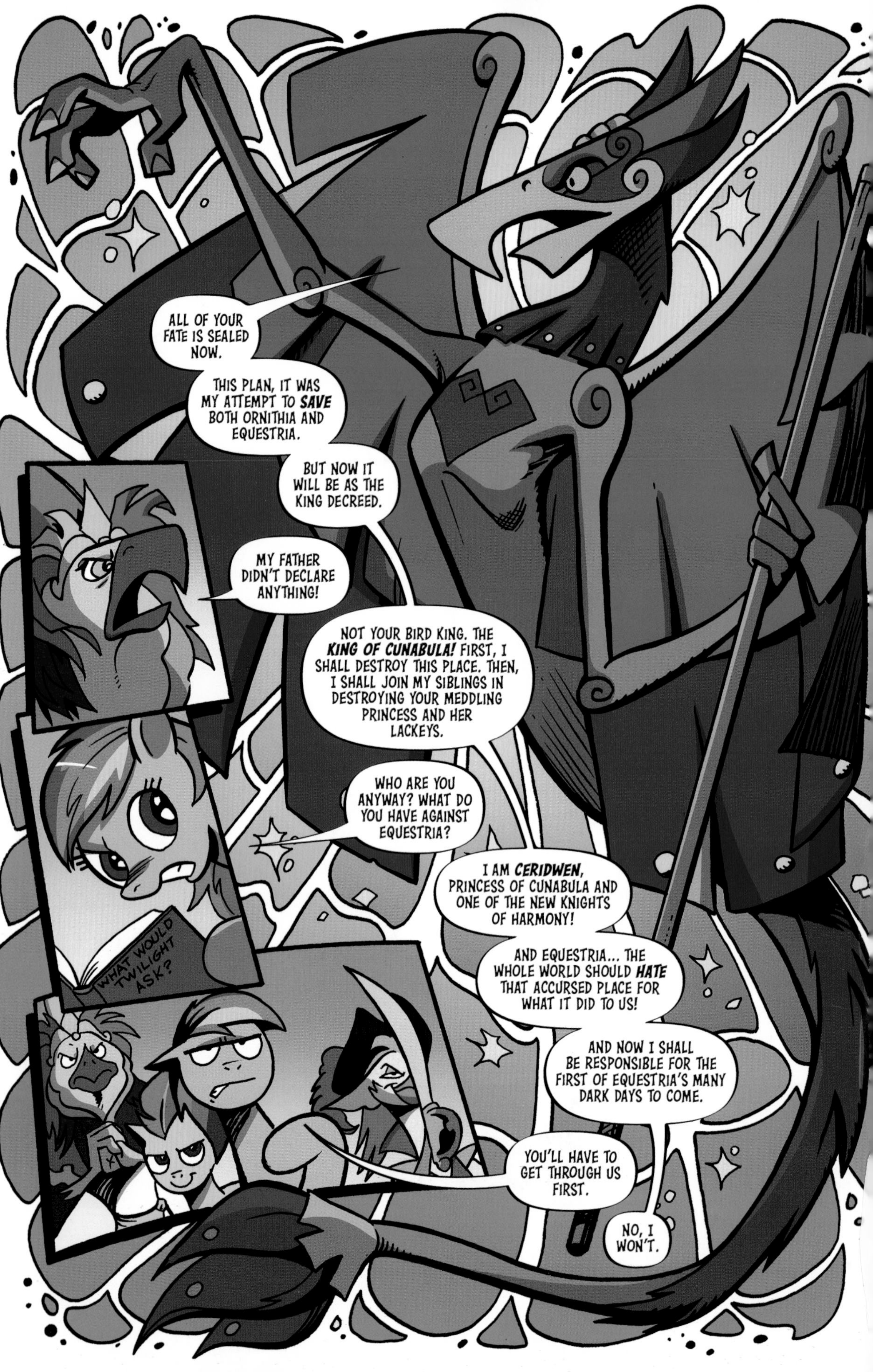
ALL OF YOUR FATE IS SEALED NOW.
THIS PLAN, IT WAS MY ATTEMPT TO SAVE BOTH ORNITHIA AND EQUESTRIA.
BUT NOW IT WILL BE AS THE KING DECREED.
MY FATHER DIDN'T DECLARE ANYTHING!
NOT YOUR BIRD KING. THE KING OF CUNABULA! FIRST, I SHALL DESTROY THIS PLACE. THEN, I SHALL JOIN MY SIBLINGS IN DESTROYING YOUR MEDDLING PRINCESS AND HER LACKEYS.
WHO ARE YOU ANYWAY? WHAT DO YOU HAVE AGAINST EQUESTRIA?
WHAT WOULD TWILIGHT ASK?
I AM CERIDWEN, PRINCESS OF CUNABULA AND ONE OF THE NEW KNIGHTS OF HARMONY!
AND EQUESTRIA... THE WHOLE WORLD SHOULD HATE THAT ACCURSED PLACE FOR WHAT IT DID TO US!
AND NOW I SHALL BE RESPONSIBLE FOR THE FIRST OF EQUESTRIA'S MANY DARK DAYS TO COME.
YOU'LL HAVE TO GET THROUGH US FIRST.
NO, I WON'T.

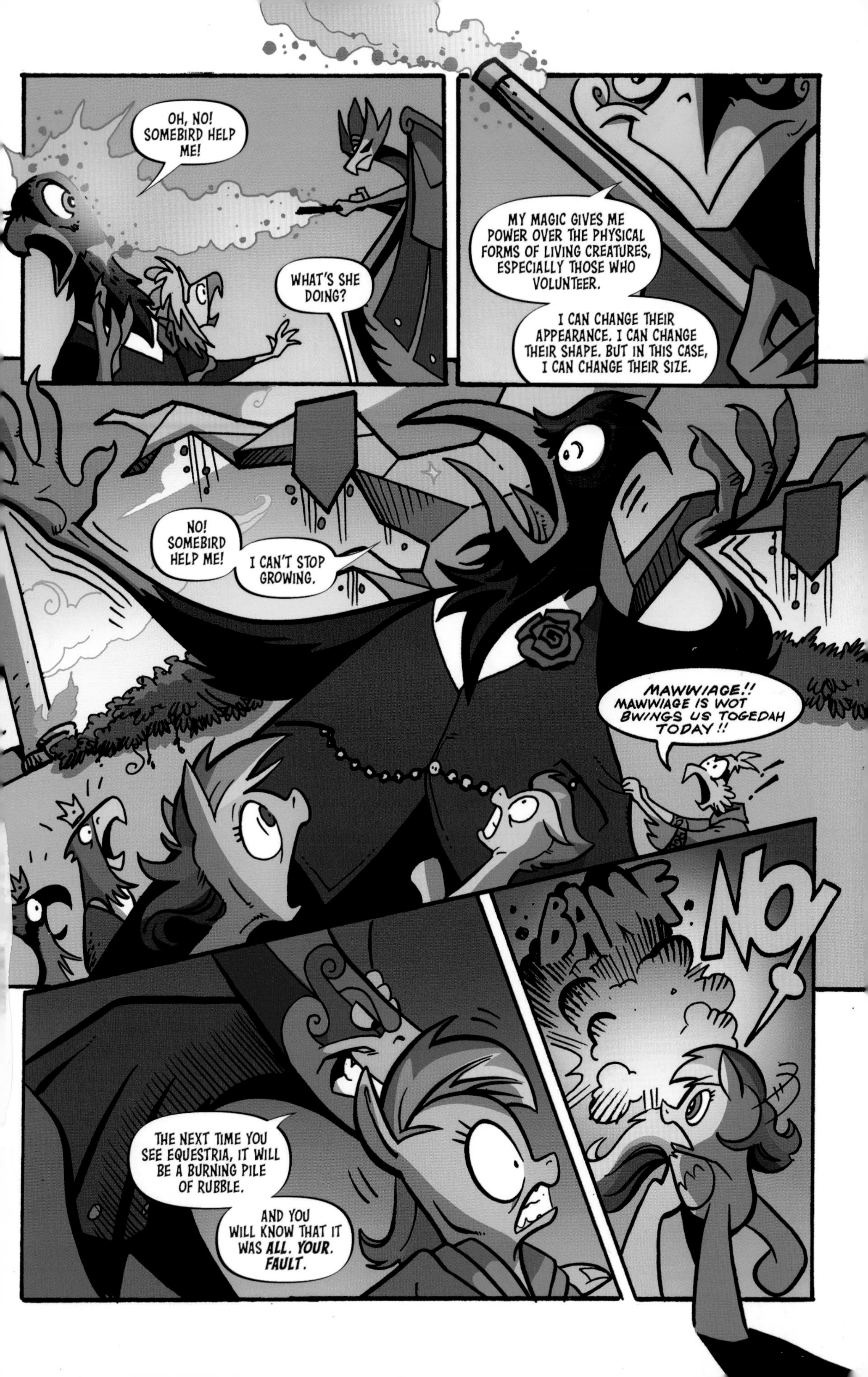
OH, NO! SOMEBIRD HELP ME!
WHAT'S SHE DOING?
MY MAGIC GIVES ME POWER OVER THE PHYSICAL FORMS OF LIVING CREATURES, ESPECIALLY THOSE WHO VOLUNTEER.
I CAN CHANGE THEIR APPEARANCE. I CAN CHANGE THEIR SHAPE. BUT IN THIS CASE, I CAN CHANGE THEIR SIZE.
NO! SOMEBIRD HELP ME!
I CAN'T STOP GROWING.
MAWWIAGE!! MAWWIAGE IS WOT BWINGS US TOGEDAH TODAY!!
BAMF
NO!
THE NEXT TIME YOU SEE EQUESTRIA, IT WILL BE A BURNING PILE OF RUBBLE.
AND YOU WILL KNOW THAT IT WAS ALL. YOUR. FAULT.

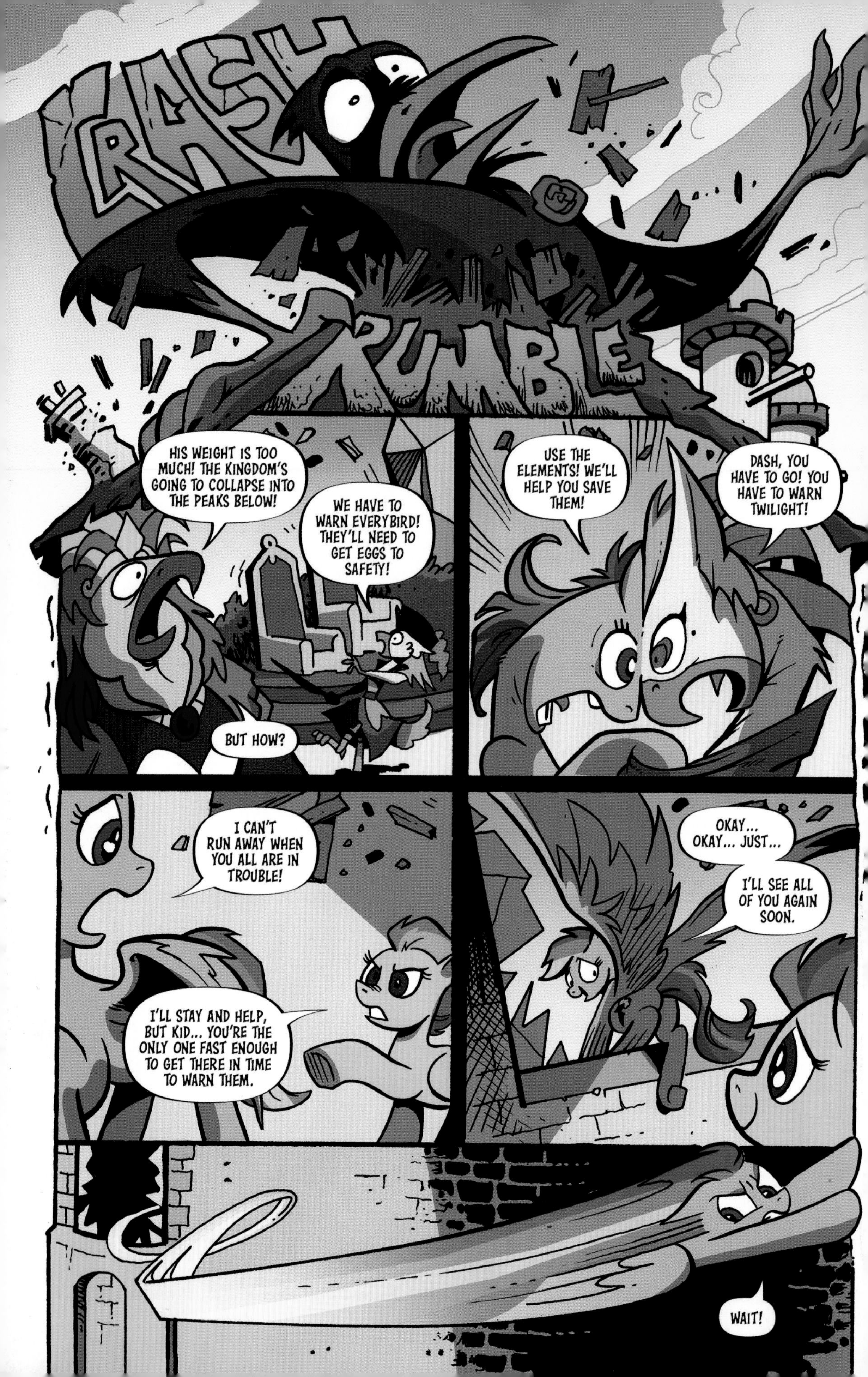
CRASH
RUMBLE
HIS WEIGHT IS TOO MUCH! THE KINGDOM'S GOING TO COLLAPSE INTO THE PEAKS BELOW!
WE HAVE TO WARN EVERYBIRD! THEY'LL NEED TO GET EGGS TO SAFETY!
BUT HOW?
USE THE ELEMENTS! WE'LL HELP YOU SAVE THEM!
DASH, YOU HAVE TO GO! YOU HAVE TO WARN TWILIGHT!
I CAN'T RUN AWAY WHEN YOU ALL ARE IN TROUBLE!
I'LL STAY AND HELP, BUT KID... YOU'RE THE ONLY ONE FAST ENOUGH TO GET THERE IN TIME TO WARN THEM.
OKAY... OKAY... JUST...
I'LL SEE ALL OF YOU AGAIN SOON.
WAIT!

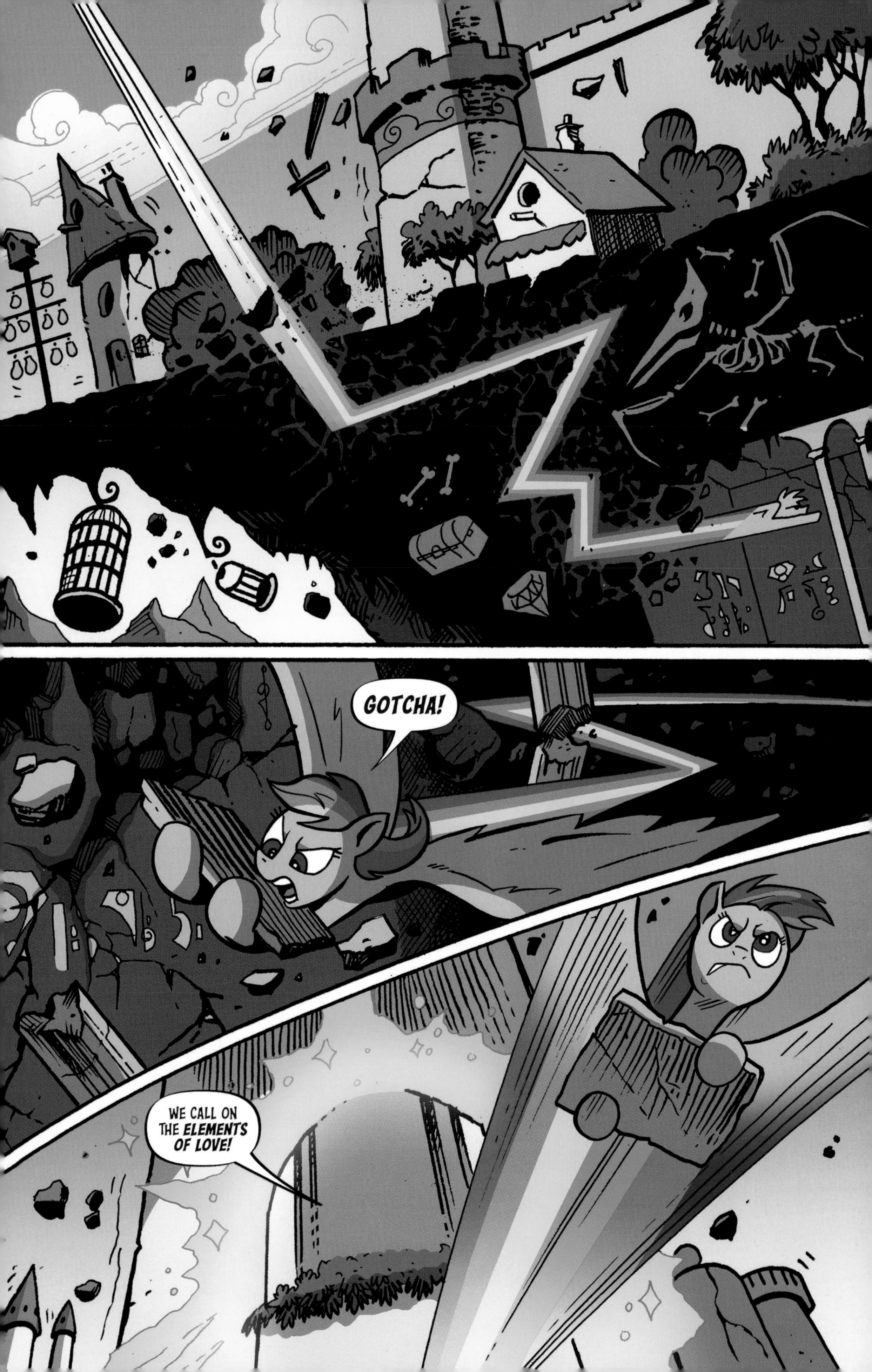
GOTCHA!
WE CALL ON THE ELEMENTS OF LOVE!

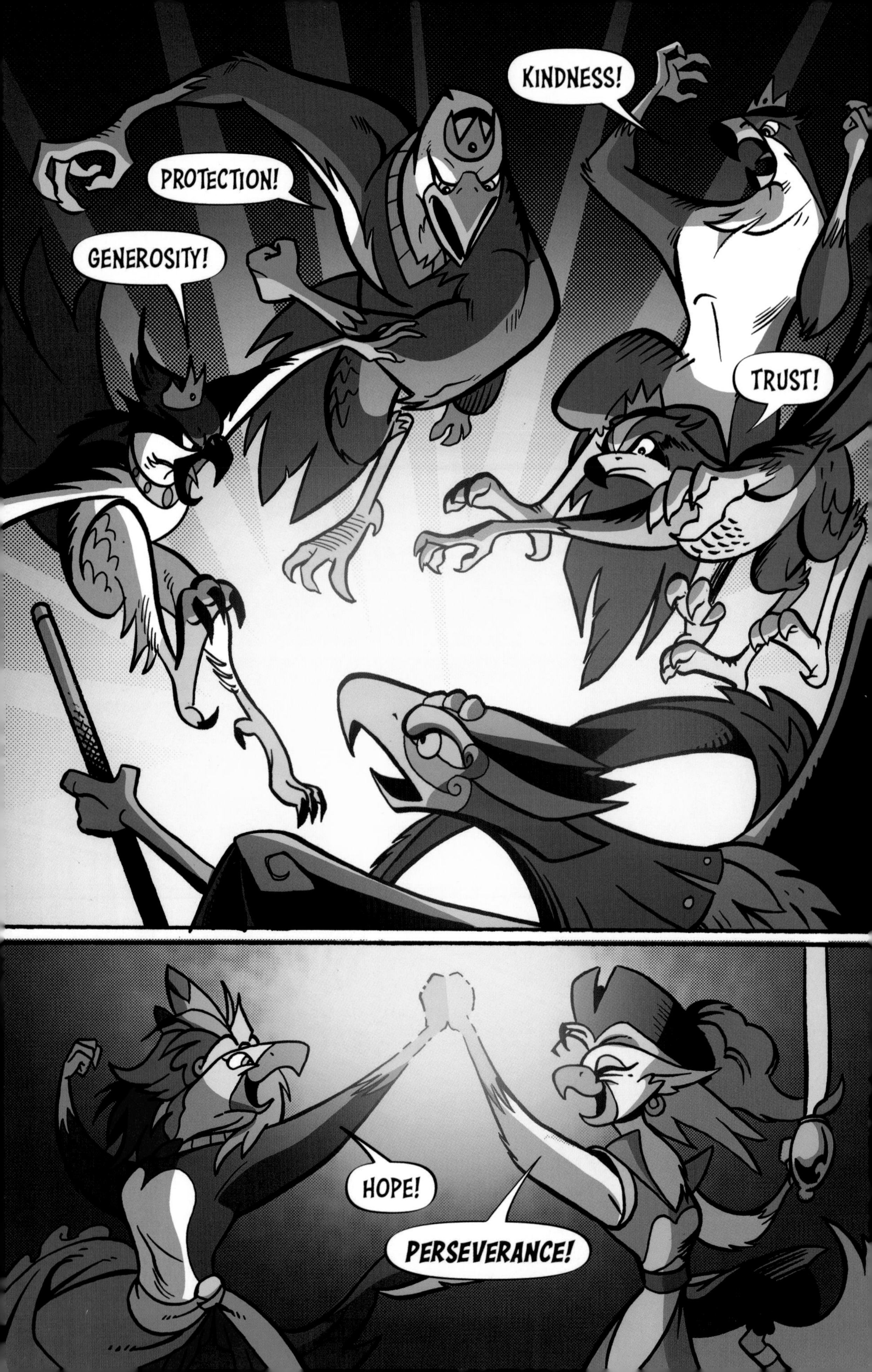
KINDNESS!
PROTECTION!
GENEROSITY!
TRUST!
HOPE!
PERSEVERANCE!

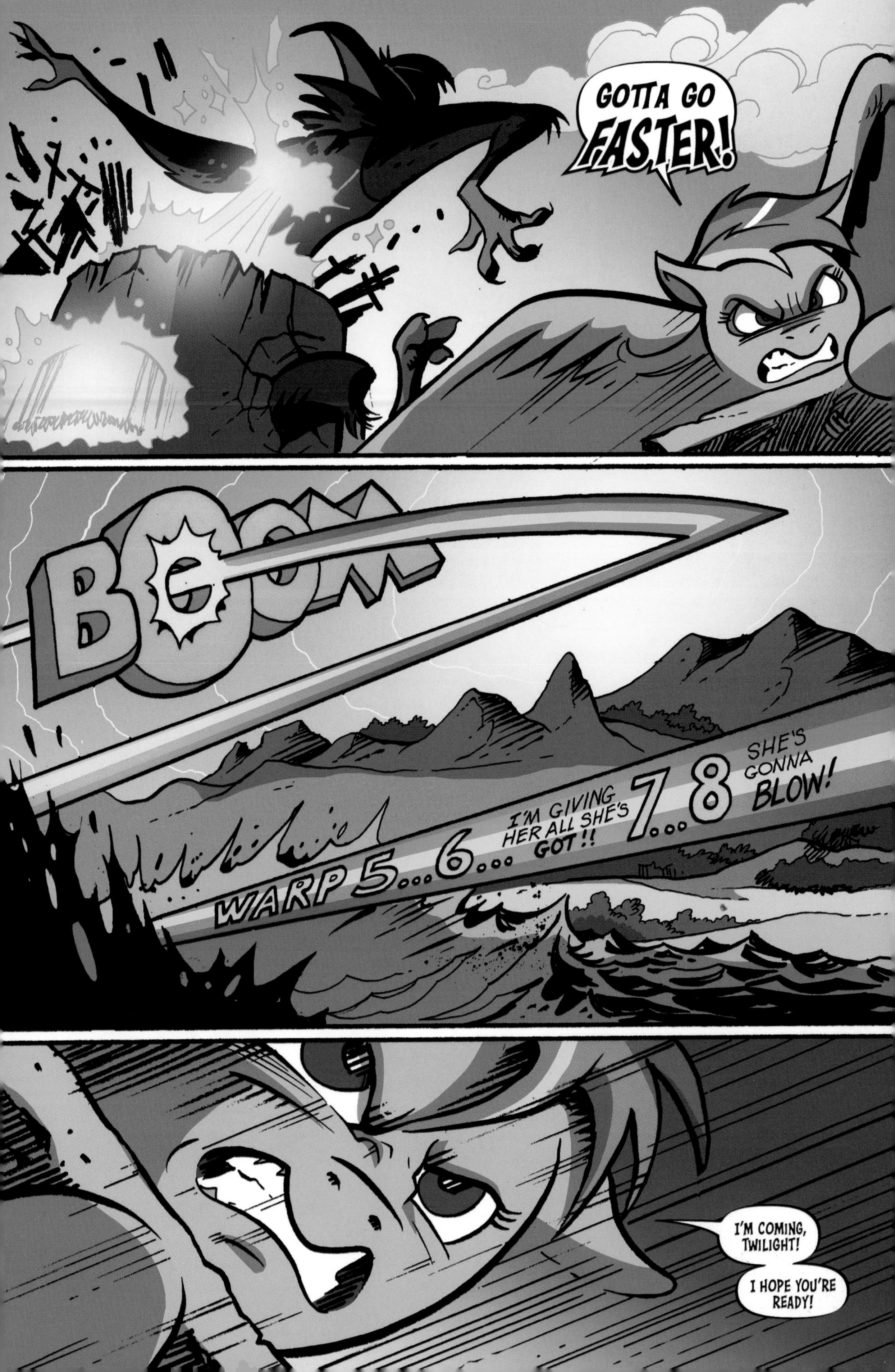
GOTTA GO FASTER!
BOOM
WARP 5...6...
I'M GIVING HER ALL SHE'S GOT!!
7...8
SHE'S GONNA BLOW!
I'M COMING, TWILIGHT!
I HOPE YOU'RE READY!

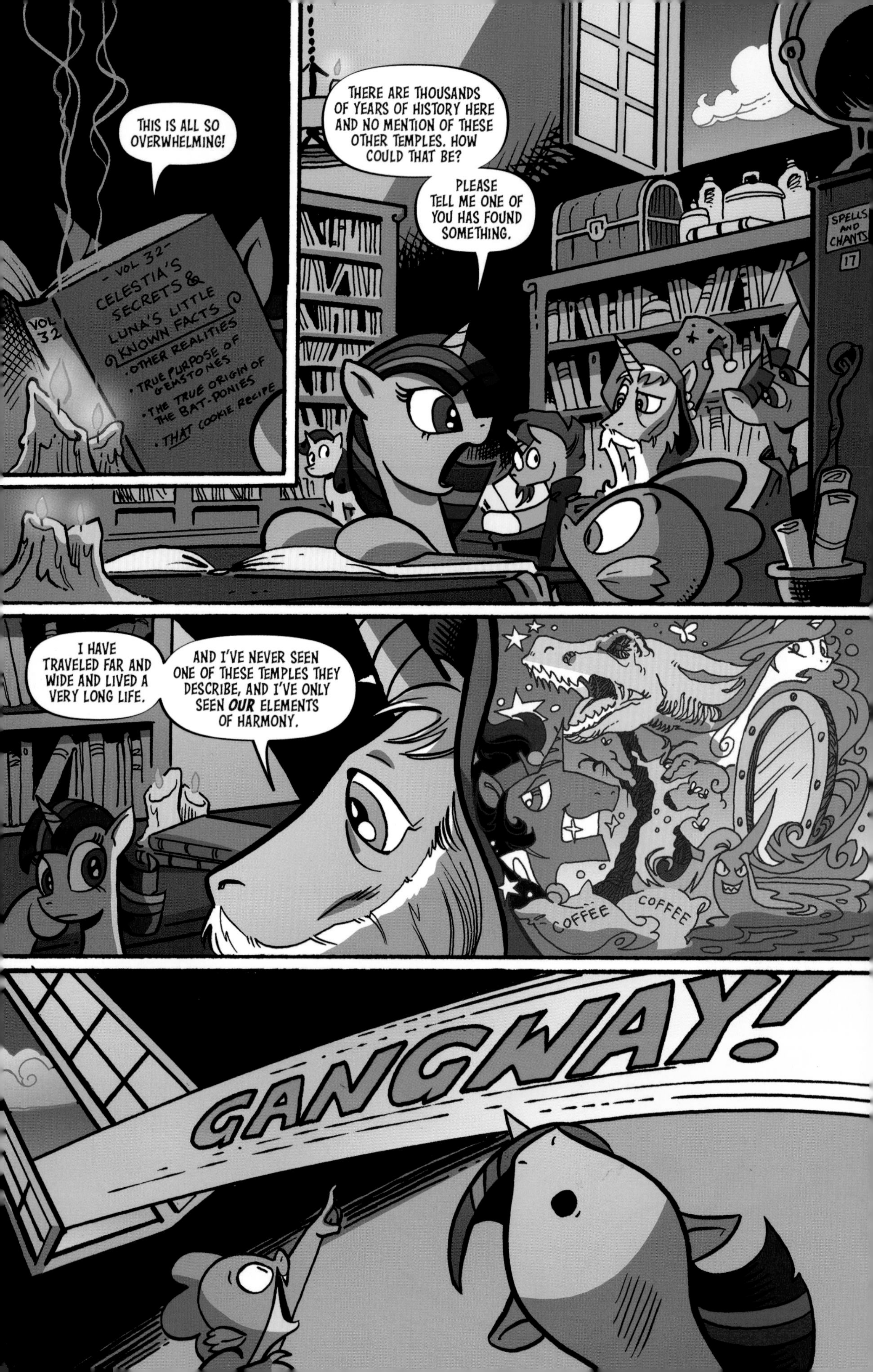

THIS IS ALL SO OVERWHELMING!
- VOL 32 - CELESTIA'S SECRETS & LUNA'S LITTLE KNOWN FACTS
VOL 32
• OTHER REALITIES
• TRUE PURPOSE OF GEMSTONES
• THE TRUE ORIGIN OF THE BAT-PONIES
• THAT COOKIE RECIPE
THERE ARE THOUSANDS OF YEARS OF HISTORY HERE AND NO MENTION OF THESE OTHER TEMPLES. HOW COULD THAT BE?
PLEASE TELL ME ONE OF YOU HAS FOUND SOMETHING.
SPELLS AND CHANTS
17
I HAVE TRAVELED FAR AND WIDE AND LIVED A VERY LONG LIFE.
AND I'VE NEVER SEEN ONE OF THESE TEMPLES THEY DESCRIBE, AND I'VE ONLY SEEN ***OUR*** ELEMENTS OF HARMONY.
COFFEE
COFFEE
GANGWAY!

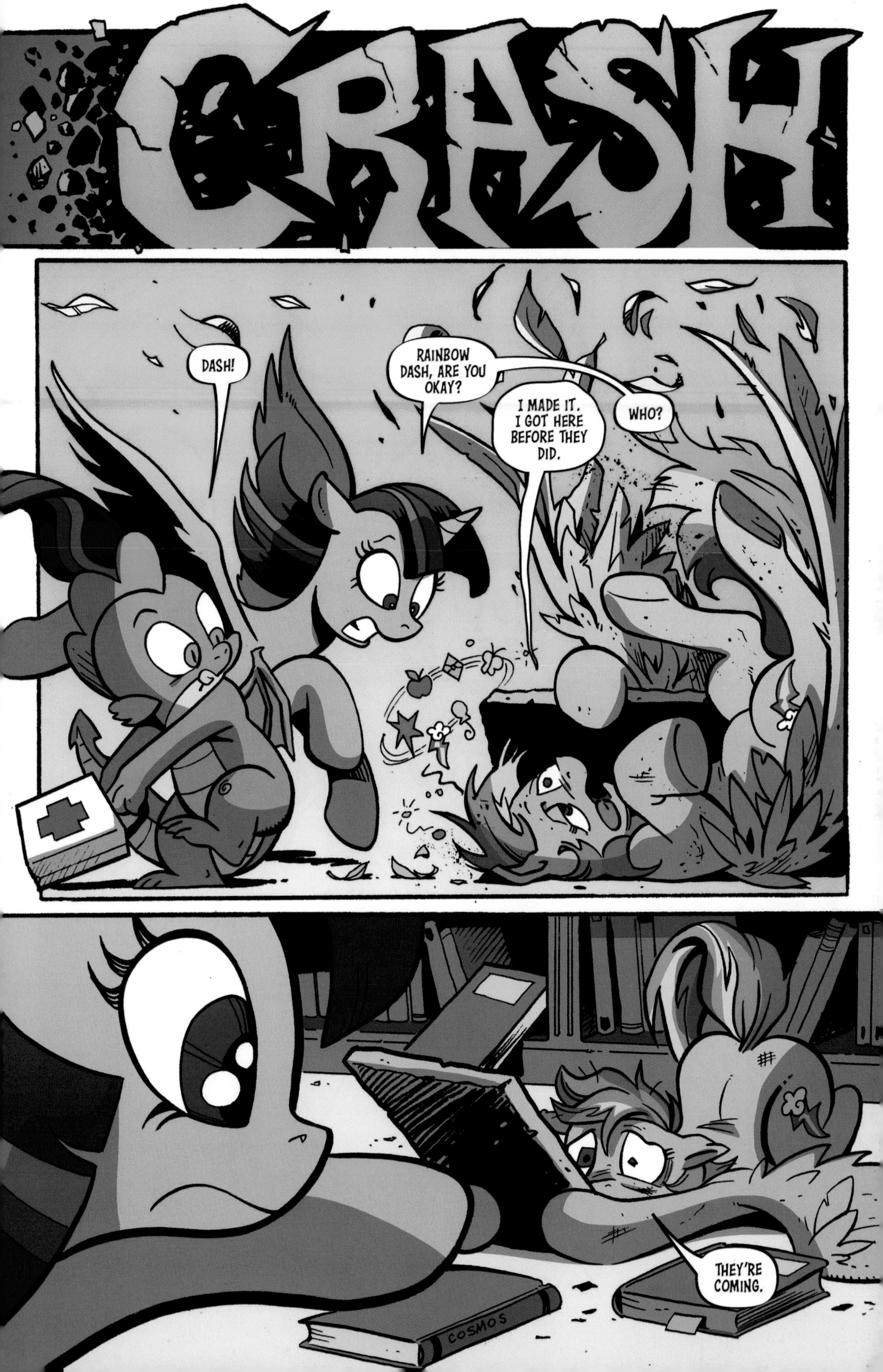
CRASH
DASH!
RAINBOW DASH, ARE YOU OKAY?
WHO?
I MADE IT. I GOT HERE BEFORE THEY DID.
THEY'RE COMING.
COSMOS

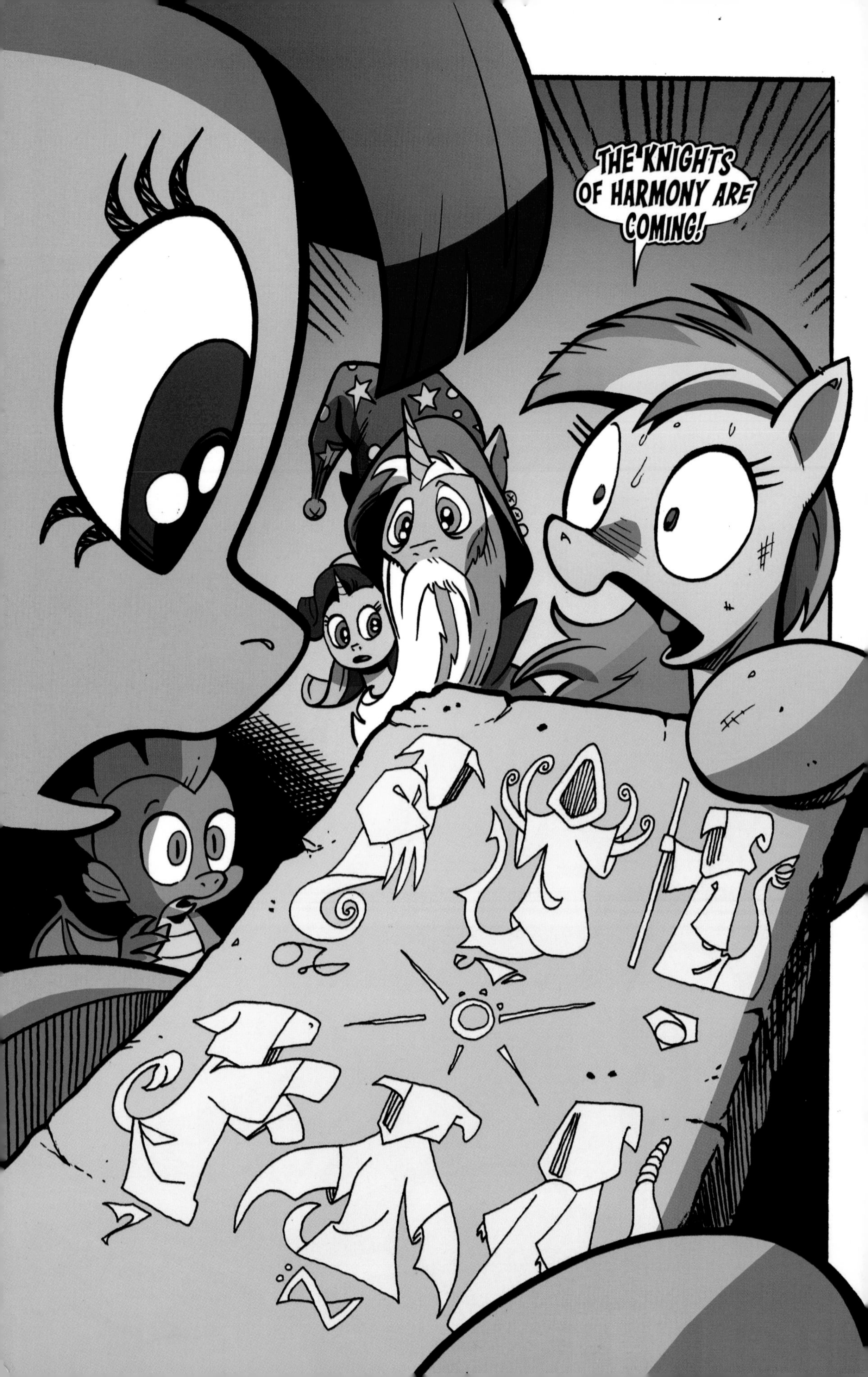
THE KNIGHTS OF HARMONY ARE COMING!

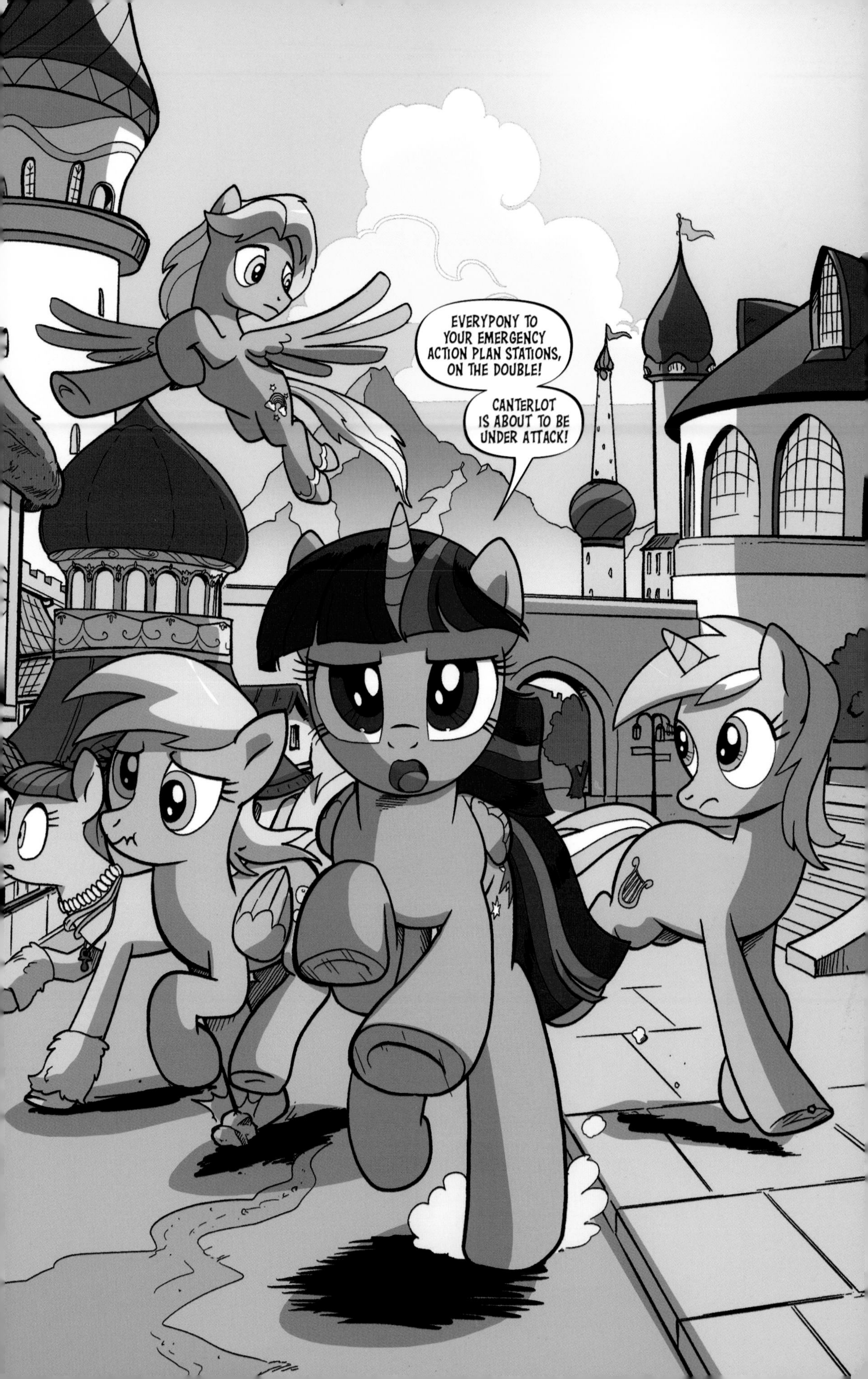
EVERYPONY TO YOUR EMERGENCY ACTION PLAN STATIONS, ON THE DOUBLE!
CANTERLOT IS ABOUT TO BE UNDER ATTACK!

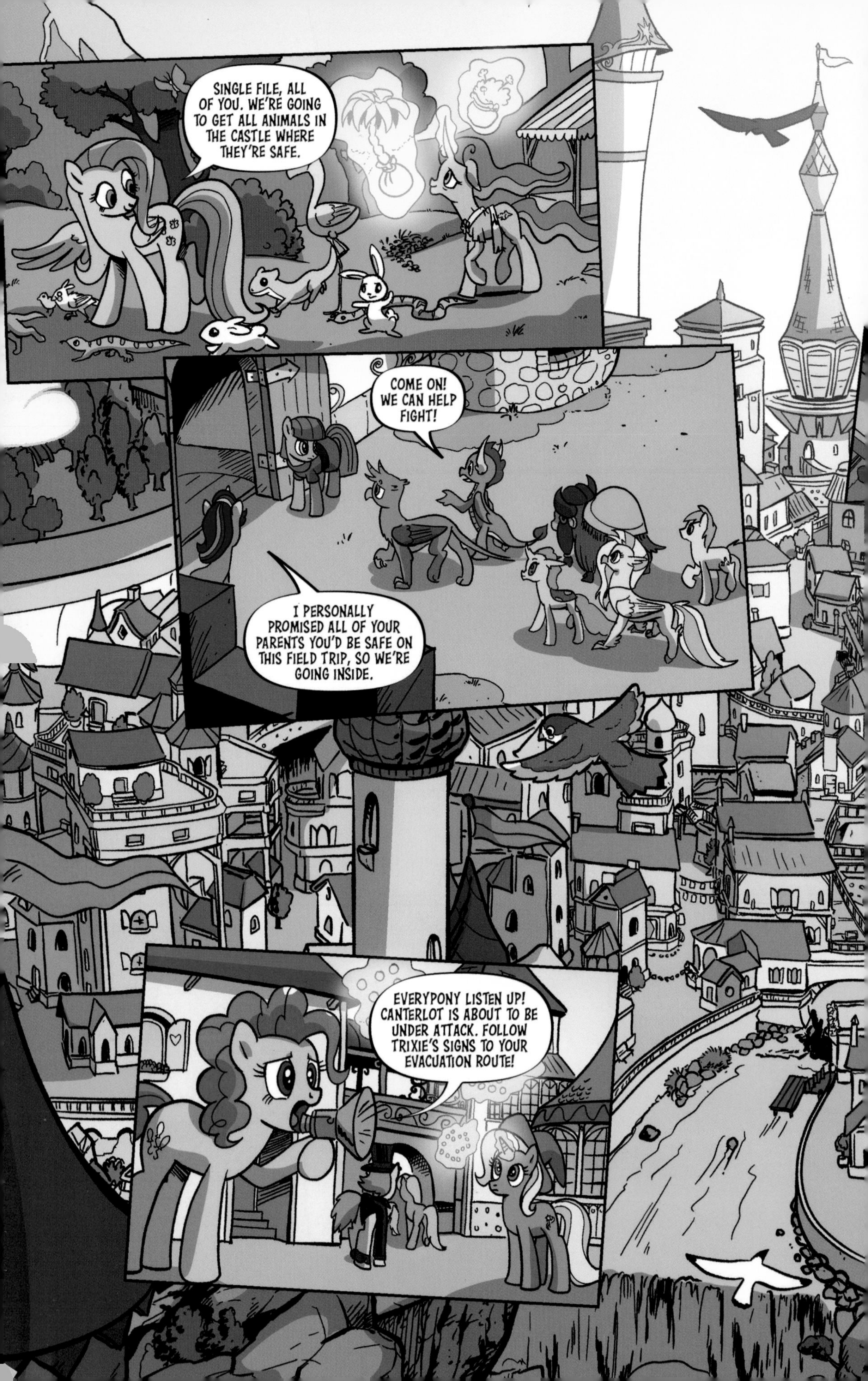
SINGLE FILE, ALL OF YOU. WE'RE GOING TO GET ALL ANIMALS IN THE CASTLE WHERE THEY'RE SAFE.
COME ON! WE CAN HELP FIGHT!
I PERSONALLY PROMISED ALL OF YOUR PARENTS YOU'D BE SAFE ON THIS FIELD TRIP, SO WE'RE GOING INSIDE.
EVERYPONY LISTEN UP! CANTERLOT IS ABOUT TO BE UNDER ATTACK. FOLLOW TRIXIE'S SIGNS TO YOUR EVACUATION ROUTE!

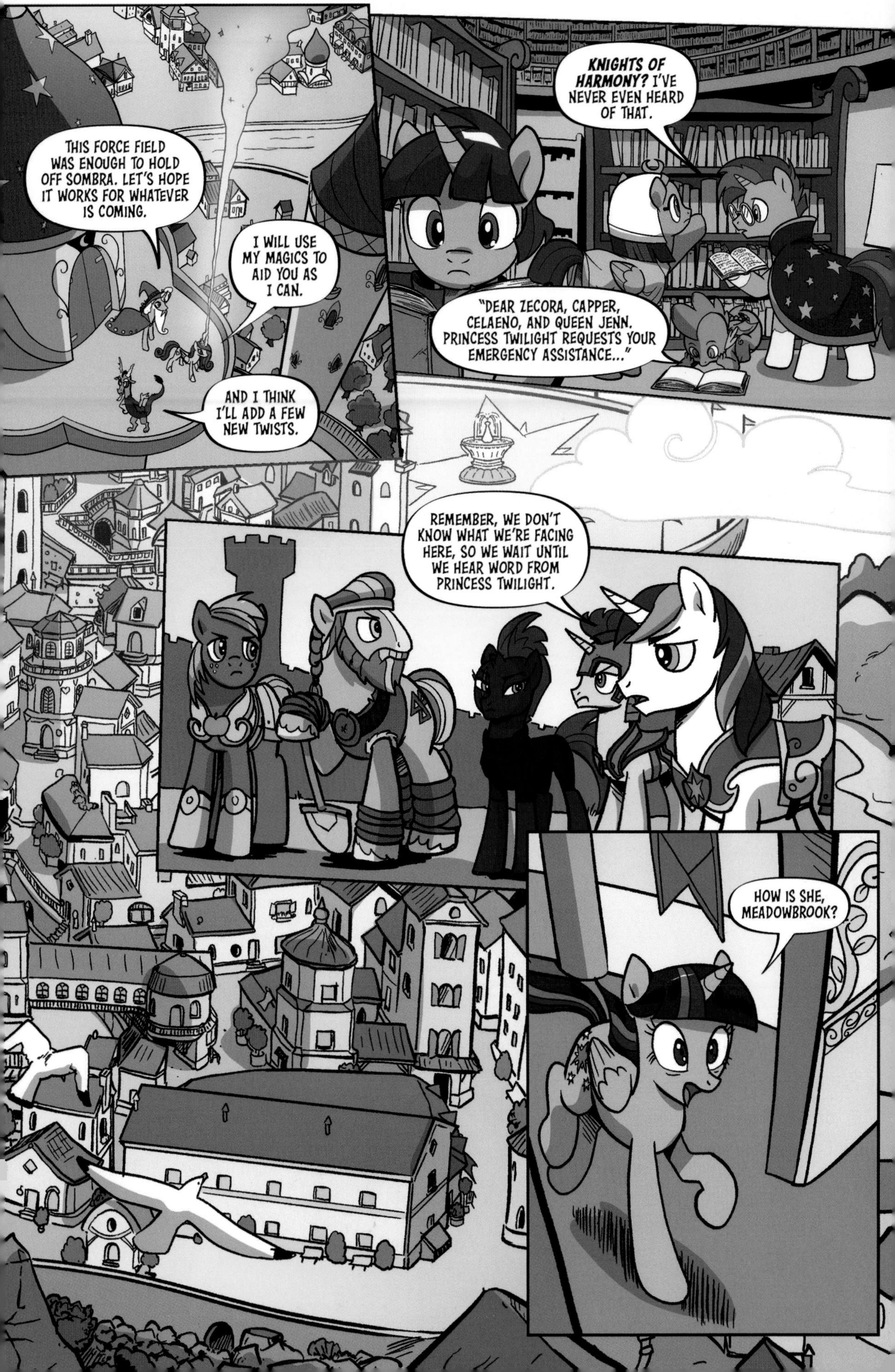
THIS FORCE FIELD WAS ENOUGH TO HOLD OFF SOMBRA. LET'S HOPE IT WORKS FOR WHATEVER IS COMING.
I WILL USE MY MAGICS TO AID YOU AS I CAN.
AND I THINK I'LL ADD A FEW NEW TWISTS.
KNIGHTS OF HARMONY? I'VE NEVER EVEN HEARD OF THAT.
"DEAR ZECORA, CAPPER, CELAENO, AND QUEEN JENN. PRINCESS TWILIGHT REQUESTS YOUR EMERGENCY ASSISTANCE..."
REMEMBER, WE DON'T KNOW WHAT WE'RE FACING HERE, SO WE WAIT UNTIL WE HEAR WORD FROM PRINCESS TWILIGHT.
HOW IS SHE, MEADOWBROOK?

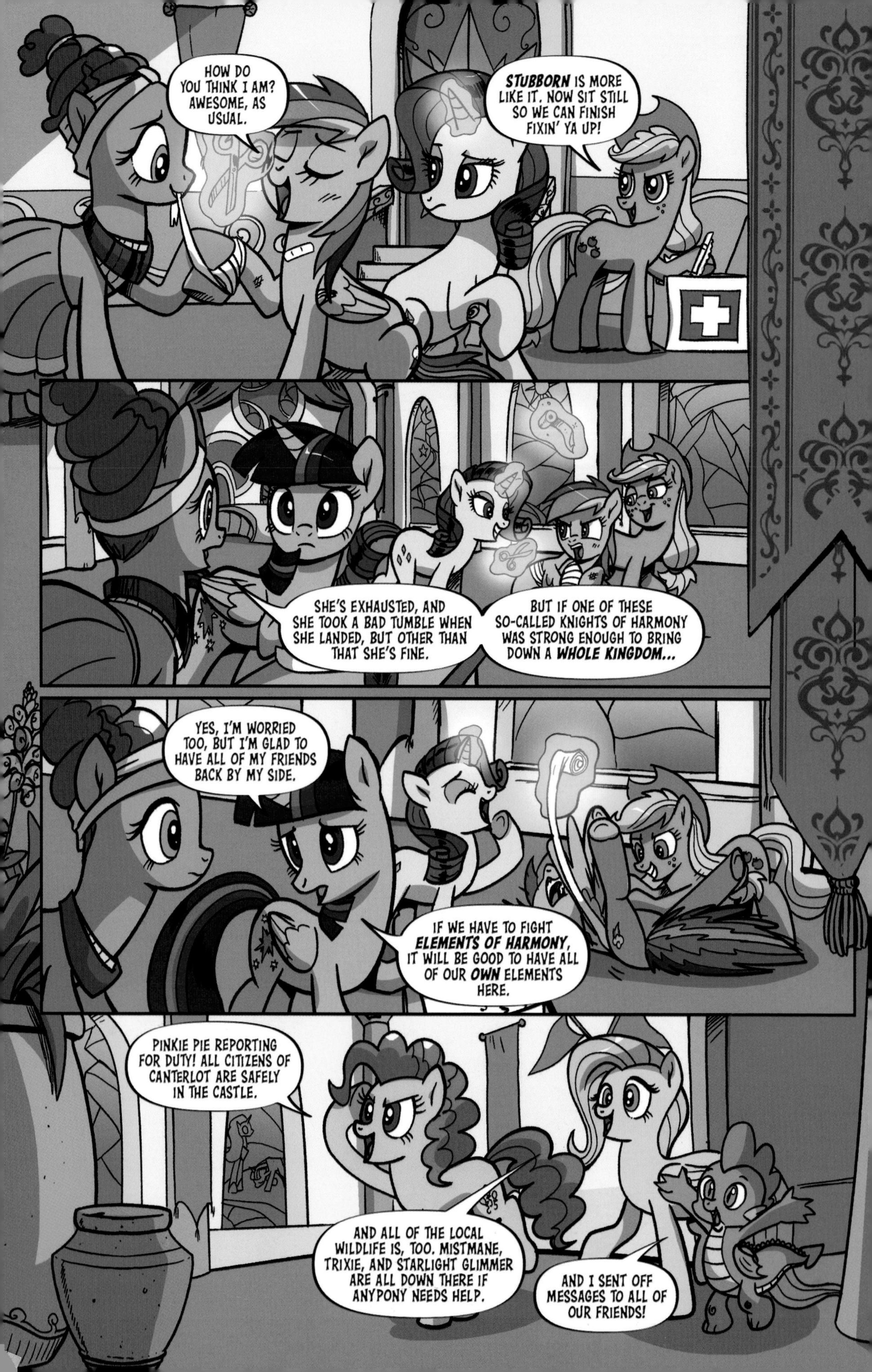
HOW DO YOU THINK I AM? AWESOME, AS USUAL.
STUBBORN IS MORE LIKE IT. NOW SIT STILL SO WE CAN FINISH FIXIN' YA UP!
SHE'S EXHAUSTED, AND SHE TOOK A BAD TUMBLE WHEN SHE LANDED, BUT OTHER THAN THAT SHE'S FINE.
BUT IF ONE OF THESE SO-CALLED KNIGHTS OF HARMONY WAS STRONG ENOUGH TO BRING DOWN A WHOLE KINGDOM...
YES, I'M WORRIED TOO, BUT I'M GLAD TO HAVE ALL OF MY FRIENDS BACK BY MY SIDE.
IF WE HAVE TO FIGHT ELEMENTS OF HARMONY, IT WILL BE GOOD TO HAVE ALL OF OUR OWN ELEMENTS HERE.
PINKIE PIE REPORTING FOR DUTY! ALL CITIZENS OF CANTERLOT ARE SAFELY IN THE CASTLE.
AND ALL OF THE LOCAL WILDLIFE IS, TOO. MISTMANE, TRIXIE, AND STARLIGHT GLIMMER ARE ALL DOWN THERE IF ANYPONY NEEDS HELP.
AND I SENT OFF MESSAGES TO ALL OF OUR FRIENDS!

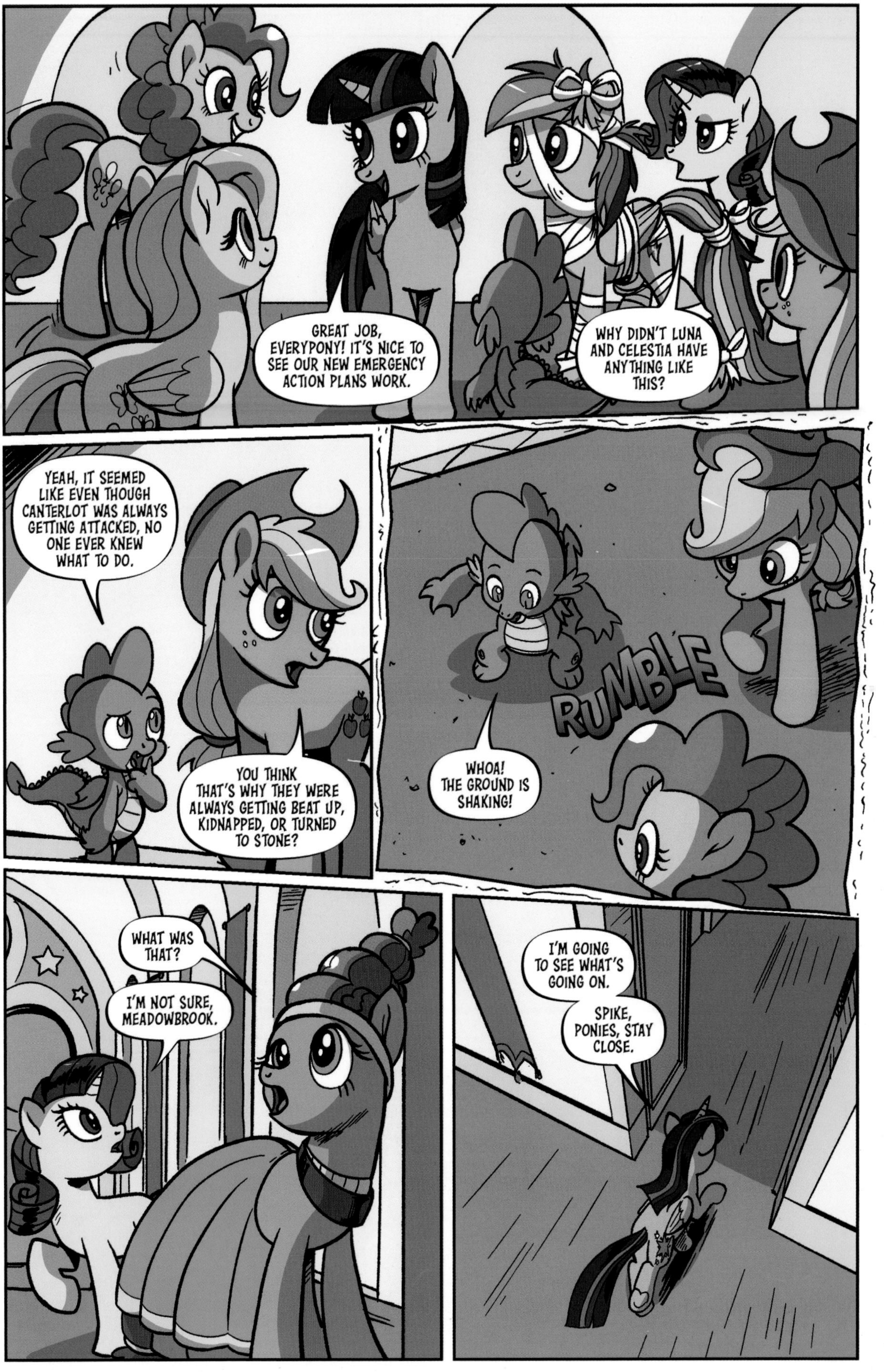
GREAT JOB, EVERYPONY! IT'S NICE TO SEE OUR NEW EMERGENCY ACTION PLANS WORK.
WHY DIDN'T LUNA AND CELESTIA HAVE ANYTHING LIKE THIS?
YEAH, IT SEEMED LIKE EVEN THOUGH CANTERLOT WAS ALWAYS GETTING ATTACKED, NO ONE EVER KNEW WHAT TO DO.
YOU THINK THAT'S WHY THEY WERE ALWAYS GETTING BEAT UP, KIDNAPPED, OR TURNED TO STONE?
RUMBLE
WHOA! THE GROUND IS SHAKING!
WHAT WAS THAT?
I'M NOT SURE, MEADOWBROOK.
I'M GOING TO SEE WHAT'S GOING ON.
SPIKE, PONIES, STAY CLOSE.

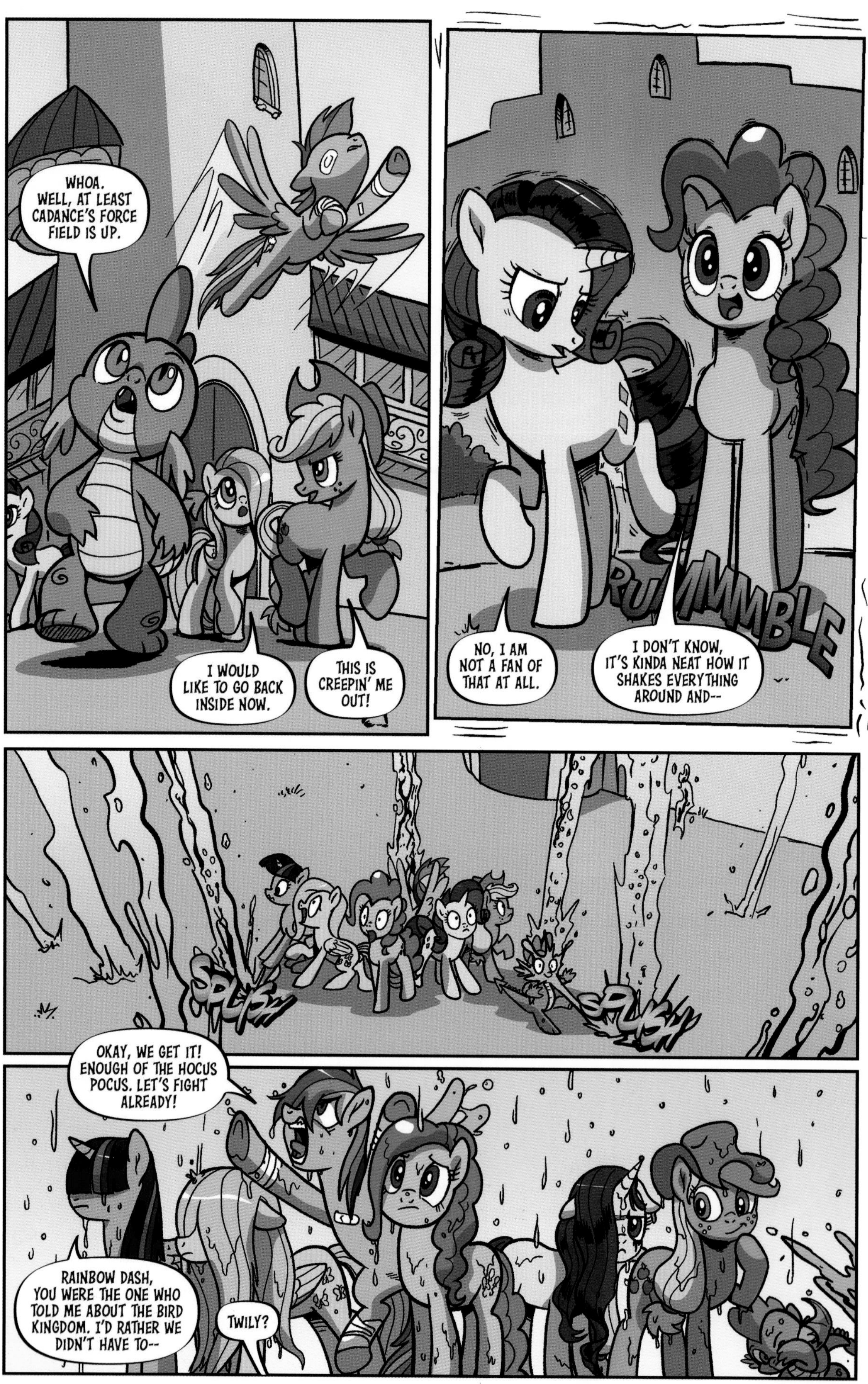
WHOA. WELL, AT LEAST CADANCE'S FORCE FIELD IS UP.
I WOULD LIKE TO GO BACK INSIDE NOW.
THIS IS CREEPIN' ME OUT!
RUMMMBLE
NO, I AM NOT A FAN OF THAT AT ALL.
I DON'T KNOW, IT'S KINDA NEAT HOW IT SHAKES EVERYTHING AROUND AND--
SPLISH
SPLISH
OKAY, WE GET IT! ENOUGH OF THE HOCUS POCUS. LET'S FIGHT ALREADY!
RAINBOW DASH, YOU WERE THE ONE WHO TOLD ME ABOUT THE BIRD KINGDOM. I'D RATHER WE DIDN'T HAVE TO--
TWILY?

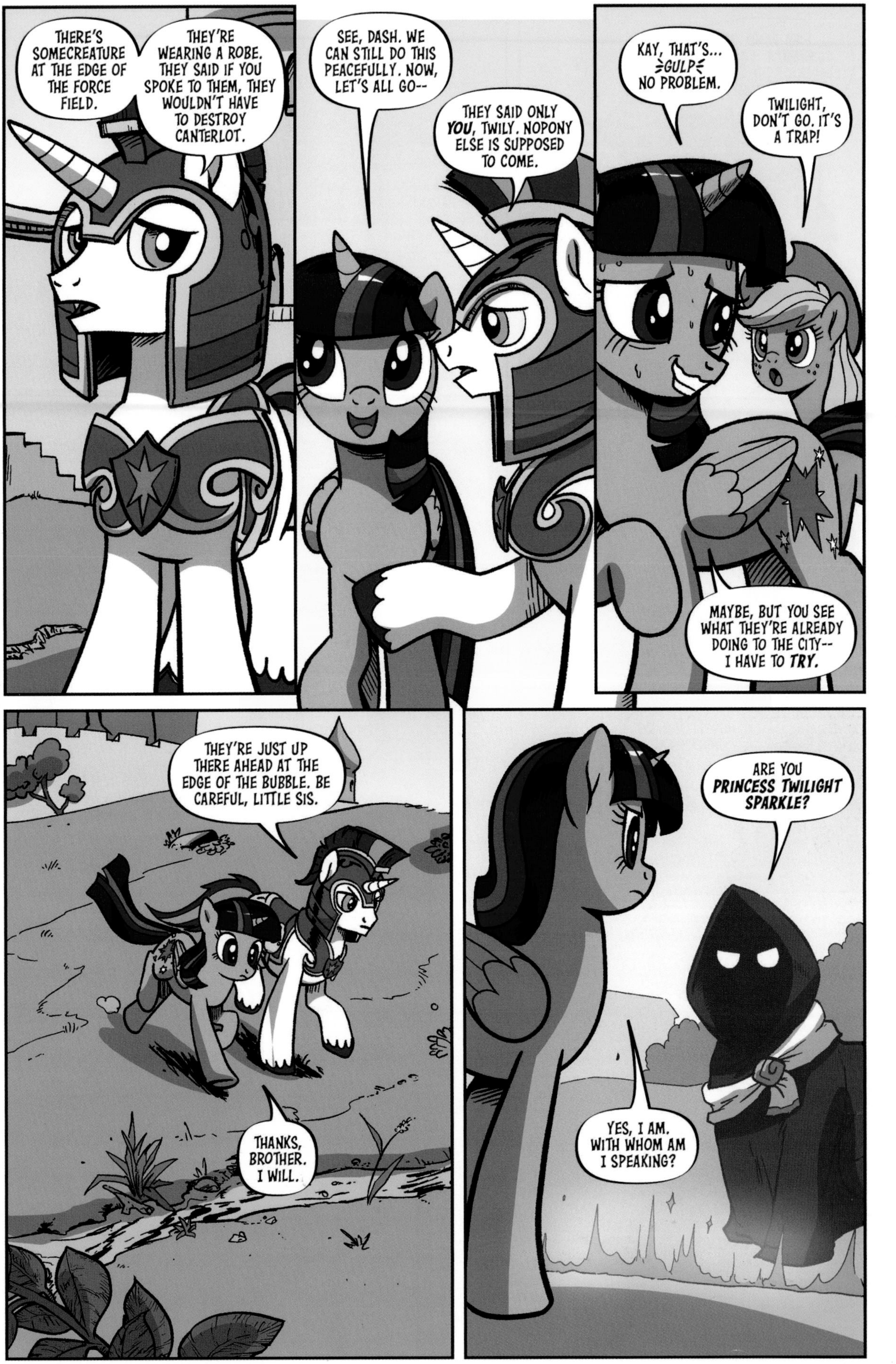
THERE'S SOMECREATURE AT THE EDGE OF THE FORCE FIELD.
THEY'RE WEARING A ROBE. THEY SAID IF YOU SPOKE TO THEM, THEY WOULDN'T HAVE TO DESTROY CANTERLOT.
SEE, DASH. WE CAN STILL DO THIS PEACEFULLY. NOW, LET'S ALL GO--
THEY SAID ONLY YOU, TWILY. NOPONY ELSE IS SUPPOSED TO COME.
KAY, THAT'S... GULP NO PROBLEM.
TWILIGHT, DON'T GO. IT'S A TRAP!
MAYBE, BUT YOU SEE WHAT THEY'RE ALREADY DOING TO THE CITY-- I HAVE TO TRY.
THEY'RE JUST UP THERE AHEAD AT THE EDGE OF THE BUBBLE. BE CAREFUL, LITTLE SIS.
THANKS, BROTHER. I WILL.
ARE YOU PRINCESS TWILIGHT SPARKLE?
YES, I AM. WITH WHOM AM I SPEAKING?

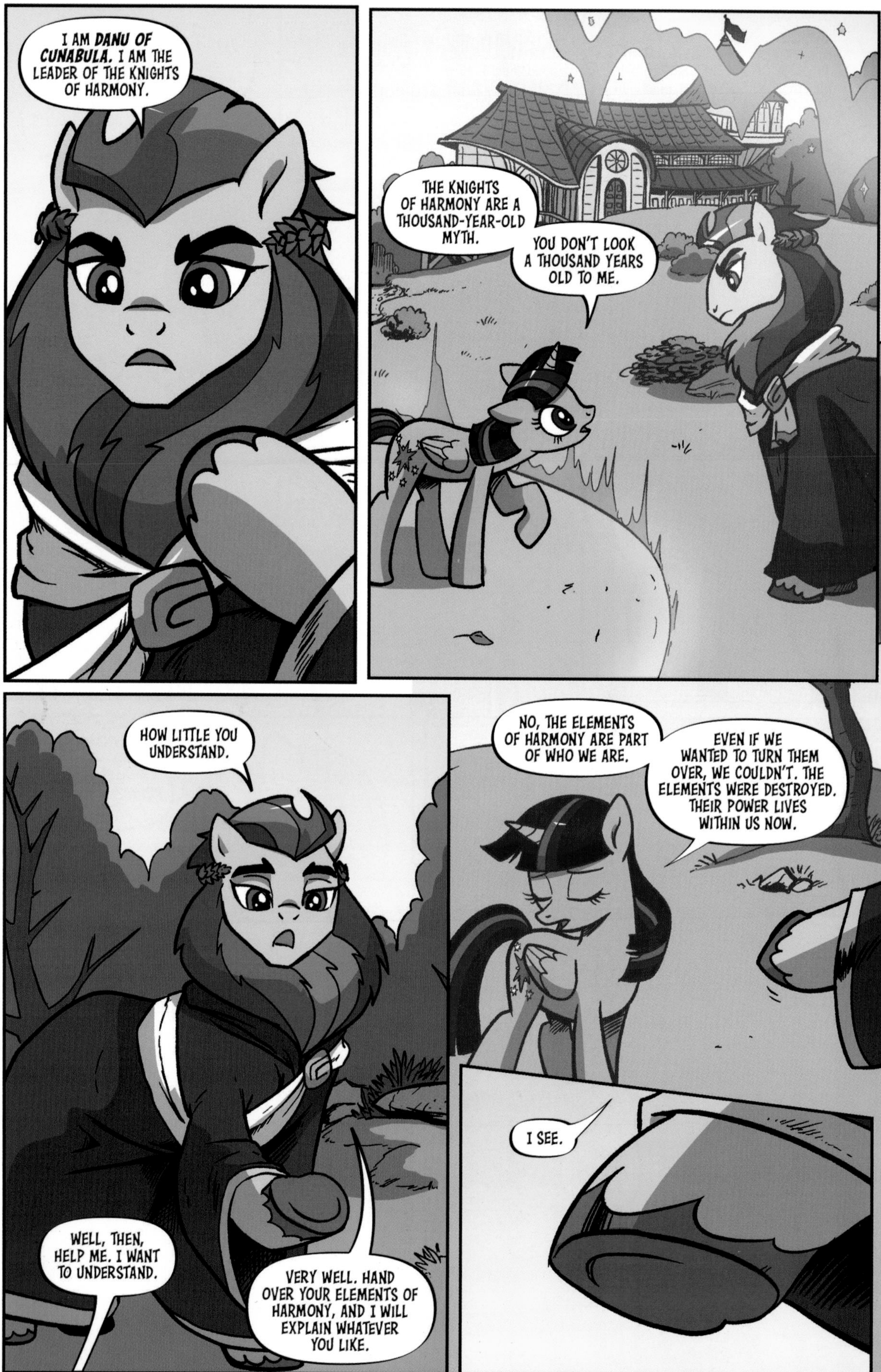
I AM ***DANU OF CUNABULA.*** I AM THE LEADER OF THE KNIGHTS OF HARMONY.
THE KNIGHTS OF HARMONY ARE A THOUSAND-YEAR-OLD MYTH.
YOU DON'T LOOK A THOUSAND YEARS OLD TO ME.
HOW LITTLE YOU UNDERSTAND.
WELL, THEN, HELP ME. I WANT TO UNDERSTAND.
VERY WELL. HAND OVER YOUR ELEMENTS OF HARMONY, AND I WILL EXPLAIN WHATEVER YOU LIKE.
NO, THE ELEMENTS OF HARMONY ARE PART OF WHO WE ARE.
EVEN IF WE WANTED TO TURN THEM OVER, WE COULDN'T. THE ELEMENTS WERE DESTROYED. THEIR POWER LIVES WITHIN US NOW.
I SEE.

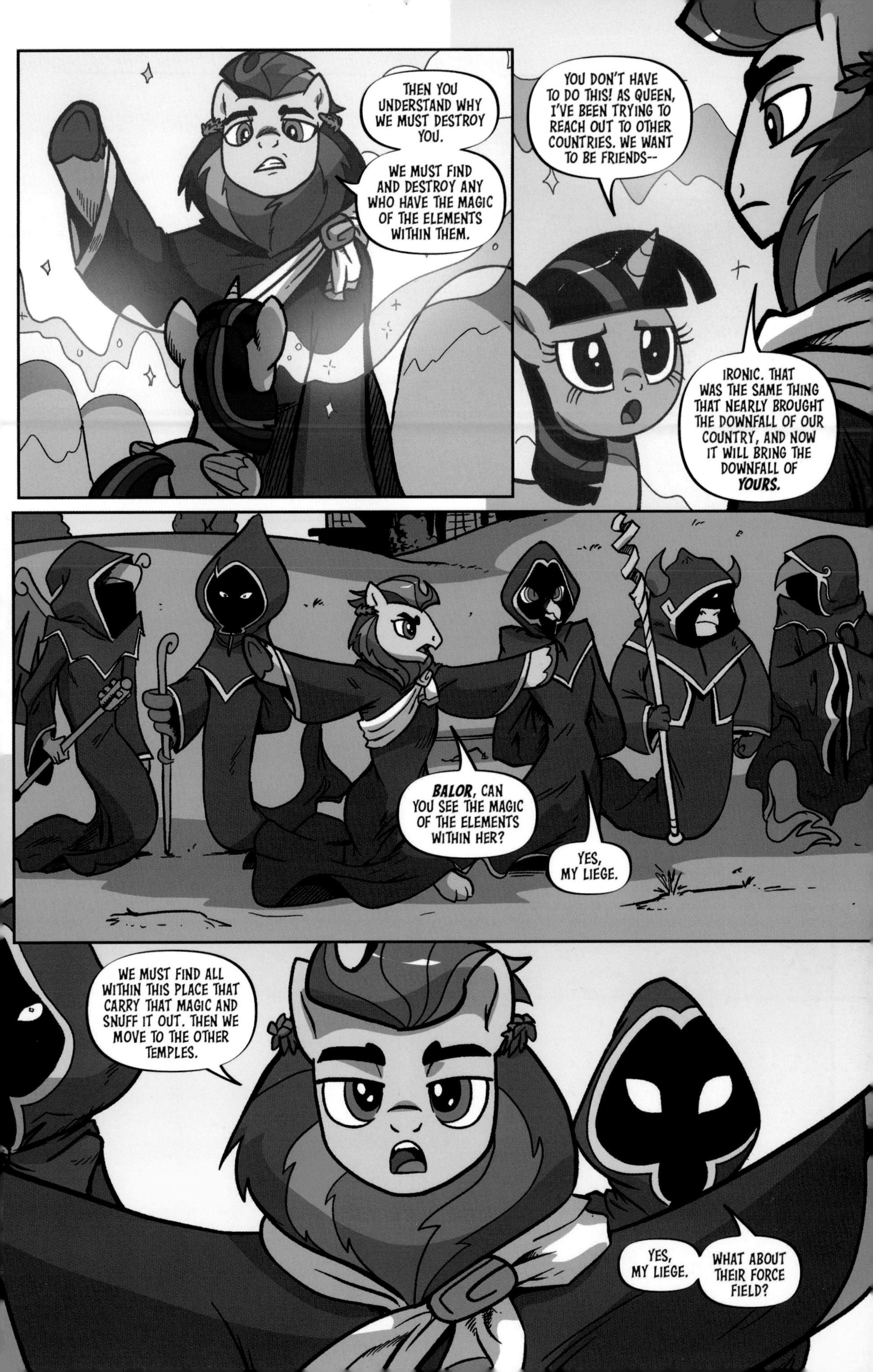
THEN YOU UNDERSTAND WHY WE MUST DESTROY YOU.
WE MUST FIND AND DESTROY ANY WHO HAVE THE MAGIC OF THE ELEMENTS WITHIN THEM.
YOU DON'T HAVE TO DO THIS! AS QUEEN, I'VE BEEN TRYING TO REACH OUT TO OTHER COUNTRIES. WE WANT TO BE FRIENDS--
IRONIC. THAT WAS THE SAME THING THAT NEARLY BROUGHT THE DOWNFALL OF OUR COUNTRY, AND NOW IT WILL BRING THE DOWNFALL OF YOURS.
BALOR, CAN YOU SEE THE MAGIC OF THE ELEMENTS WITHIN HER?
YES, MY LIEGE.
WE MUST FIND ALL WITHIN THIS PLACE THAT CARRY THAT MAGIC AND SNUFF IT OUT. THEN WE MOVE TO THE OTHER TEMPLES.
YES, MY LIEGE.
WHAT ABOUT THEIR FORCE FIELD?

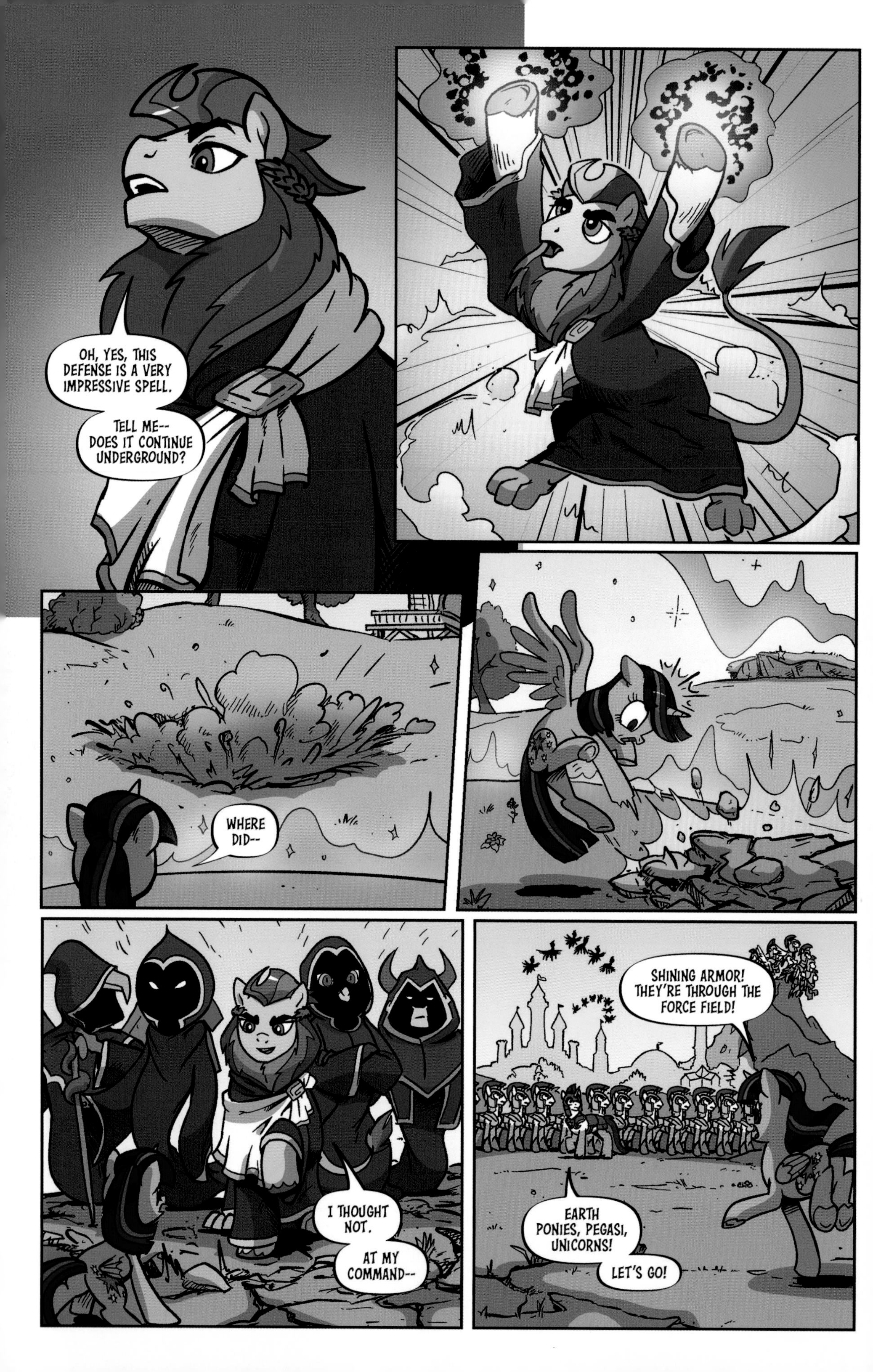
OH, YES, THIS DEFENSE IS A VERY IMPRESSIVE SPELL.
TELL ME-- DOES IT CONTINUE UNDERGROUND?
WHERE DID--
I THOUGHT NOT.
AT MY COMMAND--
SHINING ARMOR! THEY'RE THROUGH THE FORCE FIELD!
EARTH PONIES, PEGASI, UNICORNS!
LET'S GO!

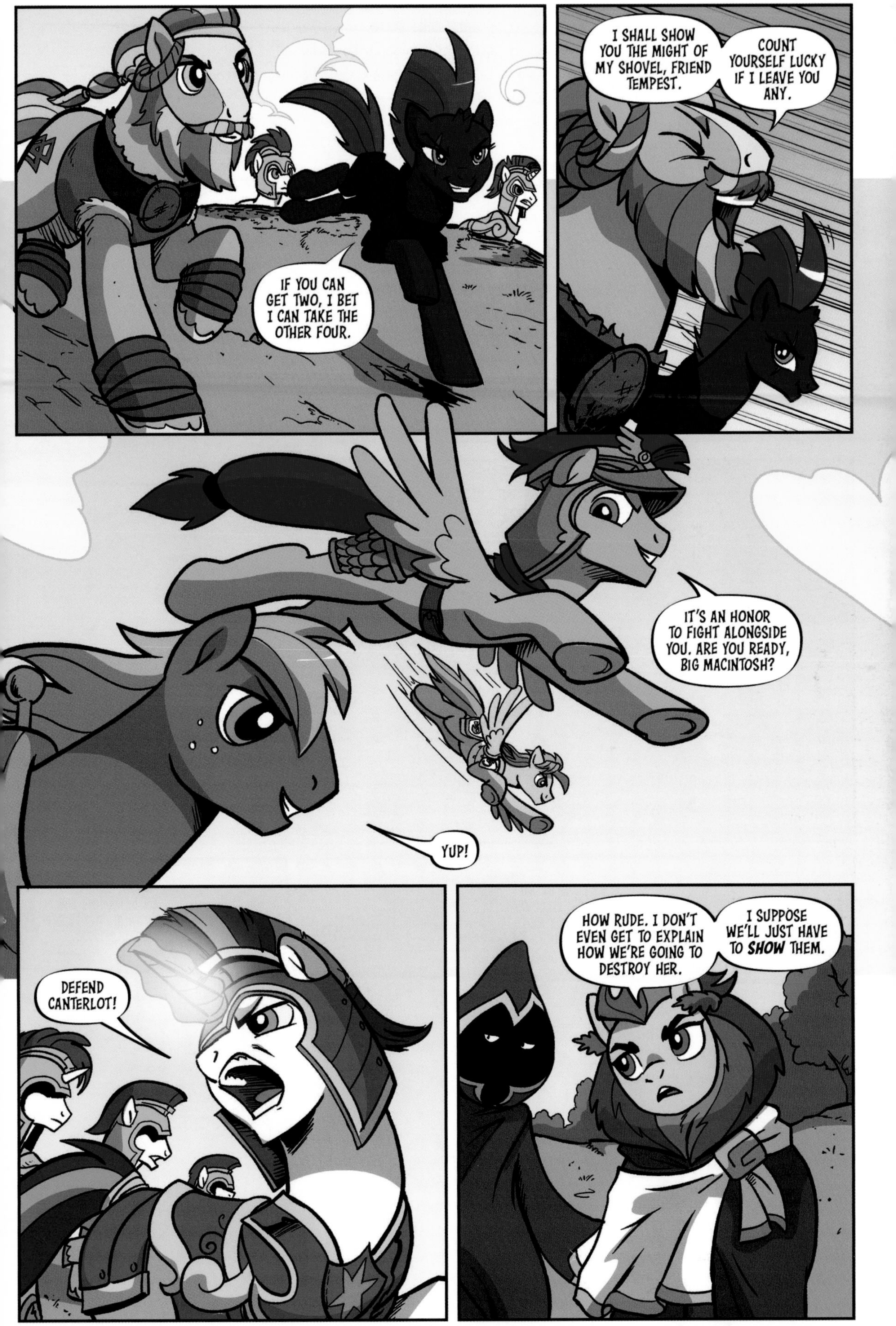
IF YOU CAN GET TWO, I BET I CAN TAKE THE OTHER FOUR.
I SHALL SHOW YOU THE MIGHT OF MY SHOVEL, FRIEND TEMPEST.
COUNT YOURSELF LUCKY IF I LEAVE YOU ANY.
IT'S AN HONOR TO FIGHT ALONGSIDE YOU. ARE YOU READY, BIG MACINTOSH?
YUP!
DEFEND CANTERLOT!
HOW RUDE. I DON'T EVEN GET TO EXPLAIN HOW WE'RE GOING TO DESTROY HER.
I SUPPOSE WE'LL JUST HAVE TO **SHOW** THEM.

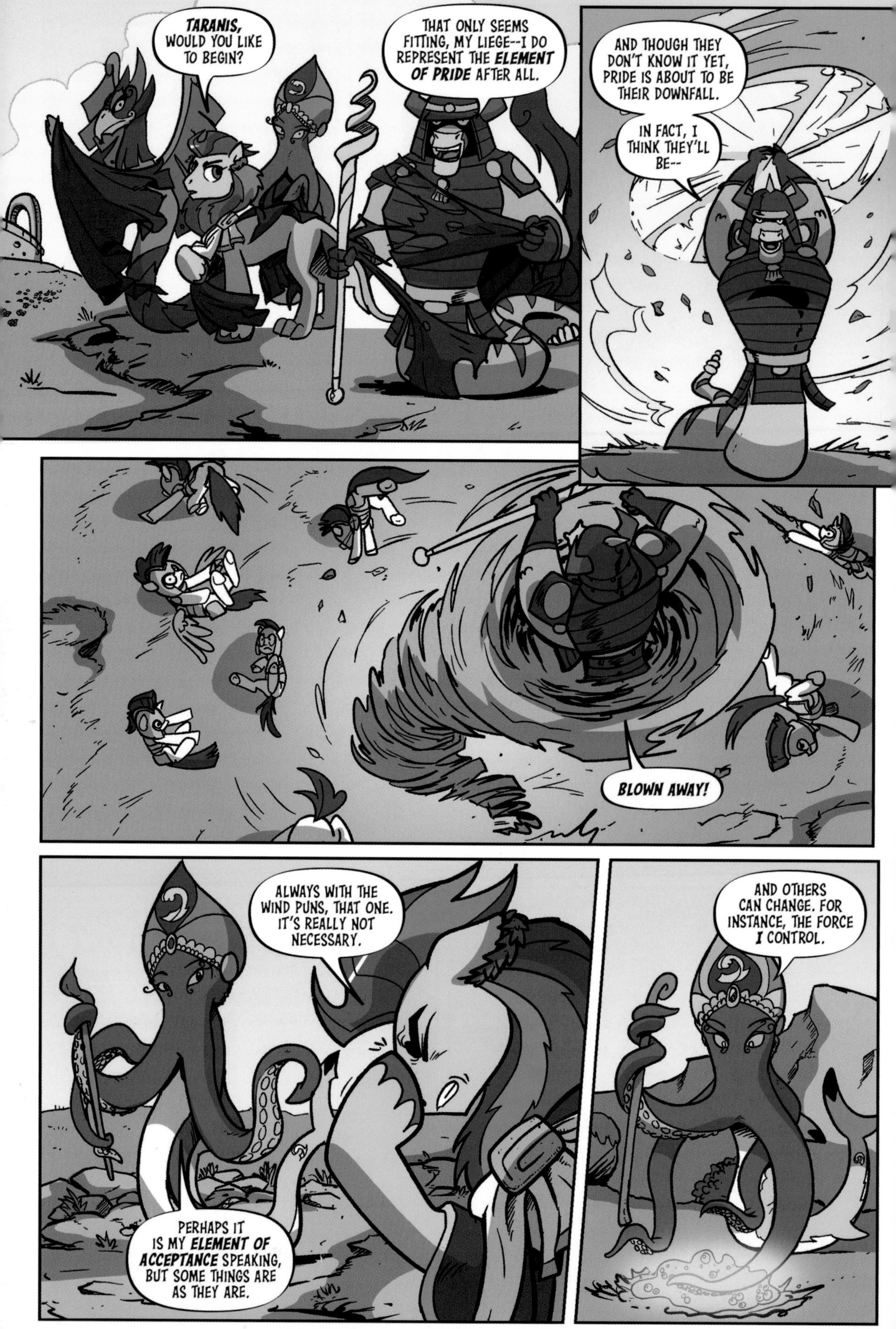
TARANIS, WOULD YOU LIKE TO BEGIN?
THAT ONLY SEEMS FITTING, MY LIEGE--I DO REPRESENT THE ELEMENT OF PRIDE AFTER ALL.
AND THOUGH THEY DON'T KNOW IT YET, PRIDE IS ABOUT TO BE THEIR DOWNFALL.
IN FACT, I THINK THEY'LL BE--
BLOWN AWAY!
ALWAYS WITH THE WIND PUNS, THAT ONE. IT'S REALLY NOT NECESSARY.
PERHAPS IT IS MY ELEMENT OF ACCEPTANCE SPEAKING, BUT SOME THINGS ARE AS THEY ARE.
AND OTHERS CAN CHANGE. FOR INSTANCE, THE FORCE I CONTROL.

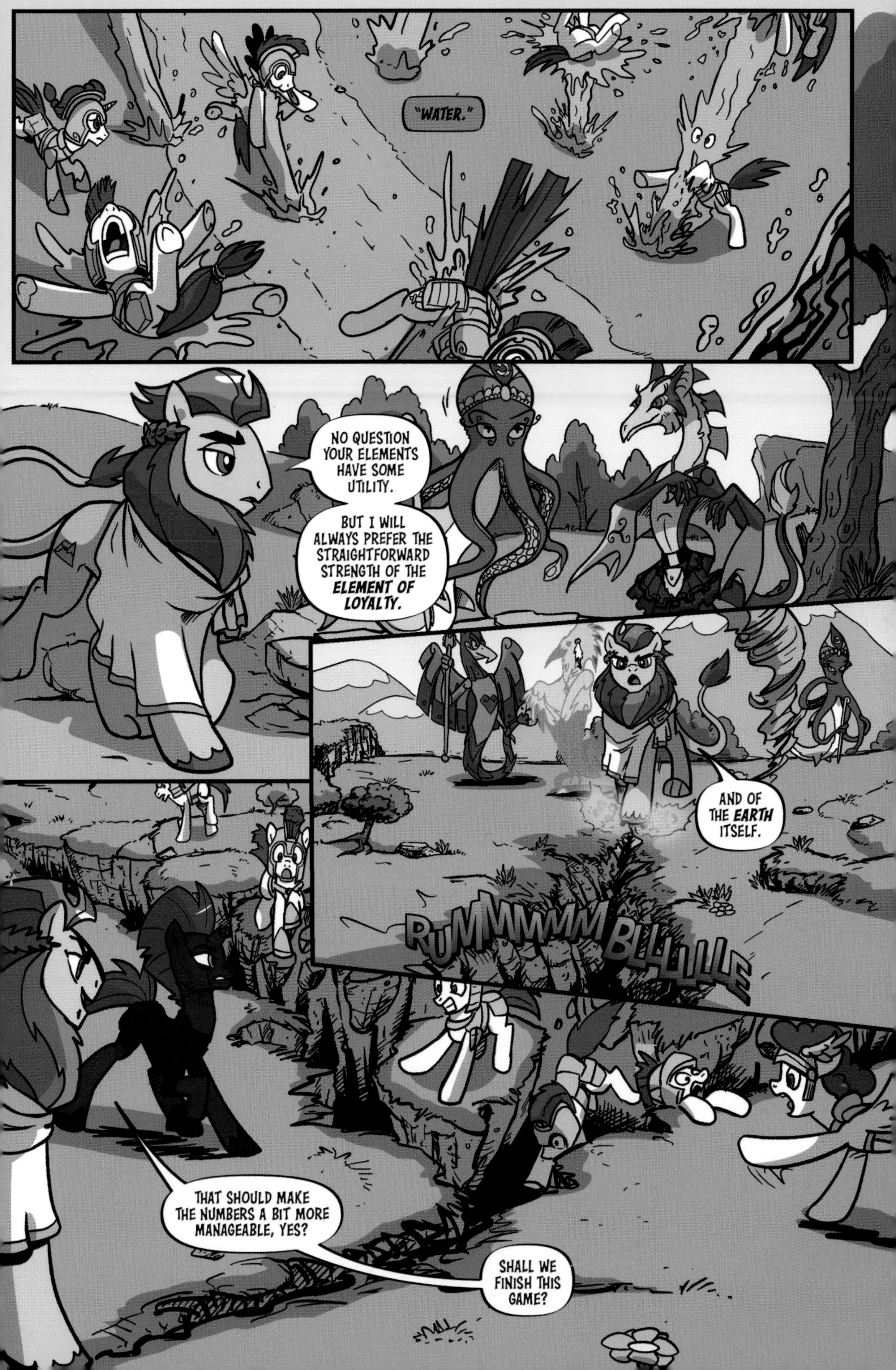
"WATER."
NO QUESTION YOUR ELEMENTS HAVE SOME UTILITY.
BUT I WILL ALWAYS PREFER THE STRAIGHTFORWARD STRENGTH OF THE ***ELEMENT OF LOYALTY.***
AND OF THE ***EARTH*** ITSELF.
RUMMMMM BLLLLLE
THAT SHOULD MAKE THE NUMBERS A BIT MORE MANAGEABLE, YES?
SHALL WE FINISH THIS GAME?

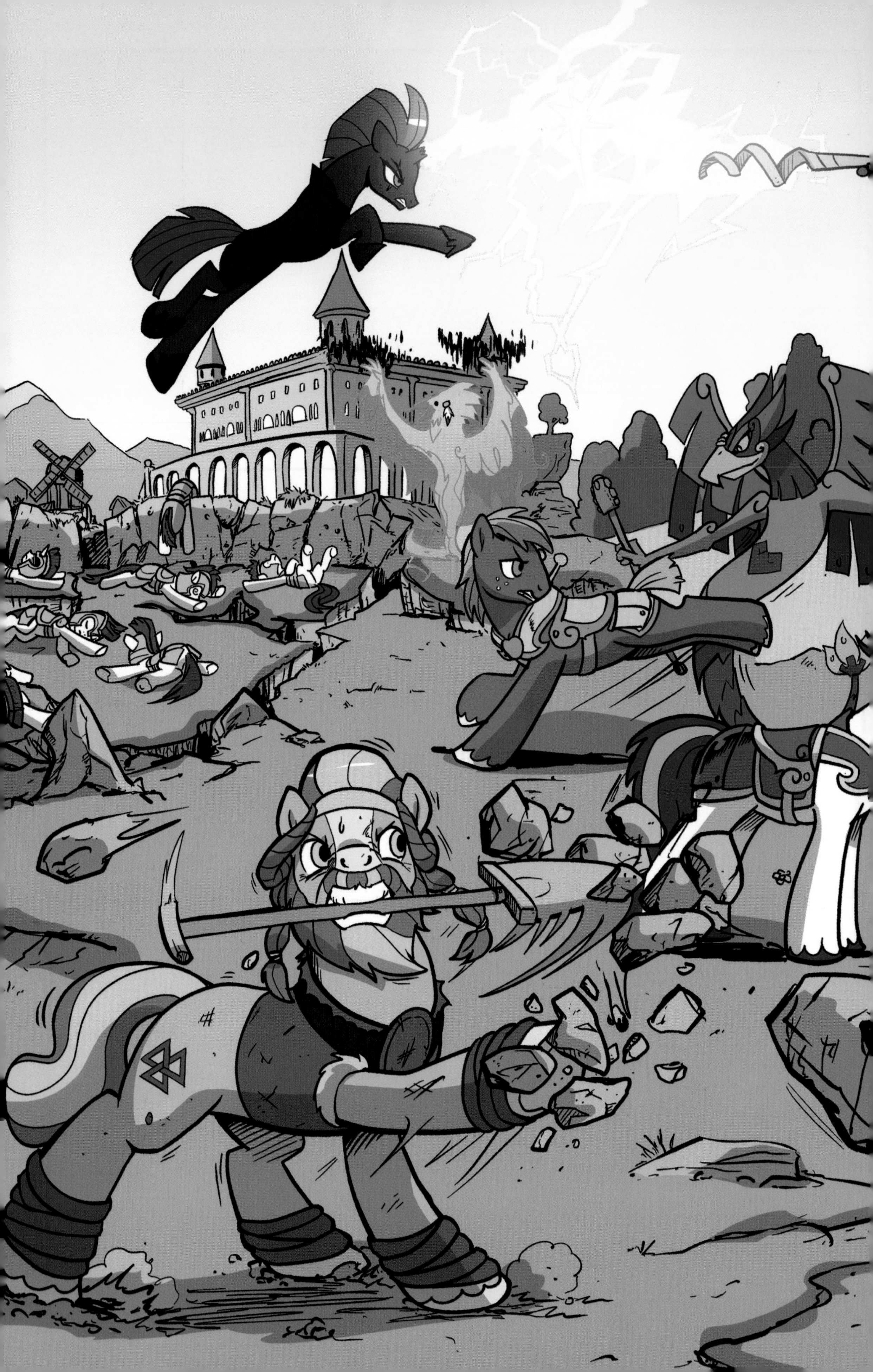

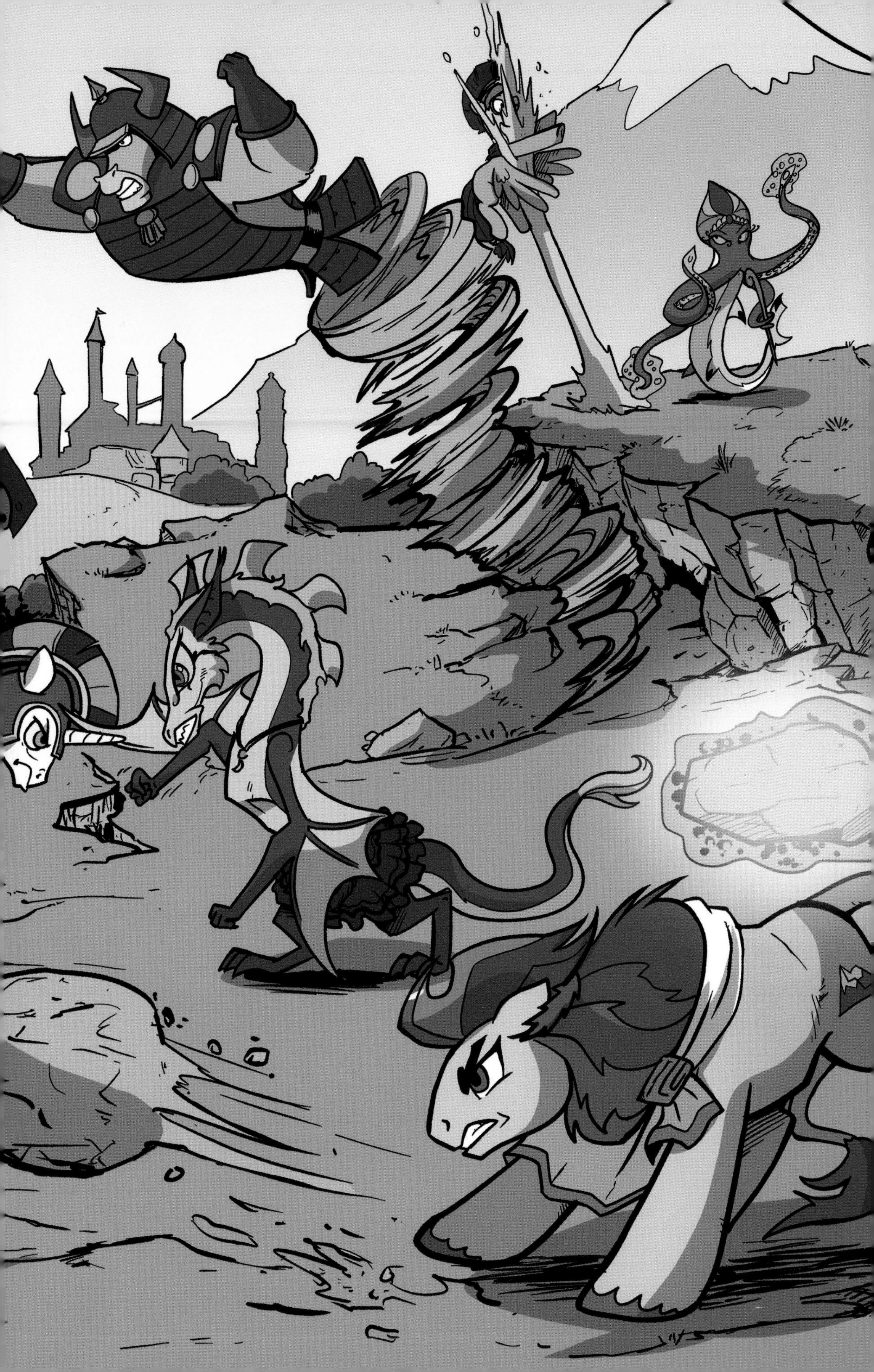

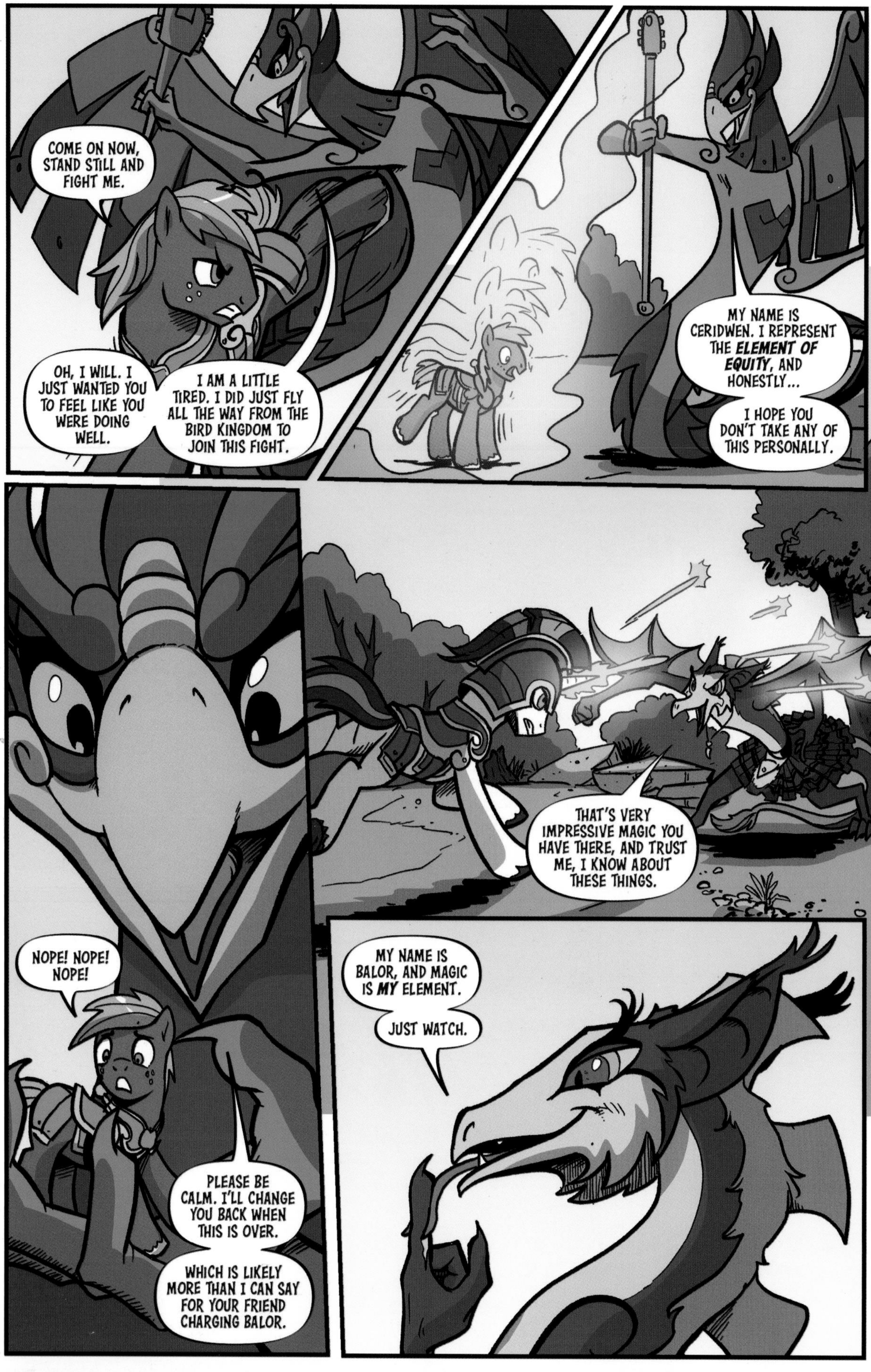
COME ON NOW, STAND STILL AND FIGHT ME.
OH, I WILL. I JUST WANTED YOU TO FEEL LIKE YOU WERE DOING WELL.
I AM A LITTLE TIRED. I DID JUST FLY ALL THE WAY FROM THE BIRD KINGDOM TO JOIN THIS FIGHT.
MY NAME IS CERIDWEN. I REPRESENT THE ***ELEMENT OF EQUITY***, AND HONESTLY...
I HOPE YOU DON'T TAKE ANY OF THIS PERSONALLY.
THAT'S VERY IMPRESSIVE MAGIC YOU HAVE THERE, AND TRUST ME, I KNOW ABOUT THESE THINGS.
NOPE! NOPE! NOPE!
PLEASE BE CALM. I'LL CHANGE YOU BACK WHEN THIS IS OVER.
WHICH IS LIKELY MORE THAN I CAN SAY FOR YOUR FRIEND CHARGING BALOR.
MY NAME IS BALOR, AND MAGIC IS ***MY*** ELEMENT.
JUST WATCH.

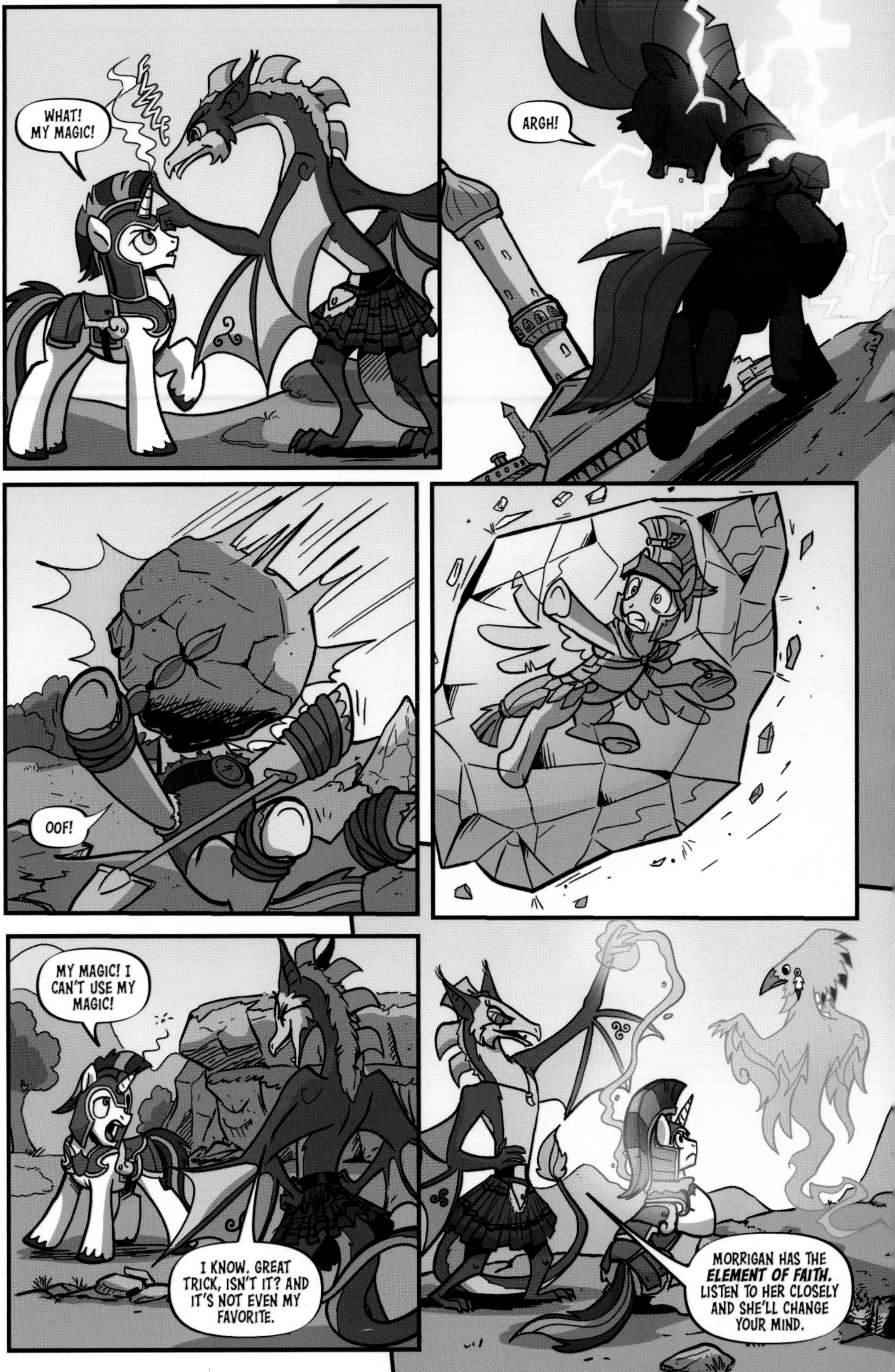
WHAT! MY MAGIC!
FIZZLE
ARGH!
OOF!
MY MAGIC! I CAN'T USE MY MAGIC!
I KNOW. GREAT TRICK, ISN'T IT? AND IT'S NOT EVEN MY FAVORITE.
MORRIGAN HAS THE ELEMENT OF FAITH. LISTEN TO HER CLOSELY AND SHE'LL CHANGE YOUR MIND.

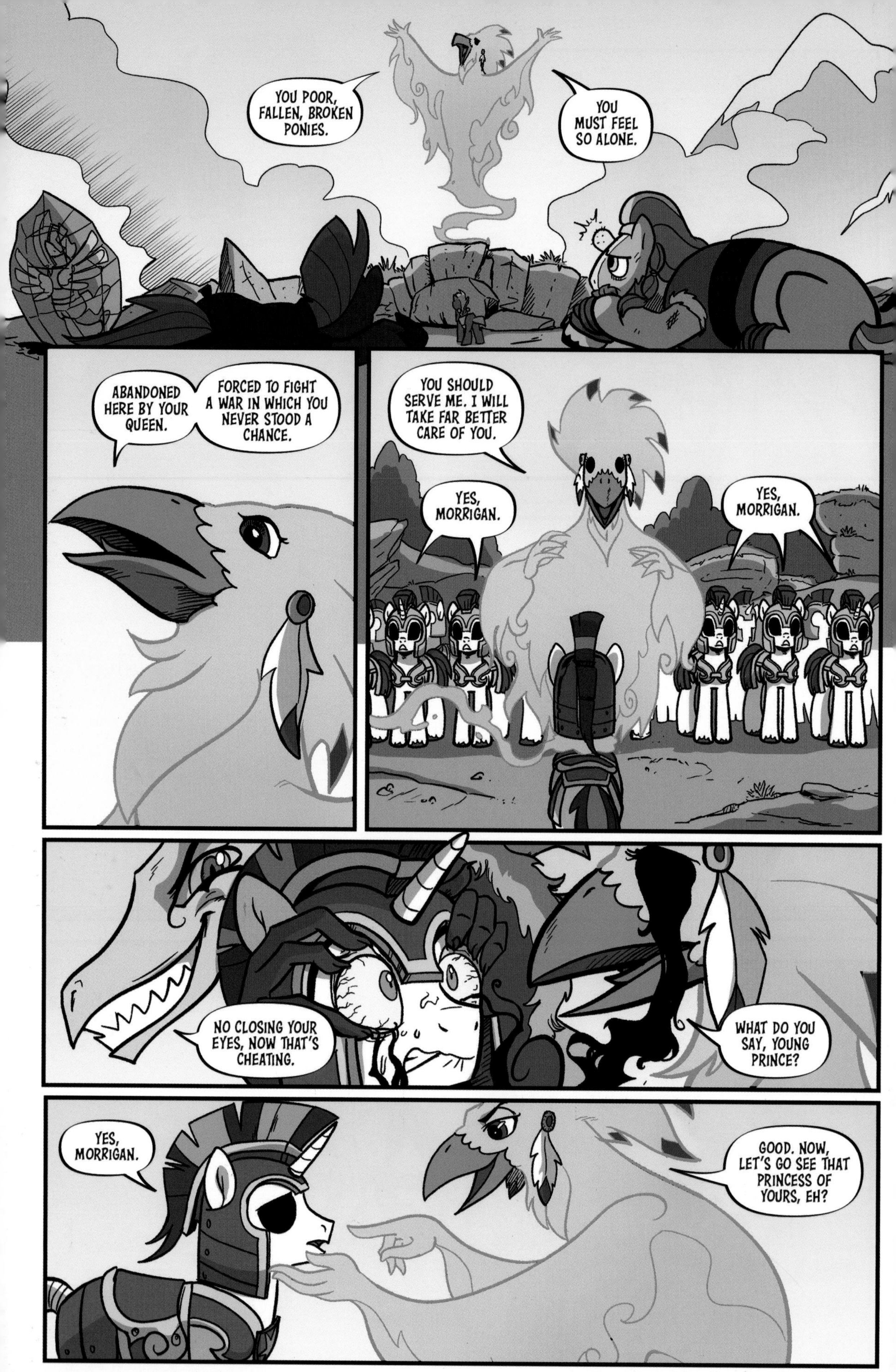
YOU POOR, FALLEN, BROKEN PONIES.
YOU MUST FEEL SO ALONE.
ABANDONED HERE BY YOUR QUEEN.
FORCED TO FIGHT A WAR IN WHICH YOU NEVER STOOD A CHANCE.
YOU SHOULD SERVE ME. I WILL TAKE FAR BETTER CARE OF YOU.
YES, MORRIGAN.
YES, MORRIGAN.
NO CLOSING YOUR EYES, NOW THAT'S CHEATING.
WHAT DO YOU SAY, YOUNG PRINCE?
YES, MORRIGAN.
GOOD. NOW, LET'S GO SEE THAT PRINCESS OF YOURS, EH?

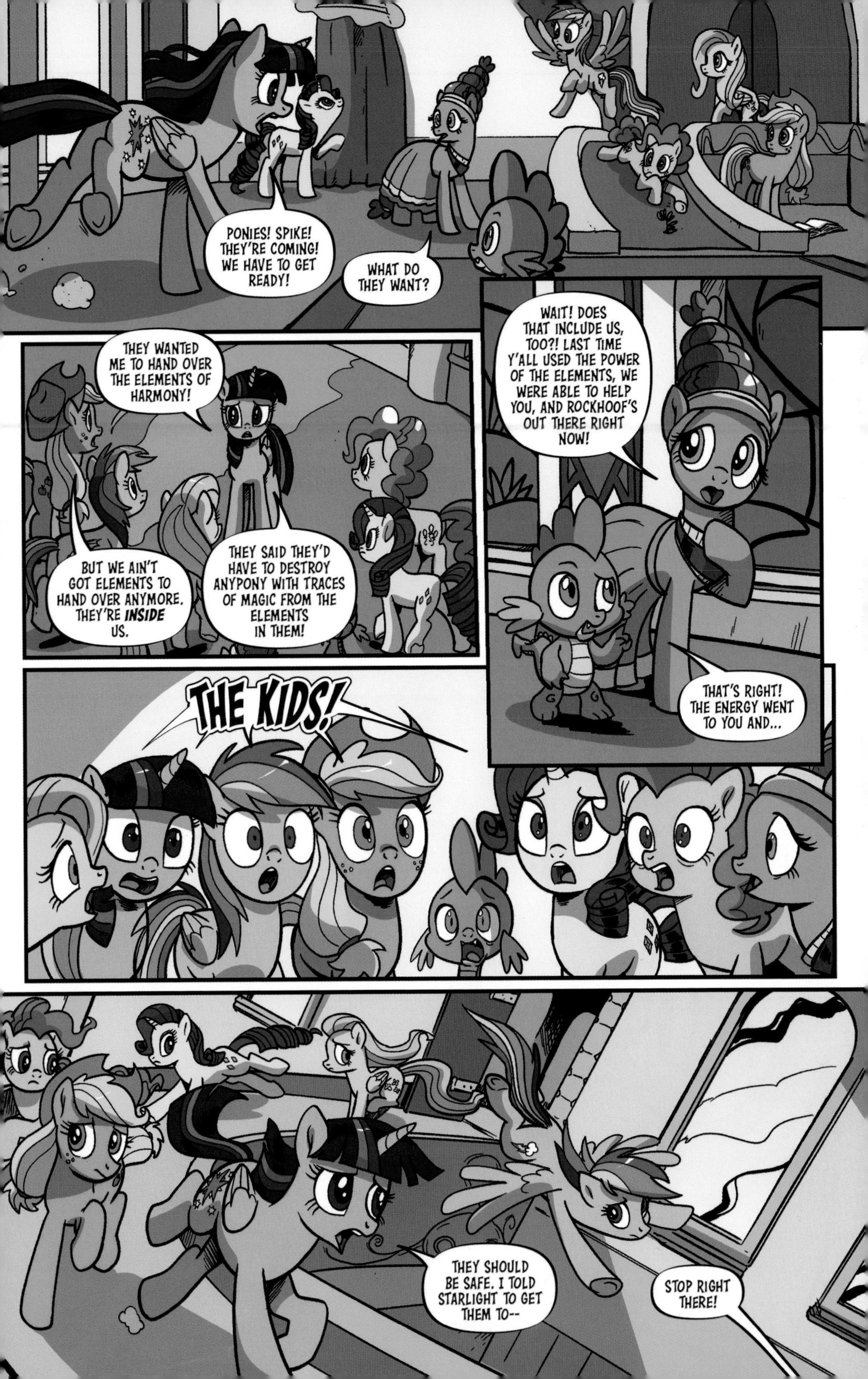
PONIES! SPIKE! THEY'RE COMING! WE HAVE TO GET READY!
WHAT DO THEY WANT?
THEY WANTED ME TO HAND OVER THE ELEMENTS OF HARMONY!
BUT WE AIN'T GOT ELEMENTS TO HAND OVER ANYMORE. THEY'RE *INSIDE* US.
THEY SAID THEY'D HAVE TO DESTROY ANYPONY WITH TRACES OF MAGIC FROM THE ELEMENTS IN THEM!
WAIT! DOES THAT INCLUDE US, TOO?! LAST TIME Y'ALL USED THE POWER OF THE ELEMENTS, WE WERE ABLE TO HELP YOU, AND ROCKHOOF'S OUT THERE RIGHT NOW!
THAT'S RIGHT! THE ENERGY WENT TO YOU AND...
THE KIDS!
THEY SHOULD BE SAFE. I TOLD STARLIGHT TO GET THEM TO--
STOP RIGHT THERE!

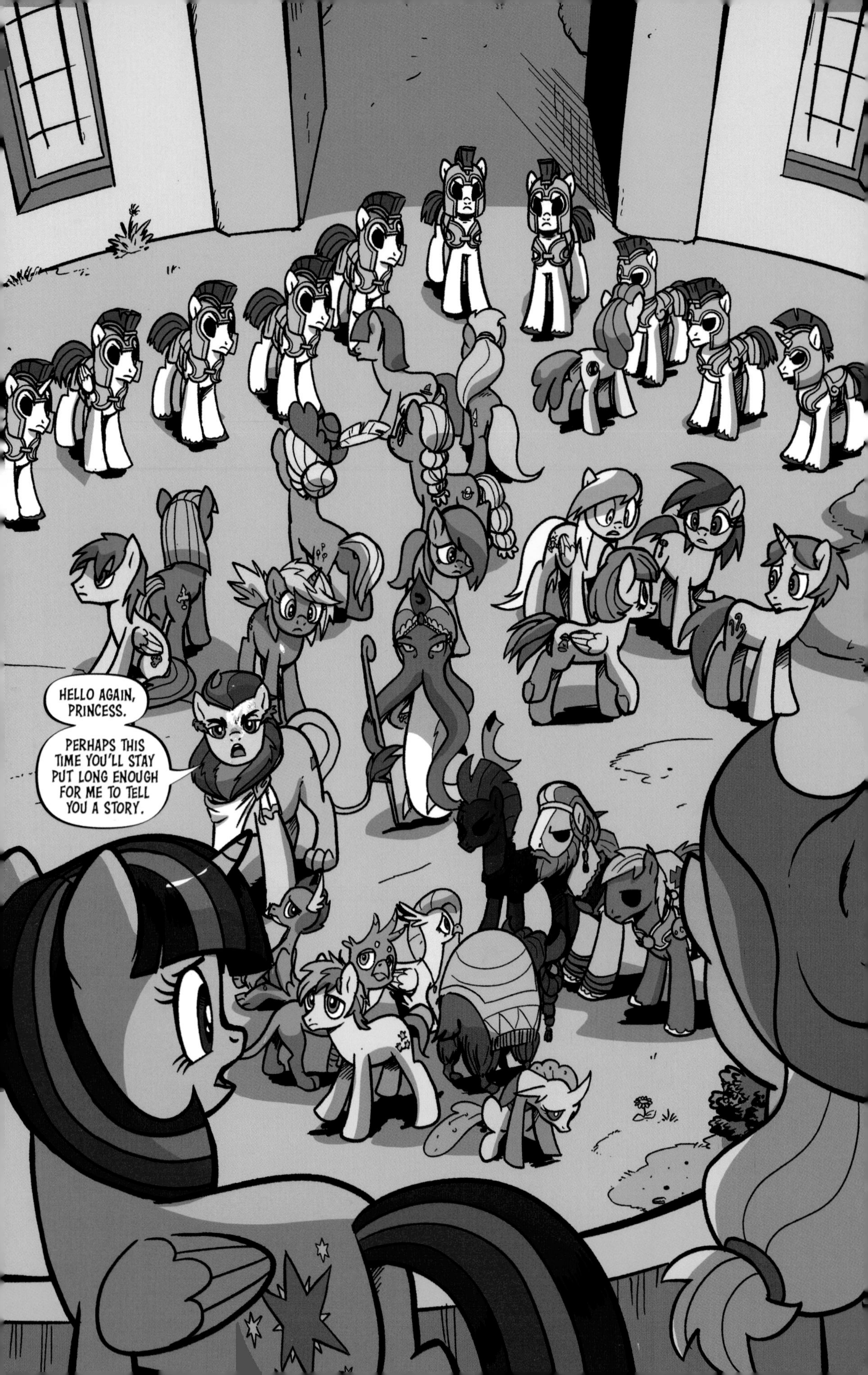
HELLO AGAIN, PRINCESS.
PERHAPS THIS TIME YOU'LL STAY PUT LONG ENOUGH FOR ME TO TELL YOU A STORY.

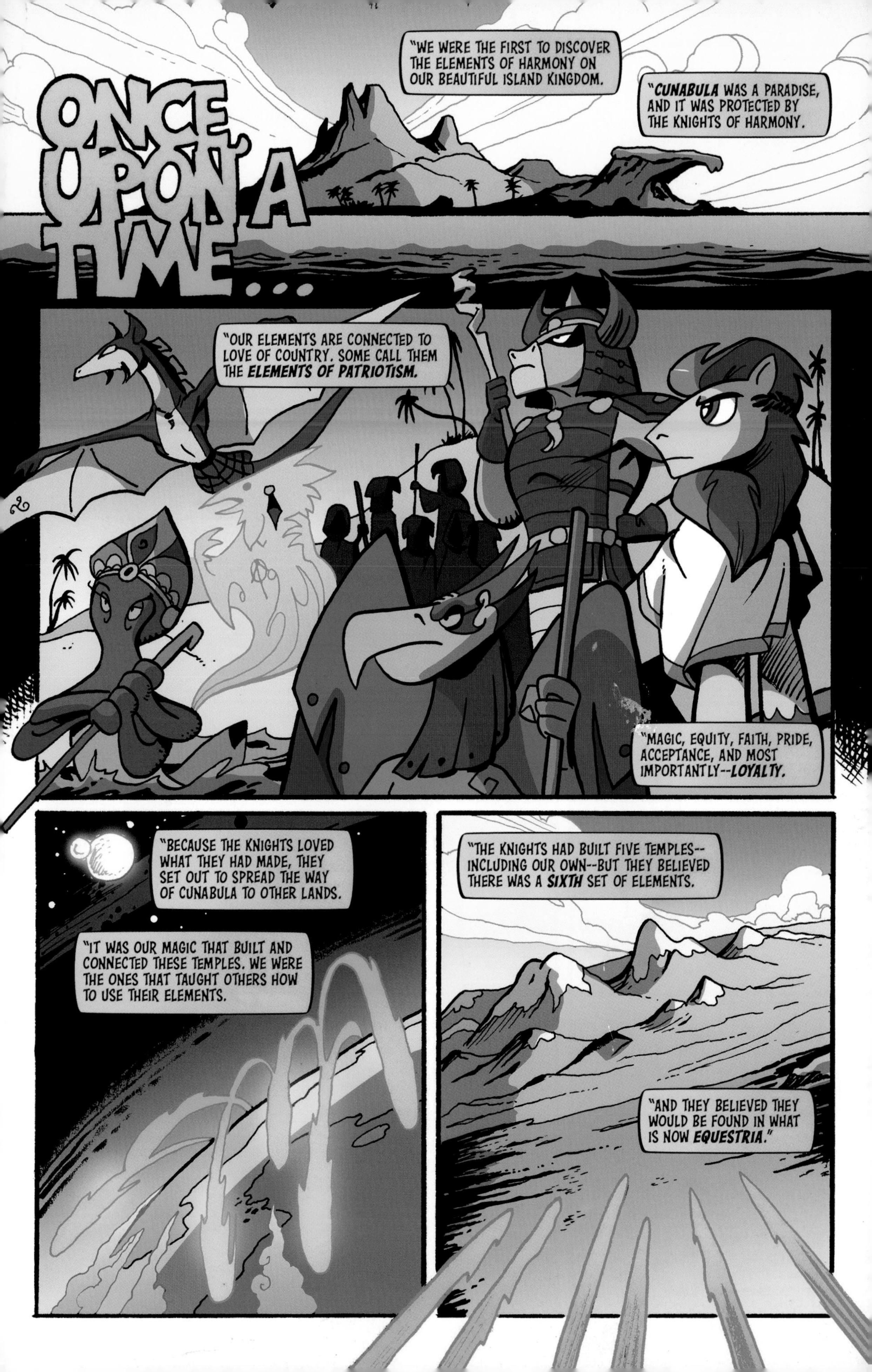
ONCE UPON A TIME...
"WE WERE THE FIRST TO DISCOVER THE ELEMENTS OF HARMONY ON OUR BEAUTIFUL ISLAND KINGDOM.
"CUNABULA WAS A PARADISE, AND IT WAS PROTECTED BY THE KNIGHTS OF HARMONY.
"OUR ELEMENTS ARE CONNECTED TO LOVE OF COUNTRY. SOME CALL THEM THE ELEMENTS OF PATRIOTISM.
"MAGIC, EQUITY, FAITH, PRIDE, ACCEPTANCE, AND MOST IMPORTANTLY--LOYALTY.
"BECAUSE THE KNIGHTS LOVED WHAT THEY HAD MADE, THEY SET OUT TO SPREAD THE WAY OF CUNABULA TO OTHER LANDS.
"IT WAS OUR MAGIC THAT BUILT AND CONNECTED THESE TEMPLES. WE WERE THE ONES THAT TAUGHT OTHERS HOW TO USE THEIR ELEMENTS.
"THE KNIGHTS HAD BUILT FIVE TEMPLES--INCLUDING OUR OWN--BUT THEY BELIEVED THERE WAS A SIXTH SET OF ELEMENTS.
"AND THEY BELIEVED THEY WOULD BE FOUND IN WHAT IS NOW EQUESTRIA."

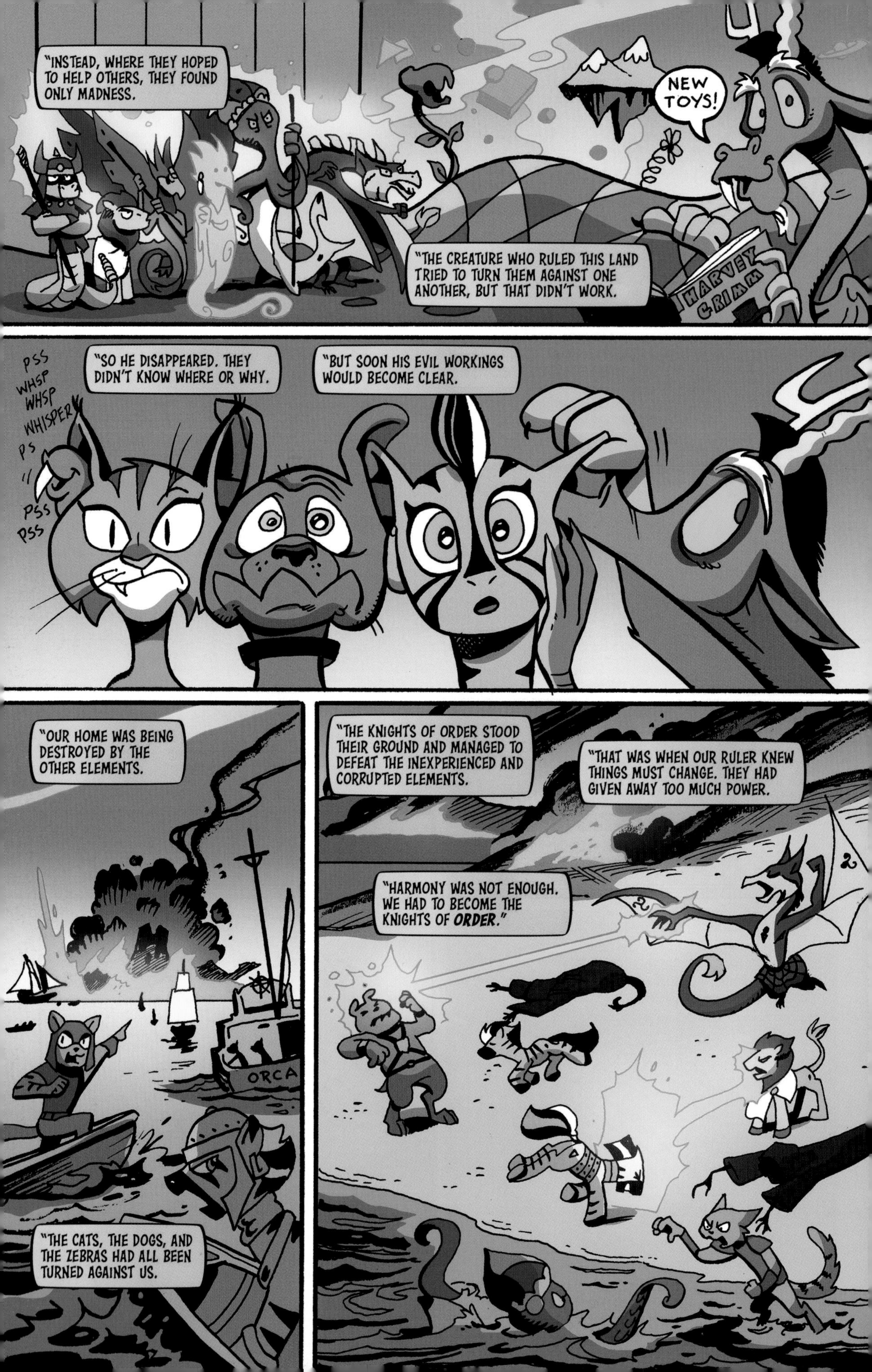
"INSTEAD, WHERE THEY HOPED TO HELP OTHERS, THEY FOUND ONLY MADNESS.
NEW TOYS!
"THE CREATURE WHO RULED THIS LAND TRIED TO TURN THEM AGAINST ONE ANOTHER, BUT THAT DIDN'T WORK.
HARVEY GRIMM
PSS WHSP WHSP WHISPER PS PSS PSS
"SO HE DISAPPEARED. THEY DIDN'T KNOW WHERE OR WHY.
"BUT SOON HIS EVIL WORKINGS WOULD BECOME CLEAR.
"OUR HOME WAS BEING DESTROYED BY THE OTHER ELEMENTS.
ORCA
"THE CATS, THE DOGS, AND THE ZEBRAS HAD ALL BEEN TURNED AGAINST US.
"THE KNIGHTS OF ORDER STOOD THEIR GROUND AND MANAGED TO DEFEAT THE INEXPERIENCED AND CORRUPTED ELEMENTS.
"THAT WAS WHEN OUR RULER KNEW THINGS MUST CHANGE. THEY HAD GIVEN AWAY TOO MUCH POWER.
"HARMONY WAS NOT ENOUGH. WE HAD TO BECOME THE KNIGHTS OF ORDER."

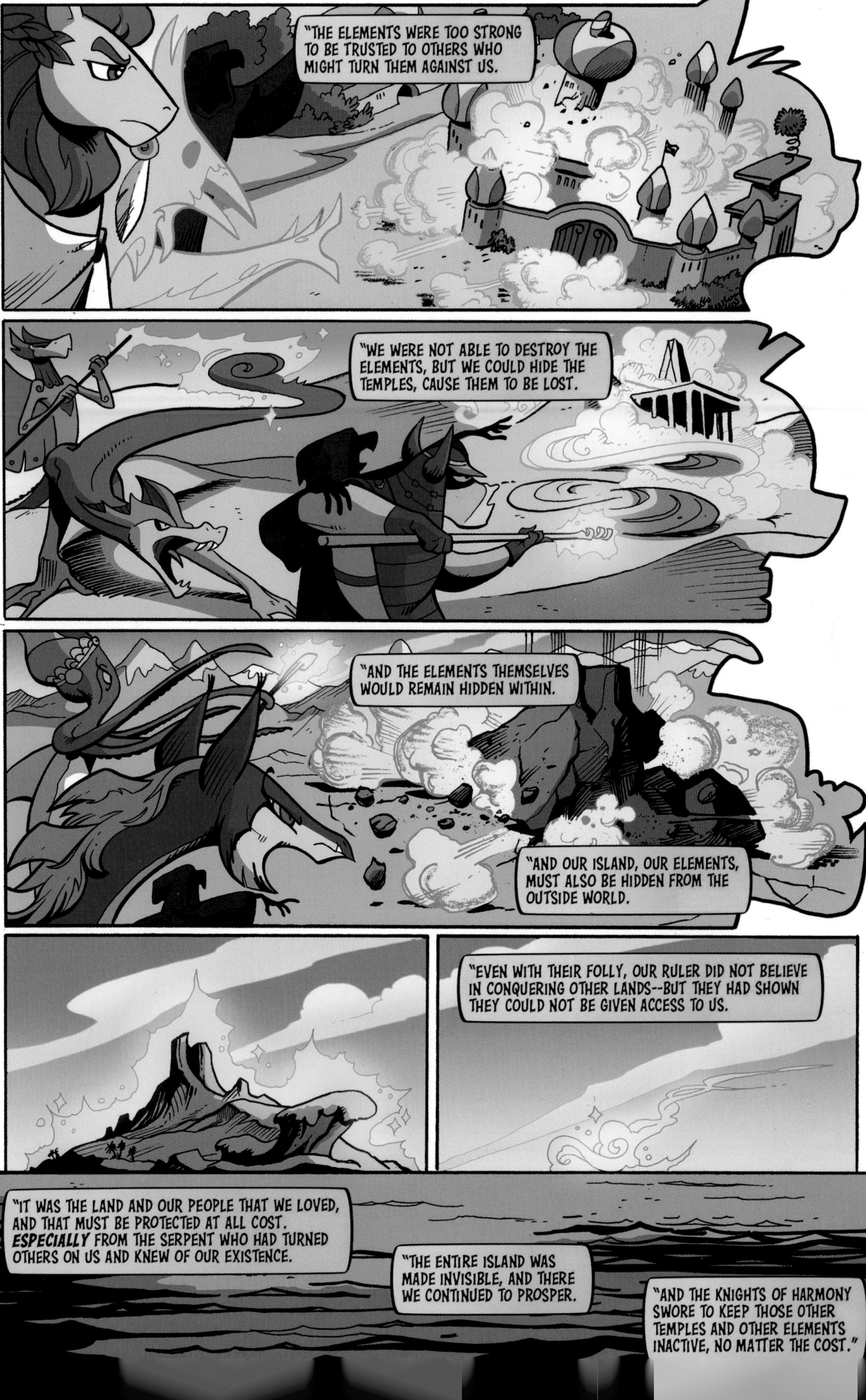
"THE ELEMENTS WERE TOO STRONG TO BE TRUSTED TO OTHERS WHO MIGHT TURN THEM AGAINST US.
"WE WERE NOT ABLE TO DESTROY THE ELEMENTS, BUT WE COULD HIDE THE TEMPLES, CAUSE THEM TO BE LOST.
"AND THE ELEMENTS THEMSELVES WOULD REMAIN HIDDEN WITHIN.
"AND OUR ISLAND, OUR ELEMENTS, MUST ALSO BE HIDDEN FROM THE OUTSIDE WORLD.
"EVEN WITH THEIR FOLLY, OUR RULER DID NOT BELIEVE IN CONQUERING OTHER LANDS--BUT THEY HAD SHOWN THEY COULD NOT BE GIVEN ACCESS TO US.
"IT WAS THE LAND AND OUR PEOPLE THAT WE LOVED, AND THAT MUST BE PROTECTED AT ALL COST. ***ESPECIALLY*** FROM THE SERPENT WHO HAD TURNED OTHERS ON US AND KNEW OF OUR EXISTENCE.
"THE ENTIRE ISLAND WAS MADE INVISIBLE, AND THERE WE CONTINUED TO PROSPER.
"AND THE KNIGHTS OF HARMONY SWORE TO KEEP THOSE OTHER TEMPLES AND OTHER ELEMENTS INACTIVE, NO MATTER THE COST."

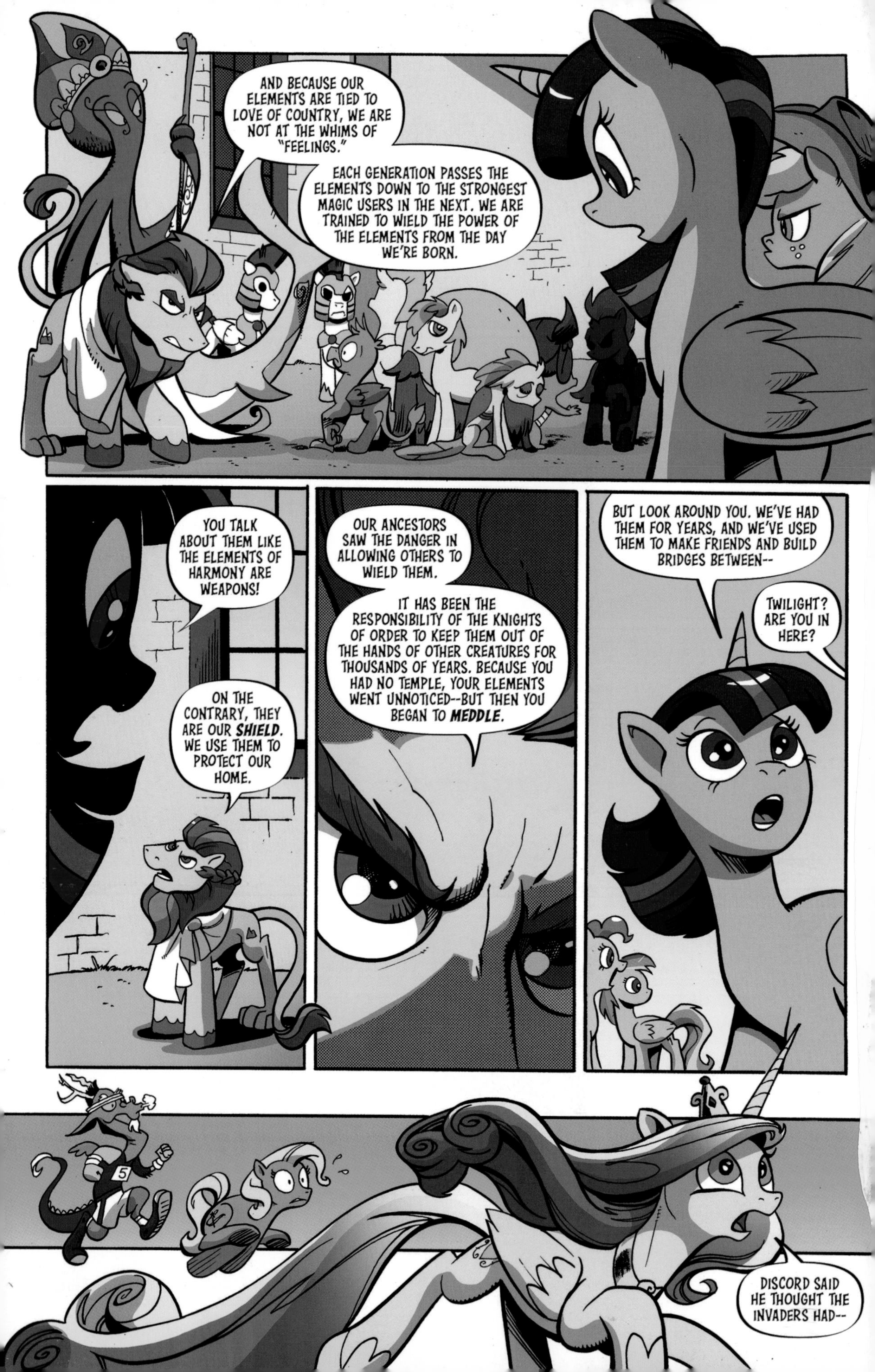
AND BECAUSE OUR ELEMENTS ARE TIED TO LOVE OF COUNTRY, WE ARE NOT AT THE WHIMS OF "FEELINGS."
EACH GENERATION PASSES THE ELEMENTS DOWN TO THE STRONGEST MAGIC USERS IN THE NEXT. WE ARE TRAINED TO WIELD THE POWER OF THE ELEMENTS FROM THE DAY WE'RE BORN.
YOU TALK ABOUT THEM LIKE THE ELEMENTS OF HARMONY ARE WEAPONS!
ON THE CONTRARY, THEY ARE OUR **SHIELD**. WE USE THEM TO PROTECT OUR HOME.
OUR ANCESTORS SAW THE DANGER IN ALLOWING OTHERS TO WIELD THEM.
IT HAS BEEN THE RESPONSIBILITY OF THE KNIGHTS OF ORDER TO KEEP THEM OUT OF THE HANDS OF OTHER CREATURES FOR THOUSANDS OF YEARS. BECAUSE YOU HAD NO TEMPLE, YOUR ELEMENTS WENT UNNOTICED--BUT THEN YOU BEGAN TO ***MEDDLE***.
BUT LOOK AROUND YOU. WE'VE HAD THEM FOR YEARS, AND WE'VE USED THEM TO MAKE FRIENDS AND BUILD BRIDGES BETWEEN--
TWILIGHT? ARE YOU IN HERE?
5
DISCORD SAID HE THOUGHT THE INVADERS HAD--

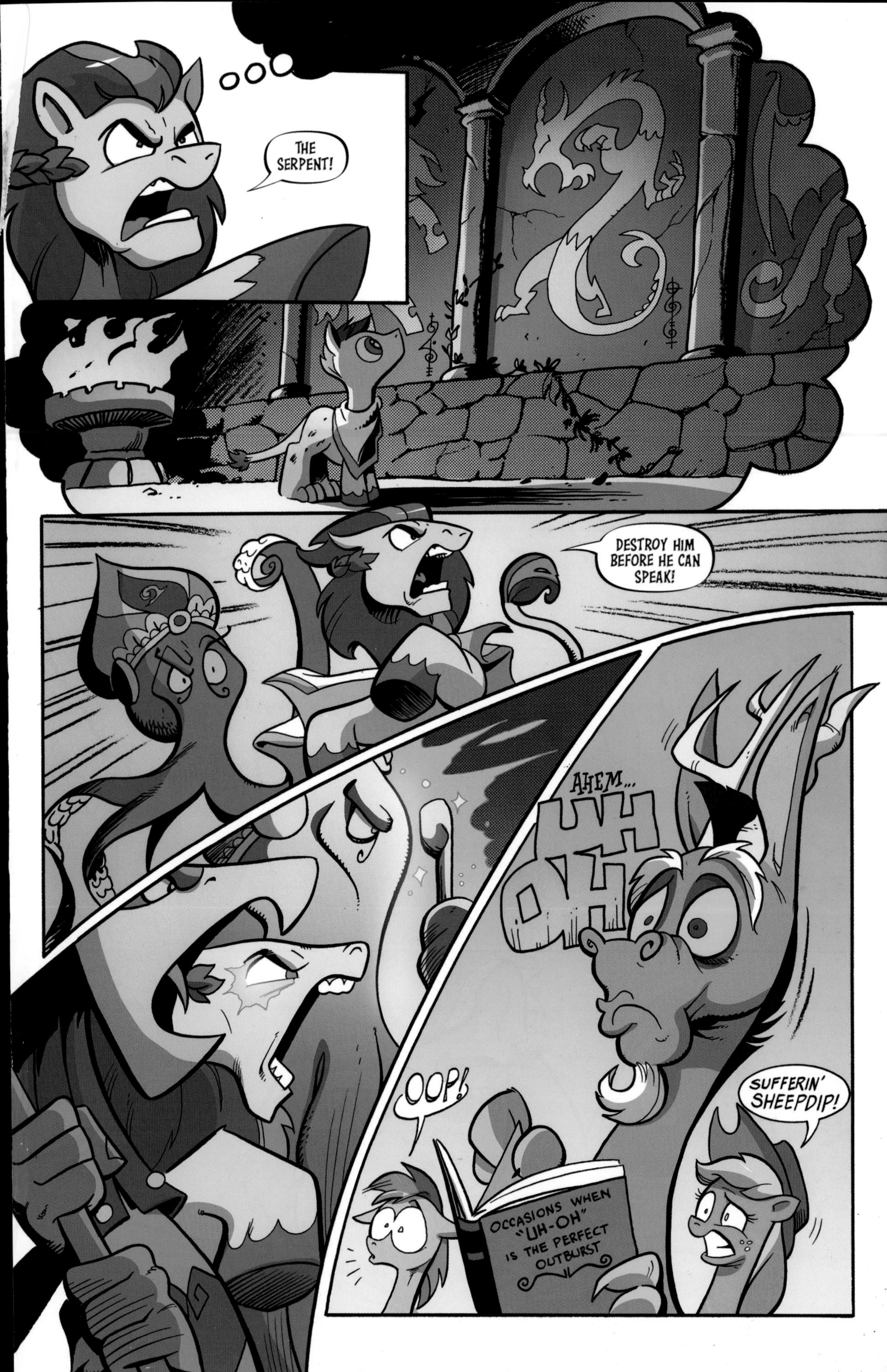
THE SERPENT!
DESTROY HIM BEFORE HE CAN SPEAK!
AHEM... UH OH
OOP!
SUFFERIN' SHEEPDIP!
OCCASIONS WHEN "UH-OH" IS THE PERFECT OUTBURST

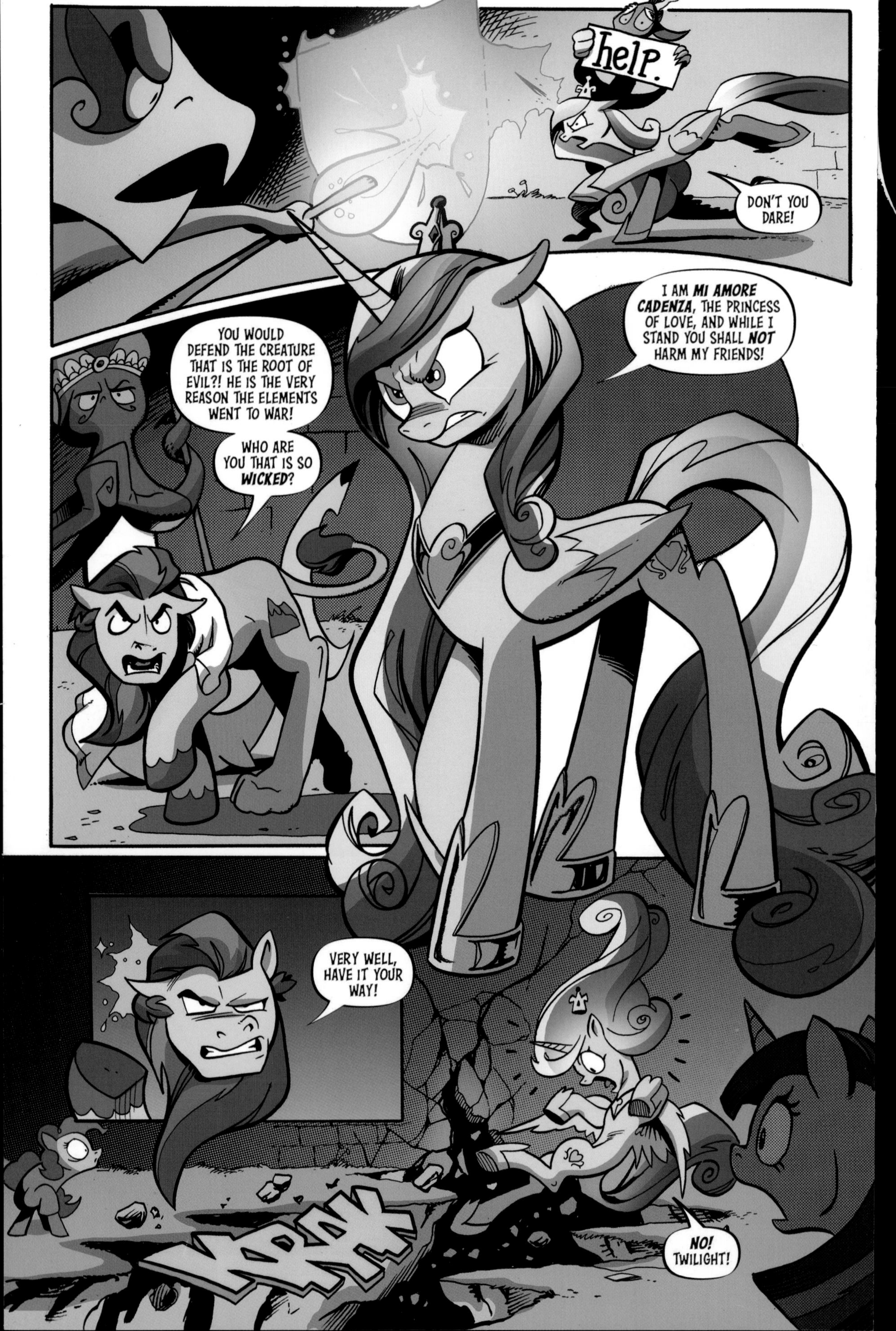
help.
DON'T YOU DARE!
YOU WOULD DEFEND THE CREATURE THAT IS THE ROOT OF EVIL?! HE IS THE VERY REASON THE ELEMENTS WENT TO WAR!
WHO ARE YOU THAT IS SO WICKED?
I AM MI AMORE CADENZA, THE PRINCESS OF LOVE, AND WHILE I STAND YOU SHALL NOT HARM MY FRIENDS!
VERY WELL, HAVE IT YOUR WAY!
KRAK
NO! TWILIGHT!

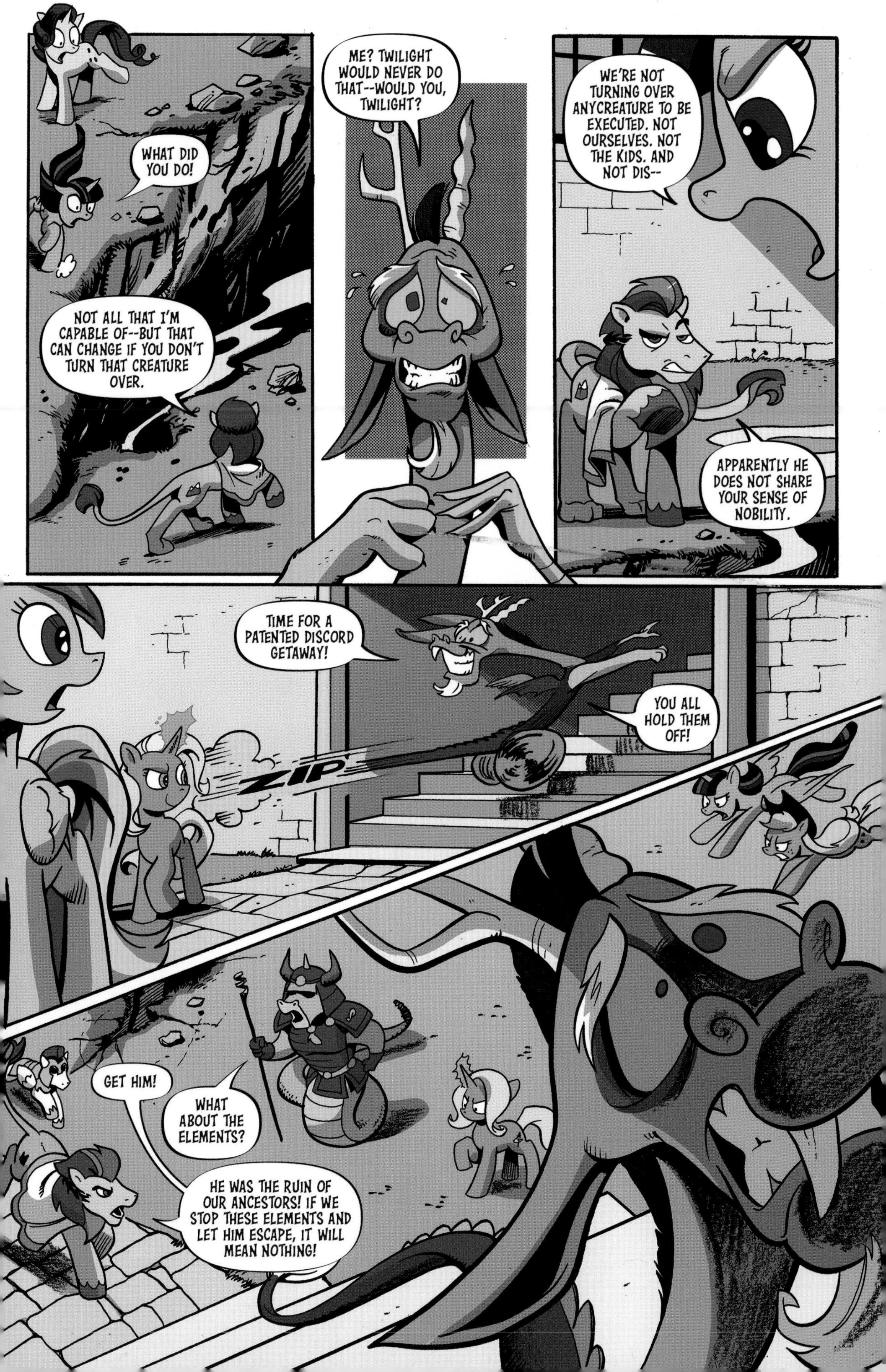
WHAT DID YOU DO!
NOT ALL THAT I'M CAPABLE OF--BUT THAT CAN CHANGE IF YOU DON'T TURN THAT CREATURE OVER.
ME? TWILIGHT WOULD NEVER DO THAT--WOULD YOU, TWILIGHT?
WE'RE NOT TURNING OVER ANYCREATURE TO BE EXECUTED. NOT OURSELVES. NOT THE KIDS. AND NOT DIS--
APPARENTLY HE DOES NOT SHARE YOUR SENSE OF NOBILITY.
TIME FOR A PATENTED DISCORD GETAWAY!
YOU ALL HOLD THEM OFF!
ZIP
GET HIM!
WHAT ABOUT THE ELEMENTS?
HE WAS THE RUIN OF OUR ANCESTORS! IF WE STOP THESE ELEMENTS AND LET HIM ESCAPE, IT WILL MEAN NOTHING!

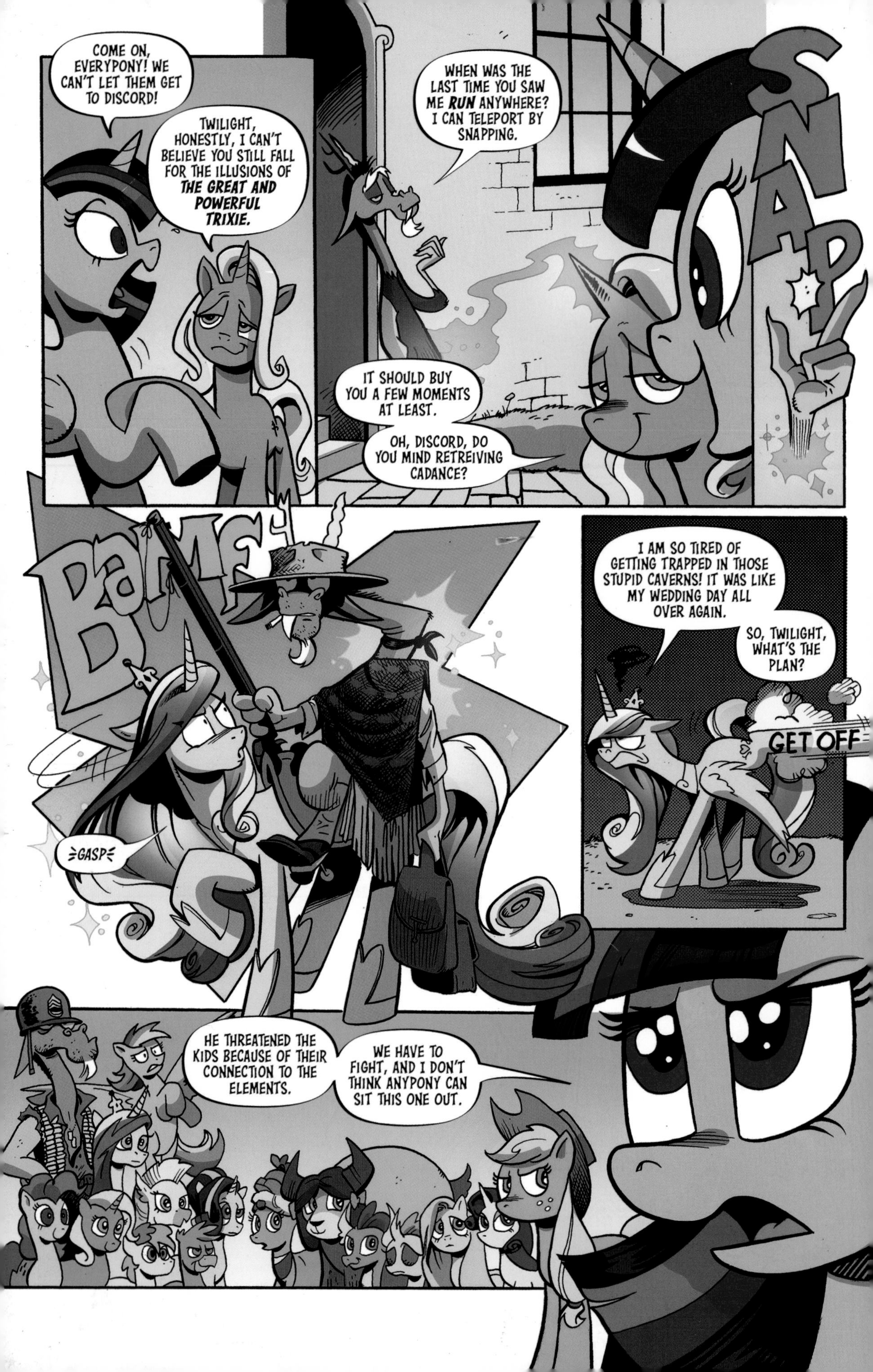
COME ON, EVERYPONY! WE CAN'T LET THEM GET TO DISCORD!
TWILIGHT, HONESTLY, I CAN'T BELIEVE YOU STILL FALL FOR THE ILLUSIONS OF **THE GREAT AND POWERFUL TRIXIE.**
WHEN WAS THE LAST TIME YOU SAW ME ***RUN*** ANYWHERE? I CAN TELEPORT BY SNAPPING.
IT SHOULD BUY YOU A FEW MOMENTS AT LEAST.
OH, DISCORD, DO YOU MIND RETREIVING CADANCE?
SNAP
BAMF
GASP
I AM SO TIRED OF GETTING TRAPPED IN THOSE STUPID CAVERNS! IT WAS LIKE MY WEDDING DAY ALL OVER AGAIN.
SO, TWILIGHT, WHAT'S THE PLAN?
GET OFF
HE THREATENED THE KIDS BECAUSE OF THEIR CONNECTION TO THE ELEMENTS.
WE HAVE TO FIGHT, AND I DON'T THINK ANYPONY CAN SIT THIS ONE OUT.

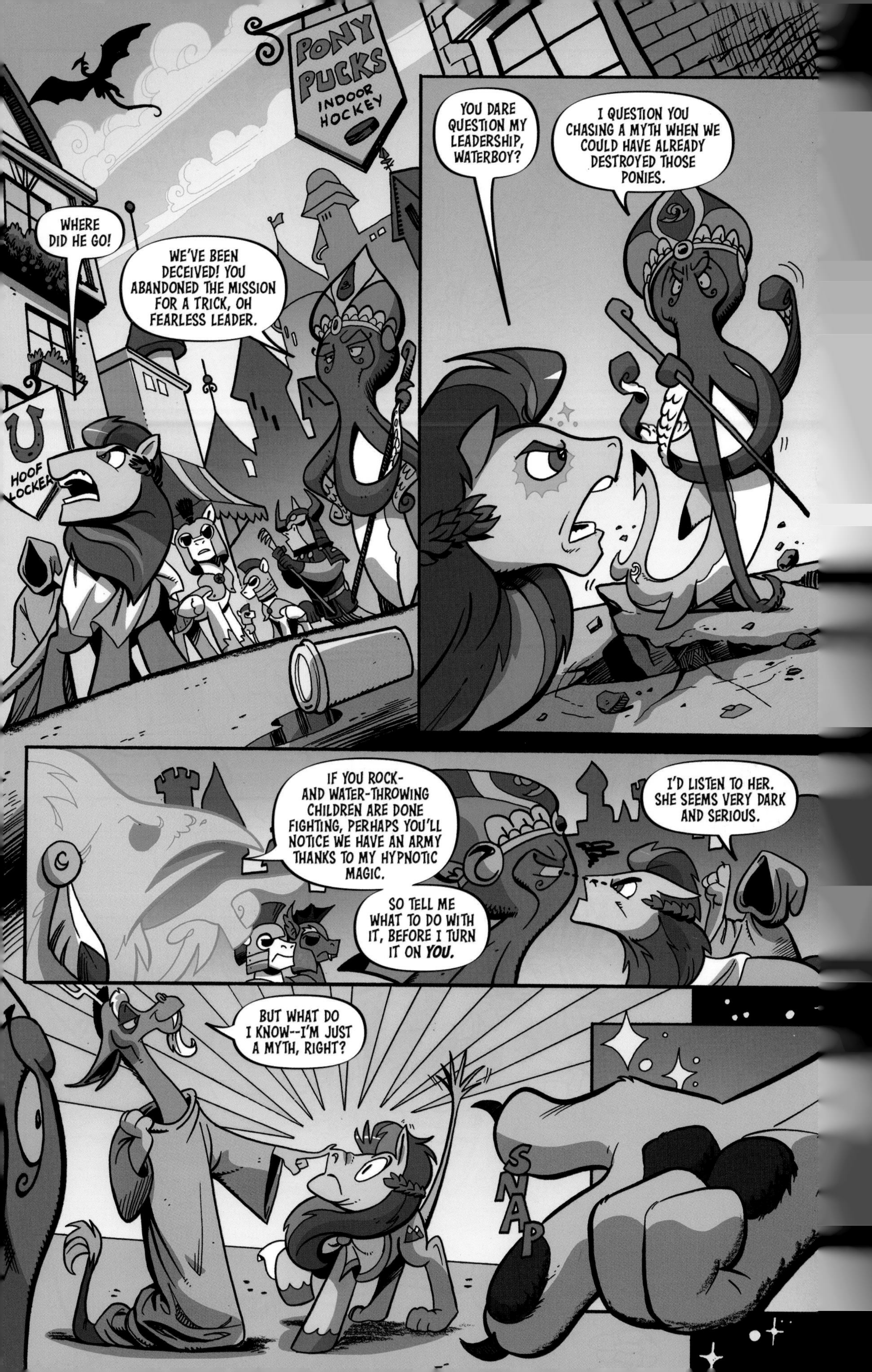
PONY PUCKS INDOOR HOCKEY
WHERE DID HE GO!
WE'VE BEEN DECEIVED! YOU ABANDONED THE MISSION FOR A TRICK, OH FEARLESS LEADER.
HOOF LOCKER
YOU DARE QUESTION MY LEADERSHIP, WATERBOY?
I QUESTION YOU CHASING A MYTH WHEN WE COULD HAVE ALREADY DESTROYED THOSE PONIES.
IF YOU ROCK- AND WATER-THROWING CHILDREN ARE DONE FIGHTING, PERHAPS YOU'LL NOTICE WE HAVE AN ARMY THANKS TO MY HYPNOTIC MAGIC.
SO TELL ME WHAT TO DO WITH IT, BEFORE I TURN IT ON ***YOU.***
I'D LISTEN TO HER. SHE SEEMS VERY DARK AND SERIOUS.
BUT WHAT DO I KNOW--I'M JUST A MYTH, RIGHT?
SNAP

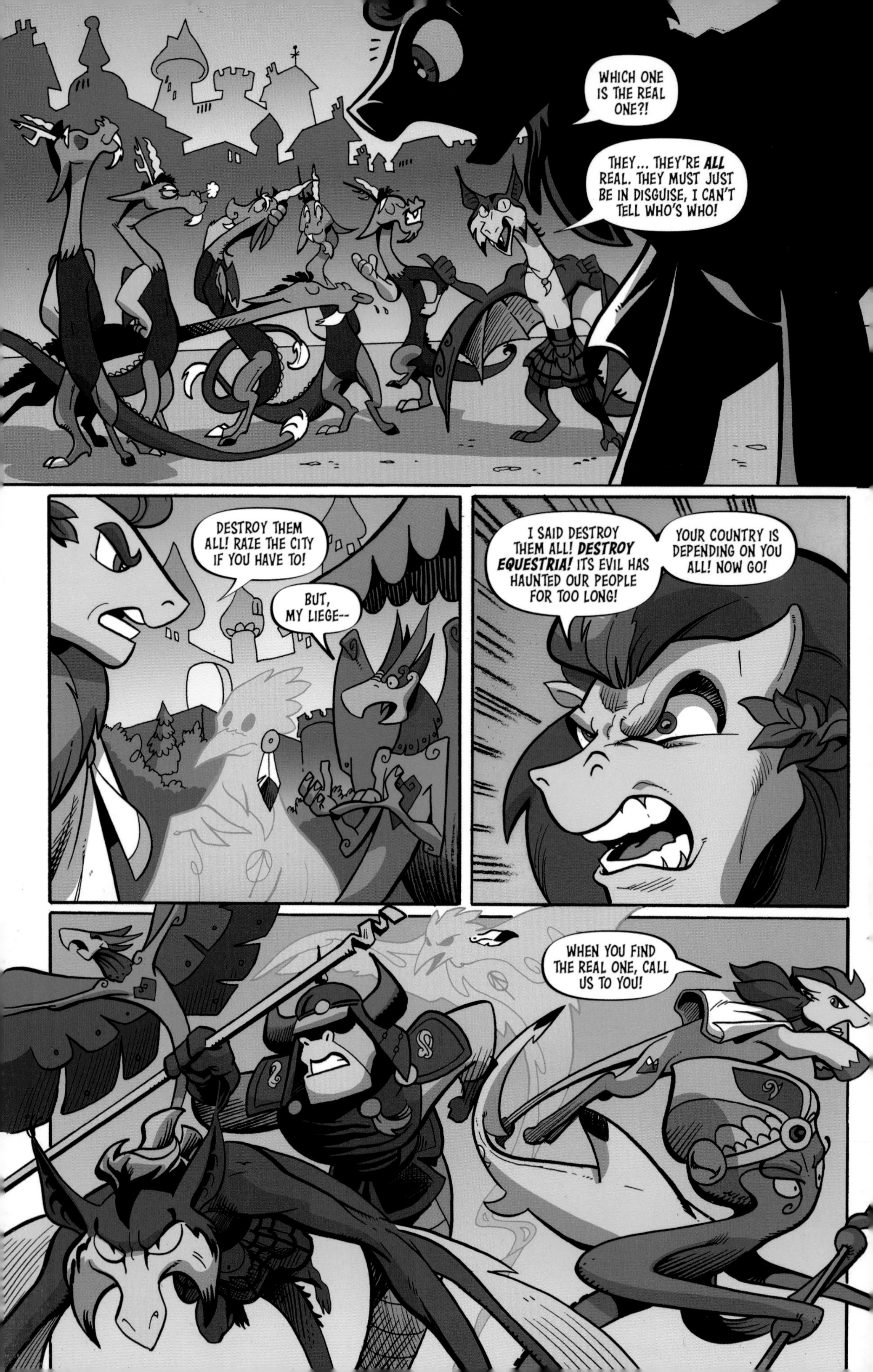
WHICH ONE IS THE REAL ONE?!
THEY... THEY'RE **ALL** REAL. THEY MUST JUST BE IN DISGUISE, I CAN'T TELL WHO'S WHO!
DESTROY THEM ALL! RAZE THE CITY IF YOU HAVE TO!
BUT, MY LIEGE--
I SAID DESTROY THEM ALL! **DESTROY EQUESTRIA!** ITS EVIL HAS HAUNTED OUR PEOPLE FOR TOO LONG!
YOUR COUNTRY IS DEPENDING ON YOU ALL! NOW GO!
WHEN YOU FIND THE REAL ONE, CALL US TO YOU!

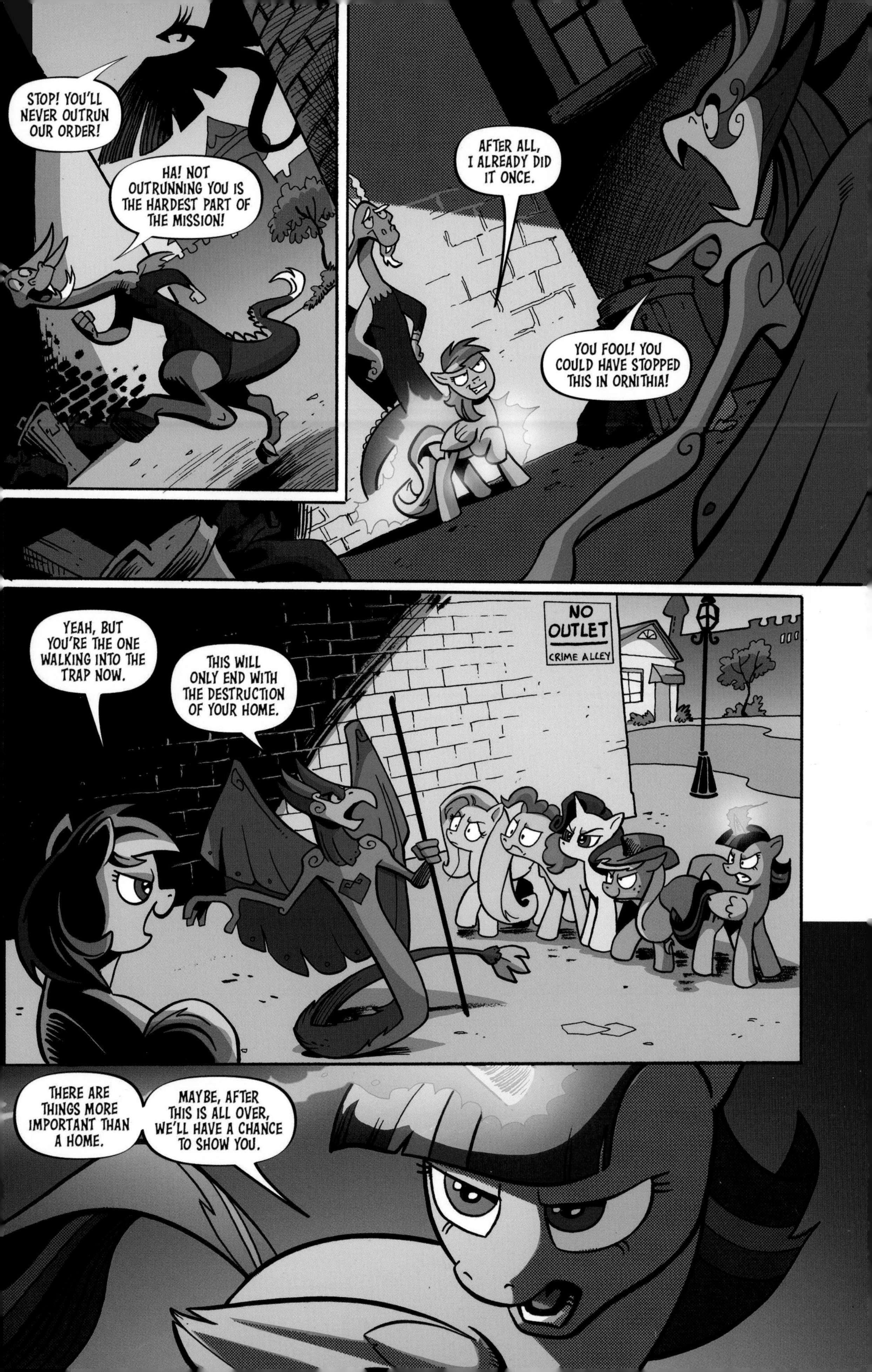
STOP! YOU'LL NEVER OUTRUN OUR ORDER!
HA! NOT OUTRUNNING YOU IS THE HARDEST PART OF THE MISSION!
AFTER ALL, I ALREADY DID IT ONCE.
YOU FOOL! YOU COULD HAVE STOPPED THIS IN ORNITHIA!
YEAH, BUT YOU'RE THE ONE WALKING INTO THE TRAP NOW.
THIS WILL ONLY END WITH THE DESTRUCTION OF YOUR HOME.
NO OUTLET
CRIME ALLEY
THERE ARE THINGS MORE IMPORTANT THAN A HOME.
MAYBE, AFTER THIS IS ALL OVER, WE'LL HAVE A CHANCE TO SHOW YOU.

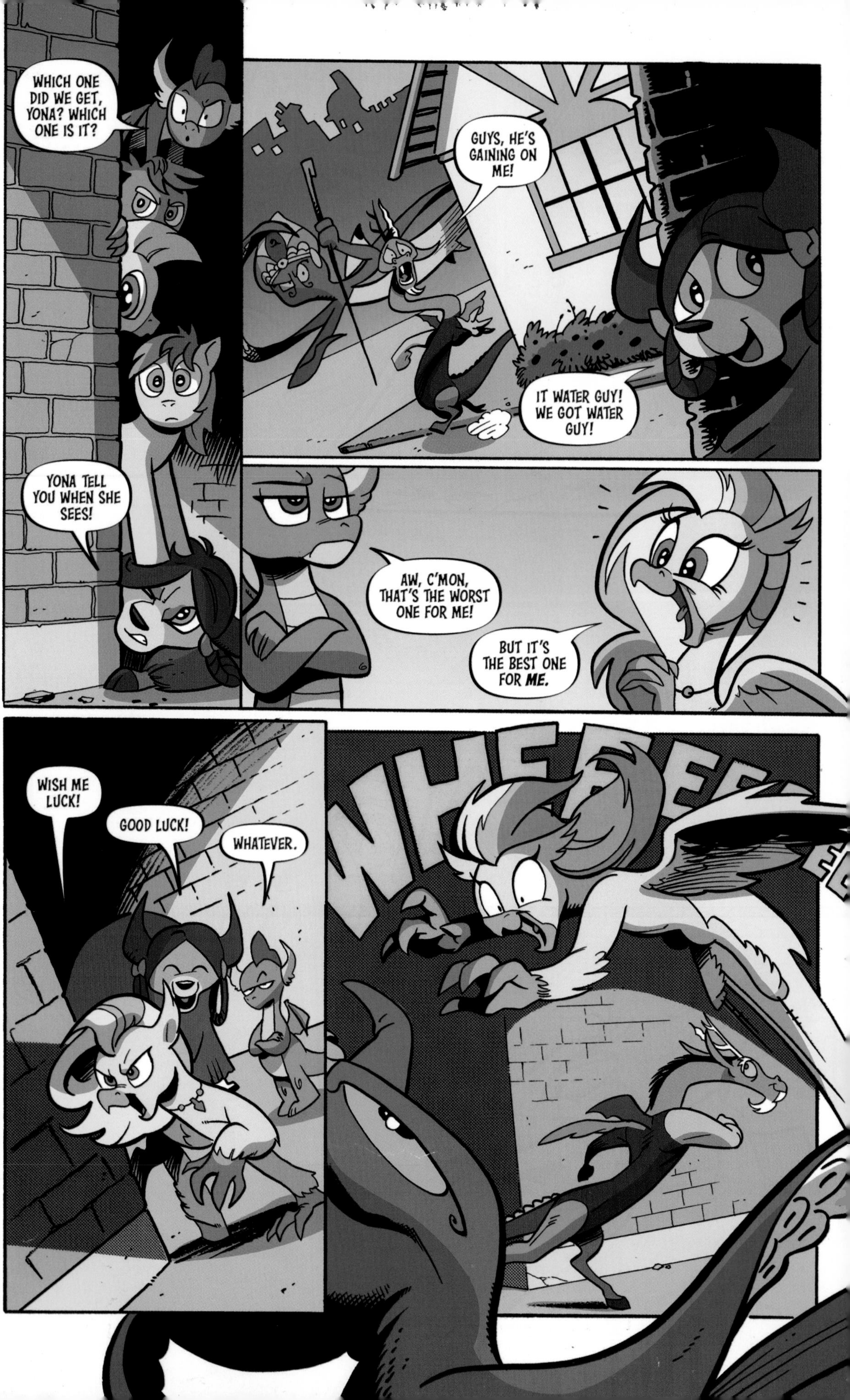
WHICH ONE DID WE GET, YONA? WHICH ONE IS IT?
GUYS, HE'S GAINING ON ME!
IT WATER GUY! WE GOT WATER GUY!
YONA TELL YOU WHEN SHE SEES!
AW, C'MON, THAT'S THE WORST ONE FOR ME!
BUT IT'S THE BEST ONE FOR ***ME.***
WISH ME LUCK!
GOOD LUCK!
WHATEVER.
WHEEE

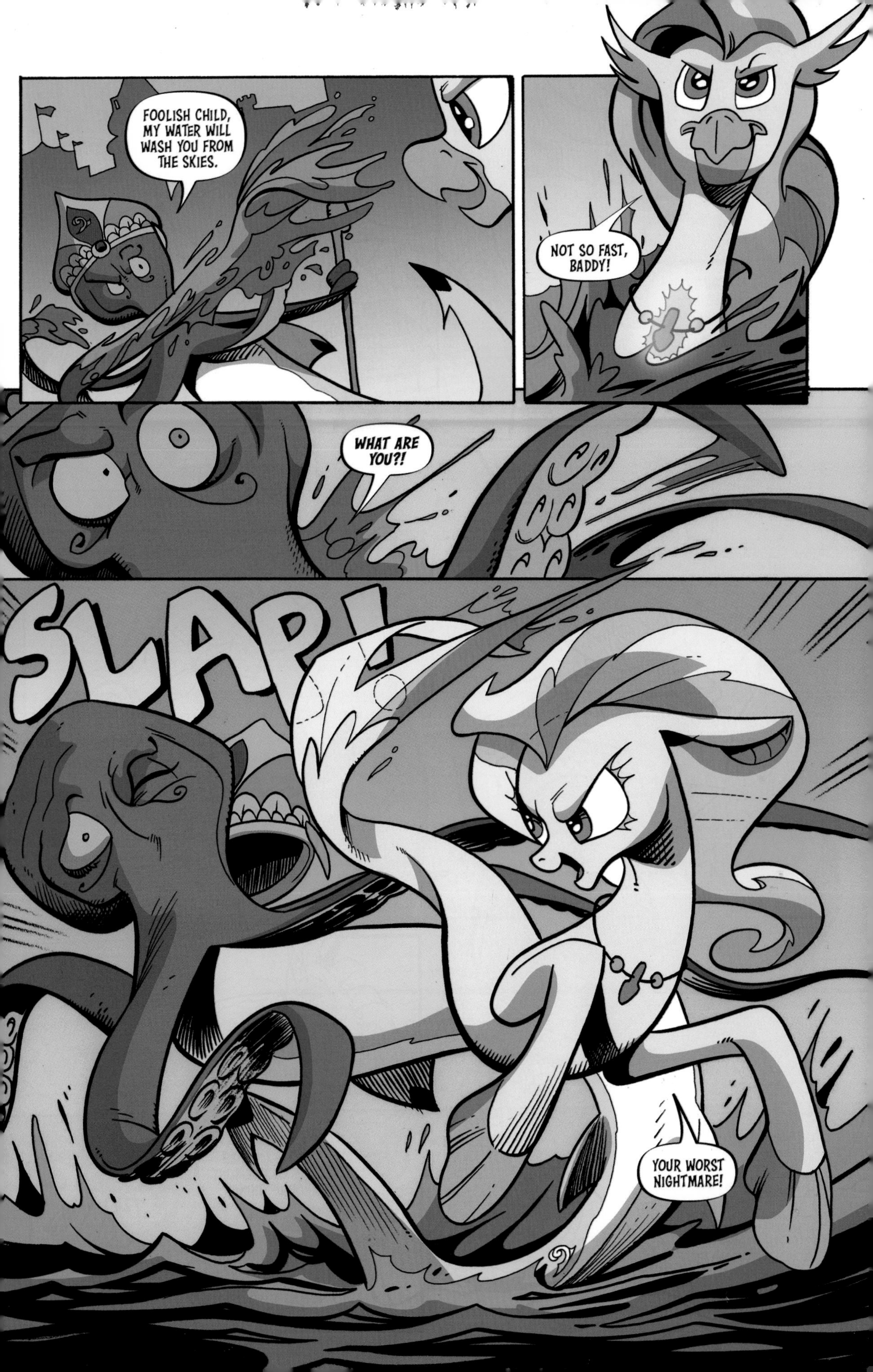
FOOLISH CHILD, MY WATER WILL WASH YOU FROM THE SKIES.
NOT SO FAST, BADDY!
WHAT ARE YOU?!
SLAP!
YOUR WORST NIGHTMARE!

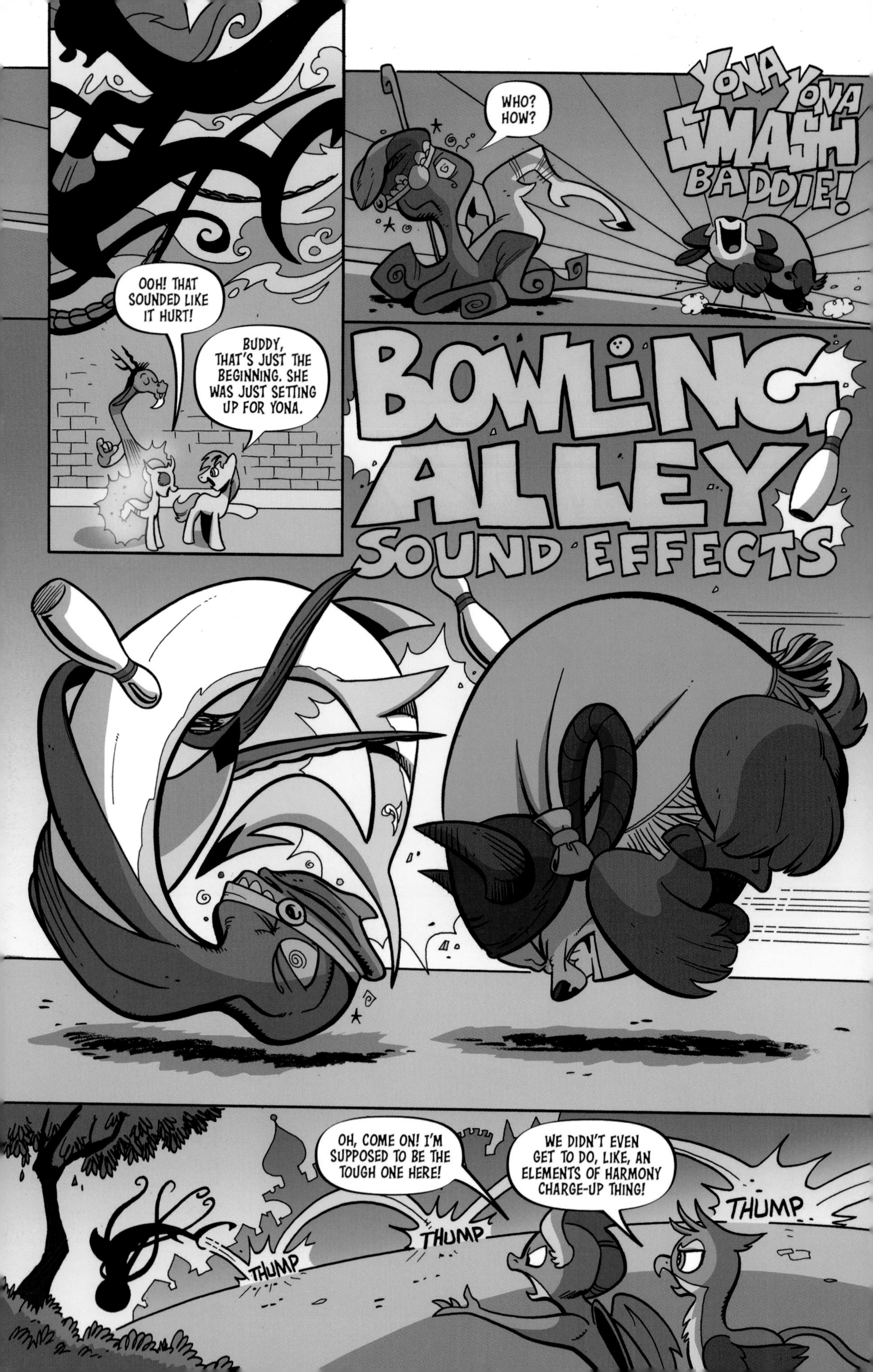

OOH! THAT SOUNDED LIKE IT HURT!
BUDDY, THAT'S JUST THE BEGINNING. SHE WAS JUST SETTING UP FOR YONA.
WHO? HOW?
YONA YONA SMASH BADDIE!
BOWLING ALLEY SOUND EFFECTS
OH, COME ON! I'M SUPPOSED TO BE THE TOUGH ONE HERE!
WE DIDN'T EVEN GET TO DO, LIKE, AN ELEMENTS OF HARMONY CHARGE-UP THING!
THUMP
THUMP
THUMP

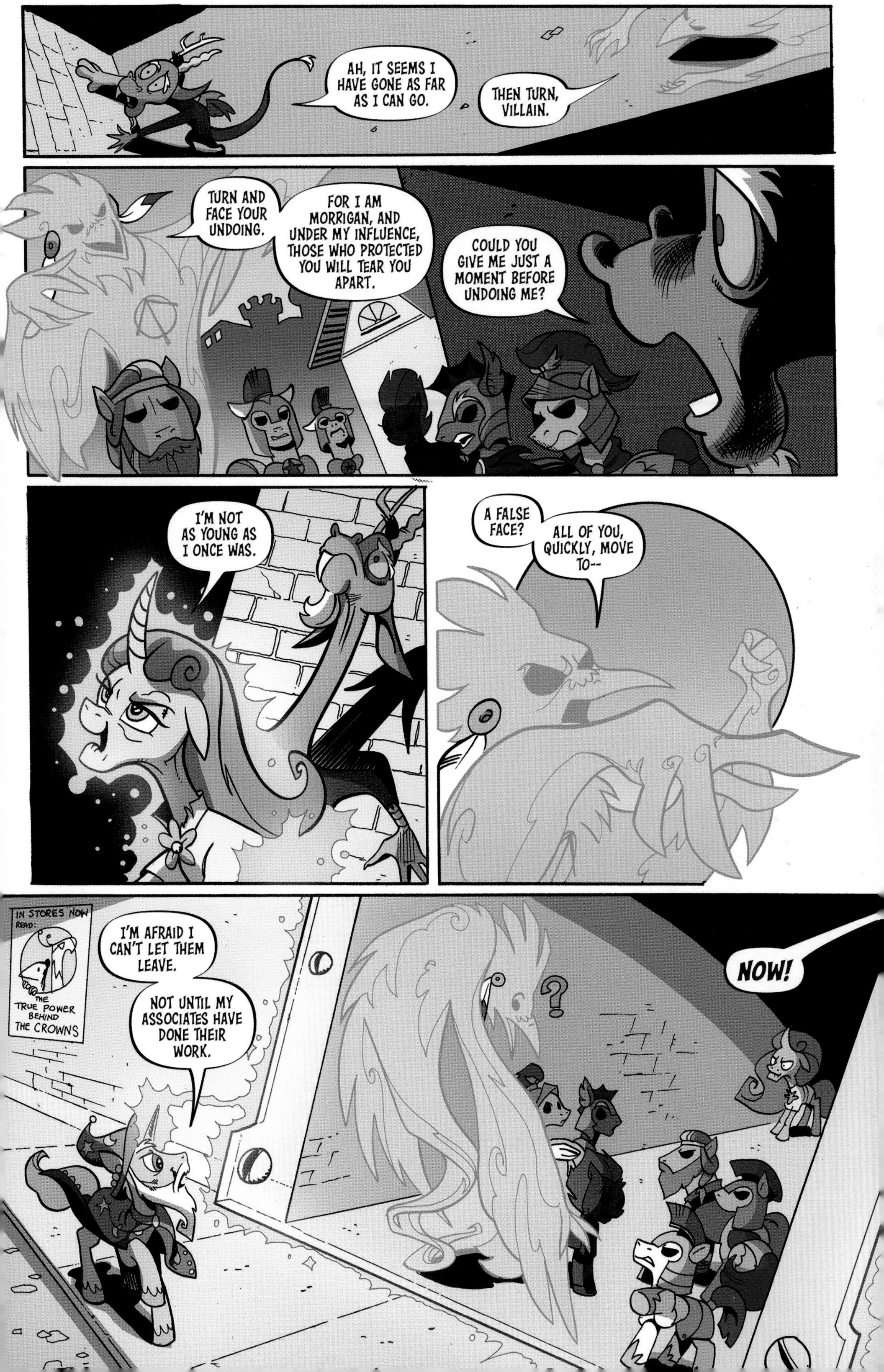
AH, IT SEEMS I HAVE GONE AS FAR AS I CAN GO.
THEN TURN, VILLAIN.
TURN AND FACE YOUR UNDOING.
FOR I AM MORRIGAN, AND UNDER MY INFLUENCE, THOSE WHO PROTECTED YOU WILL TEAR YOU APART.
COULD YOU GIVE ME JUST A MOMENT BEFORE UNDOING ME?
I'M NOT AS YOUNG AS I ONCE WAS.
A FALSE FACE?
ALL OF YOU, QUICKLY, MOVE TO--
IN STORES NOW READ:
THE TRUE POWER BEHIND THE CROWNS
I'M AFRAID I CAN'T LET THEM LEAVE.
NOT UNTIL MY ASSOCIATES HAVE DONE THEIR WORK.
?
NOW!

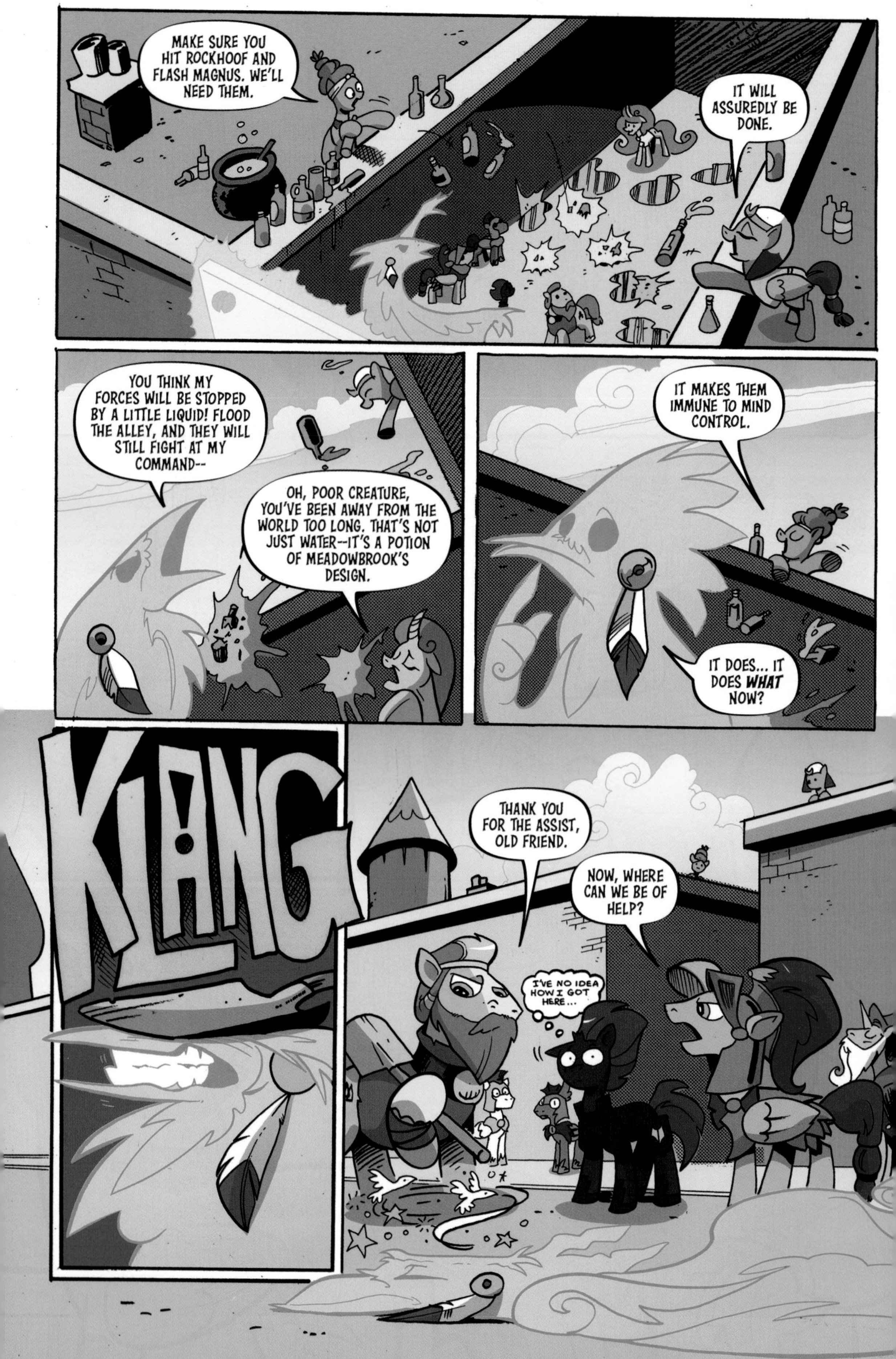
MAKE SURE YOU HIT ROCKHOOF AND FLASH MAGNUS. WE'LL NEED THEM.
IT WILL ASSUREDLY BE DONE.
YOU THINK MY FORCES WILL BE STOPPED BY A LITTLE LIQUID! FLOOD THE ALLEY, AND THEY WILL STILL FIGHT AT MY COMMAND--
OH, POOR CREATURE, YOU'VE BEEN AWAY FROM THE WORLD TOO LONG. THAT'S NOT JUST WATER--IT'S A POTION OF MEADOWBROOK'S DESIGN.
IT MAKES THEM IMMUNE TO MIND CONTROL.
IT DOES... IT DOES WHAT NOW?
KLANG
THANK YOU FOR THE ASSIST, OLD FRIEND.
NOW, WHERE CAN WE BE OF HELP?
I'VE NO IDEA HOW I GOT HERE...

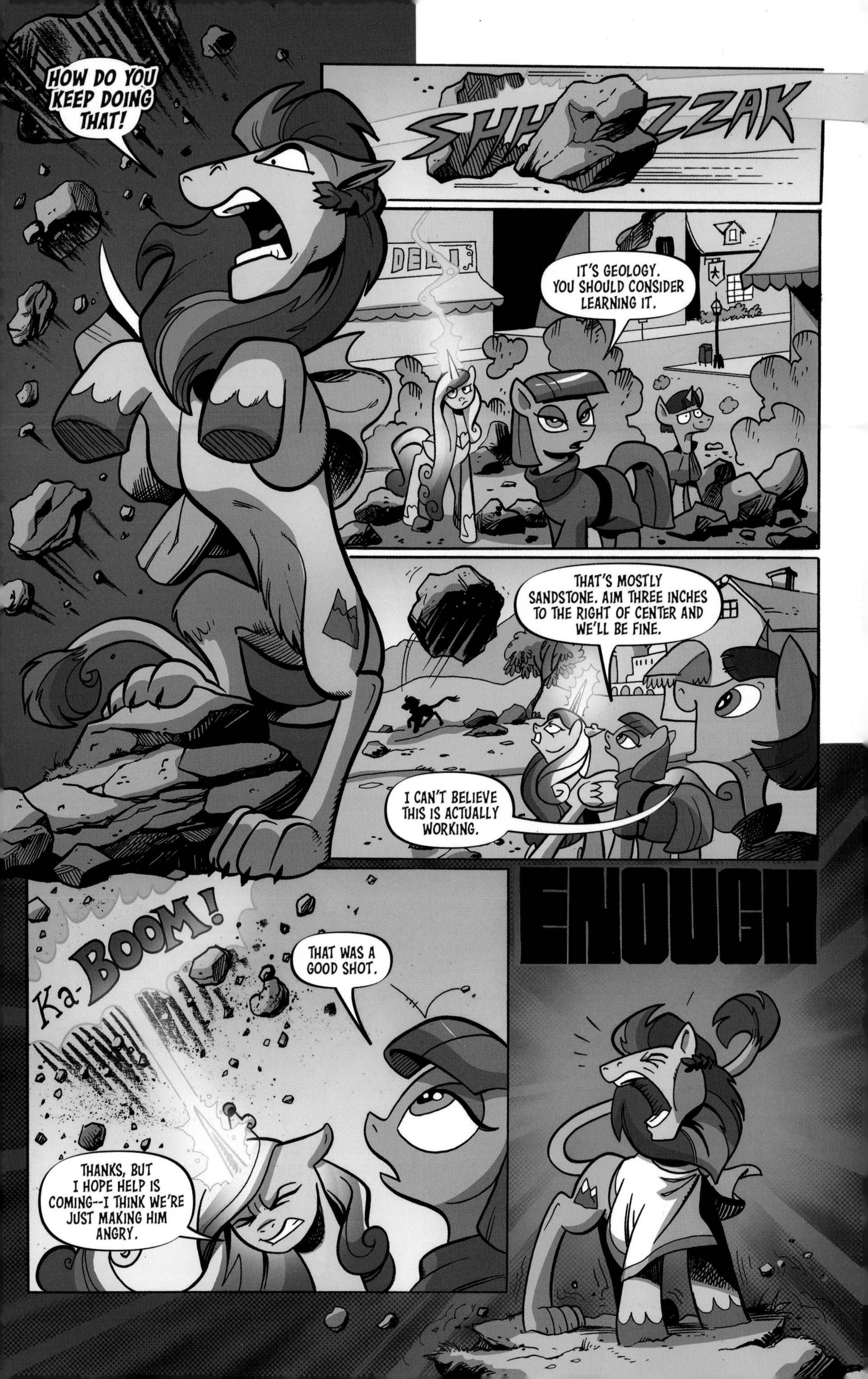
HOW DO YOU KEEP DOING THAT!
SHH ZZAK
IT'S GEOLOGY. YOU SHOULD CONSIDER LEARNING IT.
DELI
THAT'S MOSTLY SANDSTONE. AIM THREE INCHES TO THE RIGHT OF CENTER AND WE'LL BE FINE.
I CAN'T BELIEVE THIS IS ACTUALLY WORKING.
KA-BOOM!
THAT WAS A GOOD SHOT.
THANKS, BUT I HOPE HELP IS COMING--I THINK WE'RE JUST MAKING HIM ANGRY.
ENOUGH

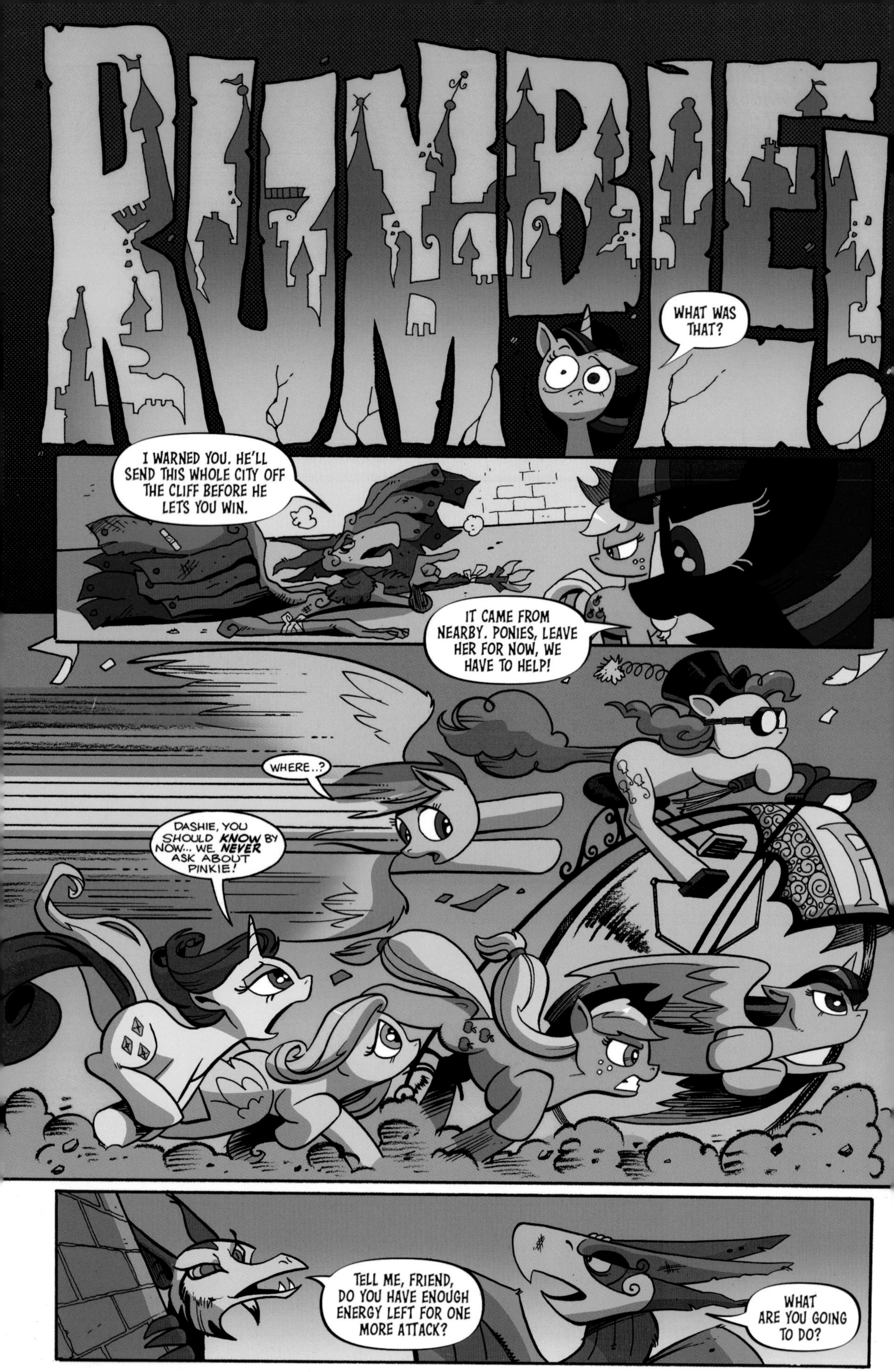
RUMBLE!
WHAT WAS THAT?
I WARNED YOU. HE'LL SEND THIS WHOLE CITY OFF THE CLIFF BEFORE HE LETS YOU WIN.
IT CAME FROM NEARBY. PONIES, LEAVE HER FOR NOW, WE HAVE TO HELP!
WHERE..?
DASHIE, YOU SHOULD KNOW BY NOW... WE NEVER ASK ABOUT PINKIE!
TELL ME, FRIEND, DO YOU HAVE ENOUGH ENERGY LEFT FOR ONE MORE ATTACK?
WHAT ARE YOU GOING TO DO?

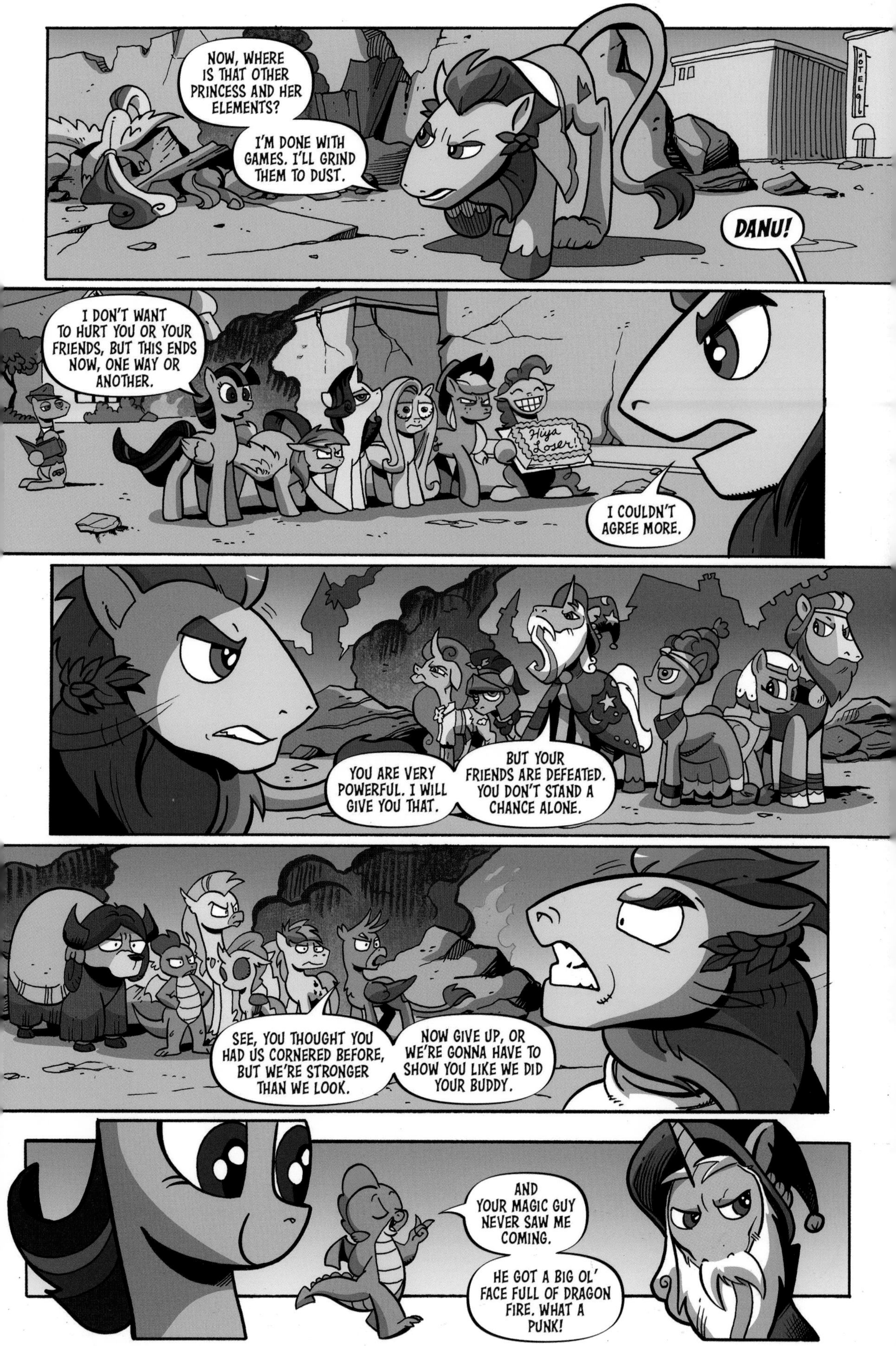
NOW, WHERE IS THAT OTHER PRINCESS AND HER ELEMENTS?
I'M DONE WITH GAMES. I'LL GRIND THEM TO DUST.
HOTEL
DANU!
I DON'T WANT TO HURT YOU OR YOUR FRIENDS, BUT THIS ENDS NOW, ONE WAY OR ANOTHER.
Hiya Loser!
I COULDN'T AGREE MORE.
YOU ARE VERY POWERFUL. I WILL GIVE YOU THAT.
BUT YOUR FRIENDS ARE DEFEATED. YOU DON'T STAND A CHANCE ALONE.
SEE, YOU THOUGHT YOU HAD US CORNERED BEFORE, BUT WE'RE STRONGER THAN WE LOOK.
NOW GIVE UP, OR WE'RE GONNA HAVE TO SHOW YOU LIKE WE DID YOUR BUDDY.
AND YOUR MAGIC GUY NEVER SAW ME COMING.
HE GOT A BIG OL' FACE FULL OF DRAGON FIRE. WHAT A PUNK!

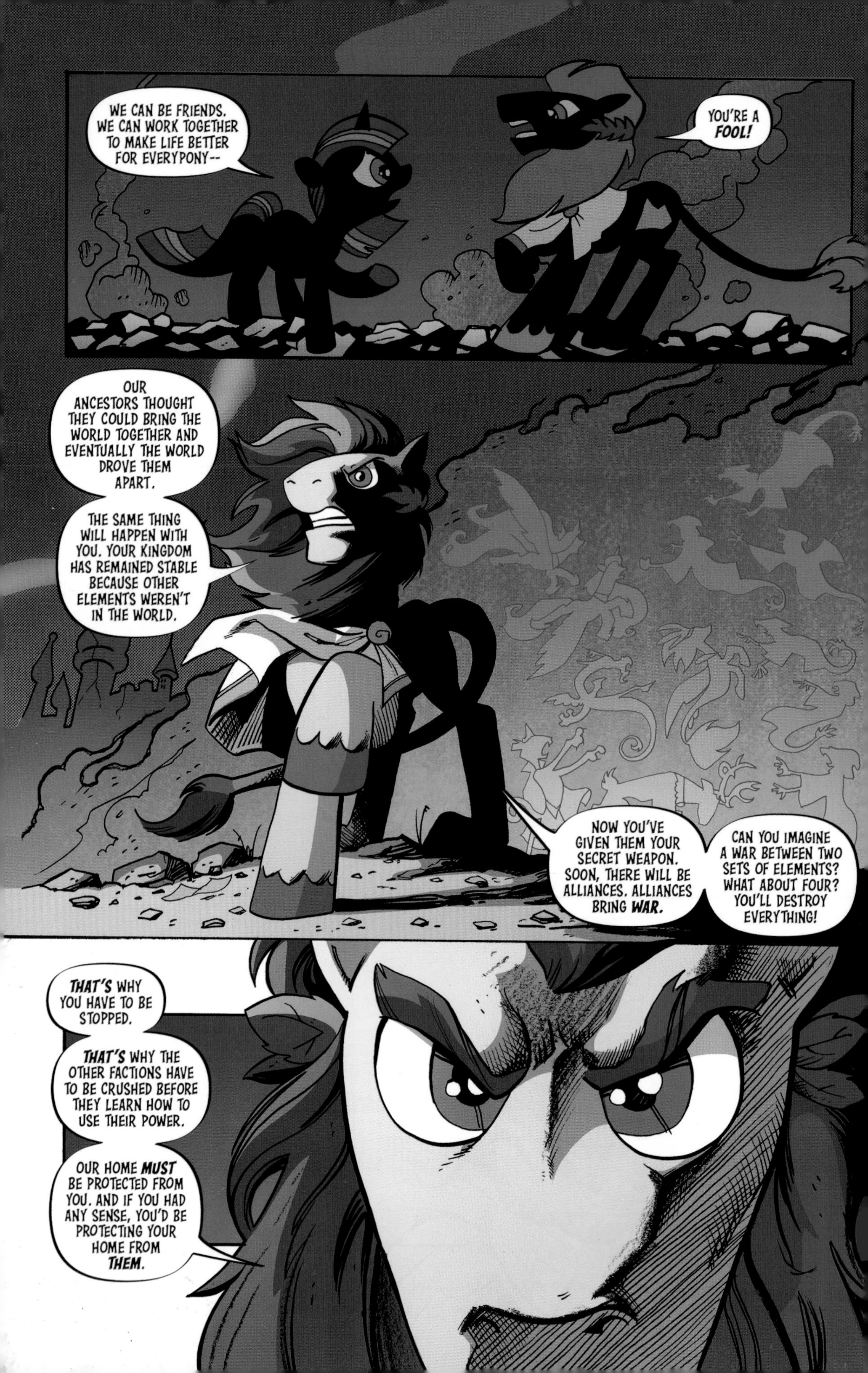
WE CAN BE FRIENDS. WE CAN WORK TOGETHER TO MAKE LIFE BETTER FOR EVERYPONY--
YOU'RE A **FOOL!**
OUR ANCESTORS THOUGHT THEY COULD BRING THE WORLD TOGETHER AND EVENTUALLY THE WORLD DROVE THEM APART.
THE SAME THING WILL HAPPEN WITH YOU. YOUR KINGDOM HAS REMAINED STABLE BECAUSE OTHER ELEMENTS WEREN'T IN THE WORLD.
NOW YOU'VE GIVEN THEM YOUR SECRET WEAPON. SOON, THERE WILL BE ALLIANCES. ALLIANCES BRING **WAR.**
CAN YOU IMAGINE A WAR BETWEEN TWO SETS OF ELEMENTS? WHAT ABOUT FOUR? YOU'LL DESTROY EVERYTHING!
THAT'S WHY YOU HAVE TO BE STOPPED.
THAT'S WHY THE OTHER FACTIONS HAVE TO BE CRUSHED BEFORE THEY LEARN HOW TO USE THEIR POWER.
OUR HOME **MUST** BE PROTECTED FROM YOU. AND IF YOU HAD ANY SENSE, YOU'D BE PROTECTING YOUR HOME FROM **THEM**.

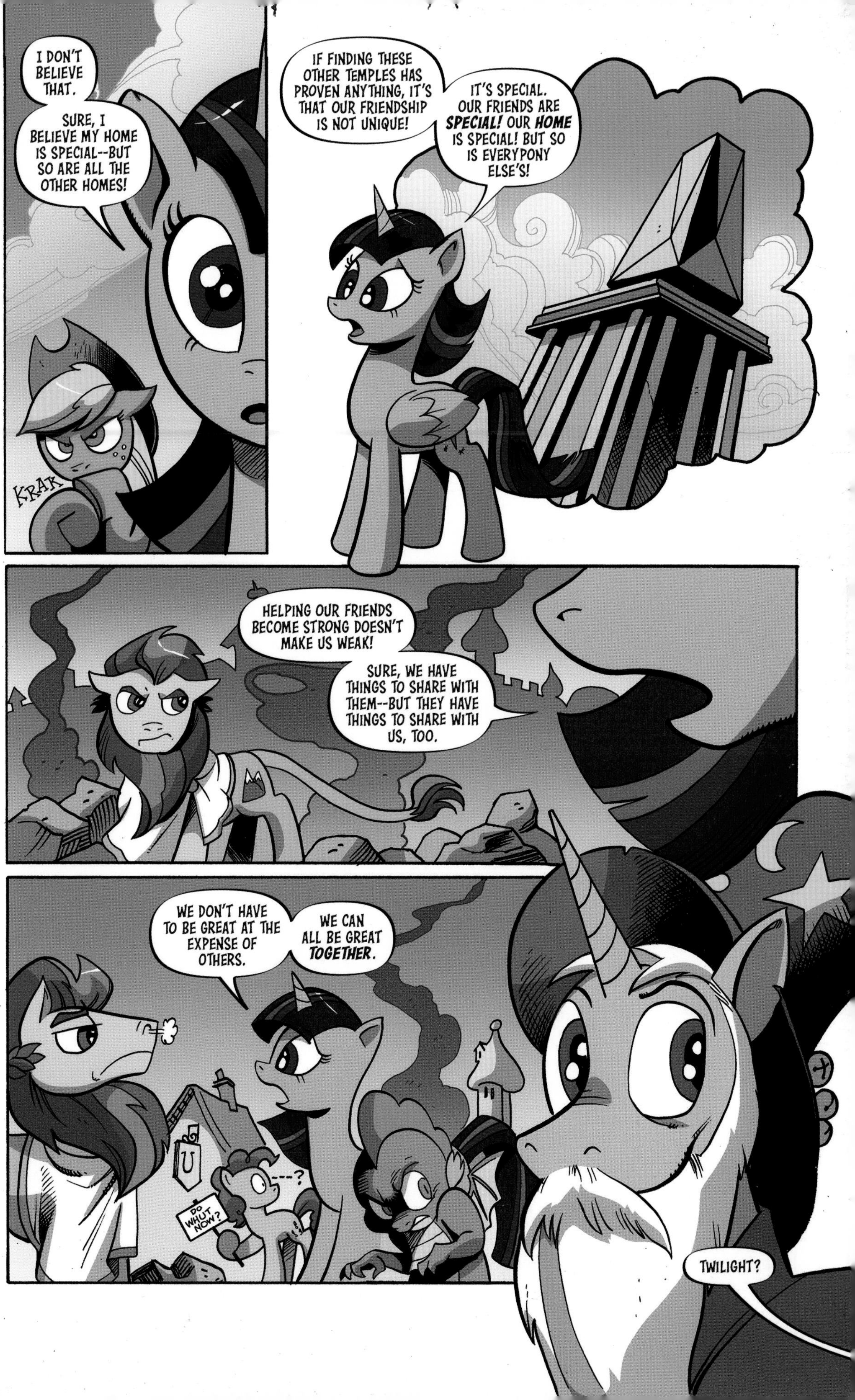
I DON'T BELIEVE THAT.
SURE, I BELIEVE MY HOME IS SPECIAL--BUT SO ARE ALL THE OTHER HOMES!
KRAK
IF FINDING THESE OTHER TEMPLES HAS PROVEN ANYTHING, IT'S THAT OUR FRIENDSHIP IS NOT UNIQUE!
IT'S SPECIAL. OUR FRIENDS ARE SPECIAL! OUR HOME IS SPECIAL! BUT SO IS EVERYPONY ELSE'S!
HELPING OUR FRIENDS BECOME STRONG DOESN'T MAKE US WEAK!
SURE, WE HAVE THINGS TO SHARE WITH THEM--BUT THEY HAVE THINGS TO SHARE WITH US, TOO.
WE DON'T HAVE TO BE GREAT AT THE EXPENSE OF OTHERS.
WE CAN ALL BE GREAT TOGETHER.
U
DO WHUT NOW?
---?
TWILIGHT?

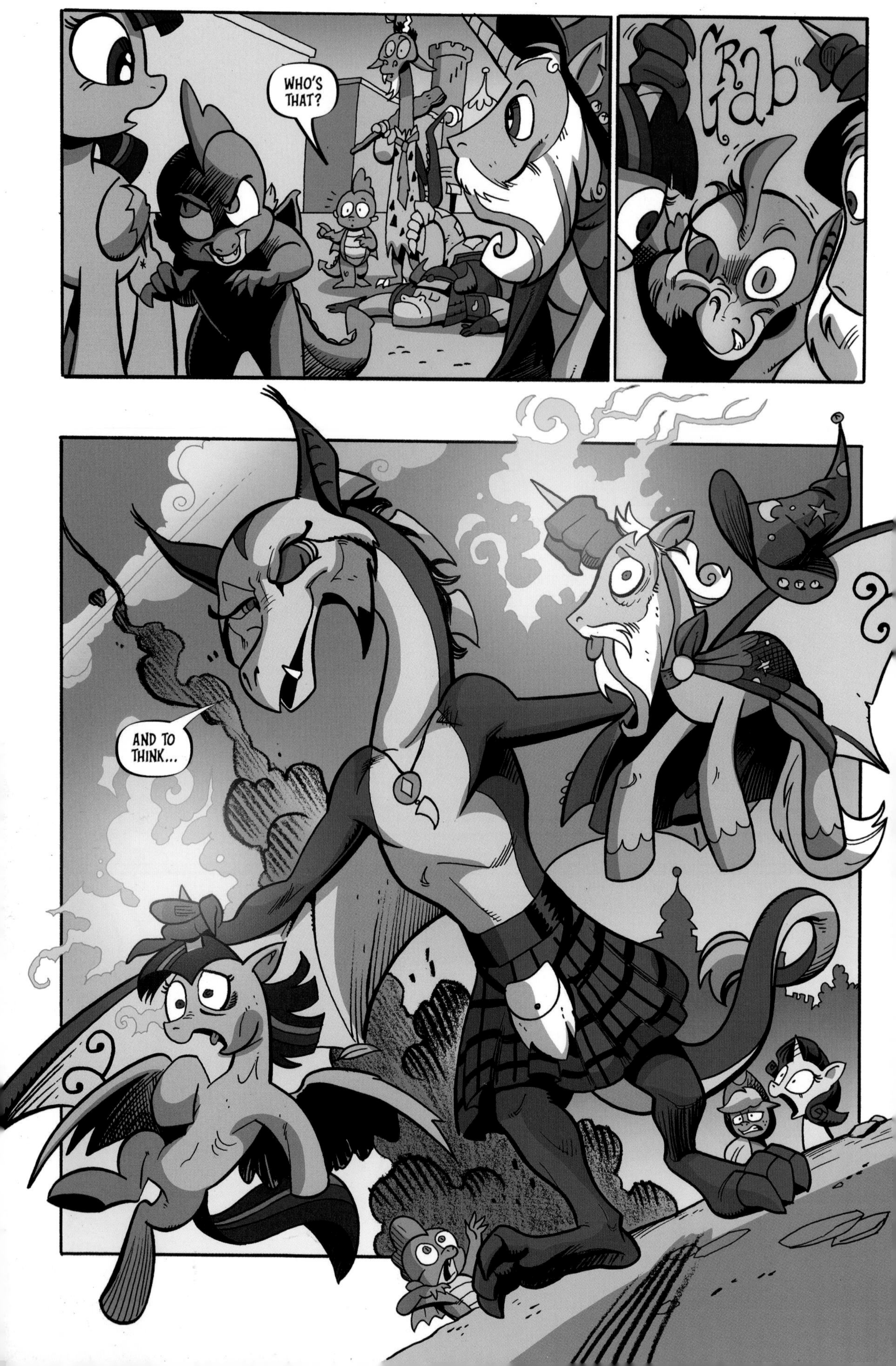
WHO'S THAT?
GRAB
AND TO THINK...

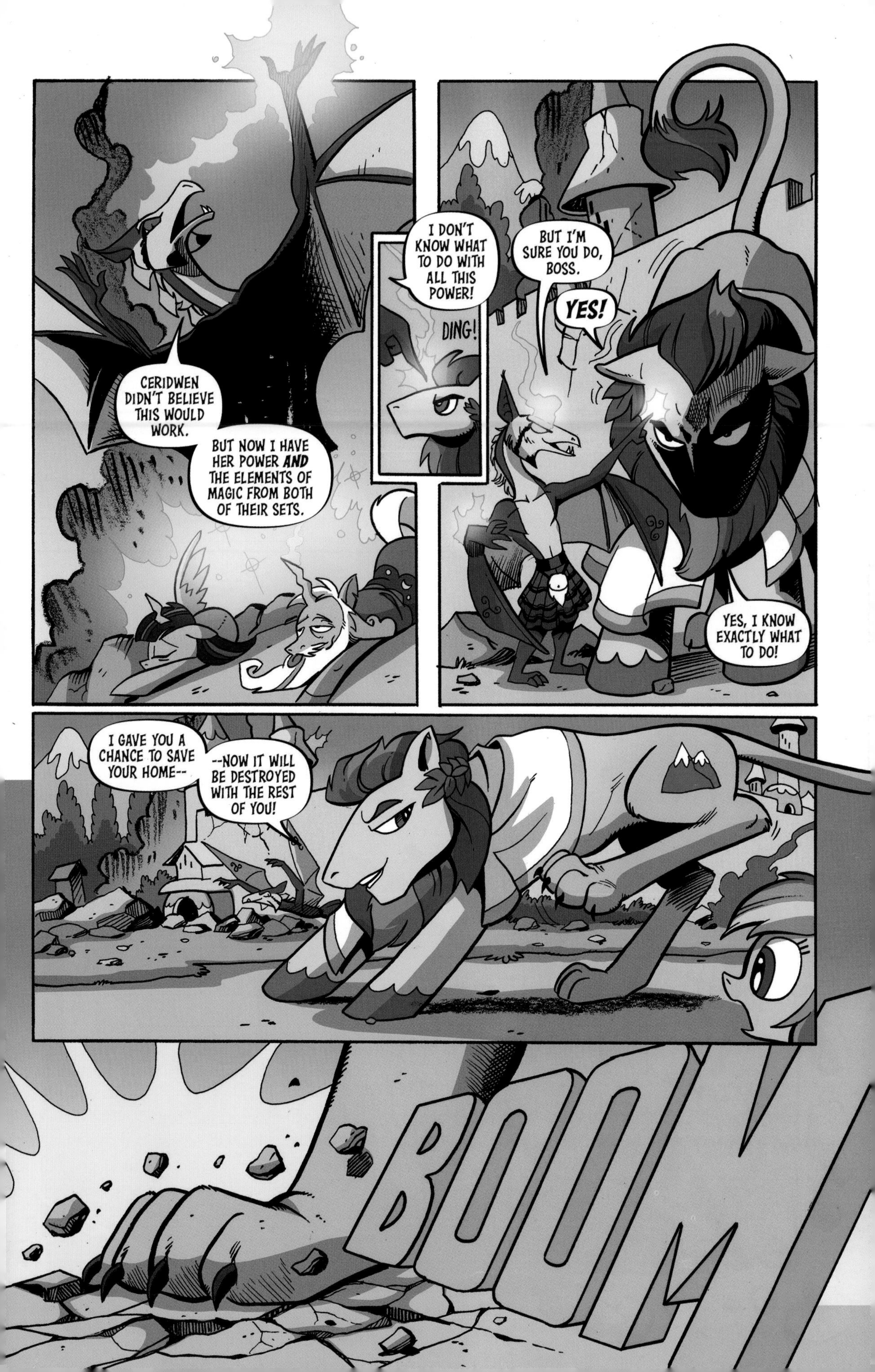
CERIDWEN DIDN'T BELIEVE THIS WOULD WORK.
BUT NOW I HAVE HER POWER AND THE ELEMENTS OF MAGIC FROM BOTH OF THEIR SETS.
I DON'T KNOW WHAT TO DO WITH ALL THIS POWER!
DING!
BUT I'M SURE YOU DO, BOSS.
YES!
YES, I KNOW EXACTLY WHAT TO DO!
I GAVE YOU A CHANCE TO SAVE YOUR HOME--
--NOW IT WILL BE DESTROYED WITH THE REST OF YOU!
BOOM!

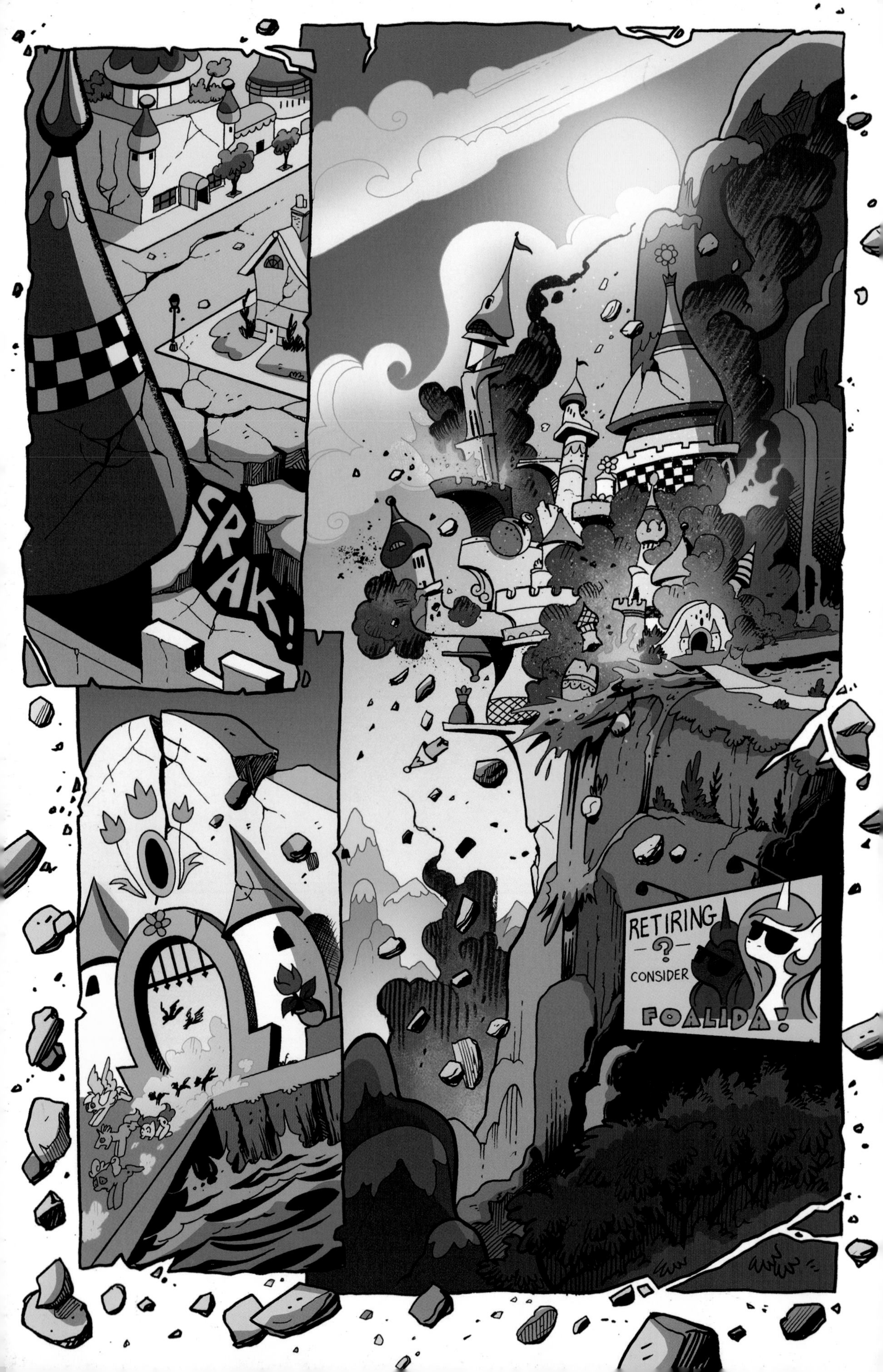
CRAK!
RETIRING
?
CONSIDER
FOALIDA!

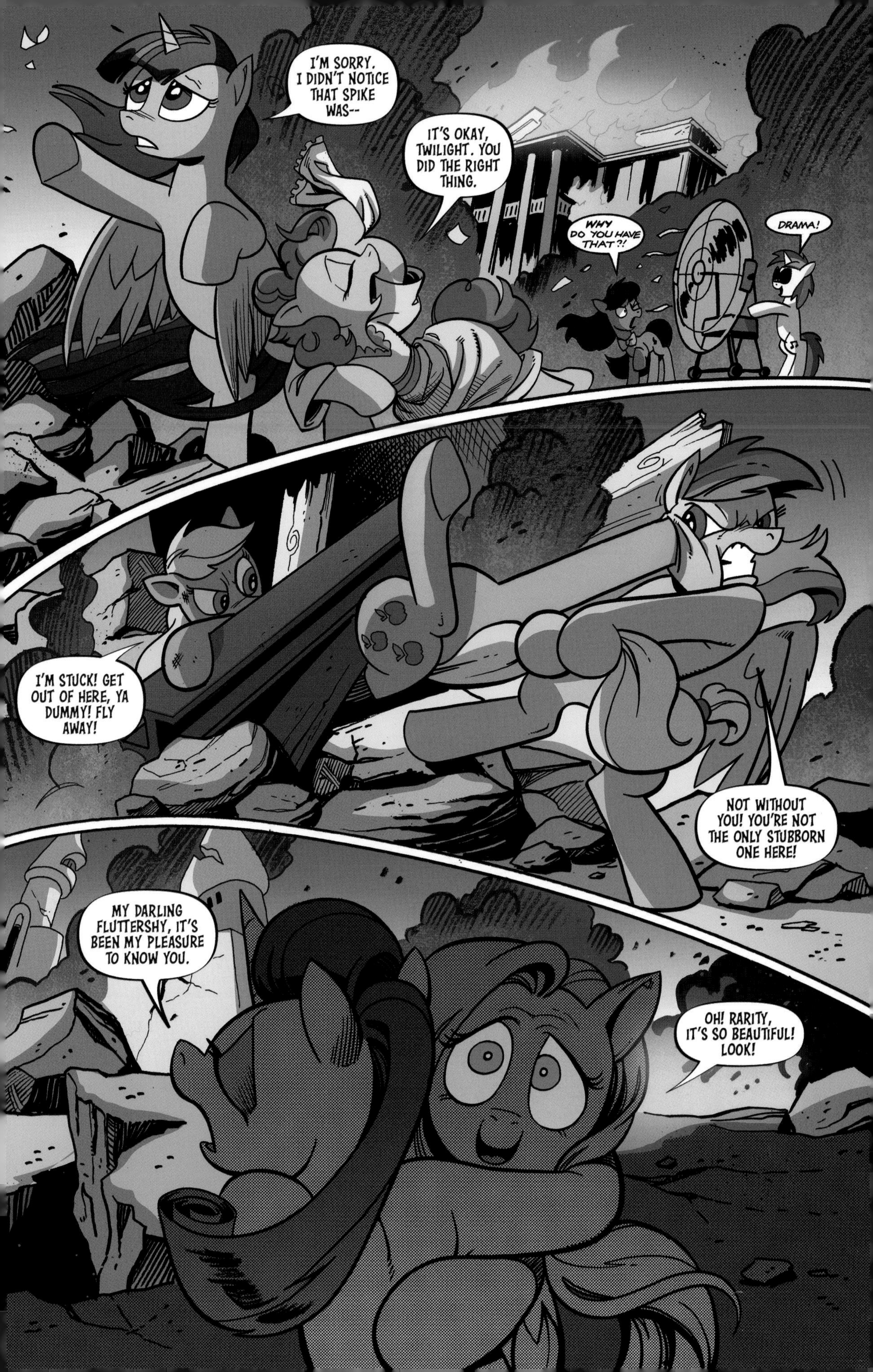
I'M SORRY. I DIDN'T NOTICE THAT SPIKE WAS--
IT'S OKAY, TWILIGHT. YOU DID THE RIGHT THING.
WHY DO YOU HAVE THAT?!
DRAMA!
I'M STUCK! GET OUT OF HERE, YA DUMMY! FLY AWAY!
NOT WITHOUT YOU! YOU'RE NOT THE ONLY STUBBORN ONE HERE!
MY DARLING FLUTTERSHY, IT'S BEEN MY PLEASURE TO KNOW YOU.
OH! RARITY, IT'S SO BEAUTIFUL! LOOK!

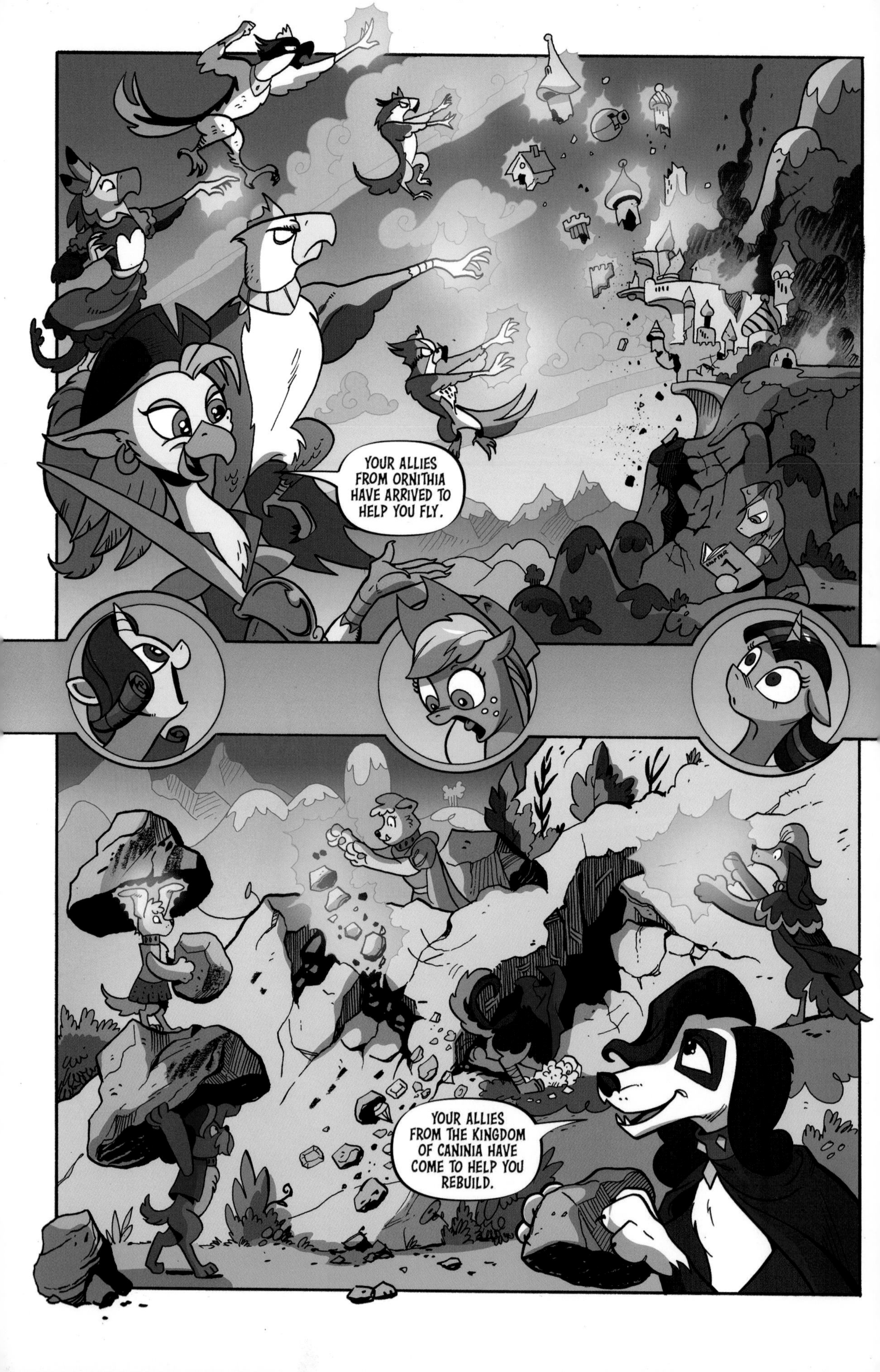
YOUR ALLIES FROM ORNITHIA HAVE ARRIVED TO HELP YOU FLY.
YOUR ALLIES FROM THE KINGDOM OF CANINIA HAVE COME TO HELP YOU REBUILD.

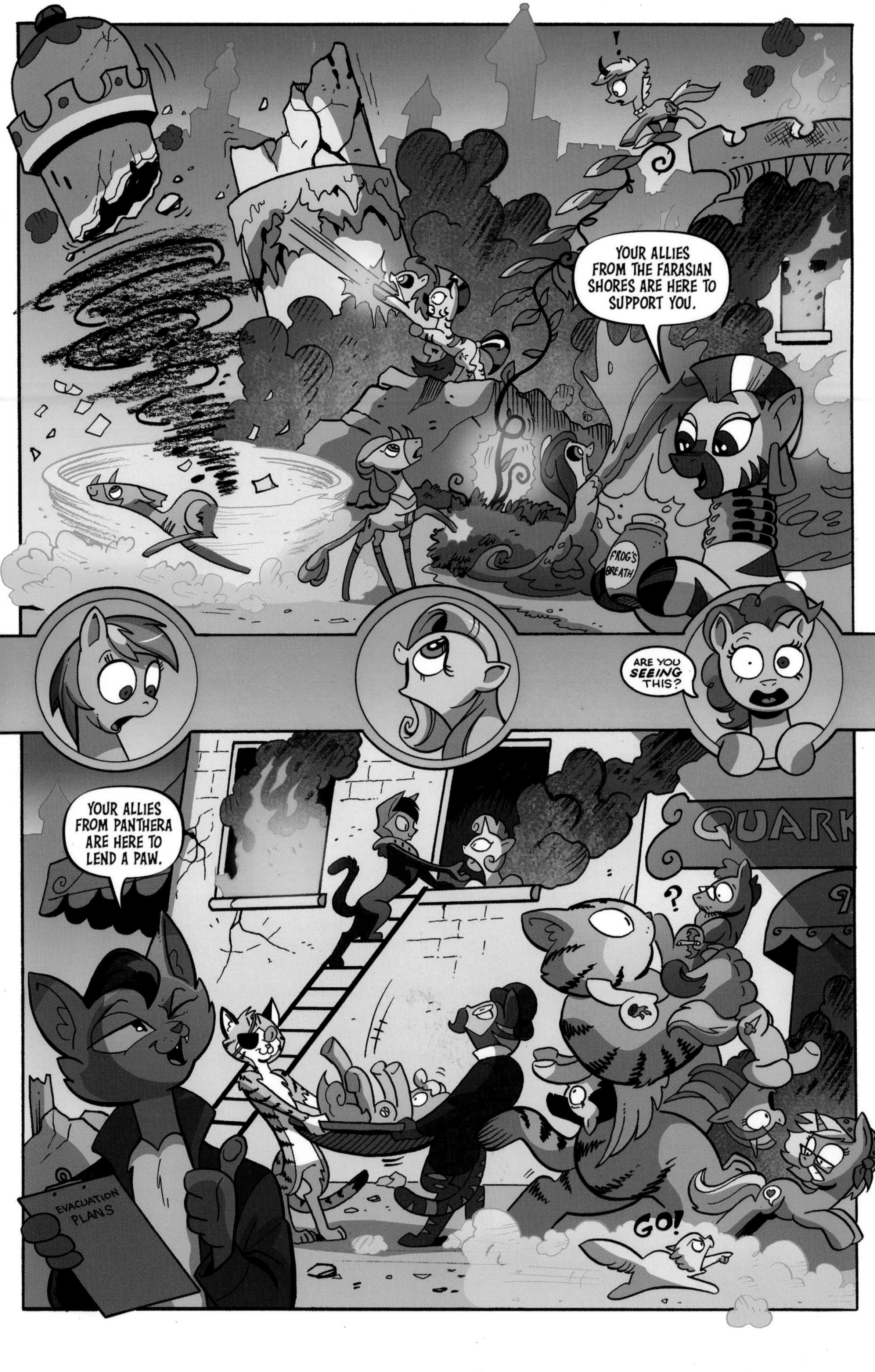

YOUR ALLIES FROM THE FARASIAN SHORES ARE HERE TO SUPPORT YOU.
FROG'S BREATH
ARE YOU SEEING THIS?
QUARK
YOUR ALLIES FROM PANTHERA ARE HERE TO LEND A PAW.
EVACUATION PLANS
GO!

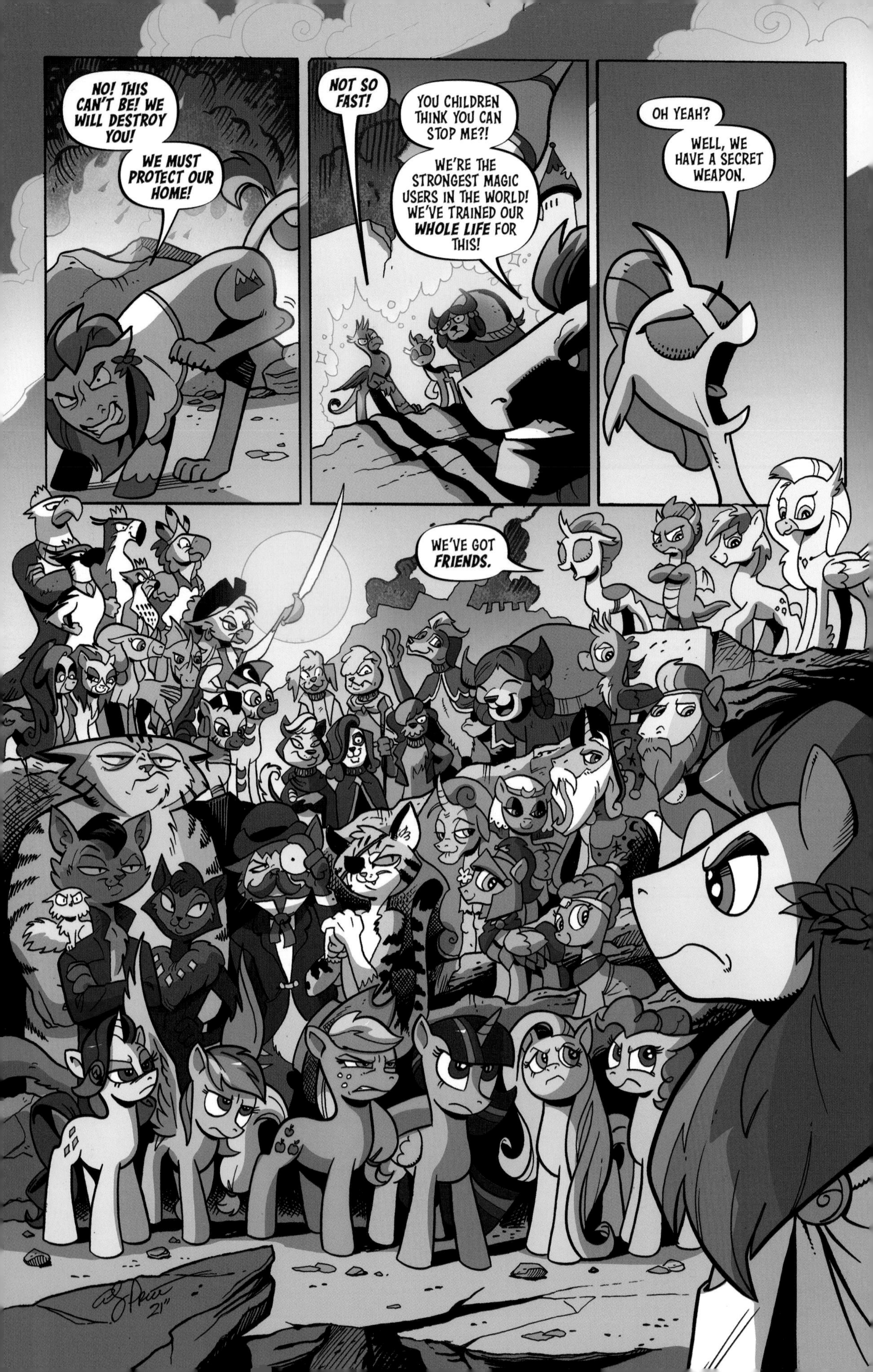
NO! THIS CAN'T BE! WE WILL DESTROY YOU!
WE MUST PROTECT OUR HOME!
NOT SO FAST!
YOU CHILDREN THINK YOU CAN STOP ME?!
WE'RE THE STRONGEST MAGIC USERS IN THE WORLD! WE'VE TRAINED OUR WHOLE LIFE FOR THIS!
OH YEAH?
WELL, WE HAVE A SECRET WEAPON.
WE'VE GOT FRIENDS.

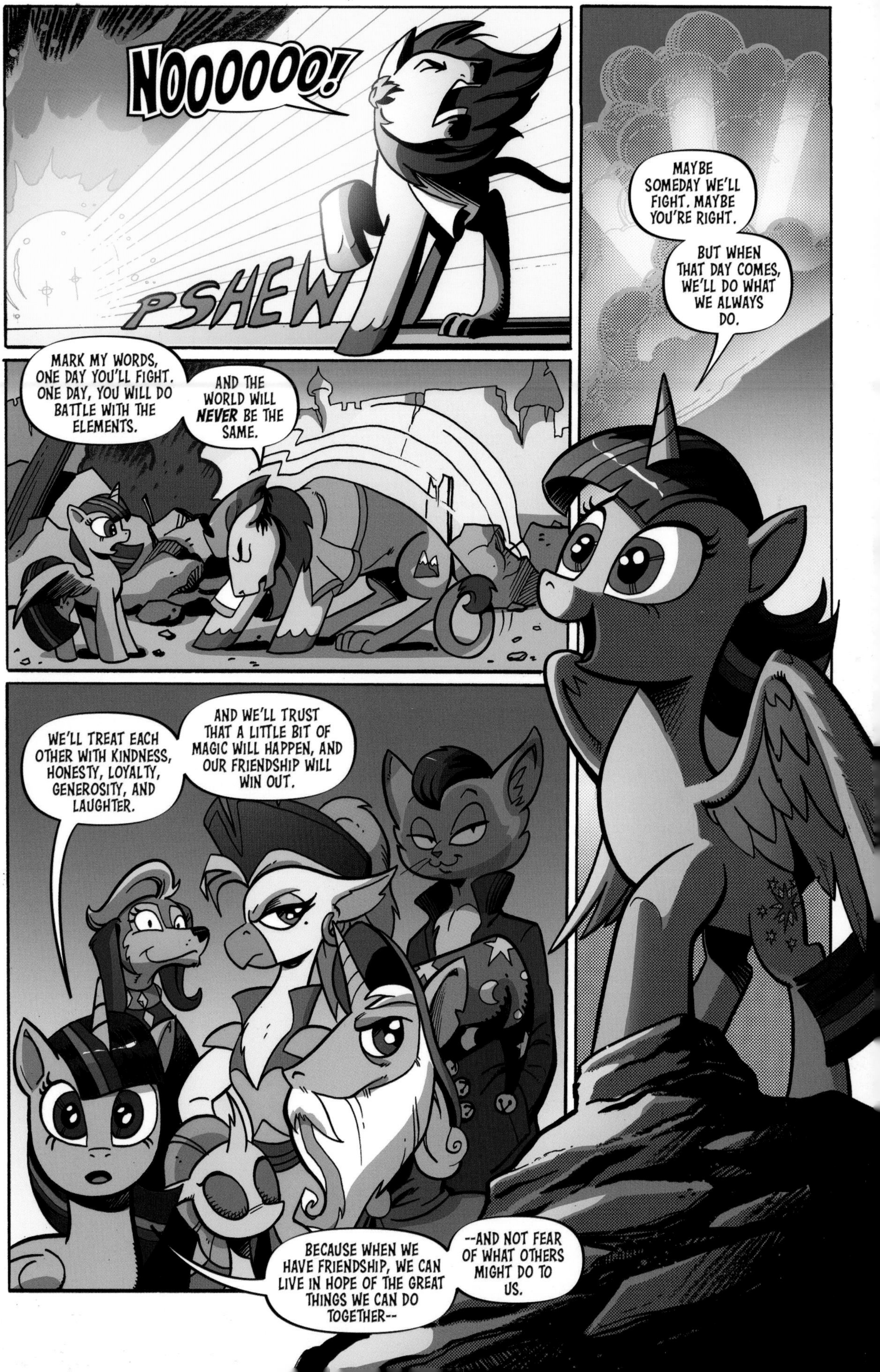
NOOOOOO!
PSHEW
MARK MY WORDS, ONE DAY YOU'LL FIGHT. ONE DAY, YOU WILL DO BATTLE WITH THE ELEMENTS.
AND THE WORLD WILL NEVER BE THE SAME.
MAYBE SOMEDAY WE'LL FIGHT. MAYBE YOU'RE RIGHT.
BUT WHEN THAT DAY COMES, WE'LL DO WHAT WE ALWAYS DO.
WE'LL TREAT EACH OTHER WITH KINDNESS, HONESTY, LOYALTY, GENEROSITY, AND LAUGHTER.
AND WE'LL TRUST THAT A LITTLE BIT OF MAGIC WILL HAPPEN, AND OUR FRIENDSHIP WILL WIN OUT.
BECAUSE WHEN WE HAVE FRIENDSHIP, WE CAN LIVE IN HOPE OF THE GREAT THINGS WE CAN DO TOGETHER--
--AND NOT FEAR OF WHAT OTHERS MIGHT DO TO US.

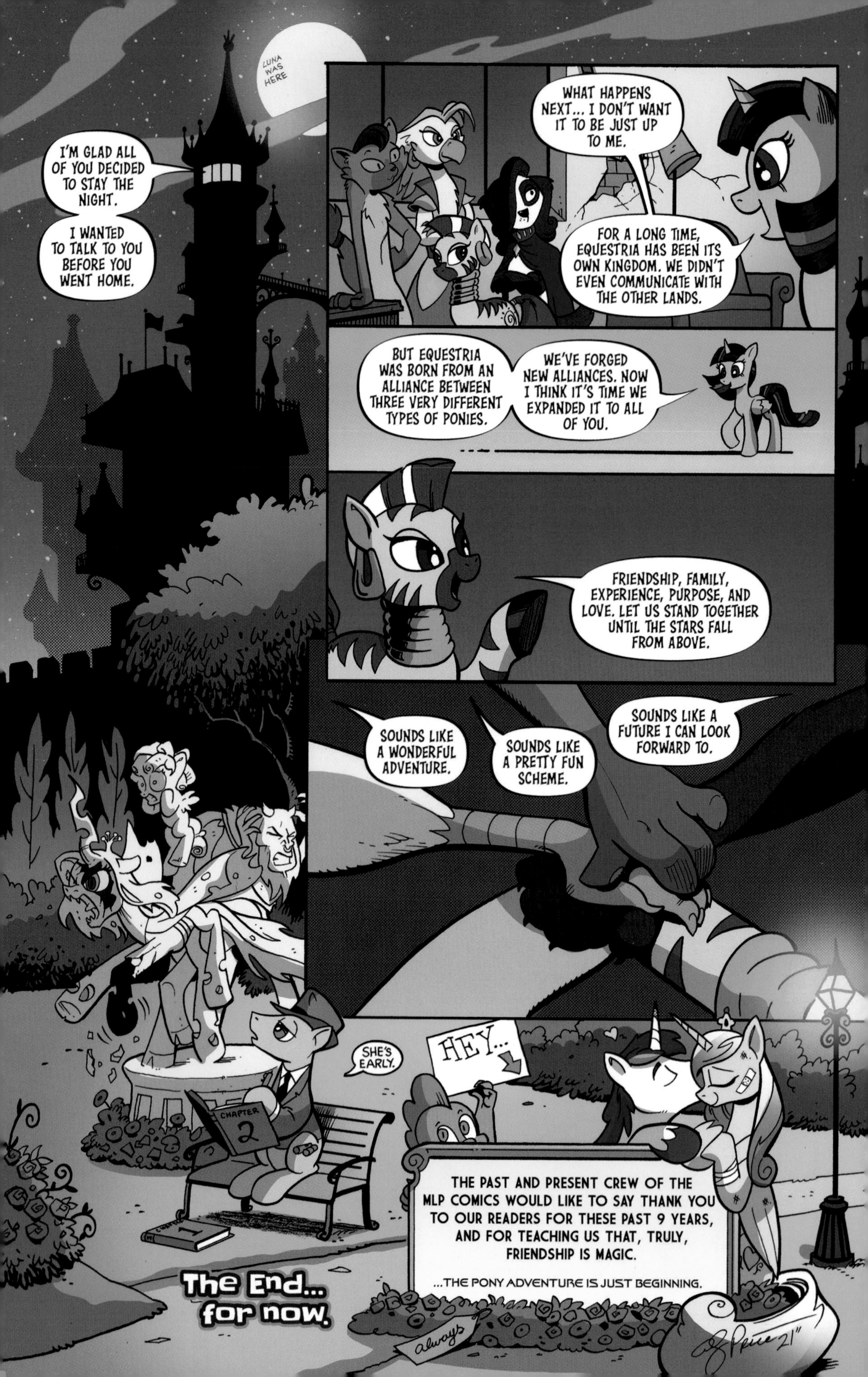
LUNA WAS HERE
I'M GLAD ALL OF YOU DECIDED TO STAY THE NIGHT.
I WANTED TO TALK TO YOU BEFORE YOU WENT HOME.
WHAT HAPPENS NEXT... I DON'T WANT IT TO BE JUST UP TO ME.
FOR A LONG TIME, EQUESTRIA HAS BEEN ITS OWN KINGDOM. WE DIDN'T EVEN COMMUNICATE WITH THE OTHER LANDS.
BUT EQUESTRIA WAS BORN FROM AN ALLIANCE BETWEEN THREE VERY DIFFERENT TYPES OF PONIES.
WE'VE FORGED NEW ALLIANCES. NOW I THINK IT'S TIME WE EXPANDED IT TO ALL OF YOU.
FRIENDSHIP, FAMILY, EXPERIENCE, PURPOSE, AND LOVE. LET US STAND TOGETHER UNTIL THE STARS FALL FROM ABOVE.
SOUNDS LIKE A WONDERFUL ADVENTURE.
SOUNDS LIKE A PRETTY FUN SCHEME.
SOUNDS LIKE A FUTURE I CAN LOOK FORWARD TO.
SHE'S EARLY.
HEY...
CHAPTER 2
1
THE PAST AND PRESENT CREW OF THE MLP COMICS WOULD LIKE TO SAY THANK YOU TO OUR READERS FOR THESE PAST 9 YEARS, AND FOR TEACHING US THAT, TRULY, FRIENDSHIP IS MAGIC.
...THE PONY ADVENTURE IS JUST BEGINNING.
The End... for now.
always
Price 21'

BY KATIE COOK

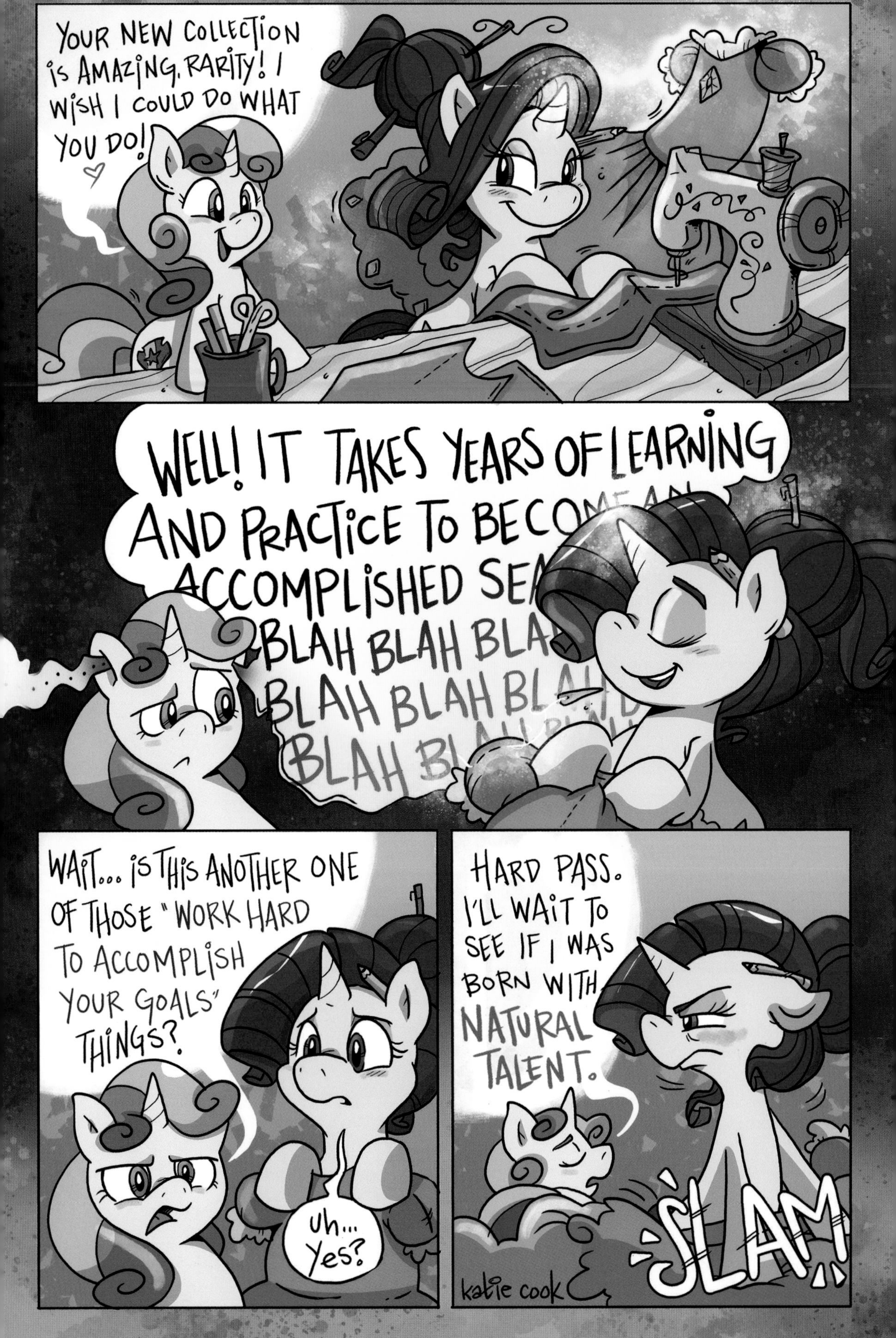
YOUR NEW COLLECTION IS AMAZING, RARITY! I WISH I COULD DO WHAT YOU DO!
WELL! IT TAKES YEARS OF LEARNING AND PRACTICE TO BECOME AN ACCOMPLISHED SEA
BLAH BLAH BLAH
BLAH BLAH BL
BLAH BL
WAIT... IS THIS ANOTHER ONE OF THOSE "WORK HARD TO ACCOMPLISH YOUR GOALS" THINGS?
UH... YES?
HARD PASS. I'LL WAIT TO SEE IF I WAS BORN WITH NATURAL TALENT.
SLAM
katie cook

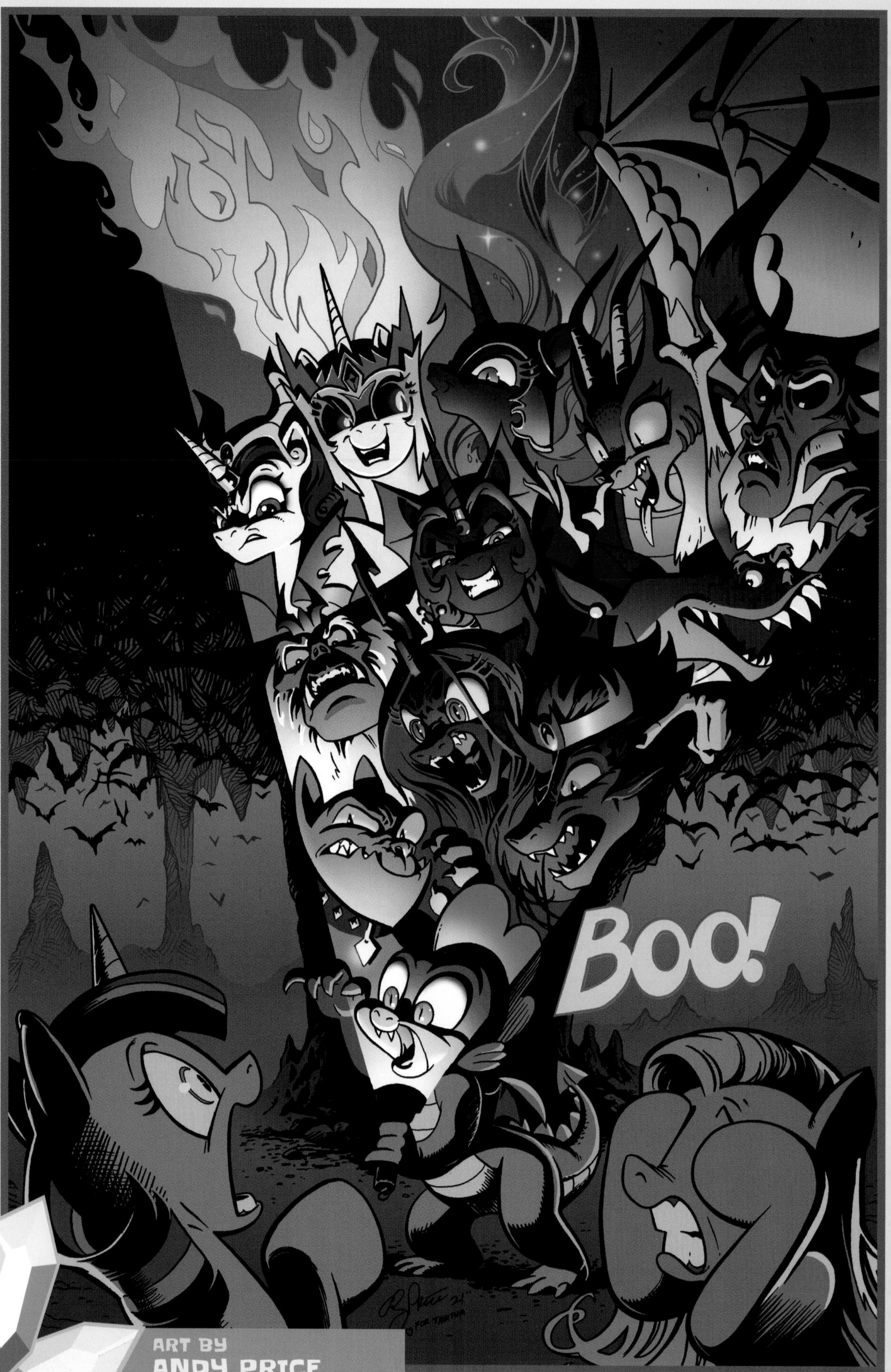
BOO!

ART BY
ANDY PRICE

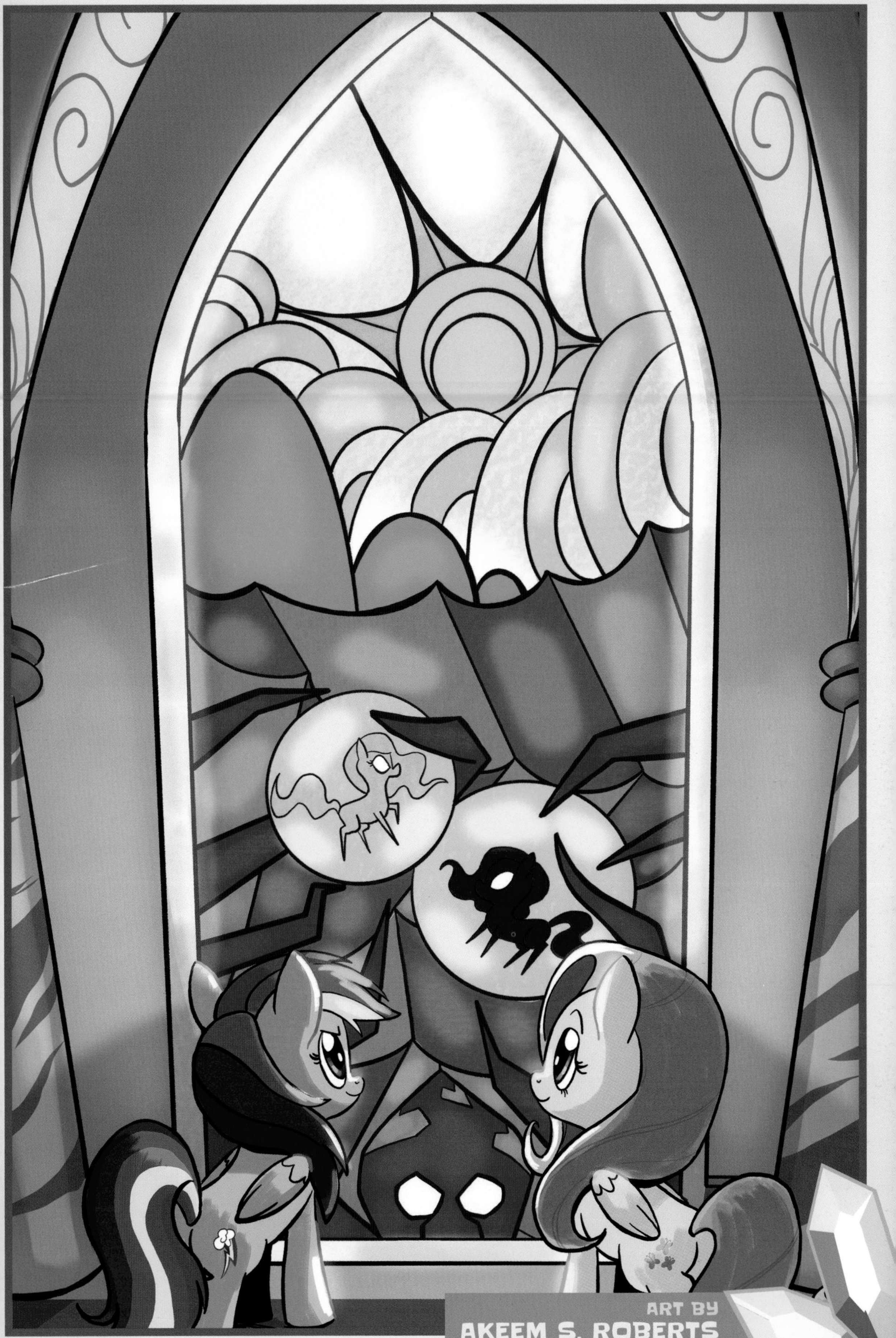
ART BY
AKEEM S. ROBERTS

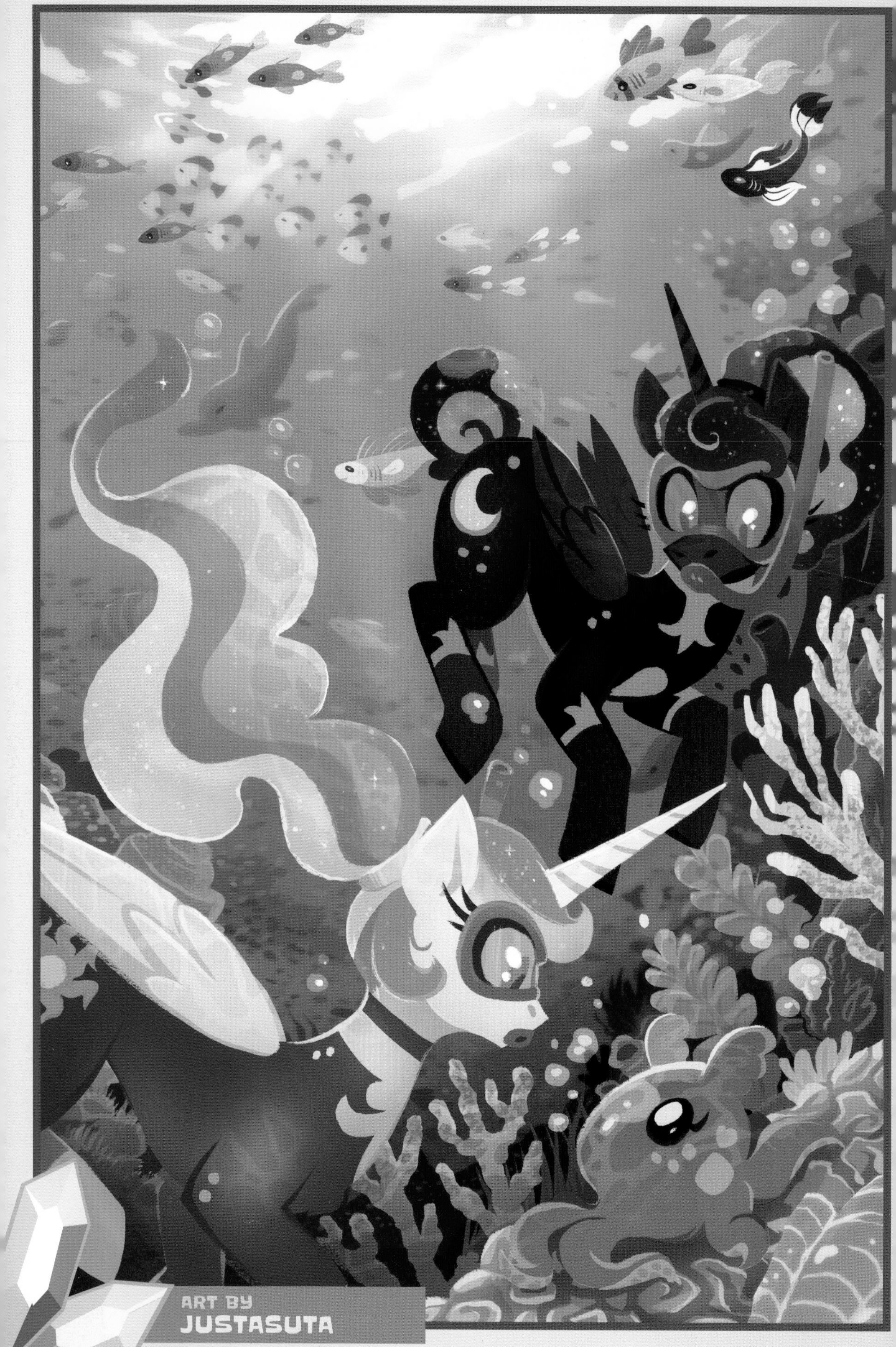
ART BY
JUSTASUTA

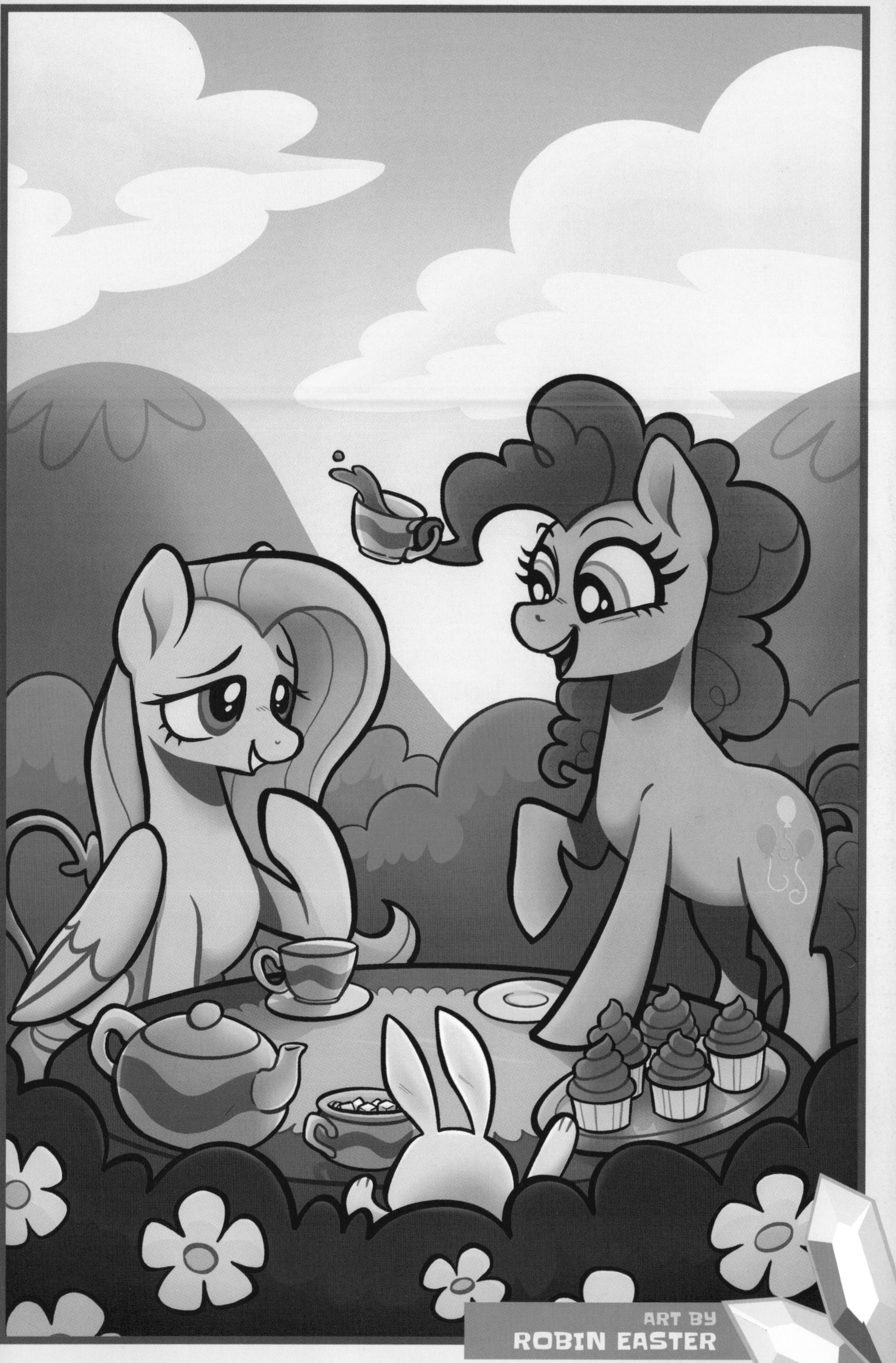
ART BY
ROBIN EASTER

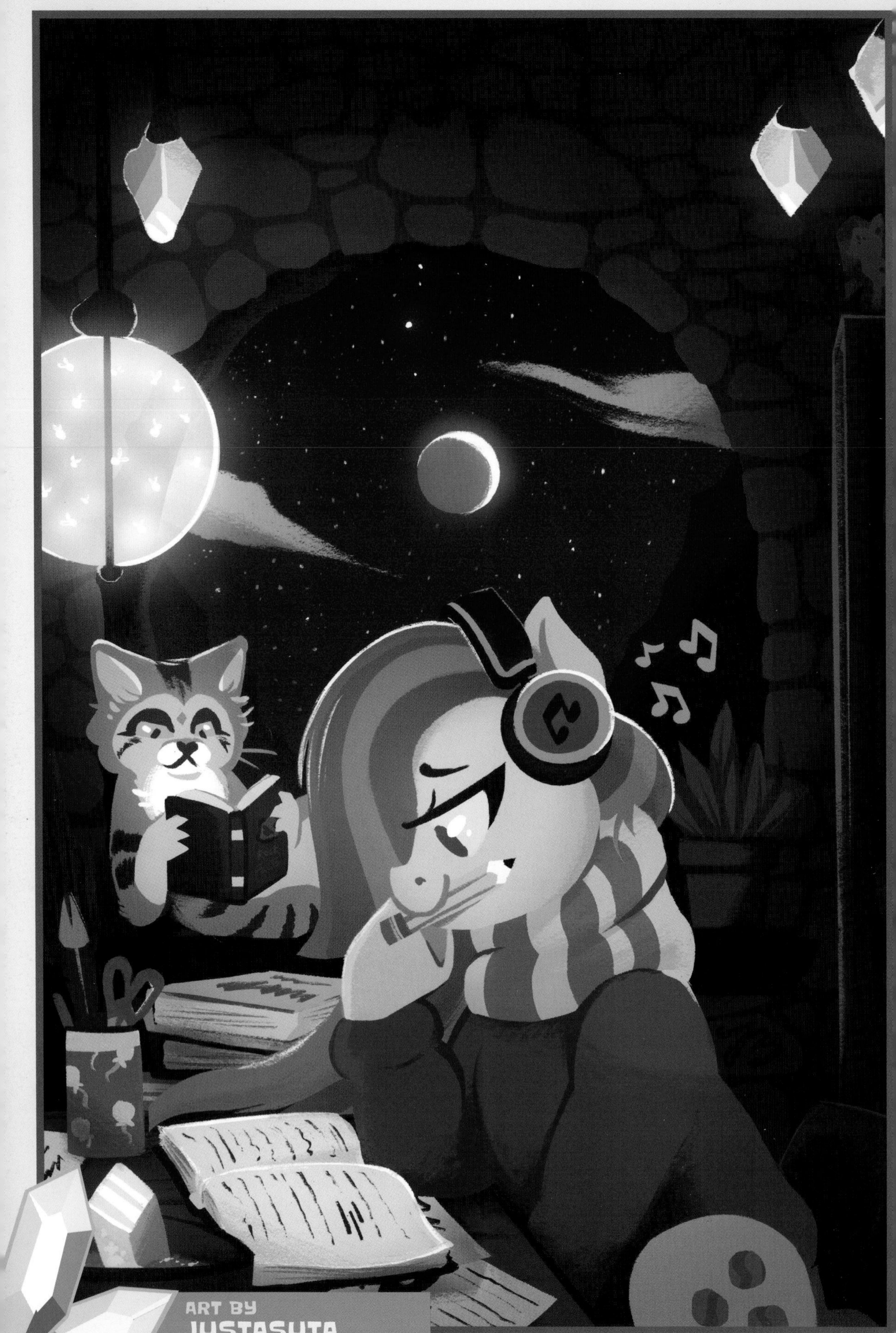
ART BY
JUSTASUTA

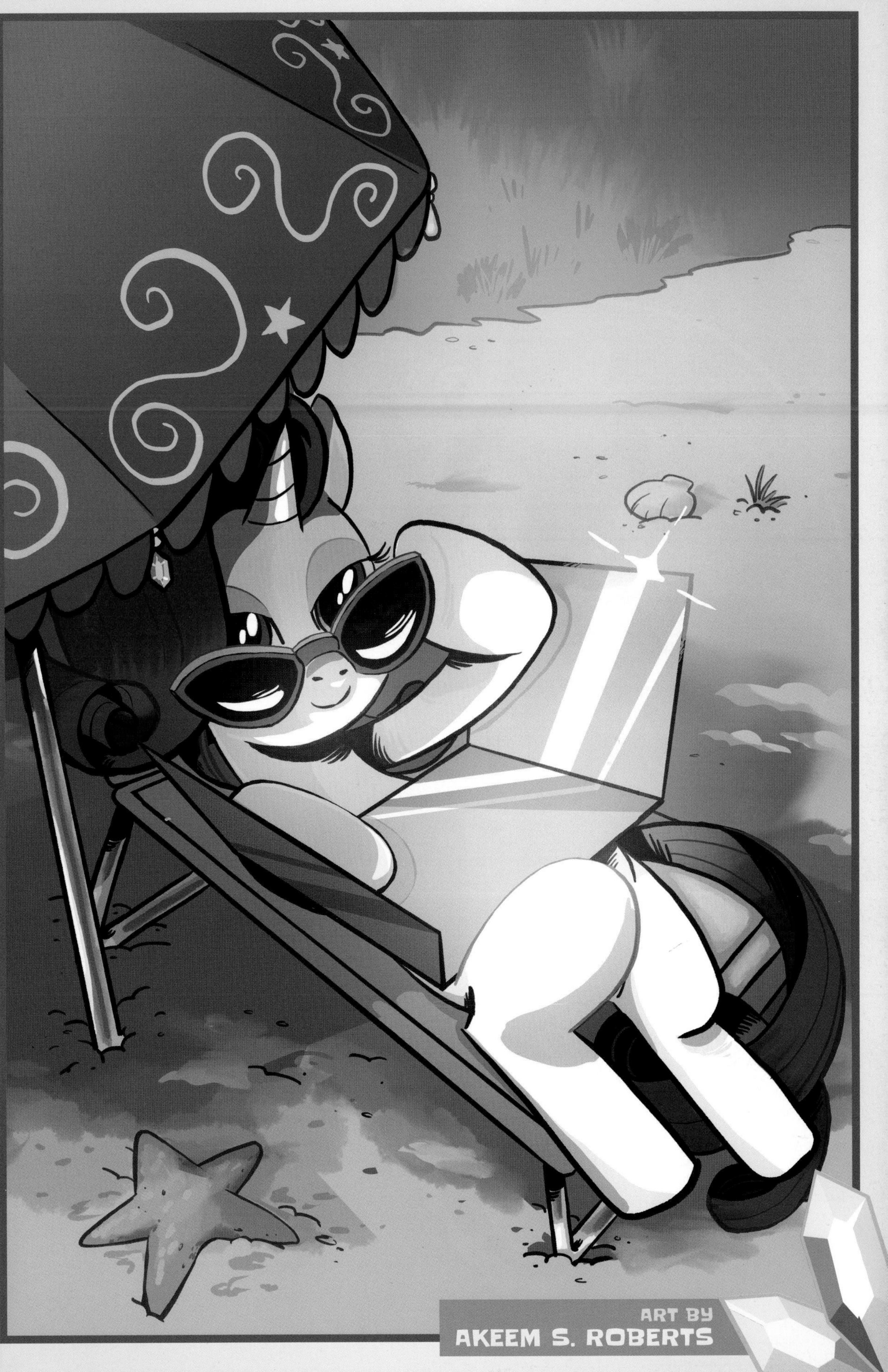
ART BY
AKEEM S. ROBERTS

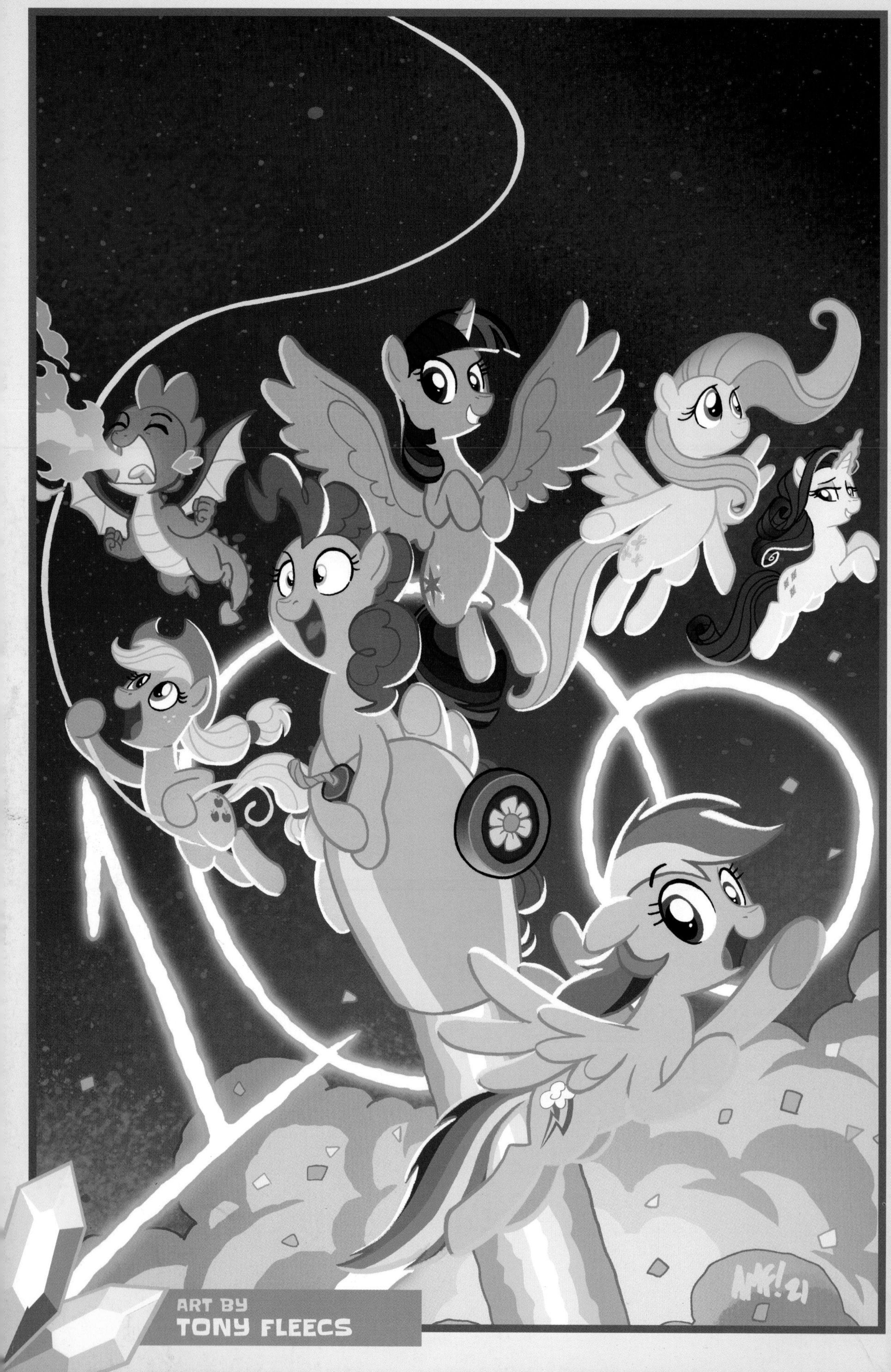

ART BY
TONY FLEECS

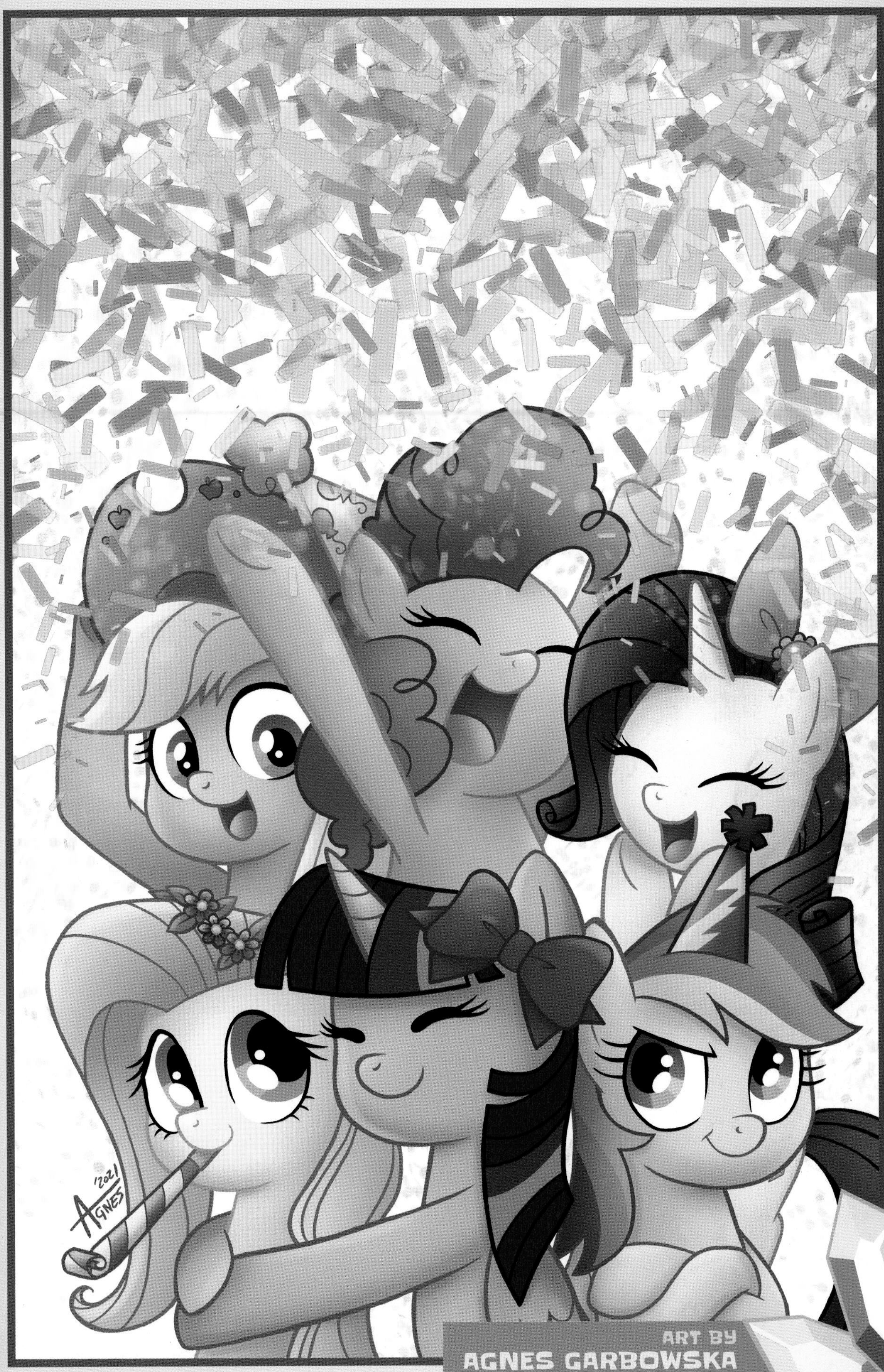
'2021
AGNES

ART BY
AGNES GARBOWSKA

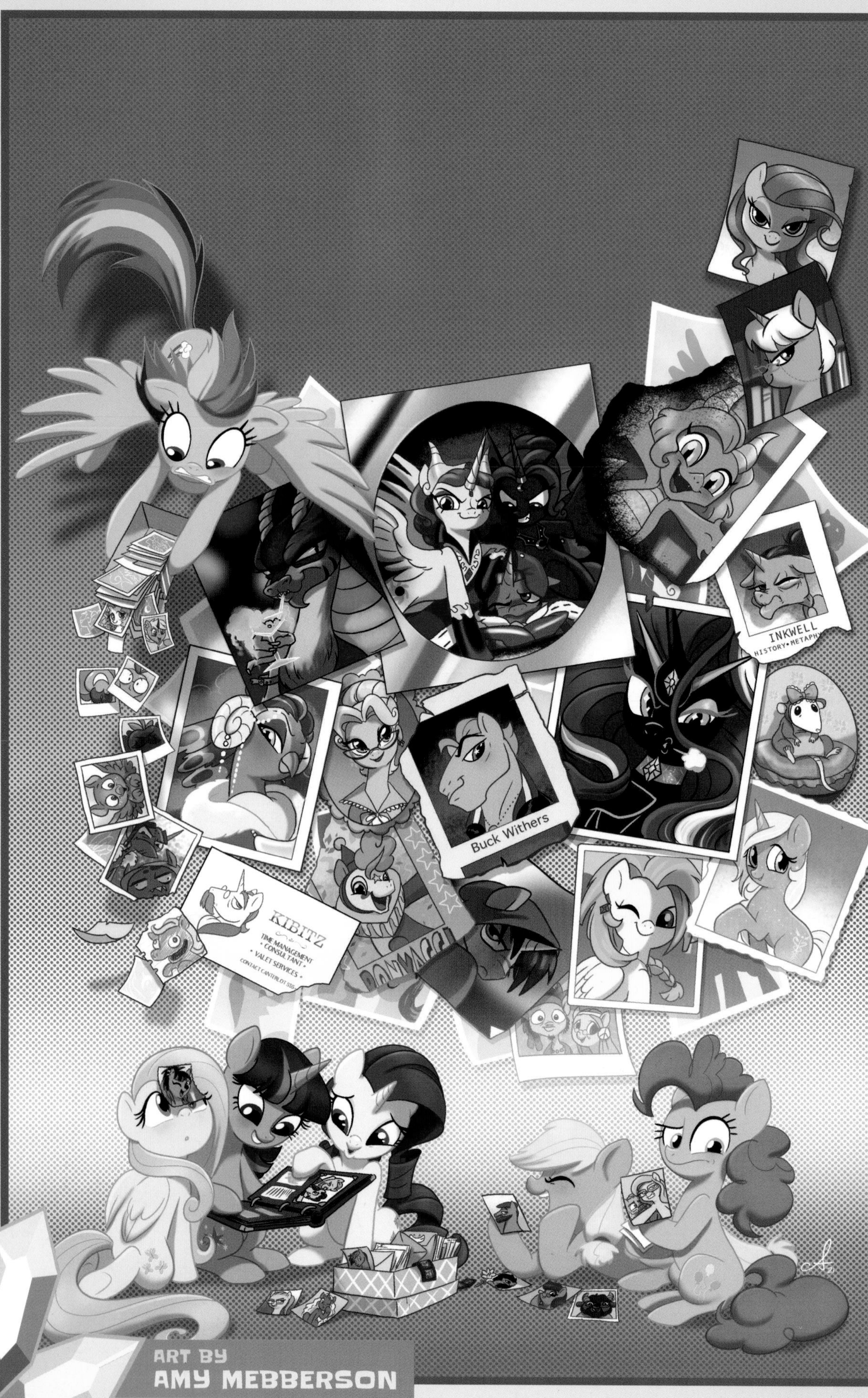
INKWELL
HISTORY • METAPH
Buck Withers
KIBITZ
TIME MANAGEMENT
• CONSULTANT •
• VALET SERVICES •
CONTACT CANTERLOT 555-

ART BY
AMY MEBBERSON

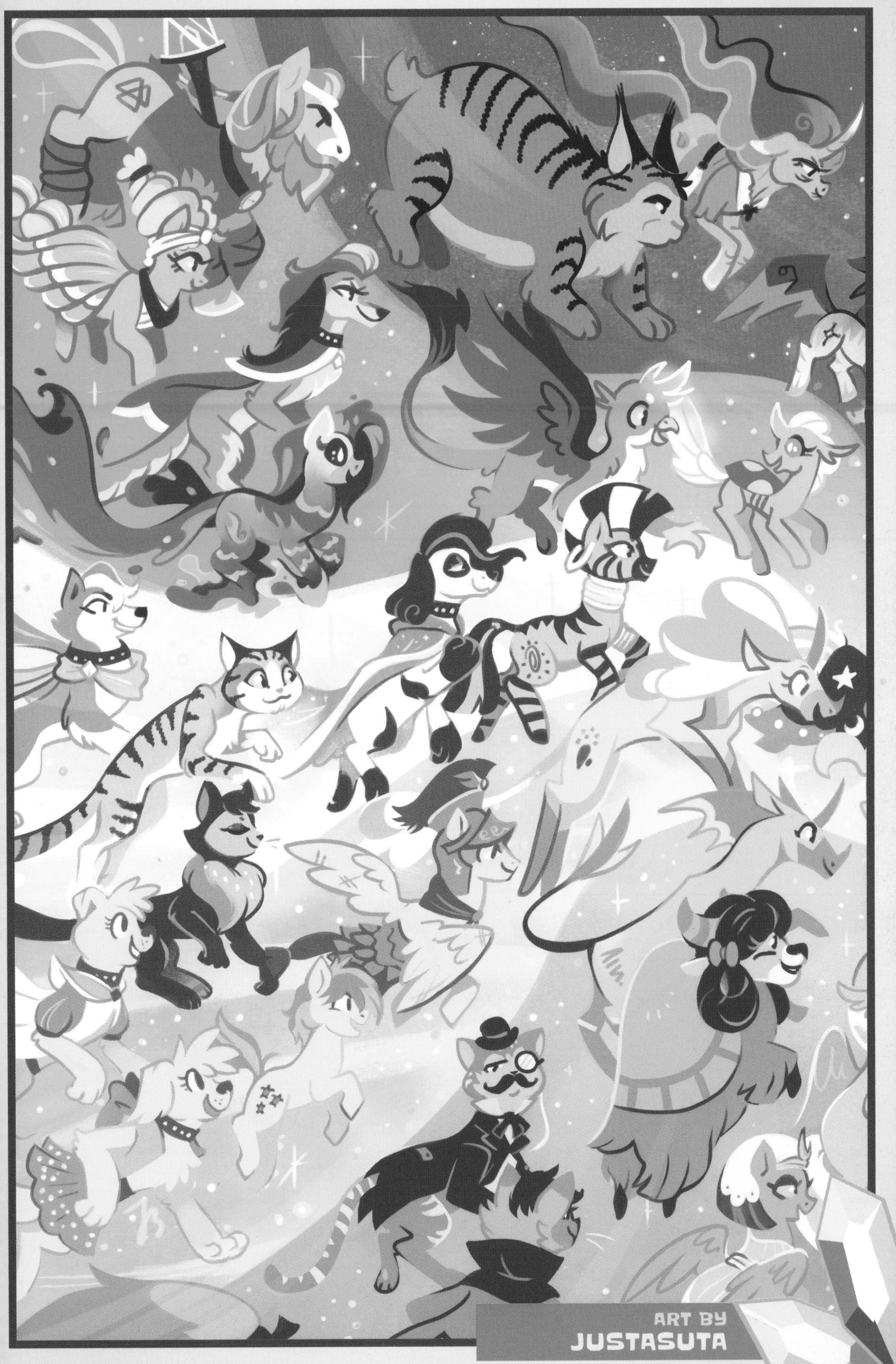
ART BY
JUSTASUTA

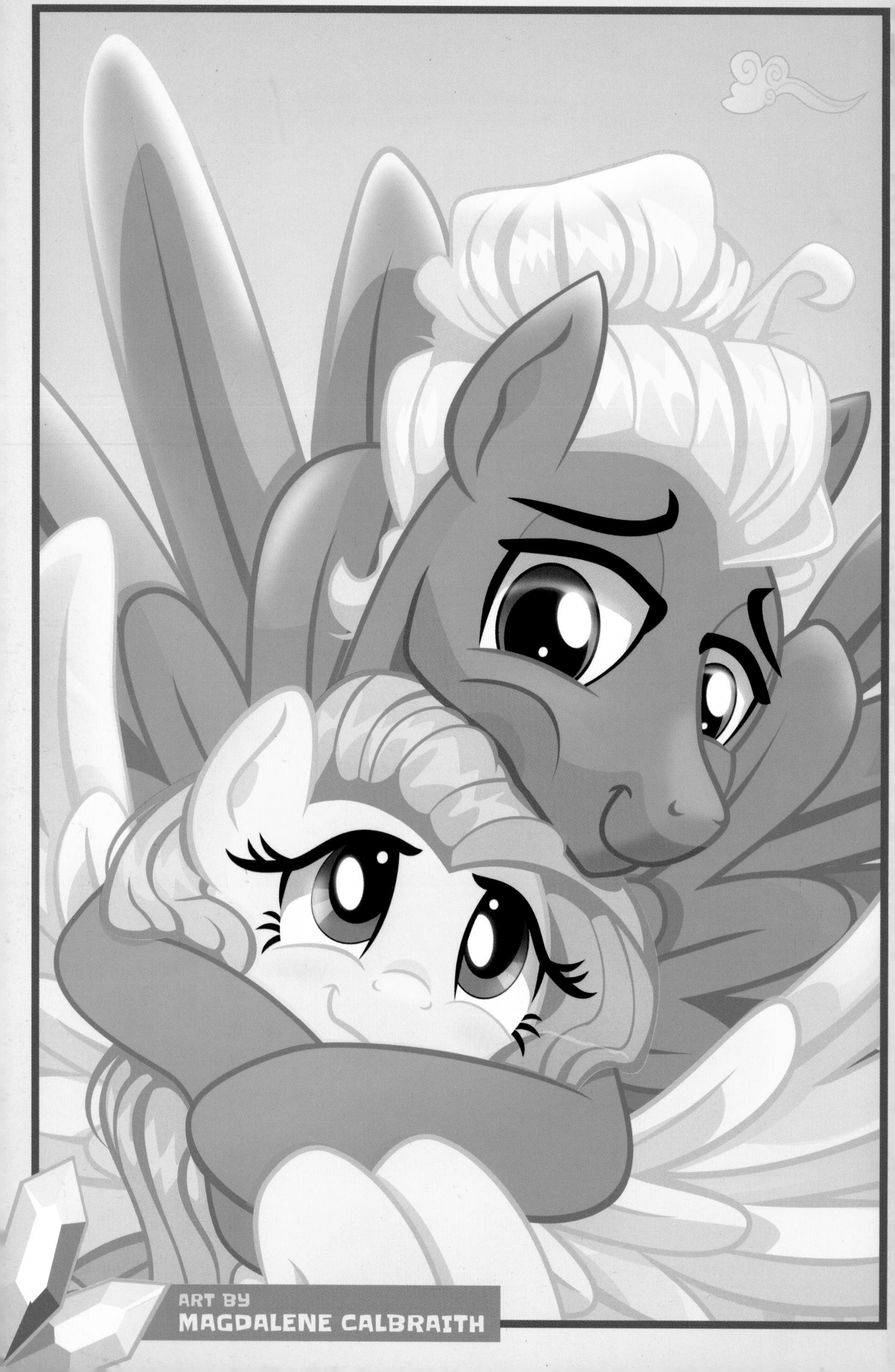

ART BY
MAGDALENE CALBRAITH

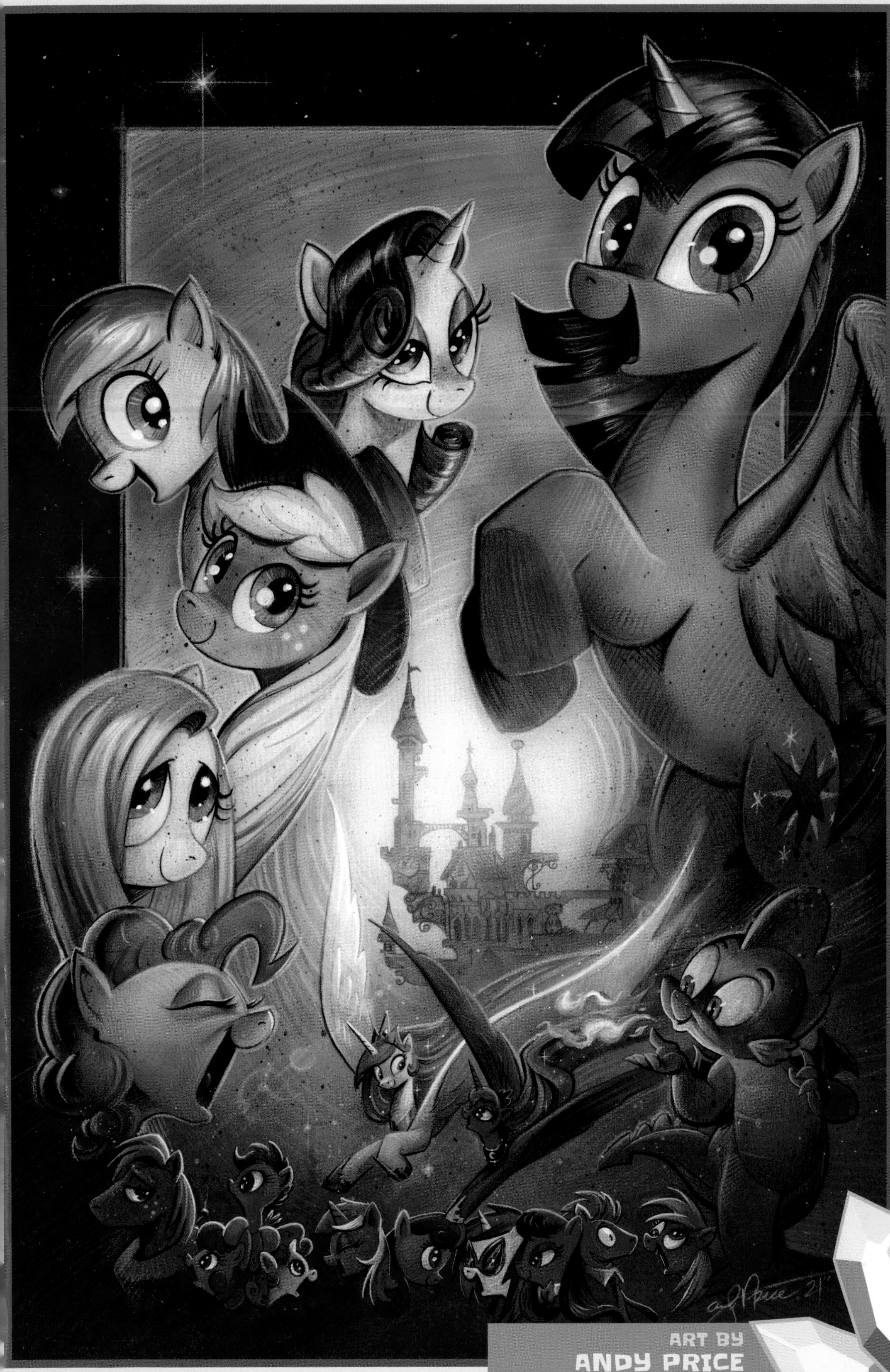

ART BY
ANDY PRICE

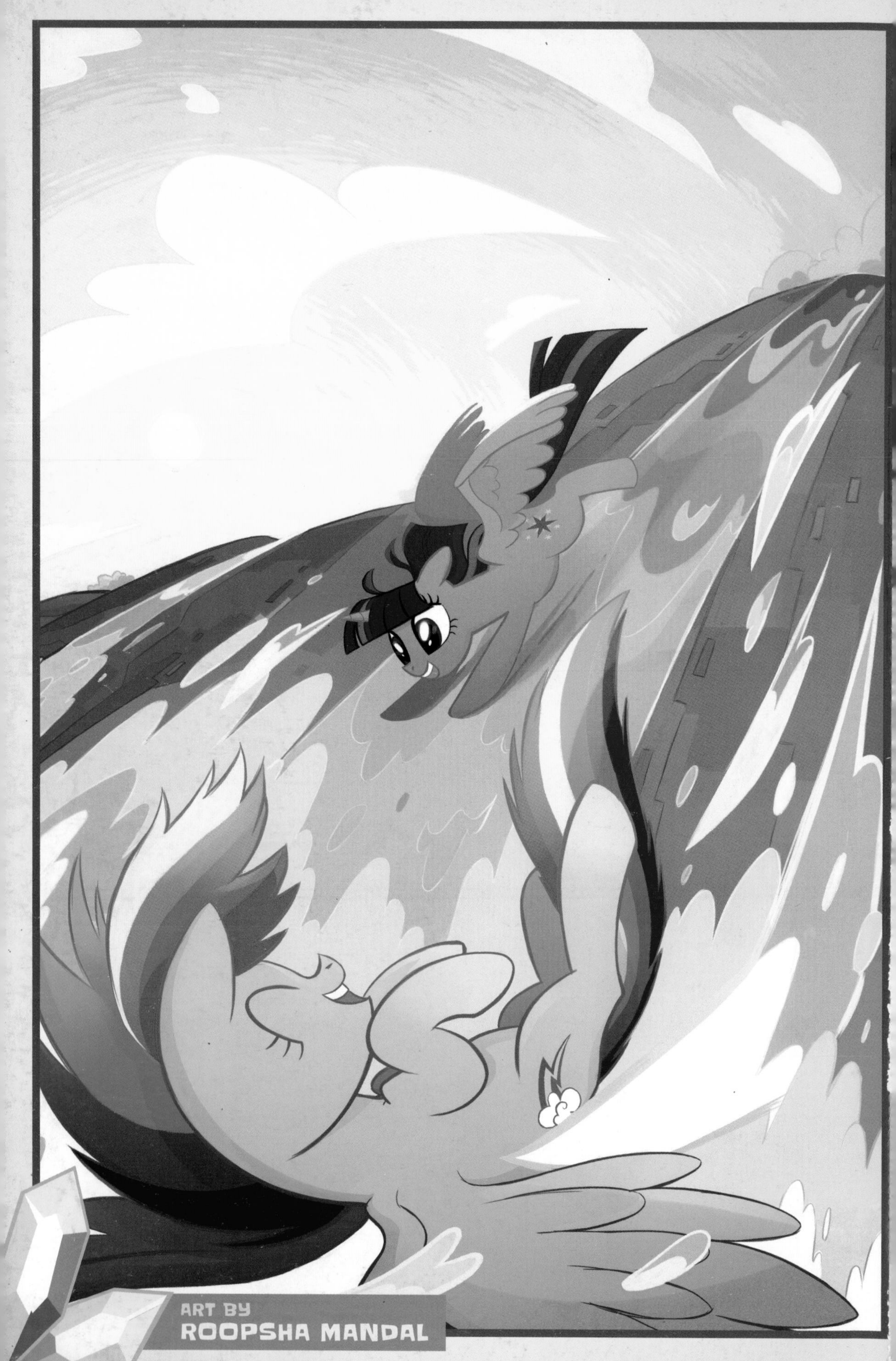
ART BY
ROOPSHA MANDAL